S

Silk

Four Days in April

Chris Durbin

Chris Durbin

Copyright © 2025 by Chris Durbin. All Rights Reserved.

Chris Durbin has asserted his rights under the Copyright, Design and Patents Act, 1988, to be identified as the author of this work.

No part of this book may be reproduced in any form or by any electronic or mechanical means including information storage and retrieval systems, without permission in writing from the author. The only exception is by a reviewer, who may quote short excerpts in a review.

Editor: Lucia Durbin

Cover Artwork: Bob Payne

Cover Design: Book Beaver

This book is a work of fiction. Characters, places, and incidents either are products of the author's imagination or are used fictitiously.

First Edition: May 2025

Silkworm

To our grandson Charlie,

the Happiness Hero

Contents

The Freedom of the Seas	v
Acknowledgements	vi
Acronyms	viii
Technical Terms	x
Arabian Gulf	xi
Straits of Hormuz	xii
HMS Winchester: Sensors & Weapons	xiii
Introduction	1
Prologue	9
Chapter One	26
Chapter Two	39
Chapter Three	51
Chapter Four	61
Chapter Five	72
Chapter Six	83
Chapter Seven	97
Chapter Eight	109
Chapter Nine	121
Chapter Ten	135
Chapter Eleven	147
Chapter Twelve	160
Chapter Thirteen	173
Chapter Fourteen	187
Chapter Fifteen	201
Chapter Sixteen	215
Chapter Seventeen	228
Chapter Eighteen	240
Chapter Nineteen	250
Chapter Twenty	265
Chapter Twenty-One	277
Chapter Twenty-Two	294
Chapter Twenty-Three	308
The Author	314
The Carlisle & Holbrooke Series	316
Feedback	317

Silkworm

The Freedom of the Seas

The most specific and unimpeachable axiom of the Law of Nations, called a primary rule or first principle, the spirit of which is self-evident and immutable: Every nation is free to travel to every other nation, and to trade with it.

The air is the common property of all, it belongs to this class of things for two reasons. First, it is not susceptible of occupation; and second its common use is destined for all men. For the same reasons the sea is common to all, because it is so limitless that it cannot become a possession of anyone.

Mare Liberum
'The Freedom of the Seas'
Hugo Grotius
AD 1609

Acknowledgements

In the 1980s, in response to Iranian aggression during its long-running war with Iraq, western nations started sending warships to accompany their tankers through the Straits of Hormuz into the Southern Arabian Gulf. Under *Operation Armilla*, Britain deployed a succession of task groups comprising a mix of destroyers, frigates, minehunters and support ships and regularly accompanied any merchant ships with a British registry or a substantial British financial interest. America, with its vastly greater naval resources, initiated *Operation Earnest Will* to escort reflagged Kuwaiti tankers, sailing under the Stars and Stripes, all the way to their home ports in the Northern Gulf. This was collectively called the *Gulf Tanker War* and it reached its deadly crescendo when, in the Spring of 1988, *USS Samuel B. Roberts* struck an Iranian mine near the Shah Allum shoal. America retaliated with *Operation Praying Mantis*, during which they destroyed a significant part of Iran's naval capability. Then, in July, while engaging a group of Iranian fast attack craft in the Straits of Hormuz, the new Aegis cruiser *USS Vincennes* shot down an Iranian Airbus – a scheduled civilian airliner full of passengers – mistakenly believing it to be an attack aircraft. *Silkworm!* is a work of fiction set within these dramatic real-world events.

All the characters in *Silkworm!* are imaginary and I have not modelled any of them on old shipmates of mine. Likewise, all the ships are fictitious although their capabilities – their weapons, sensors and machinery – correspond to real ships of the period. The fictitious *HMS Winchester* is exactly as I remember the real *HMS Exeter* to be when she deployed on Operation Armilla in the Spring of 1988. Most of the material for *Silkworm!* came from my own extensive experiences in the Arabian Gulf, dating back to my first visit in 1977, and particularly from my time as the Operations Officer of *HMS Exeter* in 1988.

Silkworm

I'm indebted to Commodore Dick Twitchen CBE RN (Retd) who refreshed my memory on Type 42 destroyers and to Lieutenant Commander Bob Eadie RN (Retd), a specialist hydrographic survey officer, who reminded me of a dramatic night on the Shah Allum shoal in April 1988.

I spent a wonderful afternoon at the Explosion Museum of Naval Firepower at Gosport, where I reacquainted myself with some of the sensors and weapons that were carried by Type 42 destroyers. The museum has a Seadart, a Seawolf, Sea Skuas, a 4.5 inch gun, a BMARC 20mm and much more; it's heaven on earth for a washed-ashore fighting sailor like me. I likewise visited the Fleet Air Arm museum at Yeovilton to view their selection of Lynx helicopters.

My research led me to a great number of online and printed sources, but I found four books particularly useful: Lee Allen Zatarain's *America's First Clash With Iran, The Tanker War, 1987-88*; Leo Marriott's *Type 42*, in the Modern Combat Ship series; Larry Jeram-Croft's *The Royal Navy Lynx, An Operational History*, and finally the *Admiralty Sailing Directions, Persian Gulf Pilot*.

We authors all stand on the shoulders of great men and women, and the inspiration to write *Silkworm!* came from two classic sea stories, both by CS Forester: *The Ship* and *The Good Shepherd*. I recommend them both, and the latter is now a superb film called *Greyhound*, starring Tom Hanks as an American convoy escort commander in the Second World War. The concept of compressing a few exciting days in the life of a warship on active duty into the dry and dusty pages of a book is irresistible.

***

Acronyms

Acronyms are pronounced by saying each letter in turn except where indicated in parenthesis.

AAW: Anti-Air Warfare
AAWC (*auk*): Anti-Air Warfare Commander
AAWO (*ay-woe*): Anti-Air Warfare Officer
APS: Air Picture Supervisor
AWACS (*ay-wax*): Airborne Warning And Control System
BDA: Battle Damage Assessment
BMARC (*bee-mark*): British Manufacture and Research Company
CASEVAC (*cas-evac*): Casualty Evacuation
CINCFLEET (*sink-fleet*): Commander-In-Chief Fleet
CPA: Closest Point of Approach
DIPCLEAR (*dip-clear*): Diplomatic Clearance
ESM: Electronic Support Measures
EW: Electronic Warfare
EWD: Electronic Warfare Director
FC: Fighter Controller
FOST (*fost*): Flag Officer Sea Training
GOP: General Operations Plot
GPMG: General Purpose Machine Gun
GTU: Gas Turbine Unit
HE: High Explosive
LAS (*laz*): Lookout Aimer Sight
MCD: Mine Clearance Diver
MCR: Machinery Control Room
MDA: Mine Danger Area
MEO: Marine Engineering Officer
MOD (*mod*): Ministry of Defence
PRF: Pulse Repetition Frequency
PWO (*pee-woe*): Principal Warfare Officer
RAS(L) (*ras-el*): Replenishment At Sea (Liquids)
RFA: Royal Fleet Auxiliary
ROE: Rules Of Engagement

RTB: Return To Base
SAM (*sam*): Surface-to-Air Missile
SITREP (*sit-rep*): Situation Report
SNOME (*snow-me*): Senior Naval Officer Middle East
SPS: Surface Picture Supervisor
TSS: Traffic Separation Scheme
TW: Territorial Waters

***

Technical Terms

Alligator: Tactical Data Link
Bird: Friendly surface-to-air missile
Bird Affirm: I can engage the target with bird
Bird Negat: I cannot engage the target with bird
Bogey: Unknown contact
Boghammer: Iranian fast attack craft
Bruiser: Friendly air-launched anti-ship missile
Bulldog: Friendly surface-launched anti-ship missile
Chirp: Helicopter's radar transponder
Cover: Order to prepare to engage a target
Dieso: Naval diesel fuel, used in most allied warships
Feet Dry: Flying over land
Feet Wet: Flying over sea
Hooter: Radar jammer
Magic: AWACS callsign
Mother: An aircraft's parent ship (or Mum)
Ops: Operations Officer
Pusser: Supply Officer
Racket: An intercepted radar signal
Skunk: Unknown surface contact
Splashed: Air target destroyed
Squawk: Response from an identification transponder
Threat Warning:
  Red: attack imminent or in progress
  Yellow: attack probable
  White: attack unlikely
Vampire: Hostile anti-ship missile
Weapons:
  Free: fire only at targets not identified as friendly
  Tight: fire only at targets positively identified as hostile

***

Silkworm

Arabian Gulf

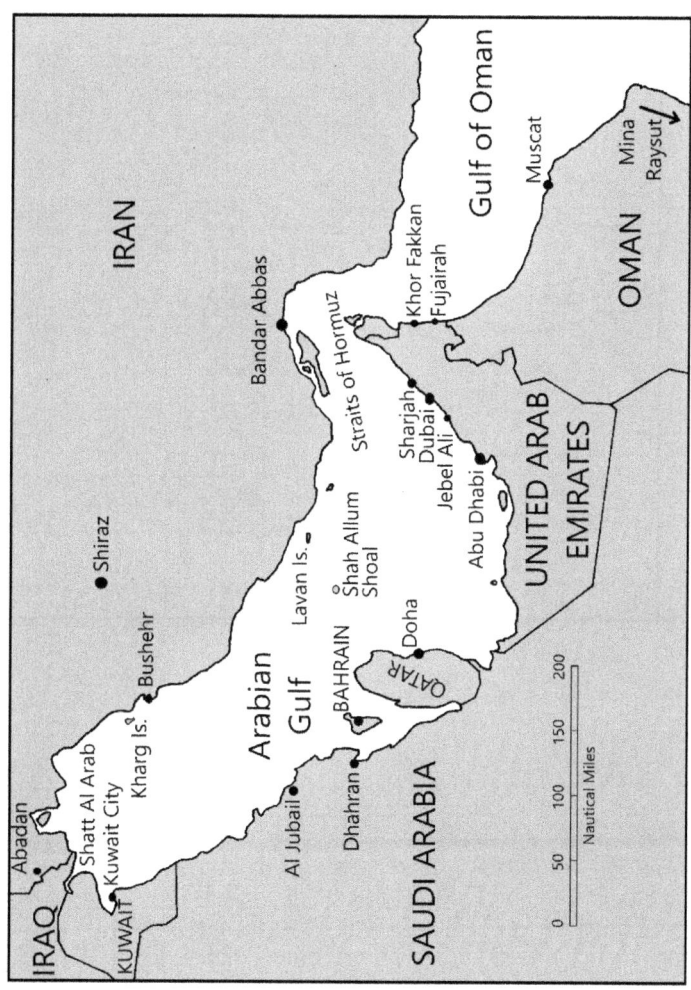

Straits of Hormuz

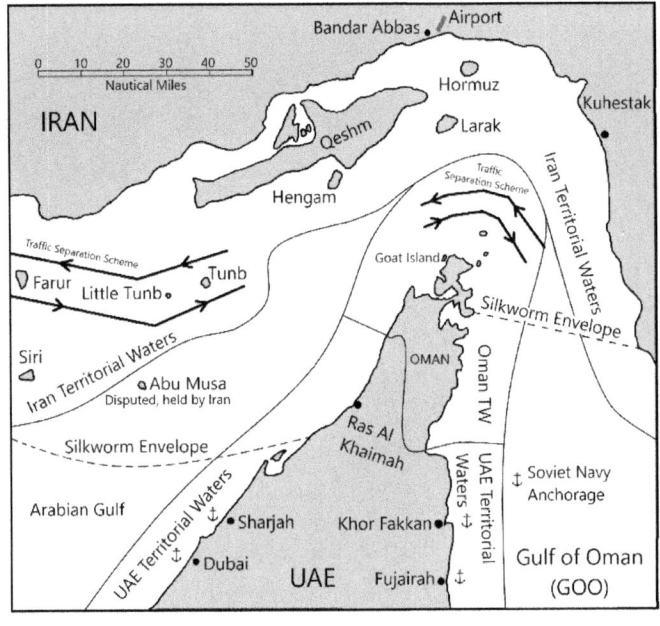

Silkworm

HMS Winchester: Sensors & Weapons

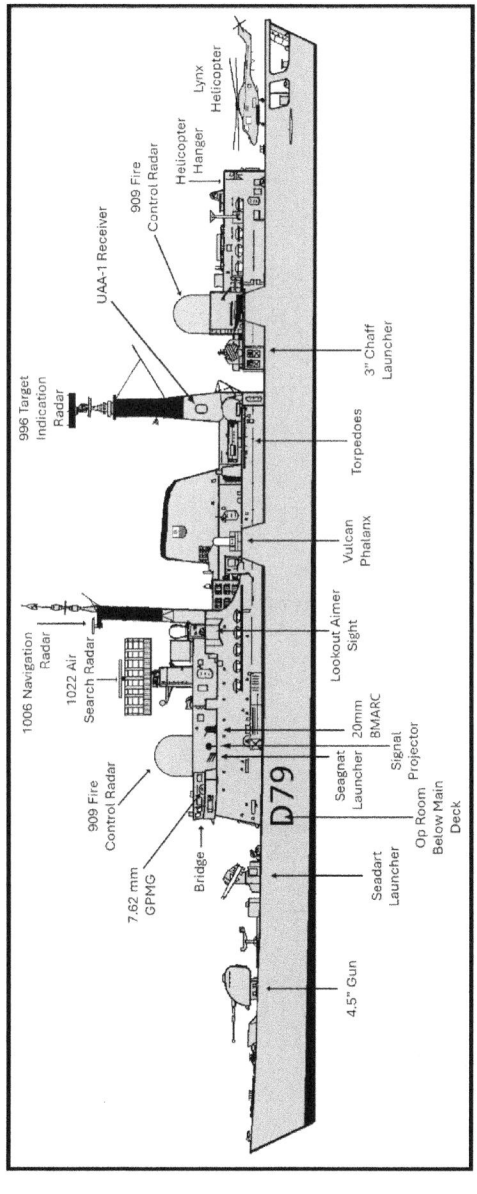

Chris Durbin

Introduction

Life, the Universe and Everything

In Douglas Adams' *The Hitchhiker's Guide to the Galaxy*, the answer to the ultimate question of life, the universe, and everything, is *forty-two*. This book has nothing to say about the greater questions of existence, but it is, nevertheless, a book about a forty-two: a Batch 2 Type 42 guided missile destroyer of the Royal Navy during the Gulf Tanker War in 1988, which I've named *HMS Winchester*. This chapter is for the reader who has little knowledge of this class of warship, and it offers enough information about the ship to help with the enjoyment of the story. If you've read this far and already know something about Type 42s, then feel free to skip this chapter and move on to the prologue.

***

The Type 42 guided missile destroyers were designed to provide defence against air and missile attack for a group of ships at sea. Sixteen were built between 1970 and 1982, fourteen for the Royal Navy and two for the Argentine Navy. Two of the British ships – *HMS Sheffield* and *HMS Coventry* – were sunk in the 1982 Falklands conflict. Twelve of the British and one of the Argentine ships have been scrapped and one hull is still in existence – *ARA Santisima Trinidad* – the only one not to be built in a British shipyard, which Argentina hopes to preserve as a national historic site.

The first two batches to be built, ten ships in all, had a full load displacement of 4,100 tons, they were 412 feet long, 47 feet in the beam and had a draught of 19 feet. The last four to be built – the third batch – were stretched to give them better seakeeping qualities and a larger missile magazine. They were 463 feet long with proportionally greater displacement, beam and draught.

***

The Type 42 destroyer *HMS Winchester* never existed; the last ship of the Royal Navy to bear that name was a W-class destroyer that was struck from the list in 1946 and scrapped at Inverkeithing. However, the fictional *HMS Winchester* is faithfully modelled on the second batch of the Type 42 class to be built. She's a *stumpy* Type 42, and she's at the modification state that's required for a deployment to the Arabian Gulf in support of Operation Armilla in 1988. Her vital statistics mirror the real ships of the second batch.

HMS Winchester is propelled by four Rolls Royce gas turbine engines that drive two shafts with controllable pitch propellers: two Tyne engines for cruising and two Olympus engines – the same basic units that powered Concorde – for high speed operations. They're installed in a Combined Gas or Gas (COGOG) configuration in which each shaft can be driven by either a Tyne or an Olympus, but not both simultaneously. The great thing about this arrangement is that it's a matter of moments to start up and engage any of the engines. *Winchester* can make fourteen knots on a single Tyne gas turbine engine if the opposite shaft is allowed to rotate under the pressure of the water flow, and in that configuration only uses a ton-and-a-half of naval diesel fuel (known as *dieso*) every hour. That's in stark contrast to running at thirty knots with the two Olympus engaged, when she burns through twelve tons an hour. *Winchester* has a fuel capacity of six hundred tons and therefore has a range of four thousand nautical miles at a normal cruising speed of eighteen knots.

***

At this point you might wish to refer to the illustration of *HMS Winchester* on page xiii.

***

HMS Winchester's principal weapon, indeed its *raison d'etre*, is the Seadart missile. This is an anti-aircraft and anti-missile system with a lesser, secondary capability against surface targets, and *Winchester* carries twenty missiles in her magazine. Seadart's nominal maximum range is forty miles, but that requires a large target that is flying high and slow and straight towards the destroyer, and begging to be shot down. Twenty miles is a more realistic combat intercept range against a target that is trying to survive, and less still against a fast enemy missile at sea-skimming heights. Of course a missile is of no use without its sensors and fire control systems, and the best way to explain *Winchester's* outfit is to describe a typical engagement, if indeed there is such a thing. Here goes:

The Type 1022 long range air search radar detects an unidentified inbound track at about a hundred-and-forty miles. The UAA-1 Electronic Support Measures (ESM) system intercepts and identifies the unknown track's radar emissions and its classification is changed from unknown to hostile. When the hostile contact reaches ninety miles tracking is handed over to the Type 996 target indication radar, which gives the ship's computer system a more accurate position, course and speed for the track. At eighty miles the Type 909 fire control radar takes over in its I-band mode to track the target in three dimensions and give fire control quality information to the Seadart system. At forty miles the 909 radar's higher frequency J-band radar starts transmitting and the 909's receiver detects the reflected energy coming back from the target. At thirty miles the system assesses that the track is a valid Seadart target, the command gives approval to engage and a Seadart missile is fired. The Seadart homes on the J-band radar energy that is reflected from the target, aiming for an intercept point between the target and the Seadart-firing destroyer. At twenty miles from the ship the Seadart's proximity fuse detects that it is within a predetermined distance from its target and detonates its warhead, destroying both the hostile target and the Seadart missile.

Now, that's a very simplified description of the process and it takes no account the hostile aircraft's countermeasures, nor of *Winchester's* counter-countermeasures, but it's enough for the reader to understand how an engagement might be carried out. Seadart had a number of combat successes in the Falklands conflict of 1982, but it was in the first Gulf War of 1991 that it made its really spectacular contribution. *HMS Gloucester*, a batch 3 stretched Type 42, shot down an Iraqi Silkworm missile that was heading for the American battleship *USS Missouri*; it was the first successful, validated, missile-versus-missile engagement of its kind. *Missouri* soon had its revenge when it destroyed the Iraqi Silkworm battery with its mighty sixteen-inch guns.

HMS Winchester has other weapons, of course. The 4.5 inch gun is used for anti-aircraft fire, anti-ship engagements and shore bombardment. It fires twenty-five rounds per minute at a maximum range of ten miles, although its range is much shorter in the anti-aircraft mode. The 4.5 inch gun can also fire starshell rounds which burst in the air over a target and illuminate it with a magnesium flare, turning night into day. Two BMARC 20mm aimer-operated belt-fed cannons are fitted, one each side, for anti-aircraft fire and to engage smaller craft at close range. As a last-ditch defence against missile attack, *Winchester* has a fully automatic Vulcan Phalanx gatling gun. It fires 3,600 depleted uranium rounds per minute, adjusting its aim frequently to have a very high probability of hitting its target. A 7.62mm General Purpose Machine Gun (GPMG) is mounted on each bridge wing. *Winchester*, however, is not only an air defence ship; it has sonar systems to find and track submarines and two triple torpedo tubes carrying Stingray anti-submarine homing torpedoes.

Defence against airborne attack is not merely about shooting the enemy's missiles from the sky, and *Winchester* has a comprehensive range of electronic countermeasures. Chaff is the most important passive defence; it consists of clouds of metallic strips cut to match specific radar wavelengths. It can be deployed by a variety of means but must always bloom in the air and descend slowly to imitate a normal radar contact. The 4.5 inch gun can fire chaff rounds far away from the ship to confuse a human operator in an attacking aircraft by offering alternative fake targets.

Three-inch chaff rocket launchers adjacent to the front of the hangar roof can do the same at closer ranges and are used against an incoming missile in its acquisition phase. Finally, if an enemy missile successfully locks onto *Winchester*, the Seagnat launcher can fire patterns of chaff close enough to the ship that they might break the missile's lock after it's already found its target. All of these countermeasures rely upon the chaff offering a more attractive target than the ship itself, and to enable that, *Winchester* has two principal means of reducing her apparent size. First, she can manoeuvre to present the smallest possible target to the inbound missile's radar; second, her superstructure is fitted with panels of Radar Absorbent Material (RAM) to soak up the enemy radar's energy rather than reflect it back. *Winchester* carries an active jammer too, a Type 675, that can blind an enemy's radar or offer spurious targets.

Like most warships, *Winchester* carries a wide variety of communication systems, including satellite transmitters and receivers and radios in every frequency band. The ship can communicate at short range with other units in sight and with the Ministry of Defence in London thousands of miles away. It has a variety of encryption devices, to scramble and unscramble long textual messages and voice communications. For the rapid exchange of positional information, *Winchester* uses a tactical data link – codeword *Alligator* – that allows the ship's computer to automatically share information with other allied ships and aircraft that are fitted with similar equipment. It means that the tactical picture that *Winchester's* operations team can see is the same – in its fundamentals – as is seen by all allied warships within radio range, and with some aircraft. It's not perfect, but it's a huge step forward in interoperability.

HMS Winchester carries a Lynx helicopter that's been extensively modified to operate in the hostile environment of the Arabian Gulf. The Lynx is fitted with a Seaspray surface search radar, and an Orange Crop electronic support measures system. On its sponsons it can carry a combination of Sea Skua semi-active homing anti-ship missiles with a range of nine miles, Stingray torpedoes and a fifty-calibre heavy machine-gun pod.

To operate this complex system-of-systems, *Winchester* has a ship's company of twenty-four officers and two-hundred-and-thirty ratings all led by a commander who is known by the courtesy title of *Captain*. The captain will usually be in the operations room when he plans to bring *Winchester* into action or when any sort of danger is threatened. However, in a close range engagement where it's important for him to see the enemy, he'll often remain on the bridge.

The Officer-of-the-Watch is responsible for the ship's safety and he'll always be stationed on the bridge, usually with a junior, unqualified officer as the second officer-of-the-watch. At action stations he'll be joined by the navigating officer.

HMS Winchester has four qualified and practicing warfare officers. Two of them are Principal Warfare Officers (PWOs) who keep watches as the captain's representative in the ops room. There are two additional warfare officers who are unique to air defence ships, having served their time as PWOs and been further trained as Anti-Air-Warfare-Officers, to co-ordinate the air defence of a group of ships; they are called AAWOs. The longest serving of the two AAWOs holds the additional role of Operations Officer, responsible to the captain for the efficiency of the warfare department and by extension for the warfighting capability of the ship. *Winchester* also carries two Fighter Controllers, who are likewise unique to air defence ships. They are junior officers who are trained in directing combat aircraft by radar and radio; most of them will eventually become PWOs and then AAWOs.

There are a few other characters that you'll meet. The Missile Gun Director Blind (MGDB) at action stations is a Chief Petty Officer Missileman who is responsible for directing all the ship's weapons. He answers to the shorthand *Blind*. The Missile Gun Director Visual (MGDV) is also a Chief Petty Officer Missileman who looks after all the close range weapons and directs visual engagements, he answers to *Visual*. The Electronic Warfare Director (EWD) is a Chief Petty Officer Electronic Warfare and he directs the electronic warfare systems including the critically important UAA-1 ESM kit. At Action Stations the Operations Room is full to overflowing with specialist officers and ratings, and the challenging task of managing all this goes to a Chief Petty Officer Radar, in his role as the Ops Room Supervisor (ORS). These are all men; the Royal Navy started sending women to sea in combat ships two years later, in 1990.

For Operation Armilla, *Winchester* has embarked a Royal Marine air defence detachment of three Javelin man-portable air defence fire units. The Javelin is a semi-automatic system that is designed to defend a very small area and is ideal to deploy to escorted tankers that are otherwise defenceless.

***

This is a book about the recent past, thirty-seven years ago as I write this introduction. I expect it will feel like ancient history to many readers, and writing it has certainly tested my memory. Type 42 destroyers are absent from the world's oceans, the Lynx helicopter is no longer to be seen on the decks of Royal Navy ships, and almost all of the sensors and weapons that have entered this story and that I and my shipmates spent so many years mastering, have passed into history. Nevertheless, British warships still ply the waters of the Arabian Gulf, keeping the sea lanes open, and they'll probably continue to do so for many years to come. I hope this book about a fictional Royal Navy destroyer with its fictional crew might preserve the memory of *Operation Armilla* for generations yet to come.

However, when all is said and done, this is a story about a grand adventure and like all the best adventures it has at its heart a noble cause. Don't get bogged down in the technology, and enjoy the ride!

***

Prologue

HMS Winchester, at Sea

'Whiskey, this is Alfa Whiskey. Sitrep. The force is under surveillance and there are indications of movements at the enemy air bases to the north, an attack is likely in the next three-zero minutes. Air threat warning yellow, weapons tight.'

The anti-air warfare officer – the AAWO – looked at the clock and noted the time on the face of his tactical display: zero-nine-thirty-two. The chinagraph pencil lead snapped on the last horizontal stroke of the figure *two* and he hardly noticed when it was taken from his hand by his assistant and replaced with an intact pencil. He kept track of his routine sitreps to avoid overloading the anti-air-warfare circuit with too much traffic while still keeping his air defence assets informed. There was also the matter of authority. He wanted the other ships to sit up and take notice when he spoke, and if he was constantly on the circuit they'd start to ignore him; familiarity breeds contempt.

As well as being the overall commander of this task group, *HMS Winchester* was also the anti-air-warfare commander – AAWC – and the AAWC owned the callsign Alfa Whiskey. As the on-watch AAWO, he carried the responsibility for co-ordinating the defence of the whole task group – callsign Whiskey – against air threats. It was a strong force: two Type 42 guided missile destroyers, *Winchester* and *Stirling*, each armed with the Seadart medium range surface-to-air missile system, and two Type 22 frigates, *Bellona* and *Biter* with their Seawolf close range surface-to-air missiles. They were escorting two replenishment ships of the Royal Feet Auxiliary, *Fort Brockhurst* and *Brown Rover*; the precious stores and fuel that they carried were vital to the task group's mission.

The captain glanced up at the clock as the AAWO finished his sitrep. He was listening to the AAW circuit in one ear but he had the ship's command open line in the other; he was in immediate contact with all of his command team. The next important call came on the open line.

'Captain, Officer-of-the-Watch. In two minutes *Fort Brockhurst* will be altering course two-three-zero in accordance with the nav plan.'

The captain glanced at the radar display in front of him. It was quite different to the AAWO's vast, horizontal tactical display. Its sweeping arm of light showed only the nearby surface contacts, for until this potential air raid developed further, his main concern was the navigational safety of the ship. He looked down the bearing of the new course, thirty degrees to port of their present heading, to confirm that his task group wasn't about to stand in towards any new hazard, or itself pose a danger to the innocent maritime traffic that continued to flow to the south of them.

'Thank you, Officer-of-the-Watch. Chief Yeoman, pass the new base course to the task group.'

'Officer-of-the-Watch, PWO. Come left two-three-zero.'

The Principal Warfare Officer – the PWO – was responsible for manoeuvering the ship in action, but he gave his orders through the officer-of-the-watch on the bridge, who could use his mark one eyeball to actually look out of the window to confirm that the manoeuvre was safe.

'Come left two-three-zero,' the officer-of-the-watch repeated.

The captain's chair groaned in its rotating socket as *Winchester* heeled gently to starboard, away from the direction of the turn. He leaned forward and adjusted the range and squelch controls on his radar display so that he could better see close-in contacts. So far so good. The navigation plan had been signalled the evening before and he'd already designated a screening sector for each ship so that the two auxiliaries were properly protected against air attack. It was the PWO's responsibility to manoeuvre the ship to stay within its sector and react to any developments, and all he had to do was monitor the flow of orders from the PWO up to the officer-of-the-watch on the bridge. Long gone were the days when a captain commanded his ship in action from the bridge; they'd been swept away in the torrent of new technology in the nineteen-sixties. The command of the ship had moved down to the operations room, in *Winchester's* case three decks below the bridge. He was young enough to have easily embraced the new way of doing things, but sometimes even he yearned for a view of the sea and the sky. He could sense that something was agitating the Electronic Warfare Director – the EWD – behind him. He was in urgent discussion with the UAA-1 operator, but the captain couldn't hear what it was about. Chief Petty Officer Quinn was new to the ship and he hadn't yet proved his worth. The UAA-1 was the equipment that picked up radar transmissions from other ships and aircraft, and it would likely be their first indication of an attack. He glanced again at the clock. He'd been doing this for four weeks and he could predict the pattern of air attacks, so any moment now…

The measured tones of the reports and orders on the command open line were shattered by the EWD's urgent call.

'Puffball! Zero-one-five. Puffball!'

This was the first positive indication of the expected air raid. *Puffball* was the codeword for a surveillance radar fitted to the Soviet-built Badger maritime attack aircraft, and in this theatre the Badgers carried the potent Silkworm missiles.

'Captain, AAWO. That racket correlates with track four-three-one-seven, forty miles to the north tracking southwest. I'm going to classify it hostile and bring the air threat warning to red.'

The captain stepped from his chair and leaned across to study the AAWO's tactical display. There it was, a single radar contact looking innocent enough among all the others. But it was moving slantwise out of the normal airlanes, and the EWD's intercept line indicating the direction of the racket passed right through the contact.

'Very well.'

The AAWO flicked his headset switch to the transmit position. Keep it calm, there was plenty of time. He took a deep breath.

'Whiskey this is Alfa Whiskey. Hostile track four-three-one-seven, ten thousand feet, assessed Badger, possibly carrying Silkworms. Air threat warning red, weapons tight. *Stirling* cover track four-three-one-seven with birds.'

Stirling, the other Type 42 destroyer in the task group, was stationed further to the west and would get a better shot at any incoming missiles. The order to cover the track meant that one of *Stirling's* two fire control radars would be locked onto the target. Any moment now the pilot in the attack aircraft would be getting a persistent shriek in his ear from his own electronic warning kit, telling him that an anti-aircraft missile system was locked onto him.

'Officer-of-the-Watch, Captain. Are *Bellona* and *Biter* in their goalkeeping stations?'

'Affirmative, sir. *Bellona's* covering *Fort Brockhurst* and *Biter's* covering *Brown Rover*.'

The goalkeeping stations required the frigates to be so close to the ships that they were to protect that it was difficult to separate them on the radar unless he wound his display's range down to the lowest setting and dialled down on the squelch knob. Then he'd lose his view of the wider task group and he didn't want to do that, not while this air raid was developing.

'Alfa Whiskey, this is Charlie Whiskey. Covering track four-three-one-seven. Birds negat track four-three-one-seven.'

Stirling's AAWO was announcing that he had a fire control radar lock on the Badger, but it was still out of range of his Seadart system.

'AAWO, EWD. Jam the Puffball, sir?'

Winchester had been fitted with a Type 675 jammer –

known as the *Hooter* – during its last refit and the EWD was eager to use all of his toys, particularly as *Stirling* didn't have one. The Hooter was capable of blinding the Badger's radar over a sector centred on *Winchester*, and it made it difficult for the attacking aircraft to pick out its target. On the other hand it unequivocally confirmed to the Badger that its target was in the vicinity.

'Negative, EWD. If they're still trying to pick us out from the other traffic, giving them a spoke will only help them.'

The captain heard the AAWOs voice on the AAW circuit again.

'Whiskey this is Alfa Whiskey. Hostile four-three-one-seven continues tracking southwest, range four-zero nautical miles, ten thousand feet, beyond birds range. Air threat warning red, weapons tight.'

So far so good, and the AAWO took a moment to look around. A Type 42's ops room was a crowded space at action stations, so much so that often the easiest way to move from one side to the other was to climb up to the deck above and walk across the cabin flat to drop down another ladder. Every seat was filled and there were at least a dozen people standing. Over to his left and partially obscured by his radar consol, the air picture team was staring earnestly at their radar displays, with their fingers on their tracker-balls, keeping tabs on everything that was moving in the air within a hundred miles. Behind him the missile gun director blind, a chief petty officer, was monitoring his weapon systems and waiting for the order to bring them into action. Over his right shoulder the EWD searched for indications of enemy radars and further to his right, in the centre of the ops room, he could see the captain looking thoughtful. Another glance at the tactical display showed him that the Badger was still tracking southwest, just beyond Seadart engagement range. If past performance was any guide, it would soon turn in, and at about twenty miles from the task group it would release two Silkworm missiles. Then the training would kick in. First the soft-kill: chaff to decoy the incoming missiles; manoeuvre to make the ships more difficult targets; perhaps the jammer to blind the missiles, but beware of the home-on-jam feature. Then the hard-kill: Seadart to shoot them down at longer range and the frigates' Seawolf missiles as a backup if they evaded the Seadart. The warships all had close-in weapon systems as a last-ditch defence, but the two auxiliaries had nothing, they were relying entirely on their escorts. So far so good, indeed. They'd done this a dozen times and the AAWO liked to think that his team excelled at it, in fact he thought they were the best. It was hardly a challenge any more. But was it too good to be true? The greatest sin in battle is to underestimate one's enemy. He dropped his headset to rest around his neck and took a step closer to the captain.

'Something's not right here, sir, this is too obvious.'

'I agree. Shore-based anti-ship missiles perhaps?'

'They're not in the intelligence summary, but it isn't always right. I'm beginning to suspect that we're being duped.'

He replaced his headset and settled it across his ears. Whether the threat came from the air or from the land, once the missiles had been launched they were an air threat and it was the responsibility of the air picture supervisor – the APS – to spot them.

'APS, AAWO. Look out for fast-moving contacts leaving the shoreline to the north and northeast.'

Winchester's computerised command system didn't have a representation of the shoreline on the tactical displays but the AAWO's assistant marked a rough approximation of its position using the chinagraph pencil. The AAWO stabbed his finger at the area that he was concerned about and his assistant adjusted the scale and offset to better see what was moving, thus making his laborious pencil marks wildly inaccurate. He philosophically set about rearranging them for this new scale. It was difficult for the radar to see a low air contact over the land and probably the first indication would come as it broke free from the clutter along the shoreline.

'Whiskey this is Alfa Whiskey. Hostile four-three-one-seven continues tracking southwest beyond birds range. Assess hostile four-three-one-seven might be targeting for a land-based attack from north and northeast. Air threat warning red, weapons tight.'

The AAWO could sense the tension rising and he could feel the sweat on his arms and chest. Something must happen soon; that Badger wasn't airborne for its own amusement. His assistant jabbed at the tactical display, at a fleeting blip close to where his chinagraph mark said that the shoreline should be. They waited the three seconds that the target indication radar took to make its next sweep… nothing. Another three seconds. Ah, there it was again, and now there were two contacts. In that six seconds they'd moved a mile closer to the task group. The local air trackers had seen it too and they were furiously punching their keyboards to create the electronic tracks that would initiate the process of countermeasures. He glanced at the EWD; the man looked uncertain, as though he was trying to decide what to do; that wasn't good enough and he'd need to address that later. He turned back to his tactical display a moment before the shrill blast of the EWD's whistle cut through the low hum of voices. His urgent shout said the rest.

'Silkworm! Zero-three-two. Silkworm!'

So that was it. As he'd guessed, the Badger was for surveillance and to distract the task group's air defences while a hitherto unknown battery of land-based Silkworms to the northeast used the Badger's information to launch their missiles.

The soft-kill manager – the off-watch AAWO – leaned across the tactical display and fired the three-inch chaff rockets then across the EWD's shoulder to fire the Seagnat chaff. That would give the incoming missiles a choice of targets to lock onto, and most of them would be decoys.

'Whiskey this is Alfa Whiskey. Tracks four-four-one-two and four-four-two-two assessed vampires. Charlie Whiskey take the left, Bravo Whiskey take the right. Weapons free, deploy chaff.'

The AAWC was ordering *Stirling* and his own ship *Winchester* – Bravo Whiskey – to engage the inbound missiles. There was no need to tell *Bellona* and *Biter* what to do, they knew that a *vampire* was an enemy anti-ship missile inbound. They were well-drilled in their goalkeeper duties and knew best how to protect the auxiliaries if the Silkworms should get past *Winchester* and *Stirling's* outer defences.

'Officer-of-the-Watch, PWO. Come hard right zero-one-two.'

The PWO was manoeuvering the ship to place the threat twenty degrees on the bow to give the Silkworms the smallest possible radar signature to lock onto, while keeping *Winchester's* weapon arcs open. There was one more thing he needed to do.

'Phalanx to auto.'

In auto mode the Vulcan Phalanx gatling gun would engage anything that met its pre-set criteria, and a Silkworm missile coming straight for *Winchester* at close to the speed of sound would be instantly assessed as a threat and automatically engaged as soon as it was in range.

'Birds affirm track four-four-two-two.'

Blind announced on command open line that his Seadart system had locked onto its target. He held his hand over the keys that the Seadart controller would need to hit to fire the missile. The AAWO was aware that the gun controller was slewing the 4.5 inch gun to follow the fire control radar that was locked onto the incoming missiles. A medium range gun had little chance against a Mach 0.9 missile, but if all else failed…

The missile gun director blind needed no more orders to bring the Seadart into action. The AAWC had declared weapons free and had designated a target to each ship. The missile gun director blind repeated the AAWO's order over the Seadart control circuit and took his hand off the Seadart controller's keys.

'Take track four-four-two-two with birds.'

Twenty miles, nineteen, eighteen. A missile travelling at Mach 0.9 covered half a mile between each sweep of the target indication radar and travelled a nautical mile every six seconds.

'This is Charlie Whiskey, birds away track four-four-two-one.'

Stirling had fired a salvo of Seadart missiles. *Winchester's* Seadart controller was waiting for the first moment that his own missiles could be launched. Now. He made the engage key and the missile gun director blind chimed in with his own report on the AAW circuit.

'This is Bravo Whiskey, birds away track four-four-two-two.'

The AAWO watched the little dots that represented the four Seadart missiles – two from *Stirling* followed closely by two from *Winchester* – as they advanced on the incoming Silkworm missiles at twice the speed of sound. He saw them merge with the targets at twelve miles range, then he shifted his eyes to the Badger to the northwest. There was still something amiss.

'This is *Stirling*, splashed track four-four-two-one.'

'This is *Winchester*, splashed track four-four-two-two.'

Splashed: the targets had been destroyed. The AAWO flicked his transmit switch.

'Whiskey this is Alfa Whiskey. All vampires splashed. Air threat warning remains red based on the Badger to the northwest and possible second salvo of vampires.'

Seconds passed and the Badger continued on its way just beyond Seadart range. Surely that wasn't all. It was the EWD's whistle that announced that the AAWO's hunch was correct, it cut through everything else that was happening to announce the immediate and grave threat.

'Silkworm! three-two-five. Silkworm!'

'Officer-of-the-Watch, PWO. Come hard left three-four-five.'

The PWO's order was hardly given before the deck heeled sharply and there was a clatter as the inevitable loose gear fell from computer consoles and tactical displays. It was imperative to manoeuvre the ship quickly because these new Silkworms could hardly be twenty miles away by now, and that meant only two minutes to impact, if they should get that far.

'Whiskey this is Alfa Whiskey. Tracks three-seven-zero-zero and three-seven-five-five assessed vampires. Charlie Whiskey take the left, Bravo Whiskey take the right. Weapons free, deploy Chaff.'

The AAWO would dearly like to have a shot at the Badger, it was within range now, but the urgent need was to defeat the inbound missiles, the Badger could wait.

'This is Bravo Whiskey, birds away track three-seven-five-five.'

'This is Charlie Whiskey, birds away track three-seven-zero-zero.'

The missile gun director blind would have time later to savour that moment. Despite being further way, his ship had engaged the incoming Silkworms first, and his old friend in *Stirling* would pay the penalty in beer when they next met. Nevertheless, it was good work from both ships to engage a new threat so quickly.

Once again the AAWO found himself able to think of the next move while the missile gun director blind dealt with the immediate engagements.

'Captain, sir, AAWO. As soon as there are no birds in the air I'd like to try to lure that Badger closer and get a shot at him. If we jam his Puffball he might try to move in to burn through the jamming. He must need to carry out BDA.'

The captain thought for a moment. Perhaps it would work. And the AAWO was right, it was standard practice for an attacker to attempt some sort of battle damage assessment if only to determine whether another attack would be required. And certainly *Winchester* mustn't use the jammer while the Seadarts were being guided to their targets. The latest trials results suggested that the hooter wouldn't interfere with the J-band receiver in the back of the missiles, but he didn't want to risk it.

'As soon as the Seadart engagement is over, AAWO,' replied the captain as he stood to watch it on the tactical display. Again he saw the contacts merge and heard the missile gun director blind's report on the AAW circuit, quickly followed by *Stirling's* report.

'This is Bravo Whiskey, splashed track three-seven-five-five.'

'This is Charlie Whiskey, splashed track three-seven-zero-zero.'

The AAWO was also watching the engagement. He snapped out an order on command open line, cutting right through the chief yeoman's report of the convoy's movements.

'EWD, take track four-three-one-seven with hooter.'

Then on the AAW circuit.

'Whiskey, this is Alfa Whiskey. Bravo Whiskey take track four-three-one-seven with Hooter. Charlie Whiskey take track four-three-one-seven with birds.'

Stirling was closer, but still at the extreme limit of the Seadart's range.

'APS, keep watching the coastline, this isn't over yet.'

Come on, come on, only a few miles closer and he's ours.

The AAWO watched intently, passionately, willing the Badger to turn towards the task group, but when it turned, it was to starboard, away from the task group and towards safety.

'Captain, Officer-of-the-Watch. *Stirling's* making a sprint to the northwest corner of her sector, it looks like she's winding up to full speed.'

The AAWO grinned wryly. Full marks for effort, but unless that Badger turned back towards the task group it was safe. Perhaps now it *was* all over.

He saw a lieutenant commander pushing his way through the crowded ops room towards the captain. He was conspicuous for being in his normal uniform and not wearing the white anti-flash protection that covered everyone else's head and hands, and he was sporting a beret. He said something to the captain who nodded in agreement and the interloper stood tall and raised his voice.

'Right, off headsets everyone. That's it, end of the air defence exercise. Your next serial is the Phalanx firing,' he looked at his watch, 'the target towing Canberra will be airborne in twenty minutes and you need to be in the firing area in fifteen. I'll debrief the command team in the captain's cabin after the firing; the Seariders will debrief the stations separately.'

***

Winchester powered west to the area that had been cleared for the firing.

'Captain, AAWO. Airmove departure received for the Canberra. We should see him soon.'

'Very well. Officer-of-the-Watch, make another pipe that the upper deck is out of bounds.'

When the Vulcan Phalanx destroyed a rushton target it was quite common for small fragments to pepper the ship's decks, like shrapnel from an air-burst shell.

The fighter controller had set himself up to control the target towing aircraft and he was watching the radar and listening to his radio to get the first contact with the Canberra. He'd read all the instructions and he knew what to do, and he was acutely aware that the success of this live firing exercise would be down to his skill in controlling the aircraft.

The Vulcan Phalanx was an automatic gatling gun designed to protect the ship on which it was fitted against missile attack, and it had its own surveillance and target tracking radar. It was programmed with a set of engagement parameters, and once it was in the automatic mode it would engage any contact that met those parameters. Today *Winchester* would be practicing against a rushton towed target representing a sea-skimming missile – an Exocet or one of the radar altimeter-equipped Silkworm variants. The rushton target was a complex piece of equipment; it had its own radar altimeter that measured its distance from the sea and adjusted its control surfaces to keep it at a set level, twenty feet in this case. The target would pass close – very close—to the ship, so close that if the Phalanx failed to destroy it, there was a significant risk that the target would smash into the ship, causing damage and casualties on the scale of a small missile hit. The fighter controller had two means of preventing this: first he directed the aircraft so that the rushton target would miss the ship by a small margin, and second, as soon as the towing aircraft passed overhead he'd order the pilot to break the target's radar altimeter lock so that it would start to climb and be above the height of *Winchester's* mast as it passed. It still had to be within the engagement criteria or the firing exercise would be a failure. There was yet another safety issue. The Canberra and the target must both pass *Winchester* on the same side, otherwise there was a risk of wrapping the Kevlar towing wire around the ship's superstructure. The fighter controller felt the pressure of the occasion.

'*Winchester* this is Eighty-two.'

'Eighty-two, this is *Winchester*. Contact, you're feet wet over Chesil Beach.'

'Roger *Winchester*, that's us. I'm starting to deploy the rushton now.'

The fighter controller saw the target apparently split into two, and the separate parts drew further and further apart as the towing line extended behind the Canberra.

'*Winchester*, Eighty-two, my target is deployed. Request a vector.'

'Eighty-two this is *Winchester*. Vector one-seven-five. When you're steady I'll be on your nose at one-seven miles.'

'Eighty-two, Roger. Let me know when I'm in the firing area.'

'Four miles to the firing area, Eighty-two. Stand by.'

The Portland exercise areas were busy today and *Winchester* had only two adjacent areas that were cleared for firing and just as importantly they were cleared for the rushton target at low level. The two areas combined were barely large enough for the Canberra to engage the rushton altitude lock and make a run at the ship.

'Eighty-two, you're entering the exercise area now and you're clear to engage your altitude lock.'

'Eighty-two, roger.'

'*Winchester*, eighty-two. Altitude lock engaged. The target looks good visually.'

'Eighty-two, you're clear inbound. Come right one-seven-seven.'

The AAWO was waiting for this moment.

'Check safety Phalanx.'

The missile gun director visual took a last look down the intended firing bearing.

'Clear visual.'

The officer-of-the-watch glanced at the flight deck camera. The Lynx was strapped down and the flight deck crew were in the hangar.

'Helicopter correct.'

The PWO did the same on his radar, watching for any new blips that might represent a tiny fishing boat bobbing among the waves, unseen from the bridge.

'Clear blind.'

The missile gun director visual checked that the Phalanx was pointing in the right direction.

'Turret correct.'

The captain noted all those essential reports but sat impassively, watching his radar display and monitoring the activity in the ops room.

'The Canberra's visual bearing zero-one-five.'

'What's its bearing doing, Officer-of-the-Watch?'

'Drawing slowly left, sir.'

'Fighter controller, are you happy that the target's drawing left too?'

'Affirmative, sir. It'll pass two hundred yards across our stern.'

Still one last report. The Canberra must actually pass clear of the ship's stern before the captain would give his approval, so that there was no chance of the Phalanx seeing the aircraft as its legitimate target.

They heard the sound of the Canberra's engines in the ops room at the same time as the officer-of-the-watch burst onto the command open line.

'The target towing aircraft has passed astern, sir.'

'Command approved,' the captain said in a calm, measured tone.

'Phalanx to auto,' cried the AAWO.

There was a breathless silence, then a sound like a supersonic chainsaw that lasted for no more than five seconds.

'*Winchester*, this is Eighty-two. Target destroyed. Keep an eye on me while I reel in and then I'm RTB.'

***

Winchester was already steaming fast for Portland Harbour when they gathered in the cabin. As always, there was no time to lose and the ship would pause only to disembark the seariding staff to boats in the shelter of the breakwaters before going about her business. The deck of the captain's cabin vibrated under their feet as the twin Olympus gas turbines thrust the destroyer through the waves.

'Well, gentlemen, those are your last exercises before you deploy.'

The Searider, an experienced AAWO himself, and the leader of a team of specialists from Flag Officer Sea Training's staff at Portland, was smiling, so perhaps he brought good news. They knew they'd done well, but FOST assessments were notoriously harsh and it only took one weak link to spoil the show.

'Here's what you've all been waiting to hear.'

The Searider allowed himself a dramatic pause.

'Your overall assessment is … *very satisfactory*.'

The PWO, a nervous newly-qualified lieutenant, let out an involuntary cheer, and everyone grinned in relief. Very satisfactory assessments were rare, particularly in Type 42s, and they came only as a result of relentless training and obsessive attention to detail, but *good* would have been better.

'You would have achieved a *good*, if the EW team had been a little quicker in spotting the Puffball first time. The Canberra had been transmitting on his Puffball simulator for at least a minute before he called it, and the Hawks' simulator pods had been in Silkworm mode for twenty seconds before he blew his whistle the first time. Twenty seconds, gentlemen, that's over three miles at Silkworm speed. You can't afford to give that time away so easily.'

He let that sink in for a moment.

Only one member of *Winchester's* command team wasn't smiling. The on watch AAWO for this exercise was also the ship's operations officer – known to all as *Ops* – the head of all the warfare team and the man responsible for its fighting effectiveness. He'd hoped with all his heart for that coveted FOST *good*. The Canberra aircraft that had simulated the Badger and the Hawk aircraft that had simulated the Silkworms were all well known to his team, they'd been attacking *Winchester* for the past four weeks at Portland, and the EWD should have done better. Was he distracted by all the new kit that had been fitted for this deployment, or was it something more deep-seated?

'My report will recommend that you concentrate on bringing your EW team up to speed, and if by the time you reach Gibraltar you think you might need some extra help, we'll send out the Warrant Officer EW for your passage through the Med. However, it'll be interesting to see how *Stirling's* team handled it, and I might be a little too harsh.'

That brought a laugh. FOST staff were always too harsh, but it was that strict demand for ever higher standards that gave the Royal Navy its fighting edge.

'So, that's all from FOST and I congratulate you on a good. No,' he corrected himself, 'a *very satisfactory* piece of work for your final exercise. I wish you well on your deployment to the Gulf. But remember this, the next time you hear the EWD shout *Silkworm!* it could be for real, and he'd better not have waited twenty seconds to blow his whistle.'

***

Chapter One

Tuesday, 0427
HMS Winchester, at Sea, Gulf of Oman
Operation Armilla Daily Sitrep: Transit from Muscat to Fujairah Anchorage…

'Captain, sir, Officer-of-the-Watch…'

Commander David Mayhew was startled out of a deep sleep by the voice from the speaker a few feet from his head. The officers of the watch always spoke in soft tones during these silent hours – unless there was an emergency – as though tentatively apologising for calling him. Their voices sounded intimate, blending easily into his subconscious. For a moment he thought it was part of a dream, but only for the fraction of a second that it took for his mind to separate reality from fiction. He reached for the black plastic microphone that nestled in its cradle beside his bunk and tugged at the spiral cable to bring it close enough to his mouth.

'Captain.'

'Good morning, sir. You asked for a call half an hour before nautical twilight. It's four-twenty-seven, the Fujairah anchorage bears three-one-zero at thirteen miles and we're steering zero-one-zero at four knots in accordance with the nav plan. *Bellona* and *Brown Rover* are in station astern. The MEO asked me to report that the port Tyne gas turbine has run smoothly overnight, but he didn't manage to get all the vibration readings that he would have liked.'

That was the new sub lieutenant who'd joined just before they left Portsmouth two months ago, Ben Saxby, a ship's diver hoping to become a mine clearance diver in the future. Well, good luck to him, there was no accounting for taste, and diving into mine-infested waters was definitely not high on Mayhew's own bucket list. Saxby had earned his bridge watchkeeping ticket in a minehunter on the west coast of Scotland, and the complexity of a Type 42 guided missile destroyer had been largely a mystery to him when he walked aboard in the last few days before the deployment. Mayhew had authorised him to stand his own watches only two days previously, just in time to have three qualified bridge watchkeepers available for defence watches.

'Thank you, Officer-of-the-Watch.'

Mayhew could have added that he'd come up to the bridge immediately, but it would have been an unnecessary comment. Saxby should be conducting his watch in the same way whether his captain was expected imminently or not. In fact there was no hurry, the tankers would be starting to weigh their anchors in the next half-hour and they'd embark their pilots at about six-o'clock. It would be at least an hour later that they'd come clear of the Fujairah anchorage and disembark the pilots, at about seven o'clock. Still, there was something compelling about being on the bridge at the first hint of daylight. Naval captains had done so for centuries, for dawn was the most likely time to be surprised by an enemy suddenly appearing from the dark at close range. In fact *Winchester* had no enemies at present, or at least none that had declared their hands, and yet there were unseen perils all around. He lay in his bunk for a few more moments rehearsing in his mind the plans for the next few hours. The ship was in cruising watches at the moment – state 3 condition x-ray – as they had been since leaving Portsmouth, except when they'd been exercising or entering port. He could maintain that state indefinitely; it allowed for all the usual maintenance routines, for the crew to sleep and eat, and for a reasonable amount of recreation time. It was important that he shouldn't increase the ship's readiness too soon, but the dangers increased with each mile that they travelled towards the Straits of Hormuz. He intended to call defence watches – state two condition yankee – at six o'clock; that would allow them all to settle into the routine while they loitered off Fujairah waiting for the convoy. They'd probably have to maintain that six hours on, six hours off routine for the next week until they left the Gulf again, except when they went to action stations, when every man in the ship was at his post. As soon as the tankers had disembarked their pilots he'd send the first lieutenant and the Javelin teams across in the Lynx.

During the two world wars the navy always placed a commodore in the lead ship of each convoy, to keep the other merchant ships in line and to maintain a liaison with the escort commander. He was a commodore by courtesy because it was usually a retired naval officer who had volunteered to be re-activated, and he could be anything from a captain to a rear admiral. *Winchester's* first lieutenant's task was not unlike that of a convoy commodore except that in this case he held the post for a matter of half a day, whereas the Atlantic convoys took weeks to plough their way between the new world and the old.

After depositing the first lieutenant and the Javelin fire unit, the Lynx could carry out a surface search along his intended route to the Straits. The tankers had to cover sixty miles of UAE and Omani territorial waters before they entered the traffic separation scheme in the Straits of Hormuz, so at a probable best speed of twelve knots, he could stay at defence watches until shortly after twelve o'clock and then go to action stations for the transit of the Silkworm envelope.

Silkworm! The very name gave him the shivers. He'd joined the navy at the height of the cold war and had trained to face the Soviet navy in the frigid waters of the strategic gap between Greenland and the Shetlands. He could recite the range, the guidance mechanism and the effectiveness of all of the Soviet navy's missiles, from the venerable but battle-proven Styx to the modern, deadly Sunburn. However, the Soviet navy wasn't the threat that it used to be and under Gorbachev the Soviet Union was groping its way towards an accord with the western alliance. Yet its missile technology had been widely sold throughout the world and the Styx had passed through Chinese hands into the arsenals of both of the belligerents in the current Iran

Iraq war.

With a few modifications Styx had become Silkworm, and it was now the principal threat to the tankers that brought the oil and natural gas from the Gulf to energy-hungry consumers throughout the world. Silkworm was the focus of the pre-deployment command team training at *HMS Dryad*, the tactical school in the Hampshire countryside to the north of Portsmouth. It was the stick with which the FOST Seariders at Portland beat the ships that passed through their hands on their way to the Gulf. Mayhew could instantly conjure it all in his mind. The slowly building tension as the enemy's surveillance forces moved into place, the change in the radar modes that hinted at a developing attack, and then the harsh blast of the EWD's whistle: Silkworm! Another blast. Silkworm! That imperative warning cut through whatever else was happening. Everyone focussed on defeating the missile, for if the Silkworm got through, all their other concerns would be solved in the most deadly manner possible. Jammers, chaff, manoeuvre, Seadart, Phalanx; everything must come together to get the ship through the next two or three minutes as the deadly missile sped across the sea. Of course, that was all a drill. At *Dryad* the missile was nothing more than a series of electronic clues injected into the tactical game. It was a step more realistic at Portland where a Canberra aircraft would simulate the missile carrier, and a Hawk or Hunter aircraft would simulate the inbound missiles, ending with an exuberant and noisy overflight at low level.

This single missile type was the reason for *Winchester* being in the Middle East. The twelve Type 42 destroyers with their Seadart anti-aircraft missile systems were the only ships in the Royal Navy that had a decent chance of defending a convoy of tankers against a Silkworm once it had been launched. Every convoy through the Straits was given a Type 42 as an escort, as well as a frigate armed with the shorter range Seawolf missiles. Command of a Type 42, as every Royal Navy warfare officer knew, carried a high probability of a deployment to the Gulf.

'Captain, sir.'

'Captain.'

'I can hear *World Antigua* and *British Solace* talking on VHF. They're coming to short stay on their anchors; they're expecting the pilots soon by the sound of it.'

Mayhew grimaced. It looked like the tankers would be underway thirty minutes earlier than he'd expected. He'd hoped for enough time to shower and shave in peace, but if the tankers were already chatting he should start to get involved.

'Very well, I'll be on the bridge in five minutes.'

***

Mayhew pulled on his white overalls and his steel-toed steaming boots and made his way to the bridge. He still hoped for that shower and shave, but now that things were moving the ship might need to go into defence watches before he had another chance to go to his cabin, and if he expected his crew to be properly rigged in their action working dress, then so should he.

The entirety of the short route was bathed in red light so that his night vision wasn't compromised, and he ran up the ladder from his cabin flat to the bridge with practiced ease. It would have been an odd scene for one not accustomed to a ship's bridge at night. Every possible source of light had been shaded or turned down to its lowest intensity so that only a few red pinpricks could be seen; even the light behind the quartermaster's gyro compass repeater was dimmed. The radar display and the chart table at the back of the bridge were shielded by a heavy blackout curtain and woe betide the junior officer that carelessly left it open. Mayhew knew how vital it was to cut down on lights on the bridge, and not only to safeguard the bridge watchkeepers' night vision. Years ago, as a newly-ticketed bridge watchkeeper, he'd once mistaken the reflection of a stray light on the bridge window for another ship on a steady bearing, and had come close to taking emergency action to avoid a collision. It was the quartermaster – the leading seaman at the wheel – who'd saved his pride on that occasion, and he'd learned a valuable lesson. He looked swiftly around. The quartermaster – a different man entirely – was at the wheel on the port side of the bridge and the radio operator was at his station on the starboard side. Saxby was standing beside the pelorus with his binoculars around his neck and looked as though he'd just replaced the microphone that connected him to the ops room, probably to tell them that the captain was on his way to the bridge. A movement of the curtain around the chart table showed where the second officer-of-the-watch, a midshipman, was marking the ship's position on the chart.

'Good morning, sir. They've stopped talking now but the last transmission was from *World Antigua* saying that she expected to be underway at zero-five-thirty.'

Mayhew climbed up into his chair. Only two people sat on the bridge: the captain and the quartermaster, all others had to stand for the duration of their watch, it was good for their souls. He picked up his binoculars and scanned the horizon. There was little to see on this dark night. To the east, far away over the Gulf of Oman, the sky was starting to lighten as the sun edged upwards towards the rim of the sea. To the west the bright deck lights of the dozen or so enormous tankers were just visible as they lay at the Fujairah anchorage awaiting orders, or pilots, or crew changes. Otherwise there were only half a dozen lights in sight, smaller merchant ships heading north towards the Straits or south into the Gulf of Oman and onwards to the solemn vastness of the Indian Ocean.

Half of the ships bound for the Gulf paused at Fujairah, mostly for a few hours or a day, but some for much longer as the wheels of international commerce worked slowly to match up ships and cargoes and destinations. Somewhere over there were the four tankers that *Winchester* and *Bellona* – the Royal Navy's on-duty task unit – were to escort through the Straits. *World Antigua, British Solace, Highlander, Eastern Heritage*; there was a harsh sort of lyrical resonance to their names that John Masefield could have used for an extra verse to his poem *Cargoes*. More prosaically, all were either British registered or with a substantial British financial interest. This was *Winchester's* second run up the Gulf, but the first where Mayhew commanded the task unit. Previously it had been *Stirling* commanding, but the commander of the whole task group was far to the south, coming back from Mombasa, half an ocean away. Whether leading or following, Mayhew hadn't done this often enough for it to become routine.

'Is Ops up and about, Officer-of-the-Watch?'

Mayhew rarely used his officers' names on the bridge but preferred the formality of a title.

'He was reading the signals half an hour ago, sir.'

Mayhew nodded. The operations officer was always about before his captain, getting a step ahead, as he put it.

'Well, call him up here, would you?'

'Aye-aye sir.'

Saxby picked up the microphone that he'd been talking on only a few seconds ago.

'Ops room, bridge.'

Three decks below the bridge, in the warm womb-like darkness of the operations room, the surface picture supervisor heard Saxby's call on his headset.

'Ops room, SPS, sir.'

'Is the ops officer down there?'

'He's in the MCO, sir.'

'Well, ask him to come up to the bridge to speak to the captain.'

The main communications office was joined to the ops room by a simple square hatch with a sliding wooden door. All signals that came into *Winchester* were printed onto paper – there was no electronic reader, at least not one that was portable – and the hatch was the quickest means of sending them through to the ops room. It was also a convenient means of quickly passing verbal messages between these two vital compartments.

'Will do, sir.'

***

Charles Allenby was young to be the ops officer of a Type 42, but he had the advantage over his contemporaries of having grown up in that class of ship. He'd been a fighter controller, a navigator and a PWO in a succession of destroyers. When he'd passed the course to become an AAWO, it was quite natural that he'd be appointed to another Type 42. He'd only spent a few months as the junior AAWO in *Winchester* when the senior AAWO – the ops officer by dint of that seniority – had, to his great joy, been selected for promotion and moved on to command a ship of his own. Allenby found himself, at the tender age of thirty-three, assuming the awesome responsibility for the fighting capacity of a four-thousand ton destroyer. He'd almost finished catching up with the night's signals when he heard the summons to the bridge. Most of the signals were irrelevant to him: stores requests, notifications of a change in the supplier for uniforms, reports on the vibrations in a gas turbine unit – known as a GTU – allocations of married quarters, that sort of thing. However, perhaps one in four were of interest and one in ten vital. Those interesting and vital signals contained the names of tankers waiting for an escort, reports on Soviet ships entering the Gulf, movements of auxiliaries carrying the task group's essential fuel and supplies. Every signal had to be read so that he was certain that he'd missed nothing. He glanced at the remaining dozen signals. It didn't look as though any of them would change the course of the next few hours, so he removed the signal that he'd been reading, clipped his own card spacer into the ring binder at the point where his reading had brought him, and returned it to its box.

'Print out another of this one, I'm taking the original to the captain, here's the DTG.'

He copied the unique date and time group from the

signal onto the radio operator's pad. His journey took hardly any time; out of the MCO and through the blackout curtain into the ops room on the starboard side, up the ladder to the wardroom flat, up another ladder to the captain's cabin flat, then the last ladder to emerge onto the bridge. Like the captain before him it took a moment to adjust to the darkness, but when he did he could see that the outside world was noticeably less black to starboard; dawn wasn't far off.

'Morning Ops, anything new?'

'Morning, sir. That Soviet task group, the Sovremenny, the Udaloy and the tanker that have been tracked all the way from the Northern Fleet are through the canal and half-way down the Red Sea. It's assumed that they'll stop at Aden, but if they don't we could see them in a week or so. Those mines that the Americans found off Bahrain, their numbers come from a batch that the Chinese sold to Iran – leftovers from the second-world-war that must have passed through half a dozen hands – so we can assume that we know who laid them. *RFA Fort Brockhurst* is asking for a rendezvous out in the Gulf of Oman for next week, here's the signal.' He handed over a single A4 sheet, 'there's nothing else of immediate concern and nothing to change our plans for the day.'

'There's no hard information on the Silkworm batteries then.'

'No, sir. I've been trying to make some sense of all the possible sightings, and really all I can say is that they could be anywhere from Kuhestak to Abu Musa, or even Siri. There's talk of a hardened shelter at Kuhestak, but nothing confirmed.'

Mayhew grimaced. When the intelligence reports were so contradictory and vague, it was as well to plan for the worst. The intelligence sources had been reporting for a month now that the Iranians were deploying their land-based Silkworm batteries to cover the Straits of Hormuz, rather than concentrating them close to the Iraqi border in the Northern Gulf, but none of them could say with certainty where they were. It was a problem, because they were inherently mobile and only needed a stretch of hardstanding to mount a surveillance radar and provide a firm base for the wheeled launchers. Even if they should be found by satellite surveillance, they could have moved before a second pass. Add to that the delay in passing the information to British warships in theatre, and the picture became hopelessly muddled. Kuhestak to Abu Musa. That meant that this inbound convoy that he had to cover would be in the Silkworm envelope from a point about sixty miles north of here, right through the traffic separation scheme and until they passed Dubai. That was about a hundred-and-fifty miles, so they'd be under threat for twelve or thirteen hours at thirteen knots, which was the normal speed of these convoys.

'I expect that's the best that we'll get. It sounds like the convoy is getting underway already. Remind me of the timings, would you?'

'Yes, sir. We'll go to defence watches at zero-six-hundred, that's an hour from now, and have the flying brief here on the bridge at zero-seven-hundred. We'll launch the Lynx at zero-seven-thirty to identify our tankers and deliver the first lieutenant and the Javelin fire units to *World Antigua*. Then they'll fly ahead to look past Khor Fakkan, check out the Soviet navy's deep water anchorage and carry out a surface search for two hours. *Bellona's* Lynx will deliver the other fire unit to *Highlander*, return to mum and drop down to alert fifteen; then they're tasked to relieve our Lynx on station. Assuming we don't waste too much time forming up the convoy, we'll go to action stations for the transit at twelve-hundred. We should be off Dubai and clear of the suspected Silkworm batteries on Abu Musa by zero-two-hundred tomorrow, and if all's well we can revert to defence watches.'

'The tankers know their order of sailing, don't they?'

'Yes, sir, and it's been impressed on them, otherwise

some of them won't get the benefit of the Javelin coverage.'

Mayhew nodded in agreement. They'd embarked a Royal Marine Javelin detachment for the deployment, three fire units of five marines each, with a lieutenant and a sergeant in command. It was better than nothing but the Javelin really was a forlorn hope. It was designed as a man-portable anti-aircraft missile and in theory it could engage a sub-sonic missile such as a Silkworm so long as the crossing rate wasn't too high. One of the fire units commanded by the sergeant was already embedded in *Brown Rover*. With fire units in the first and third tankers they should have a decent chance of offering a last-ditch defence, so long as the tankers and *Brown Rover* stayed at their ordered distances. Javelin hadn't been tested in a surface mode, but from the lofty height of a tanker's deck there was at least a possibility that it could be effective against small surface vessels. His greatest worry was his ability to control the fire units in the heat of an action, and there was only a rather fragile military VHF radio to help with that. The lieutenant, John Hook, had wanted to go with one of his fire units but Ops had insisted that he stay in *Winchester* and command them by radio.

Allenby could see what the captain was thinking. The command and control arrangements were flimsy to say the least, but with Hook on *Winchester's* bridge he could keep all three of his fire units informed and warn them of impending action. It really would have been better if the detachment had joined the ship at Portland and participated in the pre-deployment workup.

Mayhew pretended to read the signal about the rendezvous with the auxiliary in the Gulf of Oman. It was important, but the meeting wouldn't be for another week, after *Winchester* had taken the convoy into the Arabian Gulf and brought another out. His reply could wait. For now he covertly studied his ops officer. Privately, he thought him too young for the job, the second AAWO was older and had spent longer as a lieutenant commander, and perhaps would be better in the top warfare job. For that matter, the specialist underwater warfare PWO was senior to them both but as an anti-submarine specialist wasn't eligible to be the ops officer of a destroyer. He couldn't fault Allenby by any objective measure; he was knowledgeable, energetic and honest and he handled his department well, but he seemed to lack the maturity for the job. He was constantly taking on responsibilities and extra tasks and his zeal was a little overdone. He hadn't learned the value of delegation. Mayhew could attribute part of it to his personal circumstances. Allenby was newly divorced and his ex-wife was making it difficult to see his two very young children; it was understandable that he'd thrown himself into his profession. He seemed to have cut off all contact with a normal civilian existence, he even lived on board the ship while it was in port. As far as Mayhew could tell Allenby had no social life at all, but poured all of his energy into being the best ops officer that ever lived. It was unhealthy to say the least. Take this habit of spending the morning watch reading the signals before his captain was awake and when everyone else except the duty watchkeepers was sound asleep. It meant that as the captain he could be certain that his ops officer had all the answers, but could Allenby keep up that work-rate? Surely he would burn out before the deployment was over. Perhaps today would bring him to his senses. If it all went to plan, by the time they were through the Silkworm envelope and into the Gulf, Allenby would have been on his feet for twenty-four hours, and it was a fifty-fifty chance that he'd be on watch for the six hours of defence watches that followed. Could any human body stand that? Certainly Allenby had shown no signs of flagging from the moment that they sailed from Portsmouth for their workup at Portland, and that was already more than two months ago. Well, he'd bear watching.

'I suggest, sir, that we could send a holding reply to *Fort Brockhurst*, telling them our outline schedule and suggesting that we could rendezvous at midday in five days' time, on

Sunday, subject to operational needs. Nothing specific, but giving him an expectation of when we might meet.'

'Very well, draft something for me would you?'

There, he was doing it again, loading everything on the ops officer's all-too-willing shoulders.

***

Chapter Two

Tuesday, 0730
HMS Winchester, at Sea, Gulf of Oman
Armilla Daily Sitrep: Rendezvous World Antigua, British Solace, Highlander, Eastern Heritage…

The Lynx helicopter had started its life in the nineteen-seventies as a slim, streamlined thing of beauty. That aesthetic didn't last long as more and more sensors and weapons were added to cope with its expanding role. The Lynx that *Winchester* carried to the Gulf was so burdened with external additions that it was affectionately known as a *Snarling Warthog*. Yet for all that, it was still the best small-ship helicopter in the world and Carl Stevens and Joe Flanagan, the flight commander and the observer, looked upon it with affection as they strapped themselves in and started running through their pre-flight checks.

'Action Lynx, action Lynx.'

The strident tones of the main broadcast echoed throughout the ship, but elicited little response from the flight deck crew or the team on the bridge that would have to manoeuvre the ship. The Lynx was always launched in this way, and nine times out of ten it was in response to a pre-determined schedule. The timings had been set at the flying brief half an hour before, and the Lynx had already been brought to alert five so that it could be launched at five minutes notice.

'Navigator, confirm that *Winchester*, *Bellona*, *Highlander* and *World Antigua* are all clear of UAE territorial waters.'

'Confirmed, sir.'

That was the final command check that he could legally launch the Lynx and order *Bellona* to launch hers. Of course he already knew that the tankers and the escorts had crossed the twelve-mile line, but this formal question and response made the situation clear, and recorded the decision.

'Officer-of-the-Watch, PWO. Manoeuvre for a flying course.'

Saxby was still on watch. It was his bad luck to have spent the morning cruising watch on the bridge and to be the rostered officer-of-the-watch for the long forenoon. He'd been on his feet since four o'clock and he'd be on them until midday, but at least a sympathetic steward had brought him a bacon sandwich which he'd wolfed down with hardly a sideways glance at his captain who normally wouldn't have countenanced such a thing. In some ways the three officers who shared the duties of officer-of-the-watch at defence watches were lucky. Everyone else in the ship was watch-on, watch-off, but it was so important that the man with responsibility for the ship's safety was bright and alert, that if at all possible they were in this luxurious three-way watchbill. It worked well until it was interrupted by action stations or during the transition from cruising watches, when an officer could find himself spending long periods on watch.

He took another look at the flying course calculator. The northeasterly monsoon was into its dying gasps giving a true wind of zero-three-zero at six knots. The Lynx was moderately heavy, with a fifty calibre machine gun pod fitted under its starboard sponson. With the first lieutenant and five marines, the Javelin launcher and reloads in the back it needed eighteen knots of wind across the deck to launch safely. *World Antigua* had a rudimentary helicopter deck in the forward part of the ship, which meant that the first lieutenant was spared the horrors of being winched down. He had a morbid fear of any kind of flying and his worst nightmare was being strapped into a sling and pushed out of a helicopter's door, to dangle helplessly until his feet could find the firm steel of the tanker's deck. Today that wouldn't be necessary.

'Zero-five-zero, sir, thirteen knots. I can do that on the Tynes.'

Mayhew had already determined a flying course without

the aid of the calculator, and had come to much the same conclusion. That would give a relative wind of red two-zero – twenty degrees on the port bow – at the required eighteen knots. The course would take *Winchester* directly away from Fujairah and out of its station, but that couldn't be avoided, and it would only be for five minutes, until the Lynx was airborne. The fact that it could be done without engaging the fuel-thirsty Olympus gas turbines was important too. Mayhew had a refuelling tanker – *RFA Brown Rover* – under his command, but although replenishment at sea was a well-practiced art, there was always the chance that it could be forestalled by bad weather or some operational constraint. The Shamal wind that brought sandstorms to the Arabian Gulf was unlikely at this time of year, but not impossible, and an underway replenishment in a sandstorm wasn't an attractive proposition.

'Very well, make it so Officer-of-the-Watch, keep her steady.'

Saxby swivelled the pelorus ring and took one last look down the bearing. All clear, no dhows and none of the ubiquitous fishing dories. The rest of the task unit was on *Winchester's* port side and well clear.

'Revolutions for thirteen knots, starboard fifteen, steer zero-five-zero.'

Saxby was well aware of the need to keep the flight deck as horizontal as possible and fifteen degrees of helm would achieve that. Every possible safety precaution had already been taken but with the guardrails down the flight deck was an inherently dangerous place. The Lynx was held firmly by the harpoon that extended from its underbelly to catch into the steel grid in the flight deck, and the down-wash of its rotor blades would keep it in tension. The flight deck crew all knew the drill and moved in an ordered, predictable pattern, only leaving the safety of the hangar when it was necessary.

'Revolutions for thirteen knots, starboard fifteen, steer zero-five-zero,' the quartermaster replied.

He moved his engine control levers forward and turned his aircraft-style wheel to the right. He had an autopilot available but it wasn't trusted when fine steering was required. He watched as the gyro repeater ticked around until he had ten degrees to go to the ordered heading then applied a little port helm to arrest the ship's turn. The gyro repeater moved more slowly and came to rest dead on zero-five-zero. He centred his helm and watched the course carefully until he was happy that the ship had steadied.

'Course zero-five-zero, sir.'

Saxby looked at the wind indicator. It was a little unsteady showing anything between red one-five and red two-five; that would do.

'The ship's on the flying course, sir.'

Mayhew glanced at the same wind indicator and then at the screen that showed the view from the flight deck camera. He could see the flight deck officer's back and his upper arms and elbows, and beyond him the eager helicopter's whirring rotor blades. He leaned forward and pressed the *permission to fly* switch.

The change in tone of the rotor blades could be heard within the bridge as the Lynx released its harpoon and sprang clear of the deck. It immediately banked and started moving away to port to commence a wide turn to bring it on a course for the Fujairah anchorage.

Mayhew pressed the *do not fly* switch and strode across to the bridge wing to watch the Lynx depart. He could see that *Bellona's* Lynx was heading towards *Highlander* with their Javelin fire unit. He wanted the evidence of his own eyes that all was well before turning his ship back towards the west. He'd need a little more speed to regain his position at the head of the task unit and he was already making the mental calculations when the navigator broke in.

'Three-three-zero at our present speed will bring us back into station on *Brown Rover*, sir.'

'Very well, Navs. Officer-of-the-Watch, make your course three-three-zero and let me know as soon as we're back in our sector.'

'Captain, sir, AAWO.'

The bridge intercom sprang into life.

'EWD reports an Iranian P-3 Orion racket bearing zero-one-five. It correlates with a radar track at fifty miles, squawking military, a little way south of the Musandam Peninsula. That's probably the regular morning surveillance flight from Bandar Abbas. I'm releasing it to the data link and reporting it on the Gulf AAW circuit.'

Mayhew called up a mental picture of the Straits of Hormuz. True enough, if an Iranian P-3 had left Bandar Abbas soon after dawn, it would be heading to the east of the Musandam Peninsula now for its daily check on activity in the Gulf of Oman; its IFF transponder would probably be set to the military codes. The P-3 Orion was an American maritime surveillance aircraft and back in the days of the Shah, Iran had bought six of them for just this task. Somehow, since their revolution, by swapping parts from one to another and by shady purchases on the international black market, they'd managed to keep two or three of them flying, despite the embargo. The P-3 wasn't a threat in itself, at least it hadn't been up to now, but it did mean that the position and the movement of his task group would soon be known to Iran. Should he turn off his radars to hide his position?

'Hasn't the American cruiser reported it, AAWO?'

'No sir. They're showing their position on the data link to the west of the Straits and they'll have difficulty seeing the P-3 over the peninsula.'

Well then, if the American cousins couldn't track the P-3 then *Winchester* must do so. There was a high degree of co-operation between the allied navies in the Gulf, and tracks of interest were shared using a tactical data link, called *Alligator* on the radio circuits. In a few seconds the P-3's position would appear on the American Aegis cruiser's tactical screens, and one more part of the Arabian Gulf puzzle would be in place. The cruiser would retransmit the contact to all the other allied ships right up the Arabian Gulf as far as Kuwait; French, Italian, Belgian and Dutch tactical operators would all share the same picture. No, he couldn't go into radar silence, but he could order his two consorts to do so. That would make the P-3's task more difficult. In the planning for this deployment, the task group commander had issued a number of emission control plans, to cater for a variety of situations.

'What's the emission control plan that will silence *Bellona* and *Black Rover*, AAWO?'

'Plan charlie, sir. They can transmit on their I-band radars only, though we can continue with all of our radars.'

Mayhew thought for a moment as Allenby waited in silence. He accepted that the P-3 would have detected *Winchester's* search radars already, but perhaps not *Bellona's*, which was less powerful and could therefore not be detected at so great a range, and certainly not *Brown Rover's*. The Royal Navy's standard navigational radar had identical characteristics to a normal merchantman's, in fact that's partly why it had been chosen to fit to all the warships and support ships. What would the P-3 see? Initially it would be only a racket, *Winchester's* long range radar and target indication radar would show clearly on his ESM equipment. He'd know immediately it was a British Type 42; no other class of ships in the world carried that exact combination of radars. As it came close to inspect, it would see a radar contact to correlate with the racket, and even closer it would see three contacts, but two of them would be indistinguishable from the hundred or so other merchant ships in the area. He'd have to come into visual range to see that it was a naval task unit and not three unrelated ships, and that would mean he'd be in range of *Winchester's* Seadart missiles. P-3 pilots had become distinctly wary of entering a missile engagement zone since Iran had stepped up its attacks on tankers bound to and from Kuwait. With a bit of luck, the task unit would be reported as a single British destroyer.

'Very well, AAWO, execute emission control plan charlie.'

'Aye-aye sir.'

***

Mayhew picked up his binoculars to study the horizon, though there was no earthly reason why he should need to do so. There was an able seaman at each of the two lookout aimer sights on either side of the ship with far higher magnification lenses than his binoculars, and a further lookout on the bridge, besides the officer-of-the-watch, but it gave him time to think. Well, he'd made the Iranian's task more difficult, but it was unlikely that they'd be completely fooled. A British destroyer's business off the Fujairah anchorage could be easily guessed, even if they hadn't detected the frigate and the support ship, and the word that a convoy was about to start through the Straits would soon get back to Bandar Abbas. Yet what did that tell him? Britain wasn't at war with Iran and he was little more than an interested bystander in the long-running Iran Iraq war. The two countries had been fighting this bloody conflict for nearly eight years now. The front line had hardly changed, but Iran had succeeded in making the Shatt Al Arab waterway too dangerous to be used. Iraq had countered by exporting its oil through neutral Kuwait, prompting Iraq to shift its strategy to cut off Iraq's oil exports through attacks on tankers heading to and from Kuwait. That in turn had led the Americans to re-flag a number of Kuwait-owned tankers to fly the Stars and Stripes and to escort them the length of the Arabian Gulf and through the Straits of Hormuz. It was called *Operation Earnest Will*. Britain was quick to recognise what was coming next: a shift of target to British-flagged and British-owned tankers passing through the Straits. That was why *Winchester* was here, to escort any ships that could legitimately claim British protection, and to make the important point that the seas were free for anyone to use. His horizon search stopped on *Bellona*, and he could see that her radar aerial was still rotating. Of course, that didn't mean that it was radiating, but it was best to be sure. He picked up the open line microphone.

'EWD, Captain. Has *Bellona* gone silent?'

A short delay. That was the EWD that had lost the ship its *good* assessment at Portland. He'd improved under the tutelage of the Warrant Officer specialist who had joined the ship at Gibraltar, but he was still too reactive, he persisted in waiting for things to happen rather than anticipating them. When the emission control plan was changed he should have been watching for the task unit to comply. After all, his UAA-1 was the only equipment on the ship that could answer the question.

'Affirmative sir, she's only radiating on her navigation radar.'

'Are you picking up anything from the Soviet anchorage?'

'No sir, only the usual I-band radars in that direction.'

Mayhew returned to his assumed study of the horizon. He should do a ship-count of the anchorage but his priority was to get the convoy safely through the Straits, his Lynx could do the job much more quickly and efficiently without having to divert either his own ship or *Bellona*. It was unlikely that the Soviet ships would be radiating on any of their more interesting kit – their air search or missile control radars – but it was always worth checking. The latest intelligence suggested that there was an Udaloy and a Sovremenny there, presumably waiting to be relieved by the group transiting the Red Sea. Like the western allies, the Soviets only sent their more modern destroyers and frigates to the Middle East. And in any case, they were close to being allies; certainly they were no longer outright enemies.

The Iraqis weren't a problem until the convoy reached the central Arabian Gulf. They had no navy to speak of and their air force lacked the range to make attacks south of Larak Island. Their Exocet attack on *USS Stark* a year ago was probably a mistake, a deadly error that cost the lives of thirty-seven American sailors. It was a consequence of Iraq's lack of surveillance assets and its inability to identify targets with any certainty. For the next twelve or thirteen hours the immediate problem was with Iran, and its government. Iran was a theocracy, and when God came into the equation, the normal rules of international relations fled out by the back door. There was no real knowing what the Ayatollahs would do, and they had sufficient naval and air firepower to inflict real damage on Mayhew's convoy. They were hitting neutral ships sailing to or from Kuwait almost every week, and Iraq retaliated against tankers heading for Iranian ports. It was the unprotected tankers that he felt sorry for; those flagged in the Philippines, the Maldives, Panama and anywhere else that had no naval force in the Middle East. They had nobody to protect them and were forced to desperate measures. Few British convoys started out without one or two unentitled ships tagging on at the end of the line, and that brought problems of its own when those ships came under attack, either by Iran or Iraq, under the very noses of the British escorts. The Royal Navy captains must walk a tightrope between a normal humanitarian response on the one hand, and igniting the spark that might set off a wider Middle East conflict on the other. Scylla and Charybdis for the twentieth century. Well, he'd have to solve that conundrum when it happened. His immediate problem was picking up his tankers and forming the convoy.

'Captain sir, PWO. The Lynx has identified our four tankers and dropped the first lieutenant and the first Javelin fire unit onto *World Antigua*. They're all underway and starting to form a line with *World Antigua* in the lead. A boat is going from ship to ship taking off their pilots. There are two hangers-on by the looks of it, both registered in the Philippines and similarly painted, probably owned by the same company: *Sea Surge* and *Sea Scend*.'

And... and? What, therefore, did the PWO propose to do with the Lynx? That really should come out without prompting.

'What's the plan for our Lynx, PWO?'

'Oh…' he paused. 'The convoy should be visible soon so I'd like to send the Lynx on surface search now.'

Mayhew shook his head in despair.

***

Three of those tankers had been convoyed in and out of the Gulf at least once each. *Highlander* was the only novice, and it was quite possible that her captain had been convoyed while commanding another ship. Their experience showed in the way they kept in formation. The navigational radar revealed the four fat blips shuffling into line ahead, with the lead ship – presumably *World Antigua* – tracking slowly to the north as the line formed. The first lieutenant was on board *World Antigua* to help with interpreting *Winchester's* orders. It was a difficult situation, for the navy had no authority to compel the tankers into a convoy, and every ship's captain was in principle and in fact a free agent. A free agent, that is, until the ship's owners and insurers heard that he'd wilfully rejected the convoy escort's directions, placing their ship and valuable cargo in danger, and they each knew the consequences to their career.

In fact *escort* and *convoy* were forbidden words when communicating with the Ministry of Defence. They implied that there was an immediate danger, and the term *accompanied* was preferred. Mayhew and all other captains cordially ignored that prohibition and in all other than their formal communications, they freely referred to *escorting* and *convoys*.

Mayhew dropped his binoculars into the purpose-built mahogany box that was fastened to the pelorus. It wasn't a standard fit in a destroyer, but it was amazing what a carton of duty-free cigarettes could achieve in Portsmouth dockyard. He pulled the open line microphone from its holder.

'Thank you PWO. Pass that information to *Bellona* and *Brown Rover*. I want *Bellona's* Lynx to relieve ours on station,

Silkworm

and meanwhile I want her ready to launch in support. Yeoman, make to *Bellona*, bring your Lynx to alert fifteen.'

Ah, here was the *schooly* hovering for his captain's attention. As well as being in charge of education, he was the meteorology and oceanography officer and the merchant navy intelligence lead. He came bearing enormous bound volumes of Lloyds Register of Shipping, each festooned with apparently random page markers. Each volume was constantly updated as new information became available. How he did it Mayhew couldn't even guess, it was a monumental work of data management.

'Good morning, sir. I've found our two friends in Lloyds Register and found evidence of their previous activities. They're both Philippines registered and as you thought both belong to the same company based in Manilla. They have form, sir. Earlier this year they tagged onto a French convoy and last year they came through with *Newcastle's* task group. Apparently they haven't caused any trouble but nor will they be shaken off.'

***

In the hazy air of the Gulf of Oman, the upperworks of the vast tankers didn't appear at the horizon, but gradually emerged from the murk at about six miles range. To anyone used to warships, they appeared vast, ten times, fifteen times *Winchester's* tonnage and as they were in ballast their slab sides reached as high as a Type 42's mainmast. By the time they were in visual range they'd formed a very creditable line with half a mile between each ship. Mayhew could imagine how nervous that must have made their captains; in the open ocean they would rarely have been so close to another ship and when they were it would be for a few minutes as they passed upon their separate businesses. He trained his binoculars further left to see the two Filipino ships. The flight commander was right. They looked like two peas in a pod, with the same paint scheme and the same businesslike air of disdain for appearances. There was nothing unusually scruffy about them, but beside the four British ships they looked unloved. However, Mayhew had to admit that their attention to station keeping was exemplary. They'd taken the example of the four legitimate ships and were following at the same regular intervals, as though they had as much right to the Royal Navy's protection as the others.

'Yeoman, Captain. Make to the task unit, take convoy escort stations as previously ordered.'

That would put *Brown Rover* as fifth in line, he'd leave it to the auxiliary's captain to work his way into the gap between *Eastern Heritage* and *Sea Surge*. No doubt there'd be some harsh words on the VHF circuit. And that reminded him, he must talk to the two interlopers. That could only be done on the International Maritime Mobile VHF circuit, and that meant that any attempts at deceiving the Iranian P-3 were about to be rendered futile. VHF was open to anyone who wished to listen. The signal was normally constrained to line-of-sight, about twelve miles depending on the height of the aerials, but in the Gulf of Oman it often bounced between the temperature layers in the air and reached extraordinary distances.

'Navigator, call up *Sea Surge* and *Sea Scend* on channel sixteen, would you?'

***

Chapter Three

Tuesday, 0800
HMS Winchester, at Sea, Gulf of Oman
Operation Armilla Daily Sitrep: Commenced inbound transit...

The Filipino captains knew the routine well enough and must be aware that *Winchester's* relations with the hangers-on was determined by edicts from lawyers in the Ministry of Defence in London. The British escort was not responsible for their defence and would render no more assistance than was required by the normal laws of the sea. They were requested to avoid impeding the passage of the four convoyed ships and further advised to keep watch on VHF channel thirteen for bridge-to-bridge co-ordination of movements. They appeared well aware of the unspoken reality that *Winchester* would use channel thirteen to advise the convoy of any threats, and by listening in they would at least have the opportunity to take their own precautions.

'Officer-of-the-Watch, take station one mile on *World Antigua's* beam. You can expect a passage speed of twelve or thirteen knots. Navigator, how far to run to the Silkworm envelope?'

'Twenty-seven miles, sir.'

'Very well, we'll go to action stations at twelve-hundred, as planned. That should give the off watch time to have an early lunch. Let the Pusser know, and make a main broadcast pipe.'

Joe Northcott stepped across to the quartermaster's console where the main broadcast microphone nestled in its holder. He paused for a moment to mentally rehearse what he would say. It was an important pipe; it would set the timeframe for the most dangerous part of this inbound convoy escort and it would inform the whole ship's company of what they could expect. The main broadcast penetrated to almost every compartment in the ship, and the only people who had an excuse for not hearing it were the engineers doing their rounds in the machinery spaces, for they wore ear defenders as protection from the damaging sound of the gas turbines.

Northcott coughed to clear his throat.

'D'you hear there.'

The feedback from the bridge main broadcast speaker was irritating but Northcott was used to ignoring it.

'We've collected our convoy of four tankers and as usual we have two non-entitled hangers-on. The convoy is now heading for the Straits of Hormuz and we expect to come within range of Iranian shore-based missiles at twelve-thirty. The ship will go to action stations, state one condition zulu, at twelve-hundred. We expect to be in the missile danger zone for fourteen hours, so we should be able to revert to defence watches by midnight. That's all.'

Mayhew heard the main broadcast going on in the background but his mind was elsewhere, moving forward to the next stage. It beggared belief that the Iranian P-3 didn't know that a British convoy was gathering off the Fujairah anchorage, the chatter on the VHF would have given that away. If this had been a purely naval force then he could have used encrypted circuits or other less public means of communication, but there was no such facility for talking to merchant ships. Then the Iranians knew they were coming. There was no indication that the Iranian navy or indeed the more fanatical IRGC – the Islamic Revolutionary Guard Corps – was planning to take action against a British convoy, but the Iranian government didn't march to the same drumbeat as those of western nations, their inner workings were largely a mystery. An attack, if it happened, would come without any diplomatic warning, but the enemy was still constrained by the limitations of its own military power. The technical warnings would be there for an astute observer to see, but he'd already seen them every day that he'd been in the Gulf. It was too easy to believe that the daily operations of the Iranian navy were a precursor to a swift and fatal attack on his convoy.

Take that P-3 for example. Once it had reported the convoy's position, it could keep it under surveillance for the next few hours until it was within Silkworm range. The first thing that *Winchester* would know of an attack would be when the EWD detected the missile's homing head. Mayhew could take no action against the P-3 until after it had completed its deadly mission, and then it would be too late. And yet, a P-3 – most likely the same one – came out into the Gulf of Oman almost every day, and to Mayhew's belief it had never done anything more than compile a picture of the traffic on this vital approach to the Straits of Hormuz. It would be taking a very hard line indeed to claim that Iran wasn't within its rights to do so. It meant that he had to maintain his ship's sensors and weapons, and more importantly his men, at instant readiness for the whole of the transit of the Straits. Not only must they be alert, but they must examine the intentions of every ship and aircraft that they detected and be ready to meet force with force when the moment came. So the P-3 would continue on its routine patrol unhindered by *Winchester*, and it might do that for years without the slightest evil intent, until the day that it suited the Supreme Council of the Cultural Revolution to make an example of one of the hated western powers. Mayhew knew that Britain was a close second to America on their hit-list.

***

Lieutenant Paul Buckley fiddled nervously with his keyboard. This was his first deployment as a qualified principal warfare officer, and he wasn't enjoying it. He'd only completed the year-long PWO course a few months before *Winchester* left Portsmouth for its pre-deployment workup at Portland. He'd left behind a wife and two very young children and he couldn't get it out of his mind that he was in some way abandoning them. It should have helped that his wife was demonstrably able to hold the family together without his presence, but it didn't. He read and re-read every letter from home, searching for any hint of censure, but he found none, and that made him feel useless, it made him suspicious, and in the end it made him angry. How could Clara find it so easy to live without him? Her parents were far away in the northeast of the country, so who was she turning to in time of need? If he could have stood back and watched himself objectively he would have recognised the symptoms for what they were, merely the normal guilt at leaving his family behind while he sailed away to warmer climes. However, Buckley was incapable of that objectivity and he was plagued by other problems: he really didn't believe that he was up to this job. The staff at the PWO course didn't grade their students, but he knew very well that if they had, he'd have come close to the bottom of his class. He found it difficult to assimilate information quickly, to analyse it and to make rapid decisions and take decisive action. He felt that he was always one step behind the power curve, and that the lowliest seaman in the ops room was two steps ahead of him. And he knew – he was absolutely certain – that the captain thought the same.

His morbid reflections were punctured by the action picture supervisor, effectively his personal assistant, pointing to a new track on the tactical display, bringing it to his attention, when he knew that he should already have spotted it. The Lynx was reporting contacts to the north of the convoy and a large part of the ops room was engaged in compiling a picture of what lay ahead.

To a certain extent it was predictable. The traffic separation scheme started to the northeast of the Musandam Peninsula and that invisible one-way system channelled all the inbound vessels to the north, so that they took the outside track to round the peninsula, and all those outbound took the inside track. That was the case for all of the heavy ships: the oil tankers and the liquified petroleum gas carriers, and the container ships that brought manufactured goods into the Gulf. Once they were eliminated it should be easy to identify suspicious contacts, those that weren't following any of the normal patterns.

Silkworm

However, there was a constant stream of smaller vessels, everything from tiny dhows to substantial coasting ships, that crossed between the Iranian and the Omani sides of the Straits. There were fishing boats of all shapes and sizes, and a growing number of naval vessels from half a dozen nations, each with its own objectives and following a navigational plan known only to themselves. Because of that, it was the devil's own task to compile a coherent picture of the shipping between the convoy's present position and the point where they would turn decisively in towards the Gulf. The Lynx had a radar and its own electronic intercept kit, similar to *Winchester's* UAA-1. It was busy correlating its radar tracks to its intercepts, and cross-referring with *Winchester's* contacts and with the tracks that were coming in on the data link. So much information! And it was Buckley's task to make some sense of it all. At any moment the captain could ask him for a summary and he shook himself out of his gloom to do something about it so that he was ready.

This confusing mass of data required men with specialised skills to interpret it. Men such as Petty Officer (Radar) Ward. He might well have had a Christian name, but since time immemorial anybody who joined the navy with the surname Ward was known as Sharkey Ward, and that is the only name that anybody in *Winchester* knew him by. Sharkey Ward was the defence watch surface picture supervisor – the SPS – and upon his broad shoulders fell the task of bringing all this information together and presenting it to the PWO so that he could take action based upon a firm understanding of the situation. Sharkey had worked for a few PWOs in his time, he could spot a weak one half a mile away, and he recognised that weakness in Lieutenant Buckley the first day that he stepped on board.

Buckley flicked the switch on his console to speak directly to the surface picture supervisor without anyone on the command open line hearing.

'SPS, PWO.'

'SPS, sir.'

'What do you make of the situation in the Straits?'

Sharkey replied with barely a pause for thought. He could guess that whatever he said would be relayed immediately to the captain but he didn't begrudge the PWO his moment of glory. He had a job to do and he knew that he did it well. Certainly he wasted some time in keeping the PWO informed, but it was nothing compared to the distraction of talking to the captain. He would present the information to Lieutenant Buckley, how he spun that to the captain was his affair.

'Much the same as last time, sir. There's a steady flow of tankers and LPG carriers in the separation scheme. The data link is showing *USS Carter* a little to the south of Larak Island, it looks like she's barely outside the Iranian twelve-mile limit. *Carter's* reporting an Omani patrol boat close in to the Musandam Peninsula on the data link. *USS Casablanca*, the Aegis cruiser, is further around to the west of the peninsula.'

'Is *Casablanca* Golf Whiskey?'

Sharkey replied in his best non-committal voice. The PWO should know which ship was leading the allied air defence effort for the whole of the Arabian Gulf, and it wasn't *Casablanca*. The Golf Whiskey duty was being covered by one of the older cruisers – *USS Havelock* – and would be in a more central location, probably three-hundred miles away to the north of Qatar. *Havelock* had been on station for weeks now, but *Casablanca* had only recently arrived in the Gulf.

'No sir. That's *Havelock*, way off my plot.'

'Can you see anything that looks like another convoy?'

'No, sir. There's nothing in a regular formation.'

'Thanks, SPS.'

The action picture supervisor heard the whole exchange. He looked over his shoulder and rolled his eyes at Sharkey Ward who grinned and turned back to his work.

***

Silkworm

'The ship's in station, sir.'

'Very well, Officer-of-the-Watch. Match *World Antigua's* speed and then reduce to a single Tyne with the other shaft trailing. Call down to the MEO and ask him which he'd prefer, and let him know that we might need the second at very short notice. Which reminds me, Navigator, what's our fuel percentage?'

'Ninety-three percent an hour ago, sir, and *Bellona* reported ninety-one percent at the change of the watch.'

Mayhew nodded and consulted the fuel consumption chart that swung from a hook on the pelorus. He knew it almost by heart, but it was always good to check. Since the earliest days of steam propulsion the need to conserve fuel against a future need weighed on the mind of every warship's captain. Today, however, Mayhew was relaxed. He had *Brown Rover* under his command carrying enough dieso to top up both *Winchester's* and *Bellona's* tanks half a dozen times, and his ships were well practiced in taking on fuel while underway even under threat of attack, if necessary. Yet it was still wise to conserve his fuel, for at sea one never knew what new event would cause him to pile on the speed. He wouldn't willingly go below seventy percent and at sixty percent he'd have to alert his upwards chain of command, and that would be embarrassing for everyone. Ninety-three percent was good for a transit of the Straits.

'Signalman, raise the first lieutenant on his Cougar Bright.'

'Aye-aye sir'

The signalman had a small, black, handheld Cougar radio on his desk fitted with the Bright encryption device. It operated in the military VHF band and had a simple voice encryption that would probably defy the resources of any Iranian unit. It was far more private than the open VHF, and it was identical to the radio that the first lieutenant had taken with him. Mayhew could hear the signalman calling the first lieutenant's callsign as he kept his binoculars on *World Antigua*. A mile was long range to identify a person, but a figure that could have been *Winchester's* first lieutenant emerged from the bridge and came out onto the wing, presumably to get the best reception. After making contact the signalman handed the radio to the captain.

'Good morning First Lieutenant, is all well? over.'

There was little point in using callsigns when it was only the two of them on the circuit but ending a transmission with *over* ensured that they didn't try to speak at the same time, which only confused the encryption device.

'Yes sir, all's well. The captain knows what's expected of him and he'll keep his speed constant at twelve or thirteen knots throughout the passage. He's arranged with the other three that he'll call on VHF channel thirteen when he alters course, over.'

'Good. Let him know that the two Filipino ships will be listening on that channel, over.'

'Yes, he knows that already, he heard your conversation with them. He had the same situation on his last run through the Straits, over.'

'Is he happy with the emergency signals? over.'

'Yes, he says they are the same as last time, over.'

Mayhew thought for a moment. The signals were very straightforward, there was no point in coming up with anything complex and it would only lead to confusion. If there was a threat to the convoy the navigator would give a running commentary on VHF channel thirteen. If there was an imminent danger – threat warning red in navy-speak – then *Winchester* would make six blasts on her siren to reinforce the VHF message. If he thought that the tankers needed to turn, the navigator would tell them on the VHF. They all knew, they'd been told in the preparatory signals from the MOD, that the best way to avoid an incoming missile was to turn to place it on either bow. That was where the ships presented their smallest radar reflection and it gave the hope that the missile would glance off the ship's side before exploding. Six years ago in the Falklands war *HMS Glamorgan* escaped an Exocet attack with minimal damage by using that manoeuvre. The problem for the tankers was that they couldn't turn quickly enough, and even with the missile approaching from an acute angle on the bow, a tanker's radar reflection was enormous. Still, it was better than nothing, but it did reinforce the need for *Winchester* and *Bellona* to employ all of their hard kill and soft kill measures to prevent a missile finding such a big, fat target.

'We picked up an Iranian P-3 racket just after the Lynx launched. It's still out there. It looks like his normal patrol circuit but we're watching him, over.'

'Thank you. This ship's master is very keen to be kept informed, over.'

'Well, good luck, Mark, and I hope they put on a good lunch, over.'

'I'll let you know, sir. Out.'

Mayhew returned the Cougar Bright to the signalman and picked up the clip of signals that the chief yeoman had prepared for him. The ops officer had already told him all the important ones and it only took a few minutes to skim the few that had come in since the ship had gone to defence watches. He ignored the routine stuff, his heads of department could deal with those, but here was something interesting that had just come in. Classified secret, a report of an Iranian landing craft loading sea mines at Bander Abbas, and another report of a mobile Silkworm launcher – only one – being seen on the road down towards Kuhestak. Well, his convoy would be passing through water too deep for the mines that Iran had in its inventory, they were all made for shallow water use, but at some point *Winchester* would have to leave the deep channels if only to pick up stores at Dubai or Abu Dhabi. There were British minehunters in the Gulf already, two ships of the Hunt class, *HMS Exmoor* and *HMS Hambledon*, and a survey ship fitted out for mine countermeasures support, *HMS Hero*. They'd keep the approaches to the main ports clear, but it was too much to ask of such a small number of ships that they'd clear the whole of the Gulf's shallow waters. As for the Silkworm launcher, it was one more indefinite piece of information that shed more heat than light. It could have been out on manoeuvres on its own, it could have been heading for a repair depot, or it could have been one of a number of launchers heading for a pre-prepared launching site from which it could cover the eastern approaches to the Straits. The difficulty was in knowing what to do about it, except to note that the threat to *Winchester's* convoy had ratcheted up a notch or two. He leaned back in his chair but was interrupted by the buzzer announcing that the AAWO was calling him.

'Captain, AAWO. The Iranian P-3 has turned towards us, now at thirty miles bearing zero-four-zero. I'm keeping the air threat at yellow, there's no indication of an attack and we're out of land-based Silkworm range.'

'Captain, PWO. The Lynx reports that the Soviet anchorage is empty.'

Well now, where have they gone? He'd heard no report of a Soviet convoy for the past few days. In fact Soviet convoys were rare and it was always assumed that these ships were in the Gulf more to assert their right to be there than for any practical reasons. The Soviet Union was largely self-sufficient in oil and gas, and their allies around the world mostly imported their energy from the southern Soviet states, through the Black Sea and the Mediterranean. It was hard to see how these expensive deployments could be justified, with the Soviet Union seemingly in political crisis and Gorbachev trying to withdraw from the disastrous engagement in Afghanistan. 1988 felt like a watershed year where Soviet ambitions were being reined in, but still they insisted on muddying the waters with these deployments.

***

Chapter Four

Tuesday, 0915
HMS Winchester, at Sea, Gulf of Oman
Operation Armilla Daily Sitrep: Under surveillance from Iranian P-3...

Mayhew took a swift look around. The convoy was in an admirably regular order stretching away to the south: the four British tankers, *Brown Rover* and then the two Filipinos. *Bellona* was abreast of the fourth tanker – *Eastern Heritage* – at half a mile, as Mayhew's escort orders specified. That gave the Javelin fire unit in *Highlander* a clear field of fire. From *World Antigua* in the lead to *Sea Surge* at the tail, the whole column was three miles long, and the Filipinos at the far end were already indistinct in this murky weather. Lieutenant Hook seemed happy enough. He'd been given a command open line headset and he had his own marine signalman for his portable radio. He was already making his radio checks with his fire units.

'Officer-of-the-Watch, I'm going down to the ops room. Stay in station on *World Antigua* and keep a good lookout for dhows and dories. The navigator will be up here, but you have the ship.'

He dropped down the three decks and entered the perpetual darkness of the ops room. No natural light ever reached this part of the ship and the fluorescent tube lights were only switched on when the ship was safely in harbour. Heavy blackout curtains at the two entrances kept out any stray light from the passageways outside. The place was illuminated by the soft orange glow from the tactical consoles and the tracker displays, and by a myriad of multi-coloured indicator lights. Electronics ruled here; the whole combat system was fed by a bank of computers in the compartment below that took in information from sensors, manipulated it and provided it as processed information to the operators. There was one remaining vestige of the old days, and when he had the time Mayhew made that his first stop. The general operations plot beside the ladder on the starboard side was nothing more than a small-scale admiralty chart covered by a large sheet of tracing paper. Upon it the operator marked all of the non-real-time information that came in from sources other than the ship's sensors. On here the reported positions of combatants from half a dozen nations were marked: the United States, France, Italy, the Netherlands, Belgium, Iran, Iraq, Oman, Saudi Arabia, the Soviet Union and many more. It was a running commentary on the world that existed outside the range of *Winchester's* radars, beyond the coverage of the allied tactical data link picture, and a snapshot of it was frozen in time whenever the GOP operator changed the tracing paper, for the used traces were carefully saved in case of future need.

'What's new, Able Seaman Markham?'

The GOP operator hadn't noticed the captain sliding down the ladder from one-deck, and he jumped at the sound of his voice, and scrambled to collect his thoughts.

'That Soviet group is still way beyond the GOP range, sir, we had an update a few minutes ago.'

He pointed to a pencilled symbol in the southerly margin of the chart.

'That puts them past the halfway point of the Red Sea. I had an update on the mine countermeasures group; they're in transit towards Bahrain for a route clearance task. The rest is as you last saw it, sir.'

Mayhew looked at a pencilled symbol halfway between Dubai and Doha. It represented the multinational mine countermeasures force: a command ship, a support ship and four mine countermeasures vessels – MCMVs. The whole group was being led by a mobile mine countermeasures command team embarked in the hydrographic ship *HMS Hero* that had been taken from its usual surveying duties to fulfil the role. The Americans had a similarly-sized group of MCMVs based in Bahrain; it was a testimony to the very real mining threat that existed in the Gulf.

Silkworm

Mayhew nodded and stepped deeper into the ops room to where Allenby sat at his tactical console as the on-watch AAWO. He was evidently wondering when the captain would pay attention to the immediate issues, but Mayhew wasn't going to be rushed, not yet.

'PWO, are you keeping both Lynx informed?'

'Yes, sir. *Bellona's* Lynx is taking over the task and ours will be returning in about twenty minutes.'

Allenby jumped in when the PWO finished.

'There, sir. The P-3's turned away slightly but still closing. His radar loses some of its discrimination when he's pointing right at a target and he's probably aiming off to count the size of the convoy. Range twenty-five miles now. I'd like to cover him with the forward 909, that will give us his height and might warn him off.'

Mayhew studied the AAWO's screen for a moment. If the P-3 was in any doubt of the identity of the convoy, lighting him up with the Seadart fire control radar would settle the matter, for only the Type 42s and the Royal Navy aircraft carriers had that equipment, and none of the carriers were in the Middle East. Yet there were real advantages in doing so. First, it would give an accurate reading of the P-3's height, which might help in determining its intentions, and secondly, as Allenby suggested, it would be an unequivocal warning for it to keep clear.

'Very well, I-band only, let me know when you have its height.'

The 909's I-band transmitter was for tracking targets and although an aircraft would know that it was being illuminated, it wouldn't be unduly alarmed. However, there was a second component to the radar – J-band – and that was used to guide the Seadart missiles onto their target. Most aircraft had a warning system that sent an alarm straight into the pilot's headset when it detected a locked-on J-band radar. It increased the temperature of the encounter and in this case Mayhew was convinced that it wasn't necessary. There was a legal point to consider, too.

The P-3 would have its own rules of engagement and it could be justified in accusing *Winchester* of displaying hostile intent by using its J-band missile control radar; it couldn't make the same claim for the I-band tracker. ROE cut both ways in this war of shades and shadows.

Allenby dropped his microphone down to his mouth.

'Blind, height-find track five-six-one-nine with forward 909.'

The order to *height-find* told the Seadart controller that he could use only the I-band transmitter. He selected the forward fire control radar – the type 909 – that served both the Seadart and the 4.5 inch gun – and used his tracker ball to indicate the P-3's track. Far above the ops room, on top of the bridge roof, the 909 awoke within its fibreglass dome and started a search pattern around the indicated position. In three seconds it locked on, and two seconds later the height of the target appeared on his screen. The AAWO's assistant had already hooked the track and he saw the height displayed at the same time as the Seadart controller. It appeared on the AAWO's tactical display and with a few quick taps of the keyboard it was distributed to all of the allied ships that were fitted with the data link.

'Captain, AAWO. The P-3 is at four thousand feet, sir. That's his visual search height, he'd be higher if he was doing a radar sweep. He's interested in us, for sure.'

Mayhew stared at the radar contact for a moment as though he could see into the Iranian mission commander's mind. Interested, certainly, but with evil purpose? This P-3, or one very similar, was out here on patrol every day of the year and he had a legal right to do so. As long as he stayed out of the UAE and Omani twelve mile territorial limit and he complied with air traffic rules, he could exercise his right to operate over the waters of the high seas, just as *Winchester's* Lynx was doing at this moment. In fact, Mayhew had only given permission for the Lynx to launch once both *Winchester* and the ships of the convoy were more than twelve miles from the UAE coast. If he'd wanted to fly inside UAE waters he'd have had to go through the process of requesting diplomatic clearance from the UAE government, and that was only done in dire need. And yet there was undoubtedly something unusual about this aircraft's flight path. The P-3 habitually stayed on the Iranian side of the Straits and carried out its surveillance at long range, presumably to avoid confrontation. This low and purposeful approach was something new, a departure from the mode of operations that had been reported by a succession of British task groups since the Armilla Patrol – the continuous British presence in the region – started eight years ago. His rules of engagement allowed him to engage if the other party was showing hostile *intent*. That was a significant easing of the rules in the past few months; previously only a hostile *act* – essentially the release of a weapon – could allow him to fire his own weapons. Did this aircraft have hostile intent then? As far as his command team could tell him there were no Iranian units within range to fire a weapon at *Winchester* or the convoy. Despite some lurid press reports of the P-3s being fitted with air-to-surface missiles, there was no hard intelligence to suggest that they had done so, and he didn't believe they had. The worst that this P-3 could do was to identify his convoy and report its presence, and that was not in itself showing hostile intent. Then he must hold his nerve.

'Very well. Is the fighter controller ready with the warning message?'

'Yes, sir. Ready on aeronautical distress VHF.'

Mayhew looked over beyond the PWO's console where Lieutenant Gavin Beresford sat at his own radar console. He was a qualified fighter controller, but with no British aircraft carrier in the region and with no Royal Air Force squadrons to call upon, his specialist skills were largely redundant, and he was mostly employed as an officer-of-the-watch and in standing in for any of the warfare officers when things were quiet. He knew what was required and waved over his shoulder to confirm that he was ready.

'Continue to cover with the 909, AAWO, I-band only, we don't want to completely scare him, and when he's ten miles from us you can transmit the normal warning.'

'Yes, sir. Remain at air threat yellow?'

'I think so, we don't want to alarm our own people, and we'll stay at defence watches.'

Mayhew took his seat in the centre of the ops room. He was sure that he'd made the right decision; he'd chosen a path that would both defuse the situation and keep his convoy and his ship safe. There was no doubt in his mind that the P-3 was not a threat. He could have brought the ship to action stations, but it would have been a distraction at exactly the time that he needed to concentrate on determining its intentions. At defence watches, at a pinch, he could use any of his weapons, but that wouldn't be necessary. Nevertheless, he could feel the tension in the ops room rising. There was one more thing he should do. He settled the command open line headset onto his head.

'Officer-of-the-Watch, Captain. Ask the navigator to call up the first lieutenant on Cougar Bright and let him know what's happening. Make sure you don't alarm him, but it's possible that he'll see an overflight by an Iranian P-3. Javelin Commander, the same for your fire units and remind them that weapons are tight.'

The Javelin detachment wasn't used to operating under rules of engagement and he didn't want a trigger-happy marine assuming that an Iranian P-3 was automatically a valid target.

Mayhew took a moment to consider the convoy's ability to withstand an air attack. Layered defence, it was called. He had chaff to confuse the enemy's targeting process and to break a hostile missile's homing head lock, and he had a jammer to blind it. Seadart could pluck an aircraft out of the sky at thirty-five miles on a good day, and *Bellona's* Seawolf could protect the ships in its immediate vicinity. Both he and *Bellona* had close-in-weapons-systems – rapid-firing, radar controlled gatling guns – for last-ditch protection and

Silkworm

he had three Javelin fire units scattered around his convoy. There was *Winchester's* 4.5 inch gun that could certainly deal with something as large and slow as a P-3 and he had twenty-millimetre guns if it really came to a close action. It was a strong defence, but it would still be severely tested against a Silkworm at sea-skimming height, if it came to that.

'Do you want a commentary on channel thirteen, sir?'

That was the navigator, but Mayhew had already decided that he didn't want to spook the convoy. He hadn't met any of the captains of those tankers, and he didn't know how they would react. In truth, there was little chance of the P-3 coming close enough for them to see it, and what could they do anyway?

'That won't be necessary, thanks. Just let the first lieutenant know on Cougar Bright.'

'Fifteen miles, sir, and he's coming straight at us now.'

'Thank you, AAWO. Count the distances down on open line to ten miles please. Fighter controller, are you on open line?'

'Yes, sir. All ready to go.'

Beresford was absolutely the right man for this job. As a fighter controller he was trained to see things from a pilot's perspective, and he understood how aircraft navigated and expressed their position. He could be trusted to make the right calls that the P-3 would understand.

'Thirteen miles.'

Mayhew was aware of the ops room supervisor – a petty officer at defence watches – angrily turning sailors away from the doors. They'd heard what was happening and were hoping to slip into their action stations, but the petty officer was having none of it. Mayhew made a mental note to talk to Allenby after this was over. This enthusiasm was all very well but it was counter-productive. What he needed now was a calm and measured approach.

'Twelve miles.'

Beresford coughed to clear his throat.

'Eleven miles.'

'Make the first warning, fighter controller. I'll have silence in the ops room now.'

The normal chatter of orders and reports died away as every ear strained to hear the fighter controller. He'd been taught on his course at Yeovilton to pitch his voice up on a radio circuit, to make it more easily understood across the noise of the static electricity, and he sounded quite different to his everyday self. Mayhew switched his headset to the aeronautical distress frequency to hear the exchange.

'Iranian aircraft in position two-seven miles bearing zero-four-zero from Fujairah airport, squawking mode two, this is British warship ten miles right ahead of you. What is your intention please?'

Nothing, no response. Mayhew could see that the AAWO's assistant was listening to the same frequency but on another radio set, to confirm that there was nothing wrong with Beresford's radio. He nodded and made a thumbs-up gesture to the captain and the AAWO.

The ops room was completely quiet now.

'Nine miles.'

Mayhew noticed that Allenby's voice was clear and steady. If the AAWO felt any anxiety he wasn't showing it.

The fighter controller coughed quietly again.

'Iranian aircraft in position two-six miles bearing zero-four-zero from Fujairah airport, squawking mode two, this is British warship ten miles right ahead of you. What is your intention please?'

More silence, then a voice broke onto the circuit speaking in confident and only slightly accented English.

'British warship, this is Iranian aircraft nine miles to your north east at four thousand feet heading southwest. I am on a maritime patrol in international waters. I see that you have a convoy and will not approach closer than five miles. I am turning away to the southeast and I request that you cease radiating your tracking radar, sir.'

Mayhew grinned, he hadn't realised how tense he felt. It could still be a ruse, but he was prepared to bet any amount that it wasn't. That was the genuine voice of a pilot trying to complete his routine surveillance mission without causing a diplomatic incident.

'Fighter controller, tell him that we'll turn off our tracking radar and wish him a good flight home.'

'He's turning away, sir,' Allenby reported. 'Blind, cease covering track five-six-one-nine. Strangle the 909.'

Allenby was making sure that the captain's wishes were properly understood and carried out by doubling up on the command and control orders.

'Iranian aircraft this is British warship. Thank you sir and have a good flight home. Listening on VHF one-two-one-decimal-five. Out.'

Beresford's voice showed no trace of the relief at the Iranian's actions; he sounded as though he'd expected nothing else.

Mayhew watched over the AAWO's shoulder as the P-3 made a wide turn to port and moved away deeper into the Gulf of Oman. He was quietly pleased that he hadn't increased *Winchester's* readiness state, and even happier that he hadn't alarmed the convoy. He could rely on the navigator to tell the first lieutenant that it was all over, and he could hear Allenby on the UK AAW circuit telling *Bellona*. He'd switch to the Gulf circuit later to let the Americans know. Yes, it had gone well, but it might not always be like that. He must constantly be on the lookout for the time when the approaching aircraft was indeed showing hostile intent. There was one thing, however, that he must address. That misplaced eagerness for the ops room action stations team to take their places was not on, and it was the ops officer who had to stop it. Still, all-in-all it was a good performance by his team. He stood up and stretched. He could feel a dozen pairs of eyes watching him, but he couldn't relax yet, for here was the doctor.

'Your arm, sir.'

The doctor that had embarked for the deployment was young and officious and in everyone's opinion he took himself too seriously. He'd volunteered for this secondment to the navy hoping to be at the forefront of treating battle injuries, but so far he'd seen nothing other than a few coughs and sneezes, and he was frankly disgusted with the whole affair. He thought ruefully of how this six month break in his service at Guy's Hospital would affect his career.

To fill in the time and to soak up his restless energy he'd started a survey of reactions to stress. He'd obtained agreement that he could roam the ship at will during action stations and he'd been given personal instruction in closing watertight doors and hatches behind him. He'd also selected a dozen people whose pulse rates and blood pressure he wanted to monitor, and the captain and ops officer were right at the top of his list. They'd become used to it and neither paused in their conversation as the doctor took his measurements.

'Will I live, Doc?'

Mayhew always asked the same question and the doctor, who lacked any kind of social skills, had stopped even answering him. When they'd been on passage to the Middle East he'd replied by stating the pulse rate and the systolic and diastolic pressures, but it became clear that the figures meant nothing to either the captain or the ops officer, and the captain's question was nothing more than a ritual. Now he merely scribbled in his notebook, bagged his equipment and left.

***

'Captain, PWO. The Lynx is returning, twenty miles to run bearing zero-one-zero from our position. I can see his chirp.'

The Lynx was a notoriously difficult target for radars to see, and *Winchester* couldn't rely upon its normal air search and target acquisition radars. However, each of the helicopters carried a radar transponder and the mark it made with each sweep of the radar was known as a *chirp*.

'Is *Bellona's* Lynx on task?'

'Yes sir, and already reporting surface contacts. Nothing but merchant ships and local stuff so far.'

'Very well, I'll be on the bridge for the recovery.'

'Well done everybody,' he said in his loudest voice, short of shouting, 'that was well-handled. But remember that it won't always go so smoothly, and one of these days we might have to fight our way out of a situation. Every one of us must be on the lookout for anything unusual.'

He could see that the speech had gone well and when he returned to the bridge it was evident that they'd been following the incident. Saxby was turning onto a flying course and all Mayhew had to do was slip into his chair and confirm that all the preparations for recovery had been made. He glanced at the wind indicator then ducked below the level of the top of the bridge windows to see the Lynx approaching from the port side. A nod from the navigator and he made the permission to fly switch. And here, right on cue, was his steward bearing a massive mug of tea and two hobnob biscuits.

***

Chapter Five

Tuesday, 1100
HMS Winchester, at Sea, Straits of Hormuz
Operation Armilla Daily Sitrep: Boghammers operating at entrance to TSS...

Ben Saxby grasped the pelorus for support and bobbed up and down, working his knees to prevent them becoming too stiff. He'd been on watch since four o'clock in the morning and it had just been his bad luck that when the ship moved from cruising watches to defence watches it was his watch – the starboard watch – that came on duty at six-o'clock. He'd negotiated a relief for an hour to grab breakfast, but if they went to action stations at twelve-o'clock he'd be back on the bridge again until the ship passed through the Straits.

The rising sun had burned off some of the haze and he could see the mountains that rose up from the Oman coast and continued to the north until they ended at the Musandam Peninsula. Ben was interested in geology, and he had a theory that the painfully contorted shape of the Straits of Hormuz was caused by those mountains. They must be particularly hard and resistant to erosion, while the land to the north must be softer, causing that dramatic loop at the entrance to the Arabian Gulf. It was difficult to know for certain, and the Admiralty Pilot book – the mariner's fount of all regional knowledge – was unhelpful on the subject. That was one of the frustrations of being at sea, he couldn't nip down to the local library and spend a few happy hours searching among the shelves. If the information didn't exist on board the ship, then for the time being it was unknowable. Well, he'd look it up when *Winchester* returned to Portsmouth after this deployment.

The captain was on the bridge, deep in conversation with the MEO, who was still concerned about the new port Tyne gas turbine. It had been changed at Mina Raysut at the other end of Oman only a week ago, the new one having been flown out from UK in a Hercules aircraft. The Type 42s were designed to easily change any of the four GTUs, and it was a work of only a few days, with the help of the specialists from the Fleet Maintenance Unit that came out with the new equipment. The MEO wanted a steady overnight run where he could take his readings, and the captain was explaining why that was impossible until they brought their next convoy out through the Straits. Probably they'd decide to keep that Tyne in reserve until they could properly test it.

He turned to his second officer-of-the-watch who was busy at the chart table. Colin Wallace was a sub lieutenant like Ben Saxby, but whereas Saxby had joined the navy straight from school as a midshipman, and had consequently was already on his second operational appointment, Wallace had been to university and had not yet finished his fleet training time.

'What's our distance off the land now Colin?'

There was a pause and the sound of dividers and parallel rule being manipulated.

'The nearest point of land's twenty-one miles bearing two-eight-zero.'

'Come and look out the front a moment.'

Saxby wanted an officer's eyes out of the window while they were steaming at twelve knots with a giant tanker only a mile on the beam. During the day there was no need for the blackout curtain around the chart table, and that made it so much easier to step away from the front of the bridge. Wallace had been using the Decca Navigator system to fix the ship's position, and checking it by radar ranges of the nearest points on shore. He could also see the marks where the satellite navigation fixes had been recorded. It was reassuring to see that all three methods agreed and even with no visual references – the Omani mountains were too featureless to be useful – he could be confident of his position. Normally, the navigator would mark on the chart the track that the officer-of-the-watch was to follow, but today they were letting *World Antigua* steer her own course while *Winchester* kept station on her beam. That was only sensible because they must use the traffic separation scheme through the Straits, and the tanker's captain would certainly steer the shortest course to join it. It was close to heresy, and he wisely kept his opinion to himself, but Saxby could see no point in going through the laborious process of fixing the ship's position by the Decca Navigator. The entire fleet had been fitted with satellite navigation for at least the last six years, and now that it had settled down it was very reliable. He certainly trusted it more than the Decca. The Navigator had marked the chart with a dotted line where the Silkworm envelope started, only ten miles away now. He checked the clock, eleven-twenty; they were right on time to go to action stations at twelve-hundred. He pressed his face to the metal cone that allowed him to see the radar display despite the bright sunshine, and turned the range knob until the expanding circle just touched the shoreline. Twenty-one nautical miles, as Colin had said. It was always best to be certain. He glanced at the ship's log to confirm that it was being properly kept up and then turned back to the pelorus.

'Bridge, Ops Room.'

That would be the SPS. Saxby picked up the intercom microphone.

'Bridge.'

'New contact, sir. Green zero-one-zero at twelve miles, course one-five-seven at thirteen knots, CPA five miles to starboard.'

Saxby brought his binoculars to his eyes. They focussed automatically, so once he'd set them for his own eyes at the beginning of the watch, they needed no more adjustment. He looked ten degrees to starboard and there, sure enough, he saw the starboard side of a laden tanker's massive superstructure, barely showing above the horizon. It was obviously going to pass well clear to starboard and its closest point of approach – its CPA – looked about five miles.

'Roger, watch. That's a tanker leaving the separation scheme and heading outbound to the southeast. You'll probably see a number of those as we get closer. Report if their CPA is closer than four miles.'

'Ops room, roger.'

Saxby saw that the captain had used his binoculars too, and that the MEO was waiting patiently to re-start the conversation. For normal merchant traffic the officer-of-the-watch only needed to inform the captain if its CPA was less than two miles, and this one would pass much further away than that. The *watch* order meant that the SPS wouldn't report it again unless it changed its course or speed. Sometimes Saxby just loved his job. He was only twenty-two and responsible for the safety of this huge, complex and very expensive piece of floating national sovereignty. Here they were, under surveillance by a potentially hostile aircraft – he knew all about the Iranian P-3 – almost within range of deadly missiles and commanding the escort for four massive tankers, seven if he included *Brown Rover* and the two Filipinos. Yet all of *Winchester's* vital functions reported to him. The AAWO and the PWO played their part, but until the threat level increased, the responsibility was all his. Life was good!

'Captain, PWO.'

The call from the ops room reminded him that sometimes it wasn't all about him.

'Captain.'

'*Bellona's* Lynx reports a group of small craft manoeuvering right at the entrance to the TSS. They look like Boghammers, but he's not going too close.'

'How long does he have on task?'

'He can stay for another thirty minutes maximum, sir. He's holding at three miles range at the moment.'

Mayhew grimaced. Buckley should have anticipated that he'd ask about the Lynx's endurance and he should have given that information with his initial report.

'Confirm that our Lynx is at alert fifteen.'

'Confirmed, sir. Alert fifteen.'

'Very well. Tell the flight commander to come to the ops room and I'll meet him there.'

Boghammers! If the report was correct these were some of the boats that Iran had bought from Sweden five years ago. They were armed with a variety of low-tech but high-lethality weaponry, such as rocket propelled grenades, larger two-and-three inch unguided rockets and heavy machine guns. Now they were operated by the IRGC's naval wing and they were rapidly becoming one of the principal threats to merchant shipping steering for Kuwait. *Winchester* hadn't encountered them during her previous convoy escort duty, and the intelligence reports all agreed that they were stationed far to the north, where they could support the fighting against Iraq. What could have brought them all the way down to the Straits? Mayhew closed his conversation with the MEO with a promise that he'd only use the port Tyne if necessary, for safety or if the ship's mission demanded it, and hurried down to the ops room.

'Nothing from *USS Carter*, PWO?'

'No, sir, it doesn't look as though her Seahawk is airborne and the Lynx reported her position twenty miles to the northwest.'

Then the first thing was to get out a report of this sighting. The Lynx had no data link, so the only way of telling the allied nations of this sighting was to send an urgent signal and to report it on the multi-national co-ordination circuit, Navy Red.

'Have you injected a track in the system?'

'Yes sir, but I haven't released it to alligator, it's too indefinite.'

That was true enough. The position that the Lynx reported could easily be five miles out, and it wouldn't help to transmit that sort of dodgy data on the link.

'What do you think, Flight Commander?'

Carl Stevens was the Lynx pilot and as he was senior to the observer, he gloried in the title of flight commander.

He'd assumed that he wouldn't be flying again today because the ship would soon be entering Oman's territorial waters and launching the helicopter was prohibited without diplomatic clearance. Now the situation had changed, and it was quite clear that *Bellona's* Lynx needed some support. He eyed the distance that the ship had to travel before it entered territorial waters. Yes, there was time.

'We're loaded with two Sea Skua and the fifty-calibre pod, sir, and we can stay airborne for two-and-a-half hours if I take it easy. Boghammers are about forty-two feet long and nine tons, so they're a pretty good target for Sea Skua if I set the lowest sea-skimming height. I can stay well out of reach of shoulder-launched SAMs and I've got my IR flares just in case. The fifty calibre's good for warning shots.'

Mayhew watched the flight commander as he spoke. It was disappointing that he was so focussed on engaging the Boghammers rather than tracking them. Yes, it might come to a fight and then he'd need all of that aviator aggression, but it was much more likely that they would merely track them and if necessary warn them off. And yet he was getting a growing feeling that things had changed in the week since he last came this way. That P-3 sounded friendly enough, but from all that he had heard, it was unusual for them to cross the median line, and even less common for them to come so close to a convoy. And now these Boghammers – if that's what they were – operating out of their normal areas. Something was up.

'I trust that it won't come to that, Flight Commander. Your mission is to locate, identify and shadow. You're happy with the ROE?'

'Yes, sir. Hostile intent.'

Mayhew looked at him sharply.

'Indeed, and in the case of Boghammers I take that to mean that they're training loaded weapons at you, within the operating range of those weapons and that they're manoeuvering aggressively. If you see them engaging a merchant ship that's not British, then it's none of our business. Is that quite clear?'

Stevens nodded. It was clear enough but both he and the captain knew that in the end only the people on the spot could determine whether the Iranian behaviour reached the level that could be called *hostile intent*. At least it was better than last year when they were all operating under *hostile act* ROE, when in essence the enemy had to actually fire their weapons before the British ships and helicopters could respond; they had to be prepared to take the first hit. *Hostile intent* was much better but it did carry the risk of starting a war where none was wanted by either party.

'Very well. PWO, action lynx and make a pipe for the Pusser to come to the ops room. Good luck Flight Commander.'

Mayhew walked over to the general operations plot. Able Seaman Markham was still there and there was a fresh pencilled symbol showing *Winchester's* position and another showing the reported position of the Boghammers. As the PWO had said, they were thirty miles from *Winchester*, right at the southeastern end of the TSS, and that meant that they'd already crossed the median line. The Lynx would be on the scene in time to take a hot handover from *Bellona's* Lynx, that was good. But what were the Boghammers doing there? Mayhew thought that he could guess the motivations of the regular Iranian navy and air force commanders; many of them had been trained at Dartmouth in the Shah's days and that deep immersion in the naval ethos never left you. But the Revolutionary Guard was very different. Many of them were religious fanatics, and there was no telling how they would react. He saw the Pusser coming down the ladder from the wardroom deck.

'Ah, Pusser. I'm going to bring forward action stations, how quickly can you get the rest of the watch through the dining hall?'

Fred Trefoil was the ship's supply officer, responsible for anything that wasn't operational or engineering. By long custom he was called the *Pusser*, a corruption of the ancient title *Purser*. To an outsider it sounded almost like an insult, but he'd always been called *Pusser* and would have been alarmed if the captain had addressed him any other way. Today he was also covering many of the first lieutenant's roles while he was away in *World Antigua*.

'They're all through, sir, just this minute. I guessed you might want to warm the bell.'

Mayhew smiled broadly. He liked Fred, he was the only pusser that he had ever served with who concerned himself with what was going on in the ops room. Fred hated the thought of being caught out; of the ship going to action stations, or any of the other states of readiness without the men who were to go on watch being properly fed. What Mayhew didn't know was the source of Fred's information. It was Able Seaman Markham and the other GOP operators. They were unique in the ops room in being able to largely control their own work-rate and in having access to a telephone from which they could call any compartment in the ship. The chief cook was their contact into the supply world and the reward came in a steady flow of bacon sandwiches and other delicacies. The Seariders at Portland would be enraged if they knew.

'Thanks Pusser, that's a load off my mind.'

He stepped back to his console and picked up the bridge microphone.

'Officer-of-the-Watch, Captain. Pipe action stations, one-zulu.'

The bosun's mate heard the captain's order and picked up the main broadcast microphone. He adored these moments of glory, but had the sense to wait for Saxby's order.

'Hands to action stations, hands to action stations,' the main broadcast blasted throughout the ship like a brazen trumpet, 'assume damage control state one condition zulu. Close all watertight doors and hatches. Hands to action stations.'

Mayhew settled himself in his ops room chair and

thought through his next moves. In ten minutes he'd be asked to approve launching the Lynx. The Americans were being told the situation, now it was time to tell the convoy and *Bellona*.

'Officer-of-the-Watch. Tell the navigator to raise the first lieutenant on Cougar Bright and brief him on the situation. If he's unsure he can call the PWO.'

He looked around. The ops room was rapidly filling but he was looking for a particular officer. Ah, there he was, the off-watch PWO. During action stations he became the duty staff officer, responsible for all the things that the on-watch AAWO and PWO found difficult, being more-or-less fixed in their positions. He beckoned him over.

'Get hold of *Bellona* on the secure circuit and brief them what's going on. They'll know part of it because they'll have been listening to the reports from their Lynx, but fill them in on the whole picture. When you've finished, I want to talk directly to their captain. Then do the same for *Brown Rover*. Officer-of-the-Watch, what's the state of the Lynx?'

'Rotors running, sir, ready to launch in two minutes.'

'Is the navigator on the bridge?'

'Here sir.'

Saxby had handed the microphone to the navigator so that he could answer for himself.

'You have authority to launch the Lynx when all the checks are complete.'

'Aye-aye sir.'

Mayhew could feel the Lynx winding up even from this far forward of the flight deck. The rapid beat of the rotor blades as they strained against the harpoon that held them down added a real sense of urgency.

'PWO, Officer-of-the-Watch. Coming right three-zero degrees for a flying course.'

Winchester leaned to port and the rotor blades beat even faster. The ship steadied, the rotors reached their crescendo and then suddenly the sound ceased. The Lynx had released the harpoon and was transformed from an inanimate object into a thing of ethereal beauty and deadly menace as it headed away north.

'PWO, Officer-of-the-Watch. Coming left four-zero degrees to resume station.'

'I've briefed *Bellona*, sir. Her captain's on the line.'

The duty staff handed over the secure line headset.

'Good morning, Gareth. You've been copying your Lynx's reports, I assume.'

Mayhew and *Bellona's* captain were old friends and although Gareth Johnson had joined the navy two years before Mayhew, he'd been promoted to commander six months later. It was that six months difference in seniority that determined who would command the task unit, who would lead and who would follow, and neither Mayhew nor Johnson thought anything of it, it was just the way of the navy.

'Good morning, David. Yes, we've been hearing about the Boghammers, if that's what they are.'

Mayhew smiled to himself. They both knew how often reports from aircraft on surface search proved to be wildly, and sometimes hilariously, inaccurate. Back at Portland both ships had gone haring off in the wrong direction to chase what turned out to be a fleet of charter yachts being moved to their winter berths, while their real foes took their pick of the RFAs that they should have been protecting.

'Well, on balance I suspect in this case the reports are correct. Along with the P-3's close surveillance, it indicates that something might have changed in the Iranian's strategy. They certainly weren't this bullish two weeks ago, and those Boghammers must have been redeployed from the north with something in mind. I've launched my Lynx to relieve yours and I've come to action stations. I recommend you do the same.'

'Roger that, David. I'll refuel the Lynx and keep her at alert fifteen.'

'Yes, please do that and make sure your flight commander understands the ROE. We don't want any accidents.'

There was a pause on the line. Mayhew guessed that Johnson was thinking about the other incident at Portland where his Lynx blatantly disregarded the ROE to engage a simulated fast attack craft. That had earned his ship an unsatisfactory assessment for the exercise, and Johnson wouldn't have forgotten it. Rules of Engagement were handed down from the Ministry of Defence, but they originated in Cabinet policy, and had the force of law behind them. A captain or a flight commander or an AAWO, or anyone who had weapon release authority, could be prosecuted for acting outside their given ROE. Did Gareth resent him mentioning it? Probably, but it had to be said.

'If they don't move away before we get there I'll probably put on some speed to get ahead and try to move them on. In that case I'll bring *Bellona* up to take my place.'

Bellona was one of the earlier Type 22 frigates, and had no medium range gun. It was designed and built during the Cold War, before the Falklands, when it was assumed that a frigate's purpose was to hunt Soviet submarines in the wide spaces of the North Atlantic and engage surface threats at long range with missiles. Guns were seen as obsolete, but the war in the South Atlantic had decisively demonstrated the folly of that policy. *Bellona's* Exocet missiles were effective against other frigates and destroyers – the survivors of *HMS Sheffield* could attest to that – but were of little use against Boghammers.

'That's understood.'

'Well, we'd best stay alert, Gareth. Good luck.'

'Good luck, David. Out.'

***

Chapter Six

Tuesday, 1220
HMS Winchester, at Sea, Straits of Hormuz
Operation Armilla Daily Sitrep: Entered Silkworm envelope…

'Captain, AAWO. The P-3's moving north on the Iranian side of the median line, bearing one-two-zero at eighteen miles. It's probably repositioning, but it might be heading back to Bandar Abbas.'

Mayhew checked the clock, five hours on task. That was short for the daily P-3; they normally loitered in the Gulf of Oman for eight hours or more. Perhaps they'd heard about the Lynx activity, and it was always possible that they were co-operating with the Boghammers and were moving into a better position to keep all the players under surveillance. As a rule the IRGC and the regular forces operated independently, but Mayhew knew that it wasn't safe to assume that they would never co-operate with each other. With the P-3 broadcasting the convoy's position the Boghammers would find it easy to be in the right place at the right time to interfere with its passage, if that was their intention. When they were supplied from Sweden, many of the Boghammers were fitted with a normal navigational radar, but some of the radars had been removed to make way for weapon systems. Even if one or two of this group had kept them, they were mounted so low that their horizon was probably no more than twelve miles, and without any other form of identification they would have difficulty locating the convoy on their own. The P-3 could be the vital link that helped the Boghammers find their targets.

'Captain, PWO. Our Lynx has five miles to run to join up with *Bellona's* Lynx.'

Mayhew calculated quickly. The Lynx had flown twenty miles at a hundred-and-forty knots, that sounded about right. He could see the real-time radar tracking symbols on the PWO's tactical display and the non-real-time track that had been injected for the Boghammers.

'AAWO, how's the tracking on the Lynx?'

'The target indication radar is seeing it occasionally, sir. They're operating at about a thousand feet.'

'Captain, PWO. The helicopter controller can see their chirp.'

Then he had a good handle on the positions of his units. What could the P-3 see? He couldn't see the chirp unless he had the corresponding equipment, and that was vanishingly unlikely, but with the advantage of his height and his specialised radar he was probably tracking them well enough.

'Officer-of-the-Watch, let the MCR know that I might need the two Olympus at short notice.'

'Aye-aye sir,' Saxby replied, and picked up the microphone to speak to the engineers in the machinery control room.

'Captain, PWO. Both Lynx are going low for a close pass. We'll lose them for a few minutes.'

'Very well PWO. Blind, what's the state of our Four-Five and close range weapons?'

'Four-Five loaded with HE. BMARCs and GPMGs loaded and ready, Phalanx in manual, sir.'

High explosive shells for the gun, that was the only sensible ammunition for a vessel the size of a Boghammer.

Mayhew hoped fervently that it wouldn't come to shooting it out at close range, in fact he didn't want a shootout at any range. In his mind he would have failed if he had to use his weapons at all. However, his task was to bring these tankers safely through the Straits and he must be prepared for anything. The 4.5 inch gun was a formidable weapon that could be aimed using the same fire control radar that directed the Seadart missile system. Its forty-six pound high explosive projectile could be triggered by a proximity fuse, showering a small craft with a deadly cascade of shrapnel. At close range or if the radars couldn't track the target, it could also be aimed visually using the lookout aimer sights – the LASs – below the mainmast on either side of the ship. *Winchester* carried two chief petty officer missilemen and at action stations one sat in the ops room as the missile gun director blind in close contact with the captain, the AAWO and the PWO, while the other – the missile gun director visual – managed the upper deck weapons, the Vulcan Phalanx, the chaff decoys and the LAS. To keep in contact with the action he had to move from side to side of the ship through a passageway – a tunnel really – aft of the funnel.

'PWO, Captain. Make the threat warning surface red. Chief Yeoman, pass that to the task unit.'

'Javelin, AAWO. Threat warning air is yellow, surface red, weapons tight. Make sure your fire units know what's happening and are ready for a surface engagement.'

'Javelin, roger.'

Lieutenant Hook was a man of few words but he had tight control of his detachment. Allenby had spent some time ensuring that he understood how his fire units would integrate with the overall defence of the convoy, and how they would be controlled. Yet using the Javelin against a small surface unit would be a first. Allenby was still unconvinced of its effectiveness in surface mode, and there was no official policy on its use. The Javelin had a semi-automatic command-to-line-of-sight guidance system that only required the operator to keep his aiming sight pointed at the target. A tracking system in the launcher's optics compared the location of the missile to the line-of-sight and sent it commands over a radio link to guide it towards its target. It only needed the aimer to twitch and the missile would hit the sea, but there was at least a hope and anything was worth trying if an attack should get that close. At the very least it would provide a distraction.

'Captain, PWO. The Lynx is reporting sir. Confirmed Boghammers. They're all armed with what looks like a multi-barrelled rocket launcher and a fifty-calibre machine gun. No sign of SAMs but they didn't get close enough to be certain. They're loitering just this side of the separation scheme in that wedge of international waters between Iran's and Oman's twelve-mile limit; they're apparently waiting for something.'

Mayhew could imagine how difficult it was for the Lynx. They'd be hammering in at a hundred-and-fifty knots barely above the waves with the helicopter bucking and vibrating. The observer would be using a standard set of binoculars to identify the contacts and determine how they were armed, while the pilot would be concentrating on staying low and out of range of the fifty-calibre machine guns. It was hard enough to classify them as Boghammers, but it required a leap of faith to accept the identification of the weapons at face value. Well, he'd take the identification – Boghammers for sure – but he'd reserve judgement on their armament.

'Officer-of-the-Watch, Captain. Increase twenty-eight knots. Steer... what's the course to intercept the Boghammers PWO?'

Another long pause while the PWO pressed buttons and waited for the information to appear on his tote.

'Three-five-five, sir, twenty miles.'

'Course three-five-five, Officer-of-the-Watch.'

Mayhew could feel the acceleration and hear the exhilarating sound of the Olympus engines as they sucked in air through their intakes. Then, as the speed increased, he felt *Winchester's* stern settle into the trough that the bow-wave created as it passed her stern. They would soon be powering towards the Boghammers at near-maximum speed.

'EWD. I have I-band radios on that bearing.'

'Roger EWD,' Mayhew replied.

Mayhew didn't want to discourage him but that was a about as useless as anything he'd ever heard over the command open line. It would have been extraordinary if there were no navigational radars on that bearing; *Winchester* was heading right for the start of one of the busiest traffic separation schemes in the world. A good proportion of all the world's imported energy passed through the Straits of Hormuz, and every tanker and LPG carrier would be transmitting on an I-band radio. Quite possibly some of what the EWD was seeing would originate from Boghammers, but there was no way of telling the difference as the Boghammer radios were standard commercial units.

'PWO, SPS. Surface contacts three-five-six, eighteen miles. It's a small group, no more than six.'

'PWO, roger.'

Mayhew adjusted his own radar display. Ah, there they were, and he could see the two chirps from the Lynx helicopters.

'HC, PWO. Confirm that both Lynx are still in territorial waters.'

They needed diplomatic clearance to operate helicopters inside a country's twelve-mile limit, and they could only breach that rule in a dire emergency.

'PWO, HC. Confirmed, they're in the wedge of international waters this side of the TSS.'

Things were getting complicated as the convoy moved towards the traffic separation scheme and as the territorial waters – the twelve-mile-limit – closed in from the east and the west. Mayhew hated to intervene when his own team was operating so well, but he needed to ensure that the two Lynx didn't overstep the mark.

'Chief, patch me through to the secure circuit, I want to talk to our Lynx.'

The chief ops room supervisor leaned through the hatch into the MCR and watched as the secure speech circuit was patched through, then he flicked the switch on the captain's console, checked that the green indicator light was lit and nodded to confirm.

Mayhew listened for a moment until there was a gap in the chatter between the two helicopters and the controllers in the ships.

'Two-seven-three, this is *Winchester*, Charlie Oscar, over.'

There was no need for cryptic callsigns on a secure

circuit. Two-seven-three was his own Lynx side number and *Charlie Oscar* was the universal callsign for the commanding officer. *Bellona's* Lynx was two-six-eight. He heard the flight observer's reply; the Lynx communications system didn't allow the pilot to use secure speech.

'Charlie Oscar, this is two-seven-three, over.'

The observer's voice was distorted in passing through the scrambling mechanism, it sounded as though he was speaking through water. Mayhew assumed that his voice sounded the same and tried to speak slowly and distinctly.

'Two-seven-three, Charlie Oscar. I'm going to encourage the Boghammers to move away towards the northeast before the convoy comes through. Two-seven-three take the lead and manoeuvre with two-six-eight to discourage them from moving south or southwest. Fly attack profiles from the southeast but break off before you come in range of their weapons. Look out for SAMs and break off immediately if you see any. Keep outside territorial waters, both Iran's and Oman's.'

'Charlie Oscar, this is two-seven-three, roger, out.'

'PWO, Captain. I'm going up to the bridge and I'll con the ship from there. I'll be using the gun in local control from the LAS, so tell the missile gun director visual to come to the bridge for a briefing.'

Mayhew took one more look at the tactical display. On the bridge he would be deprived of the wealth of information that was available in the ops room, and he'd be reliant upon voice reports from below. However, confronting the Boghammers brought naval warfare back a half century, before the time of radar. Seadart was useless for this, and the fire control radars couldn't lock onto those small surface targets at the close ranges that he anticipated. In any case, he needed to see the Iranians' reactions with his own eyes.

***

Saxby was staring hard through his binoculars when Mayhew reached the bridge, and the missile gun director visual entered from the bridge wing at the same time, trailing behind him the long lead for his headset that allowed him to move more-or-less freely among his close range weapons and from one side of the ship to the other.

'I can see them now, sir, and the two Lynx are circling to the right.'

'Thanks, Officer-of-the-Watch. Maintain this course and speed for the time being. Make sure everyone on the bridge has their helmet on over their anti-flash.'

The navigator started guiltily. He hated both the white anti-flash hood and the heavy steel helmet. He'd left them on the chart table, and forgotten to replace them before the captain came back onto the bridge.

'Chief. I'm not sure how this is going to pan out, but my immediate intention is to put the ship between the Boghammers and the convoy and give them a verbal warning. While I'm doing that keep all your weapons trained fore-and-aft. If they need a second warning I'll ask you to train them on whichever of the targets I think best, probably the nearest or the one that looks like the leader. That includes the Four-Five in local control, the Phalanx, the twenty-millimetres and the GPMGs. That should deliver the message. Where's the chief yeoman? I'll want the signal projector to point at the targets too so your operator must follow visual's orders. I know it's daylight, but I want as much equipment as possible to be pointed at him. I don't want anybody on the upper deck who isn't involved in the weapons. Officer-of-the-Watch, make a pipe putting the upper deck out of bounds except for the weapons crews, and that goes for the flight deck too. You've got all that, Chief?'

'Yes, sir. No problem.'

'I might have to call for warning shots. If I do, be very careful to fire across their bows and don't hit anything accidentally. I'll be on command open line.'

'Right-oh, sir. If that's all I'll get back to the boys.'

Now that was the kind of response that Mayhew liked.

No puzzled looks and no hesitation, the chief clearly knew what was expected.

'Captain, AAWO. The P-3 is orbiting between Larak Island and Kuhestak.'

Mayhew heard Allenby's call but didn't respond. The P-3's actions were important and he must keep its position in the back of his mind, but the Boghammers were the real and immediate problem.

'Navigator, get onto VHF and see if you can raise those Boghammers on channel sixteen.'

It was all happening fast now and Mayhew was glad that he'd decided to come up to the bridge. The Boghammers were just becoming visible through his binoculars. There were five of them, long and low and lean, painted in camouflage and oozing aggression. They were motoring slowly towards the northwest, away from the fast-approaching destroyer. One of them was flying an outsize Iranian flag but the others were all unadorned. He noticed that they all had radar pods fitted above their cabins.

'Visual, Captain. LAS cover the Boghammer with the flag.'

He could see the two Lynx swooping towards the group, then banking away. They looked predatory too, and he knew that a Type 42 at full power had a menace all of its own. He looked down at the fo'c'sle. The gun was pointing forward as he'd ordered but to the Boghammers it must have looked as though it was following their moves.

'No reply on channel sixteen, sir.'

'Then broadcast warning number one anyway.'

The navigator brought the microphone to his mouth.

'Iranian small boats in vicinity of the southeast end of the Hormuz traffic separation scheme, this is British warship. I request that you move away to the northeast to allow my convoy to pass through.'

There was a rapid burst of what sounded like Arabic but could have been Farsi. It sounded too faint to come from the Boghammers, it was probably one of the dhows or fishing boats offering their opinion on the situation.

'Iranian small boats in vicinity of the southeast end of the Hormuz traffic separation scheme, this is British warship. I request that you move away to the northeast to allow my convoy to pass through.'

No response, not even the anonymous Arab or Iranian.

Mayhew waited twenty seconds.

'Visual, cover the targets with the gun and close range weapons.'

The chief repeated the order so that there was no doubt that it had been correctly received.

'Cover targets with gun and close range weapons.'

There was a pause as the chief flicked his headset from command open line to the weapons control intercom, then the whine of hydraulics gave warning that the 4.5 inch gun on the fo'c'sle was moving. Mayhew resisted the urge to look at it and focussed on the Boghammers. They were only two miles away now and they must be able to see the great gun turning towards them.

'Officer-of-the-Watch, reduce ten knots. Stay on the two Olympus.'

Winchester decelerated as rapidly as she'd accelerated, and her stern lifted to the changed pattern of the waves. At ten knots, even with the high-pitched whine of the twin Olympus gas turbines, it was easier to speak, and the whole situation appeared less stressed. Mayhew knew that was only an illusion. Nothing had changed, there was still no response from the Iranians. The two helicopters were operating in an increasingly confined triangle of airspace and they'd need to be recovered soon, before *Winchester* and *Bellona* ran out of international waters.

'PWO, Captain. Tell *Bellona* to be ready to recover her Lynx.'

They were only a mile away now and every detail of the great destroyer must be visible to the Boghammers. They were staring down the barrels of a big naval gun, a Vulcan Phalanx close-in-weapon system that could fire three-thousand-six-hundred depleted uranium rounds a minute, a smaller twenty-millimetre gun, two general purpose machine guns and the unblinking stare of a powerful signal projector.

'AAWO, Captain. Load the Seadart launcher and train it on the bearing.'

They probably wouldn't know that the Seadart could do them no damage at such a close range, but this was all about a show of force.

'The warning again, Navigator.'

'Iranian small boats in vicinity of the southeast end of the Hormuz traffic separation scheme, this is British warship to your south at one mile. I urgently request that you move away to the northeast to allow my convoy to pass through.'

Mayhew walked onto the bridge wing and looked astern. The convoy was still visible, about ten miles away. Did the Boghammers know that it was there?

'AAWO, Captain. What's the P-3 doing?

'Twenty miles east at six thousand feet, circling, sir.'

'Inside Iranian territorial waters?'

'Yes, sir, well inside.'

Then it must be co-operating with the IRGC. In which case it would certainly be telling the Boghammers where the convoy was.

'Cover it with 909, AAWO, India-band only.'

The forward fire control radar was immediately above and behind the bridge, and Mayhew heard it almost immediately slewing towards the target. He looked out from the bridge wing and back towards the stern. Every man in sight looked purposeful. Even the signalman had an intense stare as though he was manning a lethal machine gun rather than a harmless signal lamp. He saw the Vulcan Phalanx jerk as it followed its target. There was no response whatsoever from the Boghammers. They must have heard the warning, every vessel at sea listened to channel sixteen. The American frigate to the west would have heard, the P-3 would have heard, and the convoy would have heard. He studied the boats through his binoculars. They were forty-two foot Boghammers for sure and all identically armed with a fifty-calibre forward and a twelve barrelled rocket launcher aft. The rockets would be unguided, but they'd be accurate enough at close range and from a steady firing platform. It looked like they had about six crew, two at each of the weapon stations, a helmsman and a skipper. He could see the skipper on the lead ship, the one with the flag. He was studying *Winchester* through binoculars just as he was being studied by *Winchester*. Mayhew raised a hand and put his fist to his ear, the universal sign that he wanted to speak by radio, but the Iranian didn't react at all. Perhaps the distance was too great for his gesture to be seen. Mayhew spoke without taking his eyes off his opponent.

'Navigator, on this course how far will we be from the centre of our traffic lane?'

'It'll be a mile to the northeast, sir.'

'Then there's room for the convoy to pass to the south and west of us?'

'Yes, sir. They'll be off the centre-line of the inbound lane, but there's enough space.'

'Very well. Call the first lieutenant and tell him that the convoy might have to stay to the south side of its lane. 'Officer-of-the-Watch, reduce to five knots and come twenty degrees to starboard.'

He'd edge in towards the Iranians and see what they did. Ah, the skipper of the lead ship had ducked down into the cockpit. What now?'

'Captain, AAWO, the P-3 has started moving away to the northwest again, towards Bandar Abbas.'

'Captain, roger.'

Was that it? Had the P-3 called off the operation? There was still no movement from the Boghammers. The nearest was only four or five cables away now. Suddenly there was a flash of white at the Boghammers stern as her engine kicked into life and her twin screws churned the water. The skipper's head reappeared above the cockpit as the helmsman put the wheel hard over to starboard and it turned sharply away. They were all turning, then it appeared that their actions were commanded from the P-3. How interesting.

'Visual, Captain. Keep your weapons trained on the targets.'

They were all moving away now. There was a sudden burst of fire from the lead Boghammer, but Mayhew could see that its fifty-calibre gun was pointing harmlessly into the air. One by one each of the Boghammers joined in the defiant salute as they roared away to the north. Mayhew caught a glimpse of the chief talking to his weapon crews, keeping them calm. It was all very well for the IRGC to waste ammunition in a pointless gesture, but that wasn't the Royal Navy's style at all.

'Captain, AAWO. *USS Casablanca* has been calling on Navy Red, asking if we need any assistance. I've given him a sitrep and told him that it's all under control.'

'Thank you AAWO, quiet right. Make sure he knows the whole story, and draft an enemy contact report for me. I'll be down in twenty minutes unless the Boghammers come back.'

'Captain, sir, Officer-of-the-Watch. We can recover two-seven-zero in international waters if I give him a flying course now.'

Mayhew had forgotten about recovering the Lynx and he must certainly not do so inside Oman's territorial waters. The Oman navy had a station on Goat Island off the northwest tip of the Musandam Peninsula and they'd be alert for any infringements. Oman was a friendly nation, but like all of the Gulf states the Sultan of Oman was all too aware of the looming power of Iran. There was another option; *Bellona* was built to operate two Lynx but only carried one, and the frigate was sufficiently far astern to be able to recover her own Lynx, stow it in the hangar then recover two-seven-zero. It was tempting, but it would constrain the task unit's operations if both Lynx should be needed in an emergency. He pushed his microphone to the top of his head so that he couldn't be heard over the open line.

'Thanks for your timely advice, Ben.'

He lowered his microphone again.

'PWO, recover two-seven-zero. Tell *Bellona* to recover two-six-eight. Make it snappy, I want to be back in station before we enter the separation scheme. Officer-of-the-Watch, keep us in international waters until the recovery is complete.'

***

Mayhew sat gratefully in his chair on the bridge and let the tension flow out of him. His steward brought a cup of tea and he had even brought a hobnob. That was an event for the diary; the captain's wife had scolded the steward most severely when she'd last come aboard in Portsmouth. Two hobnobs a day, no more. His wife was a nutritionist and she took her job very seriously indeed. She had the sort of figure that was used to advertise women's sportswear and tended to become bossy and self-righteous at the slightest sign of a half inch expansion in her husband's waistline. Lee Mayhew wasn't having her husband come back from a Gulf deployment unable to fit into his clothes. Mayhew's steward was terrified of her and needed a day's notice if she was coming on board, so that he could hide the illicit cabin stores. That nervous sideways glance whenever he came into the cabin – which was at least a dozen times a day – was an instinctive check that the captain's wife hadn't come aboard with the last mail delivery.

He looked out of the window. The Boghammers weren't even in sight, and without any further orders from him his ship was on a flying course and he could see his own Lynx was on its final approach. He glanced at the wind and pitch-and-roll indicators. They were all within limits and he made the permission to fly switch. He watched the flight deck camera and saw two-seven-zero land on and engage its harpoon.

'Lynx on deck, sir. Harpoon engaged.'

With the Lynx firmly held down by the harpoon he could manoeuvre *Winchester* quite freely, bearing in mind that the flight deck nets were down for flying operations, and the flight deck crew ran a risk every time they ventured out of the safety of the hangar.

'Very well, Officer-of-the-Watch. Return to our station. Chief Yeoman, make to *Bellona*, return to previously assigned station.'

Now for the Form Red, the obligatory report of contact with the enemy. It would be studied by the Royal Navy's Senior Officer Middle East and the Ministry of Defence, and passed to US Commander Middle East Force – COMMIDEASTFOR – in Bahrain. It would be one more indicator of Iran's intentions, one more piece in the jigsaw puzzle of intelligence that allowed the allied forces in the Gulf to be ready for whatever move Iran or Iraq made next.

***

Chapter Seven

Tuesday, 1400
HMS Winchester, at Sea, Straits of Hormuz
Operation Armilla Daily Sitrep: Entered TSS…

Mayhew dearly wanted to remove his white cotton hood and gloves but the ship was still at action stations and he'd given no order to relax anti-flash; he of all people must show an example. There was a balance: wearing anti-flash for too long encouraged his men to sneakily drop theirs when they thought they couldn't be seen, but having anti-flash relaxed when a threat was imminent was more dangerous. He remembered taking survivors on board from *HMS Coventry* after she'd been bombed and sunk during the Falklands war; he'd seen the burns on exposed flesh where waves of superheated flame – *flash* as it's known in the navy – had caught some of them with their hoods down. It was one more thing to think about, another decision that in itself was a minor matter, but it could have an impact on the ship's mission. The Boghammers were out of sight now, so this was a good moment to make a change.

'PWO, Captain, what are the threat warnings?'

Mayhew knew them very well, he kept a mental tally in that part of his mind that wasn't engaged in immediate concerns, but it was as well to check that his memory agreed with the warnings that had been issued to *Bellona* and the tankers. There was a slight pause that told him that the PWO hadn't been thinking of threat warnings. Well, he should be, they were the fundamental statements of the command's assessment of the possibility of an attack and they guided the readiness states not only of *Winchester* but of the task unit and the convoy. The pause was just long enough for Buckley to have asked Allenby's advice.

'Air is yellow, sir, sub-surface is white. I was about to ask your permission to reduce the surface warning to yellow.'

As he thought, Buckley had forgotten that the surface threat should be reduced now that the Boghammers had withdrawn. He needed sharpening-up but it would do more harm than good to give him a dressing-down in public.

'Very well, PWO. Make the threat warning surface yellow. Chief Yeoman, make to the task unit, air and surface threat warnings yellow, sub-surface white. Navigator, pass that to the first lieutenant in *World Antigua*. Officer-of-the-Watch, make a pipe: relax anti-flash, relax steel helmets.'

It was always the same, the universal looks of relief as the hoods were pulled down to rest on the shoulders and the cumbersome white gloves were removed and tucked into the lifejacket belts, ready to be quickly replaced. Every man on the bridge combed his fingers through his hair, rubbed his cheeks and looked around as though the world had been made anew, and Mayhew realised that he had unconsciously been doing the same. Anti-flash gear was certainly effective but was universally hated. However, it could be worse. If there had been a biological or chemical threat then his gun crews would be wearing their anti-gas respirators and in this heat that was no small matter. Certainly both Iran and Iraq had used chemical weapons in their long-running war, but only against each other in their huge and brutal land battles far to the north. Still, the whole ship's company carried their respirators at action stations with the green webbing bags strapped to their waists. He was pleased though that the Boghammers had seen his upper deck crews properly dressed for action; he didn't want them to be in any doubt about his readiness to defend the convoy.

'Captain, Officer-of-the-Watch. The ship's in station on *World Antigua*.'

Mayhew walked onto the port bridge wing and the two-man GPMG crew moved aside to let him through. He could imagine their frustration as the starboard battery of weapons had been trained on the Boghammers, while the port side crews could see nothing of the action. Still, they appeared in good spirits with their hair ruffled from the anti-flash hood and the warm wind blowing across their faces. He looked across at *World Antigua* to see the first lieutenant looking back at him. How had it appeared from their perspective? They would have been informed about the P-3 and the Boghammers and they'd have seen the two helicopters rushing to and fro, but they could do nothing about it, they had to hold their course and speed and hope for the best. It would be better in *World Antigua* than in the other three, for the first lieutenant would be giving a running commentary, and far better than the uncertainty and perhaps fear that the Filipino ships must have been feeling. Mayhew stepped forward and looked over at the fo'c'sle where the 4.5 inch gun and the Seadart missile launcher were ready for instant action. As he watched the launcher swung upwards so that the missiles pointed to the heavens, then slewed through a hundred-and-eighty degrees. The covers for the hoist pivoted open and the missiles disappeared below with a slight hum of hydraulic machinery. That was a sensible precaution, for this transit through Oman's territorial waters must be undertaken as an *innocent passage*, and it was at least arguable that having Seadart missiles on the launcher constituted a warlike stance that wasn't at all innocent. It was a fine point, but if he got it wrong it would become a legal matter when he was called to account. Stowing the missiles would have been Allenby's call, and he quite correctly didn't bother his captain with such details. He looked across the fo'c'sle to the far horizon. *Winchester* and its convoy were entering one of the busiest international straits in the world, and yet it was curiously quiet. Tanker traffic had reduced considerably since the warring nations had started taking potshots at vessels carrying oil and gas from their opponent's fields. Nowadays, much of it was piped overland across the UAE to Fujairah and Khor Fakkan, thus avoiding the dangerous Straits, and most of the remainder was being convoyed by the allied nations. Few tankers tried their luck with a solo passage. What would have been a constant stream of ships passing in both directions was reduced to the occasional convoy and smaller local traffic.

'AAWO, Captain. Can you hand over to Gordon for a moment and join me on the bridge?'

'Aye-aye sir, I'll be right up.'

***

Gordon Kesteven was the off-watch AAWO whose action station was in the ops room, managing the ship's soft-kill defences. It was his task to co-ordinate all of the non-kinetic anti-ship missile defences – the chaff, the jammers and the manoeuvres – that were designed to defeat an incoming missile's homing head. He therefore kept a close eye on the air picture to keep himself informed of the situation, so much so that the handover was conducted in a few seconds. As Allenby headed for the door, Kesteven sank gratefully into the AAWO's seat; the soft-kill manager had no seat and he'd been standing for nearly three hours.

Allenby blinked in the bright sunlight and pulled his sunglasses from the side pocket of his respirator bag. He saw the missile gun director visual beckon the GPMG's crew back to the ready-use lockers to give the captain and the ops officers some privacy.

'Well, Ops, that was a good performance from the ops room and the close range weapons, don't you think?'

'Yes, it was, in general...'

Mayhew cut him off in mid-sentence.

'I think we agree though that there's still a question mark over the EWD. He seems to know his kit well enough, but he just hasn't yet stepped up to being part of the command team. It was the same at Portland. Any ideas?'

'You're right, sir. I've had a word with him and asked Gordon to watch him carefully and give him a bit of mentoring. It's quite a jump from being an EW operator to being the director at action stations, and he's actually quite inexperienced for a Chief. His last ship was an all-gun Leander frigate, and that was some time ago. He was in a technical intelligence post for four years before coming to us. He seems to care too much about analysis and not enough about feeding the situational awareness and calling out the threat radars.'

'Should he be replaced? Petty Officer Dickens could step up to the job, couldn't he?'

Allenby thought for a moment. Although Chief Quinn had been through the Type 42 simulators at *HMS Dryad* and he'd passed all the tests, his mental processes hadn't really caught up yet. If it was only a question of the technology he could have coped, but the action stations Electronic Warfare Director in a Type 42 had to be thinking a step ahead and he had to be contributing proactively as part of the command team. The Seariders at Portland had spotted the problem, so it was well-known. Allenby had already considered replacing him, but it was a big step to take against such a senior rating. He'd have to be flown home and a substitute would have to be found and sent out to join *Winchester*, and in the meantime they'd be a man down in what was already a very lean team. In such a small branch, every EW rating in the navy would know what had happened and it would ruin Quinn's authority and blight his career; probably he would never be promoted to warrant officer. Allenby instinctively shied away from such a drastic step. It would be better to nurture Chief Quinn and support him as he grew into the job.

'I'd rather not, sir. He's improved since Portland but I agree that it's still not enough. Gordon has a good relationship with him and will bring him along, and I'll speak to him again when we get back to cruising watches.'

'Alright, let's go with that for now, but I want to see positive improvement. Anyway, that's not why I called you up here; what do you think of those shenanigans with the Boghammers? What was that all about?'

Allenby stroked his chin and thought for a moment. This was one of the disadvantages of being a warfare officer, he was doomed to see the world through fuzzy blips on a radar screen. He hadn't seen today's Boghammers, he'd never seen any in fact, and the captain had the advantage of him. It was difficult to explain how much could be deduced from observing the enemy first hand, but there was no doubt that it was a substantial advantage. The captain had made the right decision to come up to the bridge for the encounter; Allenby only wished he'd been free to do the same.

'Well, I haven't heard of that kind of co-operation between the regular Iranian forces and the IRGC before. The Americans haven't reported anything like it, nor the French or Italians. It felt like a rehearsal, a proof of concept perhaps, not like a real, determined attack. How did it look from the bridge?'

'Just as you say. I want a debrief from the flight commander, he might have seen more than I did, but it looked to me as though the Boghammers achieved exactly what they wanted to achieve, and then they withdrew before it escalated. It's always been assumed that the Boghammers' greatest problem is to find and identify their targets and to bring enough of them to the right place to overwhelm our defences, and a P-3 for command and control would do that. Funny, isn't it, that countries like Iran without a naval heritage believe that merely buying ships gives them a warfighting capability. It seems to take them years to realise that without the command and control arrangements they're little better than nautical terrorists. I wonder whether there was an IRGC commander in the P-3, or just their normal mission commander. In any case, it's a dangerous precedent and one that we need to spell out in the enemy contact report and the daily sitrep.'

***

Allenby slid back into the AAWO's seat in the ops room. This wasn't the time and certainly not the place to discuss Chief Quinn's performance with Kesteven, there were too many people all packed into a confined space and private conversation was impossible. Little had changed in the fifteen minutes that he'd been gone, but the P-3's IFF response had faded over Bandar Abbas and it had almost certainly landed. The usual civilian air traffic was buzzing around with regular flights between Bandar Abbas, Dubai and Muscat and a few from further afield. That was the problem in the Gulf: for most of its inhabitants life went on as usual even while a bitter war was raging in the north and tankers were being attacked in the centre and the south, and it was difficult to disentangle the warlike from the peaceful. Of course both the Iraqis and the Iranians took advantage of it and regularly flew reconnaissance and attack missions through the established airlanes in an attempt to disguise their intentions. That was why the US Navy had deployed its top-flight air defence cruisers to the Gulf, *Havelock* to the north and *Casablanca* covering the Straits. There was another cruiser, perhaps two, way out in the Gulf of Oman with their Carrier Task Group and they were all connected by tactical data links. Allenby could see the large-area picture on his tactical display, but he knew its limitations. It relied upon the contacts having been accurately identified and consistently tracked, and in a busy, congested area like the Gulf, that was rarely wholly achieved. He put out an air sitrep to the task unit ending with a statement that the air threat warning was yellow. It would never drop to white while they were inside the Gulf; the warning time that they could expect was far too short to justify that level of relaxation.

He felt a tap on his shoulder; it was Kesteven, making a motion for him to talk offline.

'Chief Quinn has been showing me how we can identify those Boghammers if we see them again. Have you got a moment?'

Allenby took another scan of the tactical display. All quiet, and he'd only be a few yards away. He nodded to his assistant who gave a thumbs-up to show that he knew that he must watch the screen even more carefully while the boss was out of his seat.

Quinn was older than most newly-promoted chief EWs and he was out of place among the rest of the ops room team, most of whom were young and highly ambitious. He looked as though he'd joined the navy in a different era, before chinagraph pencils were replaced by computer symbology, and when the electronic warfare equipment was in a primitive state, and needed nurturing to give up its secrets. They'd been a small, self-contained branch in those days with little contact with the ship's command beyond brief statements of intercepted enemy radars. That was perhaps why Quinn found life in a Type 42's ops room so challenging.

'What have you got, Chief?'

'Well, sir, we've been analysing those Boghammers' I-band radars. They're all identical civilian navigational radars, low powered and with nothing fancy about them. The UAA-1 can't distinguish between them, at least not initially.'

Allenby had already assumed that was the case, but something in Quinn's tone told him that he had more to tell.

'The frequency and the scan rate is the same for all of them and exactly like half of the small boats in the Gulf, and some of the tankers too. However, Furuno – that's the radar manufacturer, sir – gave each a unique PRF; a pulse repetition frequency...'

Allenby resisted the temptation to hurry Quinn along, he knew very well what a PRF was.

'... so that they're less likely to interfere with each other. By separately off-line analysing each of the radars we can distinguish one from another. But better than that, the PRF's are all so close together that it's almost certain that these five radars are all from the same batch, all off the production line in an unbroken sequence. Now we know those PRFs we can tell these boats apart from each other and apart from any other radars in the Gulf.'

Allenby was interested.

'How long would that take you, Chief?'

'Oh a minute or so, sir, a couple of minutes to be certain.

The computer can't do it you see, not automatically, it needs the human touch.'

That short sentence told Allenby all he needed to know about Quinn's regard for the fabulously expensive equipment that he controlled. It also told him what Quinn liked doing best, analysing the technical characteristics of the enemy radars. He'd probably still be running a fascinating series of tests on a surveillance radar while a deadly missile was streaking towards his ship. He was more of an intelligence analyst than a senior member of a tactical team. However, in this case he might be onto something useful.

'That's great Chief. But I think we can do better than that. We know that the Iranians bought all of these boats, fifty or so, in a single contract from the Boghammer company in Sweden. If these five radars came off the Furuno line together, it's probable that they all did. Let's see those PRFs.'

Quinn offered a page of his notebook for inspection but didn't let go of the book, he clearly treasured it too much to let anyone else's hands on it. As its pages fell open Allenby could see that perhaps half of them were filled with pencilled notes, almost all figures with the occasional name of a ship or type of radar. This latest page was all numbers, some crossed through and repeated, but at last the jumble resolved into five lines of half a dozen columns. Each line showed a PRF, all in the low two-thousands of pulses per second and each PRF was separated from its nearest fellow by less than ten pulses. Each line continued with what Allenby could see were computer-generated track numbers. With small vessels like that jumping in and out of radar contact, it was natural that the track numbers wouldn't be stable, and this was Quinn's attempt to follow them. Good God, how could he do that in the heat of an action? That explained why he didn't seem to be following the tactical developments, he was too interested in his PRFs! And yet, this was important information if it helped to identify the

Boghammers before they became visible. He remembered something about the US Navy equivalent to UAA-1.

'Can the Slick Thirty-Two resolve these PRFs?

'The SLQ-32 basic model,' he pedantically gave the American equipment its full title, 'is more of a threat warning receiver, sir. Maybe better at that than UAA-1, but it's not so good at gathering technical intelligence. This stuff would still be interesting to the Americans though.'

Allenby stared at the page. It was absolutely routine to share this information with the allies but it wasn't considered a priority, and a technical report would go through tortuous channels before it reached the front line operators. They'd already sent an enemy contact report to declare the contact with the Boghammers, but they could send a supplement so that the information would be passed around the allied forces in the Gulf within hours rather than weeks. He glanced across to where Petty Officer Dickens – the electronic warfare controller – was pretending not to listen to them. Dickens moved up to the EWD seat when the ship was in defence watches and Quinn was off-watch, and Allenby had always been very happy hearing his confident voice on the command open line. An idea started to form, it all depended on Dickens' answer to the next question.

'Can you do this analysis on the fly, Petty Officer Dickens?'

Dickens smiled, he almost winked. Did he guess what Allenby was up to?

'Not me, sir. I could do it if you locked me away in a nice quiet office with a coffee machine for a week, but not with everything else going on, sir, not a hope.'

'Gordon, jump into the AAWO's seat for ten minutes. Chief, come out in the passageway for the moment.'

***

It was done. It was irregular but even so it was a perfectly practical solution to the problem. Allenby had buttered up the Chief, told him that nobody else could gather and analyse such vital information, and that, with his agreement he'd like him to swap seats with Dickens at action stations, only temporarily, while they were on this deployment. Chief Quinn and the leading seaman who operated the UAA-1 would make an excellent combination to gather the threat information and pass it quickly to Dickens to make his tactical assessment. Now all that Allenby had to do was square it with the captain, and he was confident that he would be pushing at an open door. There was a longer term problem to be solved in what to do with Quinn when *Winchester* returned from deployment, but there were plenty of shore-based technical intelligence drafts for men like him, square pegs who had been forced into round holes, and it only needed the right recommendations. It seemed incredible but he could already see that after only a minute or so the EW bench looked happier with the new arrangements.

***

Chief Quinn worked on the Form Red supplement, laying out how it was possible to individually and collectively identify the Boghammers. He'd be ready to show the draft to the ops officer in an hour or so, if there were no more interruptions. It had to be good for his own sake as well as for the sake of the mission, for in this Quinn was aware that he and Allenby – and he guessed the captain himself – thought as one. Quinn's highest ambition was to get away from these noisy ships and their distractions and find a nice quiet billet where he could analyse away to his heart's content, and where he could go home every evening. For he was confident now; if they could have a few more encounters with the Boghammers, he'd really start to nail down all the data. He'd talk to the navigator and to the missile gun director visual, his messmate, and see if they could find some means of identifying the individual boats by eye. Now that would be really helpful, if he could correlate an individual radar to a known identifiable Boghammer. A glassy expression crept over his face as he watched his screen with half of his attention and re-ordered his beloved PRFs with the other half.

***

Chapter Eight

Tuesday, 1800
HMS Winchester, at Sea, Straits of Hormuz
Operation Armilla Daily Sitrep: Exited the TSS, sighted smoke on the horizon...

The sun was starting to set when Mayhew climbed the last ladder up to the bridge. The convoy was clear of the traffic separation scheme and had passed out of Oman's territorial limit and into the widening segment of international waters between the Musandam Peninsula and Iran's Qeshm Island. Now he was free to launch his Lynx, to train his weapons and even to fire them, and to manoeuvre *Winchester* as a warship should be manoeuvred. He no longer had to concern himself with what the Omanis at Goat Island saw, and what conclusions they drew from it. It gave him a feeling of emancipation, a sense that he could control affairs again.

First thing's first. He wanted to know what was ahead of him, what he was leading his convoy into. In many ways this was the most dangerous part of the route, where Iran's ships and aircraft weren't constrained by their neighbour's territorial waters and yet they could still operate close to their own ports and airfields. His last act before leaving the ops room was to tell the PWO to launch the Lynx for surface search. Now the main broadcast sprang into life as he walked onto the bridge.

'Action Lynx, Action Lynx.'

'Good evening, sir. Sunset in twenty-five minutes.'

Saxby looked as bright and chirpy as ever, which was not how Mayhew felt, although he tried his best to conceal it. How many hours had passed since he was called from his sleep? He remembered the time exactly, four-forty-seven, then it was over thirteen hours ago. It seemed like longer. Then he remembered that it was Saxby who had called him; he'd already been on the bridge for forty-five minutes when he picked up the microphone to rouse his captain from his sleep and he was still on the bridge. He must have spent all but a few minutes of those fourteen hours on his feet. Ah well, the resilience of youth. Mayhew settled himself in his chair just in time to hear Buckley's voice on command open line.

'Officer-of-the-Watch, PWO. You're free to manoeuvre for a flying course.'

Saxby checked the wind indicator and looked down the bearing for his new course.

'Clear starboard,' cried the second officer-of-the-watch as he walked back from the bridge wing where he'd been checking that there was nothing lurking in Saxby's blind spot.

The navigator held his hand up to Saxby while he walked to the bridge wing, then he repeated the call: 'Clear starboard.'

Mayhew nodded at Northcott. The navigator had only held up the process by a few seconds, and that wasn't critical this time, but he'd made sure that the sub lieutenant didn't become complacent, that he really did check the ship's blind spots every time and didn't make any assumptions. He remembered the sign above the pelorus on the bridge of the old cruiser in which he'd spent his midshipman's time.

REMEMBER YOUR NEXT ASTERN

It was a relic from the days when warships manoeuvred in close formations, and every turn or speed change risked having the next ship in the line becoming far too friendly with your own ships rear end. It was still good advice.

'Coming right two-eight-zero.'

Mayhew watched the wind indicator and the flight deck camera. The ship settled on its new course; the wind indicator oscillated for a few seconds then steadied within the flying limits. The flight deck officer was in position with his hands crossed low in front of his body and he'd seen the helicopter lashings held aloft by the flight deck crew. He glanced forward to ensure that the ship wasn't standing into any danger on this new course and then he made the *permission to fly* switch. A few seconds later he saw the Lynx accelerating past the port bridge wing, climbing away as it headed out on its surface search mission. As soon as the Lynx was clear he made the *do not fly* switch and Saxby brought the ship back into its station on *World Antigua*.

Smooth as silk, as it should be. But still, the navigator's intervention reminded him that it wouldn't always be like that. One day, someone would forget an essential step in the process, a lashing would be left on, perhaps the second officer-of-the-watch would miss the fast boat that was overtaking them, with its skipper giving his passengers a close look at a destroyer. That was what he was there for, not to be a last check, he couldn't possibly monitor everyone involved in launching the Lynx, but to keep everyone on their toes.

It was getting darker by the minute as Mayhew scanned the horizon through his binoculars. The sea ahead was eerily quiet, with nothing at all to be seen right to the far horizon. By this time of the evening all the local craft and fishermen would have headed back to their home ports, and the oil fields were still far away over the western horizon, too far for the permanent glow of the gas flares to be seen. They'd passed a solitary tanker on its way outbound, a Chinese registered ship that plied the Straits in its captain's firm belief that neither Iraq nor Iran would touch it. He was correct of course, both of the warring nations benefited from a trade in Chinese weapons – most notably the Silkworm missile – and neither would willingly cause offence.

All was quiet and in about six hours the convoy would detach for the anchorages off Sharjah and Dubai. Where the Filipino ships were bound was anyone's guess, but they would likely detach with the British tankers. The furthest that neutral tankers penetrated into the Gulf nowadays was

Doha, except for the reflagged tankers that flew the Stars and Stripes and went all the way up to Kuwait under very heavy US Navy escort. *Operation Earnest Will*, it was called. The Americans took those convoys very seriously indeed and had deployed a vast armament into the Gulf to support them. British tankers, on the other hand, rarely went past Abu Dhabi and usually no further than Dubai. It wasn't for a lack of will, but the insurance rates, already sky-high for any tankers passing into the Gulf, would make the voyage uneconomical if they went any further. Mayhew was glad to leave the Northern Arabian Gulf to the Americans. With both Iran and Iraq interdicting tankers by air attack and Iran by surface attack too, there was too much opportunity for things to go wrong, and the Royal Navy would have to double or treble its force in the Gulf to operate up towards Kuwait. If they did have to go that far, if the British public rebelled against the rocketing price of petrol at the pumps, then the Type 42s would be employed doing nothing other than the Armilla Patrol. There were only enough of them to keep two-or-three in the Gulf at a time, and no other ships in the Royal Navy could provide the area defence against a Silkworm attack that a Seadart-fitted destroyer could.

Mayhew was faintly surprised that there had been no further alarms since the Boghammers had withdrawn. Perhaps that was it for this convoy, a test of his resolve and his reward was an uncontested passage. He looked at the mahogany binoculars case fastened to the side of the pelorus. He had a private superstition – at least he imagined it was private – that he should touch wood whenever he thought that things were going too well, but he'd need to lean forward to touch the box, and it was so pleasant to just let his back rest against the chair. A foolish superstition, he thought, and if his wife heard about it her eyes would roll so far that she'd be looking out of the back of her head. He'd force himself out of it; he resolved never to touch that binocular box again. He was feeling pleased with himself already, and then the command open line burst into life.

'PWO, Visual. LAS reports smoke on the horizon green zero-five-zero.'

Mayhew's resolution faded as quickly as it was made and he leaned forward to touch the binocular box, but he knew it was too late, the Fates would not be toyed with. He swung his binoculars to the bearing, five degrees off the starboard bow. At first he could see nothing, but as he swept in a small arc from side to side, he thought he could see it, a thin plume of smoke stretching a few degrees above the horizon, some way to the left of the setting sun. This is what his predecessors in the two world wars must have felt like, before the revolution in tactical information started in the nineteen-fifties. They'd have been staring at a smudge of smoke just like he was, wondering whether it was an enemy fleet about to appear on the horizon, or a smoky old fishing boat on its way home with its engine on its last legs. But in the late twentieth century warships made little smoke, and no fishing boat's engine could create that quantity, however much of its lubrication oil it was burning.

'What's out there, Navigator?'

Northcott knew the answer without having to look at the chart.

'Nothing, sir. That would be about the extension of the border between Oman and UAE, but outside either's territorial waters. There are no rigs in that area. Tunb Island's about thirty-two miles in that direction. I suppose it could be a fire on the island, but it looks closer than that.'

'PWO, Captain. Bearing two-four-five, do you have anything?

It came as second nature to convert the relative bearings that lookouts used to true compass bearings for the ops room. The ship was steering two-four-zero so add the five degrees on the starboard bow that the LAS operator had seen and without conscious calculation he came to two-four-five degrees.

Silence from the PWO. It was Petty Officer Ward, the surface picture supervisor, who replied.

'SPS, sir. Contact bearing two-four-three at eighteen miles, course two-four-zero, eight knots. No CPA. It could be two contacts, sir, it's hard to tell at this range. I'm reporting it on alligator as a Skunk.'

That would be it, only two degrees different to the LAS report, that was a normal margin of error with radar bearings. The Americans would see it now that the SPS had released it on the data link, they'd see an unknown surface contact – a *Skunk* – and they'd think nothing of it until its classification changed.

'Captain, EWD. There are two separate I-band navigation radars on that bearing.'

Mayhew nodded silently. Dickens sounded much more confident than Quinn had ever done, and Quinn would never have thought to add this piece of information without being asked. Probably Quinn was happily analysing the heck out of those two innocuous radar intercepts while Dickens brought it all together into tactically useful information.

'PWO. Report the contact to the Lynx and tell him to investigate. He should have enough daylight left.'

'Already done, sir. The Lynx has radar contact and is going in low for a visual.'

My word, Mayhew thought, this team was really coming together now. He'd be redundant soon. Yet Buckley still bothered him. He'd sounded confident enough but he'd seen how the team dynamics worked at action stations. Without a doubt Harling, the duty staff officer, or Kesteven would have prompted Buckley to keep the Lynx informed, and Ward had certainly covered for him with that Skunk report. That was well and good and showed that the team was pulling together in the same direction, but when things started happening really quickly, every member of the team had to pull his weight, and he wasn't sure that Buckley was capable of doing that.

***

Twilight didn't last long in these latitudes. The sun would set at eighteen-thirty and fifty minutes later it would be quite dark. Nevertheless, that was plenty of time for the Lynx to tell him what he was steaming into. There were two contacts moving slowly towards the southwest and at least one of them was pouring out a quantity of smoke; it didn't sound good. He'd kept up with all the intelligence and the enemy contact reports from all of the allied navies operating in the Gulf, and there was one Iranian ship that was invariably mentioned when merchant ships found themselves under attack. He had a sort of intuition about it now.

'PWO, what's the last known position of *Sabalan*?'

'Stand by, sir.'

Mayhew knew what that meant, he was asking the GOP operator.

'*Casablanca* detected her operating around the Tunb islands this morning, sir.'

That might tie in. Tunb and Little Tunb were between thirty and forty miles on the starboard bow. They were Iranian islands, occupied and formally annexed when the Trucial Oman States – the forerunner of the United Arab Emirates – lost British protection in the early nineteen-seventies. Iran also occupied the island of Abu Musa a little deeper into the Gulf, but Sharjah had never given up its claim and international law didn't recognise Iran's sovereignty over that island. They were all useful surveillance outposts and obvious places to site Silkworm batteries, although there was no positive indication of the Iranians doing so. What was certain was that they were all known haunts of the Iranian frigate *Sabalan*, and the ship's captain was notorious for his relentless attacks on unescorted tankers if he had evidence that they were bound to or from ports that Iraq used to export its oil. He had a bad reputation and his *have a nice day* VHF sign-off after attacking some helpless tanker, often firing into the bridge and accommodations to cause the maximum casualties, had earned him the nickname *Captain Nasty*.

Sabalan was one of four *Alvand* class frigates built for the

Shah of Iran by Vickers at Barrow-in-Furness on England's northwest coast, and now ranged against British interests. She carried the same 4.5 inch gun as *Winchester's* and over the years had been fitted with a bewildering variety of surface-to-surface missiles, mortars and machine guns of varying effectiveness. *Sabalan's* captain had proved himself determined and capable, and was a byword for Iran's aggressive attitude in the Southern Arabian Gulf and the Straits. Well, it still might be nothing other than a smoky old engine, but it was better to be prepared.

The daylight was fading and the smoke was barely visible now. Mayhew took a few seconds to find it again. If he didn't know that it was there he'd probably miss it in a normal surface sweep with his binoculars. Yet even as it faded against the darkening sky, he could see that it had grown in volume, and was soaring upwards to be lost in the night's blackness.

'Captain, PWO. The Lynx reports a tanker on fire around her accommodation spaces. She's moving slowly southwest and appears to be still under command. The second contact is a small frigate – it looks like an Iranian *Alvand* class – less than a mile to the northwest of the tanker and apparently holding station, on the same course and speed.'

'Captain, Chief Yeoman. There's a distress call on five-hundred kilohertz, sir, a Panamanian tanker under attack in a position one-two-five degrees, twenty-three miles from Tunb Island. Requesting assistance.'

'That distress call is coming through on VHF as well sir,' the navigator chipped in. 'The tanker's name is *Western Promise* and they claim to be under fire from an unknown warship. They sound panicked, sir.'

'Officer-of-the-Watch, increase to twenty-eight knots and steer for the tanker's position. Make a pipe, surface and air threat warning red. On anti-flash, on steel helmets. Chief Yeoman, make to the task unit, *Winchester* investigating mayday call and possible Iranian frigate sixteen miles ahead.

Bellona take station five cables on *World Antigua's* beam. No sound signals, there's no imminent threat to the convoy.'

'Should we reply to the distress calls, sir?'

'Negative, Navs. That will commit us and I don't know the full situation yet. There are plenty of tugs on the UAE coast listening to five-hundred kilohertz, they make a living out of it. Let me know if there's any new information from the tanker.'

Mayhew flicked the switch to talk to the machinery control room.

'MCR, Captain. MEO to the bridge.'

Then he lowered his headset microphone and spoke on the command open line.

'PWO, Captain. Tell *Bellona* to cover the Iranian frigate with bulldogs and hold her Lynx at alert five for surface action or casualty evacuation. If it's a CASEVAC he's to take his doctor along. Cover the Iranian frigate with Seadart in surface mode, and with the Four-Five when it's in range. Visual, we might need the close range weapons for a surface action.'

The Lynx could easily carry four-or-five patients the fifty miles to Sharjah airport and CASEVAC was a well-practiced role that any Lynx pilot could carry out. The problem was in finding a large enough space on the tanker's deck. Many of them had a flat area, usually near the fo'c'sle, and a few had a real marked-out helicopter landing platform with a wind indicator, but there was no knowing whether *Western Promise* had either and if they had whether it was usable after being bombarded by 4.5 inch shells.

Bellona carried Exocet sea-skimming missiles – *bulldogs* in the brevity code – which were more than a match for *Sabalan's* weapons. By telling *Bellona* to cover *Sabalan*, Mayhew was sure that he had an instant response if it came to a shootout with the Iranian frigate. Exocets had proved their value in a spectacular fashion in May 1982 when an Argentinian Super-Étendard aircraft had fired two at *HMS Sheffield*, sinking the destroyer and ushering in a new era of naval warfare. *Sabalan* likely had no answer to an Exocet attack and that was an important trump card in Mayhew's deck. This was where it became a positive advantage to have been under surveillance as they started this passage. The P-3's electronic warfare operator would certainly have recognised the unique radar emissions from a Type 22 frigate and – Mayhew now hoped – the aircraft's mission commander would have passed that on to *Sabalan*. No naval captain was unaware of the danger from a sea-skimming missile, and it would prey on every captain's mind when they were in range of an Exocet-fitted enemy.

So many factors to consider, yet Mayhew was certain of one thing: *Winchester's* doctor would be furious that he wasn't involved.

***

'Ah, Richard, it's good to see you this far above the waterline.'

Although he had wide-ranging responsibilities for anything in the ship that couldn't be called a weapon or a sensor or a communication system, the marine engineering officer – the MEO – was obsessive about his beloved engines and could rarely be lured away from them. Richard Pengelley was a good-natured soul and accepted the captain's banter without a murmur. In fact he'd been doing the rounds of the damage control stations when he heard the two mighty Olympus gas turbines wind up, and he'd been hurrying towards the MCR. That was no easy task when the ship was closed down into condition zulu with all watertight doors and hatches firmly clipped shut. Then he'd had to fight his way up to the bridge, but as always his white overalls were spotlessly clean and pressed, as though they hadn't seen a machinery space in their life.

'What's afoot, sir? We seem to be in a tearing hurry.'

'It seems that there's an Iranian frigate taking potshots at a Panamanian tanker, twelve miles ahead now but moving slowly away from us. We'll be there in thirty minutes or so. I don't yet know how bad it is, and we can't linger there, not with our convoy to consider, but we might get half-an-hour or so when we can help. I want the fire hoses rigged on the upper deck and the damage control teams ready to man them.'

Pengelley nodded slowly. *Winchester* would have to be very close to the burning tanker, dangerously close, for the fire hoses to do much good. That wasn't his concern, it was up to the bridge team to ensure there was no collision. His concern was dealing with the fire.

'I know it's unlikely, sir, but I'll get the portable pumps ready in case we have a chance to get them over there. Can you warn the seaboat crew that they might be needed?'

Mayhew thought for a moment. He'd done this before when he'd been in the North Sea in a patrol frigate, protecting fisheries and oil rigs. One of the rig supply vessels had caught fire five miles off Aberdeen and had promptly been abandoned by its crew. His ship had sent a portable pump over and had put the fire out before the Aberdeen lifeboat had finished picking up the survivors and long before a tug with proper firefighting kit had arrived. The weather that day had been much like this, just as dark, with a calm sea, although the North Sea was far colder than the Arabian Gulf. A small rig supply ship was a different matter to a supertanker, but if the fire was confined to the accommodation, it might be possible. If necessary, and if *Sabalan* withdrew, he could leave the firefighting team on board the tanker. They could rejoin at Dubai or wherever the ship was bound. At action stations the boat that was at short notice to be launched was manned by taking aimers and loaders from the close range weapons. Well, it was almost certain that only one side of the ship would be engaged tonight.

'AAWO, tell visual that he's to be ready to man the seaboat if needed; he can use the crews from the disengaged side. They might need to carry a portable pump over to the tanker.'

Pengelley was already on his way back to the MCR from

where he could co-ordinate the preparations. There, with the ship's damage control centre in the adjacent compartment, he had all the levers of his command right to hand. Once everything was in place he'd come to the upper deck to direct the firefighting operation. He deplored *Sabalan's* actions, certainly, but he was grateful for the opportunity and was looking forward to tackling that fire. He felt the vibrations of the twin Olympus engines through his feet as *Winchester* leapt through the darkening sea, and he was happy. The ship was throwing a monstrous bow-wave on either side as it sped towards the stricken tanker, but that wasn't his reality. For him it was the engines, all day and every day, and today he could add to that his firefighting arrangements. The drama of this dash to the southwest was wasted on him.

***

Chapter Nine

Tuesday, 1900
HMS Winchester, at Sea, Straits of Hormuz
Operation Armilla Daily Sitrep: Encountered IRIS Sabalan attacking Panamanian tanker...

Mayhew could sense that things were moving fast in his ship. It was as though he'd taken an orderly sequence of playing cards and rapidly shuffled them, changing their order and their hierarchy of importance. But this was what the ship was trained to do. The details were all handled by his highly skilled and experienced team; he merely had to give the top-level orders in the certain knowledge that they would be obeyed. He felt like the Roman Centurion in Matthew's gospel: *I tell this one, 'Go,' and he goes; and that one, 'Come,' and he comes. I say to my servant, 'Do this,' and he does it.* His wife often chided him by claiming that all he did at work was tell everyone else what to do, never doing a damned thing himself. It was true and furthermore it was the right and in fact the only way to run a destroyer, all other ways led to anarchy and tragedy.

And yet, it was important to avoid getting ahead of himself. The purpose of his task unit was to escort the four entitled tankers to their anchorage off Dubai, all else was secondary and not to interfere with the primary task. In international law the belligerent nations had certain rights in respect to stopping, searching, detaining and even, as a last resort, firing upon merchant ships; after all, the Royal Navy had done exactly that all over the world for centuries. He needed to be careful that he didn't leave his convoy exposed to attack and that he didn't do anything that could heighten tensions between Britain and Iran. His every instinct might tell him to take on *Sabalan*, but the constraints of his mission said otherwise. This must be a humanitarian task only, the threat to sink *Sabalan* must be credible but ultimately unfulfilled.

'AAWO, is there any sign of other Iranian activity, surface or air?'

'None, sir. There's nothing at all on the data link and there are no threat radars showing, except for *Sabalan's*.'

'Very well, but we'll stay at air and surface threats red based on *Sabalan* and whatever missiles she's carrying today. Chief Yeoman, a signal pad, please, I'll dictate this one.'

At action stations and indeed at any time that the captain was on the bridge, the chief yeoman didn't stray far from his side. He produced a pad of signal forms on a clipboard and stood beside the captain waiting for him to dictate a signal.

'Thank you Chief. Immediate to SNOME, info MOD, CINCFLEET, CTG 316.2, *Bellona* and *Brown Rover*. Am responding to a mayday call from Panamanian tanker *Western Promise* in position – you can get the latitude and longitude from the navigator – under attack from Iranian frigate assumed to be *Sabalan*. If the tanker has casualties I intend to evacuate them by *Bellona's* Lynx to Sharjah airport. Request emergency DIPCLEAR.'

That should do it. The Senior Naval Officer Middle East could arrange the diplomatic clearance and both the Ministry of Defence United Kingdom and the Commander in Chief Fleet would know what was happening in case it hit the press or escalated into a significant encounter. The commander of his task group – the CTG – was somewhere in the Indian Ocean at this moment, approaching the Gulf of Oman, and he needed to know out of courtesy if nothing else.

The chief yeoman nodded and followed the navigator behind the chart room curtain, to find the position of the tanker.

'Captain, AAWO. I have a low-and-slow air contact squawking civilian, outside the airlanes. It seems to be coming from Sharjah airport, it could be a press helo.'

Damn! That was all he needed. The press knew no constraints in their search for a story and their helicopter would soon be circling the tanker taking photographs and video recordings of all the gory details. They'd probably keep a respectable distance from *Sabalan*, knowing the ship's reputation, but they'd be all over *Winchester* and the tanker. A polite warning might keep them half a mile away, but that was the best that he could hope for.

'Very well, AAWO. See if you can raise him on aeronautical distress. Tell him the situation and advise him that British Navy helicopters will be operating in the area. Request that he keeps two miles clear, although I see little hope of that working.'

Mayhew glanced ahead and was shocked to see how far they had come since he last looked out of the window. The burning tanker was clearly visible now, but there was no sign of *Sabalan*; she was presumably lost in the darkness beyond.

'PWO, where's *Sabalan* in relation to the tanker.'

'The Lynx is reporting that she's moving towards the tanker again. On her starboard quarter at a mile now and closing.'

What was the Iranian captain's intention? He would hardly be concerned with saving life, more likely he was coming in for another attack. It was well known that his Seahunter fire control radar was inoperable, and he aimed his 4.5 inch gun visually using a LAS, restricting his engagement range to half a mile or so. Military supplies to Iran had been embargoed for years, and they must be short of the spare parts they needed to keep equipment running.

'How far to the tanker, Officer-of-the-Watch?'

'Three miles, sir. I can see the frigate now to the right of the tanker.'

Ah yes, he could see it too. The glow from the burning tanker illuminated the surrounding sea and the sleek, low silhouette of the frigate was captured in its ghastly orange light with its masts and antennas seemingly touched with fire as they reflected the glow from their burning victim. At this range it looked very like a British Type 21 frigate. They'd both come from the same designer and the same shipyard, but the *Alvand* class were all smaller than the Type

21s. Now that the sun had set and twilight was over, everything outside the fire's immediate glow was cast into an even deeper gloom, and the two ships – the tanker and the frigate – looked like set pieces in a theatre tableau.

'Captain, Visual. That's *Sabalan* alright, sir. She has a different radar to the others.'

Then he knew who he was dealing with.

'Captain, PWO. The Lynx reports a small helo deck forward with a couple of casualties being laid out. The accommodation is on fire but the bridge seems to be manned. He estimates it's doing about eight knots, steering southwest.'

Mayhew took another long look at the situation.

'Navigator take the ship. Steer to take station on the tanker's starboard side at half a cable.'

This time Mayhew did tap the wood of the binocular box. He needed all the luck he could get as *Winchester's* Olympus engines ate up the final miles to what now seemed like an inevitable confrontation. *Sabalan* was clearly manoeuvering to attack the tanker's starboard side, and Mayhew intended to prevent that happening.

'Officer-of-the-Watch, get onto VHF channel sixteen, tell *Sabalan* – you can use the name – that this is British warship *Winchester* – you can use our name too – and I intend to offer lifesaving assistance to the tanker. He is requested to keep well clear.'

It was a matter of keeping his nerve now, and steering for the narrowing gap between the frigate and the tanker. He could see the MEO hovering to speak to him.

'I'm going to take her as close as I dare, Richard. You can see that the cargo isn't alight and those fires in the accommodation spaces don't look too bad. Keep the water away from the bridge if you can.'

'Aye-aye sir. I've got six hoses rigged on the port side and it will get a little wet as soon as I start.'

Mayhew nodded. He could leave the details of fire-fighting to the MEO.

Silkworm

'PWO, ask the Lynx if the conditions are suitable for casualty evacuation by *Bellona's* Lynx.'

'Captain, AAWO. The press helo is ten miles away and closing. The FC's requested that he keeps clear and he's acknowledged.'

'Captain, PWO. The Lynx says affirmative to the casualty evacuation.'

'Very well. Tell *Bellona* the situation and to launch her lynx for CASEVAC from the tanker to Sharjah.'

'Eight cables to run, sir.'

Saxby was reading off the ranges from the bridge radar display.

'Seven cables.'

The VHF sprang into life, and the accented voice sounded very close.

'*Winchester*, *Winchester*, this is an Iranian frigate. I am exercising my rights in international waters and this is no concern of yours. You must withdraw immediately.'

Bang!

A single shot from *Sabalan*. There was no indication of a hit on the tanker and it was clearly not aimed at *Winchester*.

'Visual, Captain. Train the Four-Five and all the close range weapons on the frigate's bridge. Signal projector stand by. AAWO, load the Seadart launcher.'

Mayhew had deliberately left this until the last minute so that *Sabalan* could see what he was doing, it was much more effective that way. It occurred to him that there was a fair chance that *Sabalan's* captain had been trained at the Royal Naval College at Dartmouth. Many of the Iranians spent a year there during the Shah's reign, and to be the captain of a frigate he must have been a midshipman in the late sixties or early seventies. Perhaps he would understand that *Winchester* wouldn't be intimidated. He picked up the VHF microphone.

'*Sabalan*, this is *Winchester's* captain. My intentions haven't changed. Keep clear of my ship and the tanker.'

'Five cables.'

'Edge in a bit closer, Navigator, and reduce speed to hold station on the tanker. I want to give the fire hoses a chance.'

'Captain, PWO. *Bellona's* Lynx airborne, five miles to run.'

'Good. Tell our Lynx to do a fly-by on the frigate so that it can clearly see the Sea Skuas, then position itself a mile on the frigate's stern and hover there. I want *Sabalan* to know that he's being covered by anti-ship missiles and that we can engage her at any moment. The flight commander will know what I want.'

The fire was spectacular, but Mayhew could see that it looked worse than it really was. Nevertheless it was dramatic enough and licks of flame were reaching almost to the bridge. He could see that the bridge was still manned and he had a moment to marvel that those men had stuck to their posts even when there was an obvious risk of the fire cutting off their escape. His ship was still running at nearly thirty knots with the huge tanker less than half a mile away, filling the bridge window with its massive bulk. *Sabalan* was another half mile on his starboard beam.

Bang!

Another shot from the frigate, it must have passed a few cables in front of *Winchester*. That was too close. *Sabalan's* captain was playing a very dangerous game. If it came to a shooting-match, he must know that his frigate was heavily outgunned.

'Visual, Captain. Light up the frigate's bridge with the signal projector.'

The light sprang into life and after a few seconds the signalman found his target. At less than half a mile the twenty-inch signal projector illuminated the frigate's bridge, revealing the people inside shading their eyes. A sailor hurried out onto the bridge wing to retaliate with his own signal projector, but it was a poor performance, and his tiny light – it looked like a standard ten-inch affair – couldn't compete with *Winchester's*.

'Visual, Captain. Keep the weapons trained on the bridge. We've made our point with the signal projector, now use it to see what's happening on his upper deck. Are his weapons ready? Anything else of interest. I want him to know that he's being inspected.'

Mayhew felt the deceleration as *Winchester* slid into position alongside the tanker's aft island. God, it looked a mess. He had no leisure for an accurate count, but at least half a dozen 4.5 inch shells had hit the superstructure and it was riddled with smaller calibre holes from *Sabalan's* machine guns. He could trust the navigator to hold the ship in place, this wasn't much different to manoeuvering alongside *Brown Rover* for a replenishment at sea. *Sabalan* was less than half a mile away now, three-or-four cables he estimated, and was showing no signs of coming closer. Her 4.5 inch gun was still trained to port, but it wasn't moving.

Channel sixteen on the VHF was becoming congested as the tanker continued to plead for help and the press helicopter manoeuvred around the group of ships trying to get anyone to talk to it while shooting the footage that would make it into the news within hours.

'Officer-of-the-Watch, break in on that channel sixteen chatter and tell the tanker that a navy helicopter is coming in from his port side to pick up the casualties. He is to maintain a steady course, keep the landing platform clear and not to attempt to assist the helicopter.'

Bellona's Lynx would find this transfer straightforward, as long as *Sabalan* didn't interfere. The tanker was a much, much more stable platform than a destroyer and the landing platform was far forward of the burning superstructure and the jets of water from *Winchester's* fire hoses. He could see the effect of the hoses already. There looked to be two seats of the fire, both in the accommodation areas a couple of decks below the bridge, and each one had three jets of water playing upon it. The range was greater than the ideal, of course, but there was plenty of water going in through the smashed windows and the shell holes, and already the fire was dying down.

'What's *Sabalan* doing, Visual?'

'Just sitting there, sir. Her weapons haven't moved at all. They get right agitated whenever the signal projector reaches the bridge.'

'Good. Light them up once in a while, Chief.'

'*Bellona's* Lynx is moving in from the port side, sir.'

Saxby really was excellent at keeping his captain informed, anticipating his every need for information. Well, there was no point in going to the port side to gawp at the Lynx, like some kind of spectator. The navigator was handling the ship admirably, and the missile gun director visual was keeping *Sabalan* entertained. He needed to stay in the centre of things and there was no better place than his chair.

'AAWO, PWO, Captain. Anything new?'

'Nothing worth noting, sir. The press helicopter asked for information so I've given them an outline.'

That was Allenby's voice, he would be keeping his finger on the whole picture, surface and air.

'Quite right, Ops, there's no harm in keeping the press onside.'

And that was a good point. The press helicopter would be getting great footage from this, with a blazing tanker, a British destroyer and an Iranian frigate all in close proximity and two navy Lynx helicopters buzzing around. A few casualties always helped to sell the story, of course. He had to hope that they didn't get close enough to impede the CASEVAC operation.

'Captain, Chief Yeoman. Immediate from SNOME. DIPCLEAR approved, two Lynx to Sharjah airport with casualties. DIPCLEAR expires in twenty-four hours.'

Hell! He'd clean forgotten that he must wait for a response to his signal about the diplomatic clearance request. It would have caused a dreadful fuss if he'd sent the Lynx in without having satisfied the formalities. SNOME had clearly moved quickly and that was a good idea to include both Lynx, just in case. He should have thought of that himself.

He didn't need to look at the tanker but it was a mesmerising sight. A few stray flames were still licking up the tanker's superstructure, although they were much reduced by the MEO's firefighting party and he guessed that they'd be extinguished soon. The Lynx had dropped onto the helicopter platform abaft of the stubby foremast and was using downward thrust on its rotor blades to keep itself firmly in place. He couldn't see the tanker's deck from *Winchester's* bridge – it was too high – but he could hear a running commentary on the VHF. It looked like there were four wounded sailors, three of them could walk and were being helped on board the Lynx, but the fourth was in a stretcher with *Bellona's* doctor supervising the lift. It only took a few minutes and then suddenly, like a clay from a trap, *Bellona's* Lynx sprang into the air and banked away towards Sharjah.

'Captain, PWO. I'm sending an airmove departure, one Lynx, seven persons on board, bound for Sharjah airport, and I'm requesting an ambulance for four injured persons.'

'Thank you, PWO.'

Now, that dealt with the immediate lifesaving issue. Mayhew knew that tugs would be on their way as soon as they heard about the incident; after all, that was how they made a living. Their crews slept on board, waiting for a call, and they'd surely be here within the hour.

'PWO. How far away is the convoy?'

'Ten miles bearing two-three-zero, sir, making thirteen knots towards Dubai.'

Mayhew calculated quickly. The injured tanker was still making eight knots, so the convoy was moving away from them at an aggregate of five knots. If he wound up his Olympus engines again, he could catch the convoy with an overtaking speed of fifteen knots. How far could he let the convoy go before he must break away from the tanker? *Sabalan* was still there and he had the horrible suspicion that if he left now the tanker would be in grave danger again. Did *Sabalan's* captain guess that was the case? Was he waiting for the opportunity to have another go at the tanker? Another quick look told him that the fires were almost extinguished and he could see that the tanker's crew, perhaps emboldened by *Winchester's* presence, had rolled out their own fire hoses. It was only smoke now and the tanker didn't appear to be in immediate danger. He walked to the starboard bridge wing and looked again at *Sabalan*, and he hated what he saw. There was no place on the high seas in the late twentieth century for this kind of bullying behaviour. However it was dressed up, it was close to piracy, and two hundred years ago the frigate's captain and its officers would be in danger of death by hanging.

'Visual, Captain. Light up his bridge with the signal projector again. PWO, tell the Lynx to close to half a mile.'

He studied the distance between the two ships.

'Navigator, edge away from the tanker and towards *Sabalan*. Watch out for the pressure waves.'

That was probably an unnecessary order, but it was possible that with everything else going on the navigator had forgotten the strange effects that a large ship had on a smaller when they were very close together. If he came too sharply to starboard his stern would likely be drawn in towards the tanker and there could even be a collision. Meanwhile his bows would become uncontrollable and there would be a danger of collision with the frigate. Slow and steady was the order of the day.

He watched the helm for a moment. The helmsman was using no more than five degrees of rudder; that was good. He strode over to the starboard bridge wing again. The signalman had a look of ferocious concentration as he kept his twenty-inch light squarely on the frigate's bridge. A quick look showed that all the close range weapons were trained the same way. Slowly *Winchester's* bows moved to starboard. The ship pitched slightly as it crossed the tanker's bow wave and then steadied as reached the clear water. The destroyer was closing steadily on *Sabalan* now, on a course that angled perhaps five degrees towards the frigate's track. Ah, there was the Lynx, moving in purposefully. In this strange, unnatural light the helicopter looked lean and menacing, and the Sea Skua missiles appeared squat and muscular and intimidating, like their brevity codeword: *Bruisers*.

'Captain, Officer-of-the-Watch. Two tugs are on the way from Ras Al Khaimah, estimated time of arrival thirty minutes.'

'Captain, PWO. I have two contacts on radar bearing one-two-zero range nine miles. Course three-zero-five at thirteen knots. If those are the tugs then thirty minutes is about right.'

'They're calling us on VHF now, sir,' the navigator reported.

Mayhew took another look at *Sabalan*. There was no movement at all, she was stubbornly holding her position. *Winchester* was much the larger vessel, eighty feet longer and three times the displacement, and her sheer size must have a psychological effect. If it came to push-and-shove, *Winchester* would win easily. Did *Sabalan's* captain believe that *Winchester* would go that far? If he'd read his recent history he'd know that Royal Navy frigates had done exactly that in the dispute with Iceland over cod fishing rights, and that was barely more than a decade ago. Mayhew had been the navigator in a Leander class frigate at the time, and he well remembered the dreadful sound of steel grinding against steel as they shouldered-off an Icelandic gunboat. And just like in the Iceland affair, Britain could afford to lose a ship or two while they were being repaired, while Iran with only two or three serviceable frigates could not.

However, there was another factor at play. *Sabalan* was on *Winchester's* starboard side, and the rules for preventing collisions at sea were quite clear that in this case *Sabalan* was the stand-on vessel and *Winchester* was obliged to keep clear. If it came to a court that was only interested in compliance with the international regulations, *Winchester* would certainly be deemed to be in the wrong. Who would blink first?

The gap was closing inexorably; soon he'd have to decide whether he could risk the collision. He felt that everyone on the bridge was watching him, trying to guess what his decision would be, and thanking their lucky stars that it wasn't theirs to make.

The watertight doors were all closed at condition zulu, so there were no additional actions to be taken to prepare for a collision. However, Mayhew knew how even the slightest impact jarred the whole ship, and how seamen who thought nothing of the normal pitch and roll of a destroyer at sea could be thrown off balance by something unexpected. Steel ships were unforgiving, and broken bones were quite likely.

'Officer-of-the-Watch. Standby to make a pipe *brace for collision*. Wait for my order.'

The bosun's mate would be holding the main broadcast microphone now. He'd be enjoying this moment, damn him.

They were so close that by the light of the signal projector Mayhew could clearly see into *Sabalan's* bridge. The Iranian officers and crew were all shielding their eyes against the blinding light, but he could see no signs of panic. Well, his bluff was being called. He saw the MEO coming towards him, his usually pristine white overalls now soaked and dirty from his work directing the fire hoses.

'The tanker's fires are out, sir, I won't need the portable fire pumps…'

Richard Pengelly gasped when he saw how close they were to the Iranian frigate.

'…You're going to push him away, sir? He deserves to be sent to the bottom!'

At that moment Mayhew realised that he wasn't bluffing, he really intended to do this. He'd make the contact as gently as possible and perhaps he'd get away with some scraped paint, but he wasn't going to back down now. He turned to give the orders for the main broadcast pipe and to take the ship from the navigator. If he was going to deliberately collide with another vessel it would be on his shoulders and nobody else's.

The navigator spoke first.

'He's turning, sir, turning to starboard.'

Mayhew brushed past the MEO as he hurried to the starboard bridge wing. He stared, willing it to be so. He slapped the signal projector operator on the shoulder.

'Move the light aft to his wake.'

The light revealed the tell-tale signs of a rudder being moved more than was needed to maintain a straight course. *Sabalan* was turning to starboard, away from *Winchester* and away from the Panamanian tanker. There was enough stray light to see a figure appear on the port bridge wing. The man raised his arm in a lazy greeting then turned back into the sheltered bridge.

Mayhew stepped swiftly back into the bridge to get to the VHF and was just in time to hear the sarcastic farewell.

'*Winchester* this is *Sabalan*. Until next time, have a nice day.'

***

'I don't think we should flatter ourselves, Ops. That was probably nothing to do with us, most likely he felt that he'd done enough.'

Allenby badly wanted to ask his captain whether he really would have physically pushed the frigate away, but that wasn't the sort of thing one asked one's captain, and perhaps it was better that he didn't know. It wouldn't appear in the enemy contact report, nor in the daily sitrep. Perhaps Mayhew would send a private note to his fellow captains, but it wasn't something that the upwards chain of command needed to know, it would raise far too many issues.

'You're right, sir, but it does seem like quite a coincidence after the Boghammers…' Allenby suddenly looked startled '…do you know, that was only six hours ago? It feels like a lifetime.'

'Yes, and it's dangerous to underestimate the enemy, but

everything we've heard suggests that they simply don't have that level of co-operation between their services. *Sabalan* has been doing this for a couple of years now and it's probably become a routine, although I'm not sure they'd try the US Navy's patience as much as they tried ours. You have to give him credit for holding his nerve with all that weaponry staring at him and four-thousand tons slanting down on his beam. Still, we need to be careful what we say in the sitrep.'

Mayhew was in the ops room again and *Winchester* was almost back in station on the convoy. They'd stayed with the damaged tanker until the tugs arrived and started to usher her away to the south. *Sabalan* hadn't waited to see anything of that and the familiar sound of her own Olympus gas turbines proved her desire to be away. That in itself was an interesting piece of information, for all the intelligence reports suggested that with Rolls Royce's support being cut off, her gas turbines were no longer serviceable, and she was reduced to a much slower cruising speed on her diesels. The huge wake that she kicked up and the glorious sound of her mighty blowers proved otherwise.

'Captain, PWO. The Lynx is requesting to return and refuel. They used a lot of fuel hovering behind *Sabalan*.'

'Very well, PWO, bring them back.'

He heard the routine sounds of the ship turning for a flying course. He glanced at the wind indicator and when the navigator asked permission for the Lynx to land he gave his approval, but otherwise he was engrossed in his talk with Allenby.

'Well, the convoy didn't slow down at all and we'll be off Dubai at midnight. We still have to get past Abu Musa but there's been no more intelligence of Silkworms since that report about a hard standing being constructed for launchers.'

'Then let's hope for the best. I'm going back to the bridge now.'

***

Chapter Ten

Tuesday, 2200
HMS Winchester, at Sea, Southern Arabian Gulf
Operation Armilla Daily Sitrep: Targeting radar detected on Abu Musa...

'Captain, sir. Immediate signal from SNOME.'

Mayhew had barely reached the bridge when the chief yeoman pounced upon him. He was a man with decided opinions on the importance of his job and the access it gave him to the captain; no force on God's earth could stand between them for long when he had a high precedence signal to deliver. To emphasise his relation to the ship's command, he had long ago determined that no ordinary clipboard would do when he was offering his captain a signal. This clipboard was made of varnished mahogany – solid, not plywood – and it had a polished brass clip with a spring so powerful that it took two hands to open it. The back of the board was emblazoned with the ship's crest: a turreted castle and a red rose against a white-and-red background, the whole encircled by a golden cable and surmounted by a naval crown. Its owner was announced in stern gilded block capitals: *Captain HMS Winchester*. The chief yeoman had no use for the legally correct title of *commanding officer*, he felt that it demeaned his own position to acknowledge that *Winchester* wasn't commanded by a four-ring captain. Mayhew had been intimidated by this clipboard when he first took command, and despite daily use he still handled it with something approaching reverence.

Mayhew read the signal by the red light of a torch that was kept beside the pelorus for this purpose. Not even the chief yeoman's signal board could breach the firm rule about white lights on the bridge at night.

1800D. USS Cranston damaged by suspected mine position – it offered a latitude and longitude – *near Shah Allum shoal.*

MDA established – further latitudes and longitudes – *all vessels keep clear.*

These signals – particularly when they had a high precedence – were necessarily terse as they were transmitted over a slow teleprinter circuit. Every unnecessary word was removed to free up the bandwidth for other messages and it sometimes took a second reading to get the sense of what was attempting to be conveyed. MDA, for example, wasn't a term often seen in signals, but it was an acronym for *Mine Danger Area*, and it was as well to know that.

'Well, that'll put the cat among the pigeons. Navigator, mark this position on the chart and tell me where it is in relation to somewhere I know. Chief, make sure the ops officer sees this.'

'I've already sent him a copy, sir.'

The chief yeoman quickly recovered the signal board from the captain before he could hand it over. With studious formality his massive hands opened the clip, removed the signal, and passed the single sheet of paper to the navigator. There was no way that a mere lieutenant was getting his hands on the captain's signal board.

Mayhew picked up his binoculars and scanned the horizon while he thought through this latest development. Of course he knew roughly where the Shah Allum shoal was, but he still wanted the navigator's confirmation. It was a well-known dangerous patch of shallow water right in the centre of the Arabian Gulf, a little closer to Lavan Island than to Qatar. There was a beacon at the shoal's shallowest point, but it had suffered the close attentions of too many dhows and suchlike over the years; it leaned drunkenly and its light was uncertain. He could see that the officer-of-the-watch was listening intently. Saxby's last ship had been a minehunter and as he hoped to become a mine clearance diver, the subject was of deep interest to him.

'What do you think, Officer-of-the-Watch?'

'It'll be a tethered contact mine, sir, almost certainly. Whoever laid it would have been looking for those

Silkworm

intermediate depths on either side of the shoal, deep enough for ships to pass through but shallow enough for the mine to ride near the surface. The Iranians do you think, sir?'

'Probably, but we shouldn't be too quick with our conclusions. They've certainly done it before, those landing craft of theirs are to blame.'

'Yes, sir. It's easy to lay a mine from a landing craft deck. They're shipped on their own skids generally, and with the bow door down it only takes a good shove to launch it.'

The navigator came out from behind the blackout curtain.

'Would you like to see it on the chart, sir?'

Mayhew followed the navigator behind the curtain to where the chart was illuminated by a red glow. He'd marked the position of the mine in pencil and drawn the danger area around it.

'There, sir. It won't bother us unless we get re-tasked, but it's a great position to lay a mine field if all you have are old-fashioned shallow water tethered mines. All of the Iranian tankers transit through their own territorial waters, so they won't be in danger, but everyone else will, unless they're warned. I expect the Earnest Will convoys shave the Shah Allum shoal quite closely, and perhaps that's what happened today.'

'There's been no American convoy for a few days, Navs. This is probably one of the escorts making its way south after delivering a convoy to Kuwait. In fact, I think I saw *Cranston* on the data link when the last convoy ran through.'

'Captain, MCO.'

Mayhew returned to his seat and picked up his microphone, flicking the glowing red switch that announced that the main communications office was calling him.

'Captain.'

'We're picking up the news on the BBC World Service, sir. They're saying that *USS Cranston* is still afloat but in a bad way. I haven't heard about casualties, but she's being taken in tow. They're speculating that the mines were laid by Iran, and they're quoting the *Iran Ajr* incident from last year.'

'Thanks Chief, keep me informed of anything new.'

Everyone knew about *Iran Ajr*. The Japanese-built Iranian landing craft had been caught red-handed laying mines, and she'd been attacked, captured and scuttled by the US Navy. It certainly suggested Iranian involvement, but then it could be Iraq trying to muddy the waters, hoping that Iran would take the blame. What was that quote? *Truth is the first casualty of war.* Yet it did sound like something the Iranians would do. They had limited naval and air resources, and were no match for a carrier battle group with A-6 attack aircraft and F-14 fighters. They were constantly looking for new ways to make an impact within their means. Mines were cheap – particularly if they bought old ones from China – and deniable, and if they were used intelligently they were highly effective.

'Captain, AAWO. There's a lot of activity on the tactical circuits. It looks like MCMVs are deploying from Bahrain and Dubai.'

That made sense. Mines were never laid singly and with the Earnest Will convoys passing so close, the US Navy would want no delays in clearing the route. They had a half dozen mine countermeasures vessels – MCMVs – in the Gulf, and there was a multi-national MCMV force also: two British Hunt class a Dutch and a Belgian minehunter, a Belgian support ship and a British command ship – *HMS Hero* – a survey ship that was adapted for the purpose. Would they be deployed too? Well, for now he still had a convoy to take to Dubai. He settled back into his seat, listening to all the reports and orders on the command open line.

***

'AAWO, EWD. I'm picking up an I-band surface search radar on Abu Musa again, the same one as the last time we came through, bearing two-seven-five.'

'Thanks EWD. Report it to *Bellona*.'

Silkworm

UAA-1 and its ilk gave the bearing of a radar transmission, but couldn't offer anything better than a very approximate range, near or far, and often not even that. However, if two units held the same radar transmission, and if the units were far enough apart, they could achieve a location of the transmitter by cross-fix. This one was almost certainly on Abu Musa, but it was also possible that it was coming from a ship on the same bearing.

'APS, AAWO. Keep a sharp lookout for pop-ups bearing two-seven-five.'

Should he call air threat warning red? Doing it too often was like calling *wolf*, his own command team and the other ships would soon start to disregard it. Yet raising the threat warning was a vital tool to focus everyone's attention. Abu Musa was an obvious place to site Silkworms, and it had been under suspicion for a few years. Reconnaissance flights and satellite surveillance had shown that the Iranians had made some substantial hardstandings, just the sort of thing that was needed for their mobile launchers, but nobody had ever seen Silkworms deployed to the island. Perhaps there was a sensitivity because the ownership of Abu Musa was still disputed between Iran and UAE, although with Iran's generally bullish attitude, that sounded unlikely. There was another Iranian island twenty-six miles deeper into the Gulf – Siri – that had shown a lot more activity, but there was no question of who owned Siri. The convoy was about twenty five miles from Abu Musa now, and its closest point of approach would be about twenty-two miles. Even though the Silkworm range was variously advertised as fifty or sixty miles, twenty-five miles was much more achievable with their rather antique surveillance and targeting equipment. Nevertheless, that surveillance radar that the EWD reported probably operated twenty-four hours a day, and it was better to watch it but take no reaction unless they wanted to be at air threat warning red every time they passed. On balance it was better to stay at warning yellow.

'Captain, AAWO. We've detected the surveillance radar

on Abu Musa. Air threat warning remains yellow.'

'Very well, AAWO.'

Allenby made the switch to speak on the UK AAW circuit.

'Whiskey, this is Alfa Whiskey. The convoy is under radar surveillance from Abu Musa, there is no indication of targeting. Threat warning air remains yellow.'

Allenby swung his chair around and looked at the UAA-1 display. Chief Quinn was so engrossed in it that he didn't even see the AAWO leaning over his shoulder. Ah, there it was, a rectangular group of blips and lines on the screen that would mean nothing to the untrained eye, and meant hardly more to him. He swung back to his tactical display and had another look at the space of sea between the convoy and the island. He heard Dickens and Quinn talking offline behind him.

'AAWO, EWD. The Abu Musa radar's PRF is changing, it's increased, that could be an indication of a targeting mode.'

'Have you seen that before?'

'No sir, it's new to us.'

'Captain, AAWO. Indications of a targeting mode from the Abu Musa radar bearing two-seven-nine. I'm calling air threat warning red.'

Again, it could be nothing, but dual use radars often had a higher PRF mode for targeting. It gave them a more accurate bearing for the target although it also reduced their maximum surveillance range.

'Very well, AAWO. Officer-of-the-Watch, make a pipe, on anti-flash, on steel helmets. Then make a pipe that we're under surveillance with a threat of surface-to-surface missiles. Six short blasts for the convoy.'

The anti-flash hoods made a difference to the ambience of the ops room. Suddenly everyone became anonymous and only their eyes could be seen peering through the slit in their white cotton hoods. Now, without some consideration, Allenby couldn't tell whether it was Able

Seaman Jones or Able Seaman Young sitting at the tracker position to the right of the APS. It might make the management and leadership task more challenging but it was a necessary precaution with potentially lifesaving consequences. If an inbound missile was detected there would be no time for the operators to pull their hoods up and readjust their headsets, no time before the jarring impact and shattering explosion, and no time before the expanding fireball sought its meal of exposed flesh.

'Whiskey, this is Alfa Whiskey. Air threat warning red based upon possible Silkworm targeting radar bearing two-seven-nine. Weapons tight.'

Weapons tight; that order put some constraint on the force. They could only fire at targets that are confirmed hostile. The next step would be weapons free, which would give the ships the ability to fire at targets that are *not* positively identified as friendly. The difference appeared subtle at first, but the change from *tight* to *free* put every ship and aircraft in the vicinity in danger, whether they were enemy, friend or neutral.

'Javelin, you're keeping up with this?'

'Javelin roger.'

Allenby found the marine lieutenant's brevity unnerving. Did his Javelin fire units really know what was going on? Did they really understand *weapons tight* and how would they interpret *confirmed hostile*? He came to a snap decision.

'Javelin fire units, weapons hold.'

Now he had control. The Javelins needed a specific order to open fire, and he felt better about that. He heard the detachment commander repeating the order on open line.

'Javelins weapons hold.'

'AAWO, EWD. The PRF's increased another step.'

Everyone was poised now. If this was an attack upon the convoy, the next thing they'd hear would be the EWD's whistle. Allenby could see from the set of the shoulders on the air picture team that they were concentrating fiercely on being the first to see the fast-moving blip of an incoming Silkworm.

'Blind, AAWO. Load the Seadart launchers.'

Allenby made himself look away from the tactical display. It wasn't his job to spot the missiles and he had at least half a dozen people on that already. He had to look at the bigger picture. Was this part of a coordinated attack? Would a group of Boghammers suddenly appear two miles away, streaking towards them, armed with their rockets and machine guns?

'PWO, AAWO. Any sign of surface activity?'

'Just the usual.'

'Threat direction is north and west. Keep looking.'

Buckley might well resent being told how to do his job, but that was his hard luck. What a ridiculous response: *just the usual*. It hardly reassured him that the PWO knew what he was about. Probably he'd been day-dreaming and not watching the plot at all. There'd be some hard words later.

The soft-kill manager was already leaning over, ready to fire the three-inch chaff at the first sign of incoming missiles, but Allenby and Kesteven had the same opinion on this matter. The three-inch rockets threw their chaff a lot further than the shorter range Seagnat launchers and could – in principle – be used to disrupt the missile targeting before it was fired. But it took about ten minutes to reload the launchers and meanwhile the chaff would be dispersing in the wind and drifting down into the sea. The process of targeting a Silkworm missile could take a lot longer than that and it was better to wait and fire it while the missile was in its early acquisition mode. Now, if it was an air launched threat it would be different, everything happened much more quickly in an air attack. Nevertheless, there might come a time when a pre-emptive pattern of three-inch chaff would pay dividends.

Allenby saw the captain come into the ops room. He was immediately recognisable, even in full anti-flash gear, because he was the only man on board with three fat gold rings on his shoulders.

'What do you think of this PRF change, Chief?'

The captain addressed Quinn rather than the EWD. He knew all about the swap of responsibilities but he also knew that Chief Quinn was the man to ask about technical matters.

'There it is, sir,' he replied stabbing at the screen with a chinagraph pencil, 'the PRF has stepped up twice and that's exactly what I'd expect to see when they're trying to sort out one target from another. See, they're looking at nine ships and they'll have their orders whether they take a tanker or a warship, or one of the unentitled.'

And that was the question that was exercising Mayhew's mind. Was this merely Iranian routine, trying to pick off a Filipino or Panamanian tanker without involving the Americans, the Brits or the French? If so it was a dangerous game with so many politically unsuitable targets in close proximity. If it was a direct and intentional attack on a British convoy then that was another matter. Of course, if there were Silkworms on Abu Musa, the crews would know the composition of the convoy and its disposition; they'd have received reports from the P-3 at least, and probably the Boghammers and *Sabalan*. Yes, they could be trying to discriminate between the contacts, to work out which were the escorts, which the convoyed ships and which the hangers-on to ensure that they took the correct target.

'Another step-up, sir.'

Now Mayhew, Allenby and Kesteven could see the change in the PRF as Quinn pointed his finger at the flickering numbers on the side of the screen. It no longer looked like a series of changing numbers but it had taken on a sinister aspect, as though the numbers themselves were malevolent, and the object of their hatred was *HMS Winchester*.

'I've been holding back the three-inch sir, but I think…'

'I agree, AAWO. Make it so, Soft Kill. There's time to go through the safety checks'

'Check safety three-inch starboard,' Kesteven announced over the command open line.

'Clear visual,' from the missile gun director visual.

'Clear blind,' from the PWO who was staring at his radar screen.

The missile gun director visual waved his crew back from the three-inch mounting and called 'mounting correct.'

Saxby checked the flight deck camera.

'Helicopter correct.'

Mayhew glanced at his own radar display looking for any small contact that might have been missed.

'Command approved.'

Kesteven pushed the buttons above the AAWO's head and eight rockets flew into the night sky with a whooshing sound that could be heard in the ops room.

'Visual, clear and reload,' Kesteven said calmly.

For the next ten minutes while the upper deck weapons crews furiously reloaded the launchers they would have to rely upon the Seagnat and the port side, down-threat, three-inch rockets to deploy chaff.

Mayhew turned back to his own radar display. It might lack the tactical picture with all the tracks labelled and identified that the AAWO and PWO enjoyed, but it had much greater resolution and it could distinguish close-range contacts that wouldn't show on the other displays. He made sure that his navigation radar was selected and he wound down the range. There they were, eight blooms on the starboard side. They didn't look like ships from here, but from twenty-five miles away and to the homing head of a missile, they might be persuasive. Well, they'd both shown their hand now. *Winchester* had already gained valuable intelligence about the surveillance radar on Abu Musa, and at the radar station on the island they knew that the group of ships to the east was capable of deploying chaff, and therefore not an innocent cluster of unaccompanied tankers. No action is without its consequences and the wise

Silkworm

warrior carefully balances the benefits against the risks.

The atmosphere in *Winchester's* ops room was still tense as the destroyer slid through the warm, soft seas like a knife through butter. Eight minutes passed and the three-inch rockets were declared reloaded. fifteen minutes, and now the island was dead abeam and with every passing ten-minutes the range would be increasing by a mile. The optimum point had passed. Thirty minutes later and the EWD spoke on command open line.

'Captain, AAWO, EWD. Abu Musa radar's PRF has stepped down to its original surveillance mode.'

Mayhew and Allenby exchanged a glance. That performance from Abu Musa wasn't a random exercise, and taken together with the day's previous incidents it looked very much like a rehearsal, like a new tactic had been practiced. They felt like lab rats waiting for the next test of their intellect. Yet, it also felt like the end of today's alarms, even though the ship was still in range of missiles from Abu Musa and the convoy was still in international waters. In a little over an hour they'd be in UAE territorial waters and it was highly unlikely that Iran would make even more enemies by attacking them there.

'Captain, Navigator. We're slanting in towards UAE waters, the twelve mile limit is two miles on our port beam.'

'Very well, tell *World Antigua* that we'll send our Lynx to pick up the first lieutenant and the Javelin fire unit before they cross the twelve-mile line. Tell *Highlander* that they'll be next. Helicopter controller, have you heard anything from *Bellona's* Lynx?'

'Stand by, sir, he's just coming on now. He's feet wet and asking *Bellona* for her position.'

Feet wet. That was the universal call for an aircraft crossing the coastline from the land to the sea. *Feet dry* was the opposite. The Lynx had only fourteen miles to fly.

'Chief Yeoman, patch me through to *Bellona* on the secure line.'

There was a pause as Mayhew waited for the tone telling

him that the electronic switches had been made and his conversation would be encrypted.

'*Bellona* this is *Winchester*, Charlie Oscar, over.'

'*Bellona*, Charlie Oscar.'

'Good evening, Gareth. I'm hoping that's the excitement done for now, over.'

'Indeed. My Lynx will be on deck in five minutes and once they've taken a suck of fuel they can collect the Javelin boys from *Highlander*, over.'

'That won't be necessary, my Lynx will do both *World Antigua* and *Highlander*, I expect yours has had a tiring night. I'll pick up *Brown Rover's* Javelin fire unit after we've replenished tomorrow. I'd like to see a brief summary from your doctor as soon as possible so that I can add that to the daily sitrep, over.'

'Will do, I expect my people will be grateful, over.'

'I'll be passing out stations for the night soon, but I think we'll track gently up the Gulf, in case we're called for the *USS Cranston* affair. Well, good night to you. Out.'

***

Chapter Eleven

Wednesday 0430
HMS Winchester, at Sea, Southern Arabian Gulf
Operation Armilla Daily Sitrep: RAS(L) Brown Rover, passage to Bahrain…

'Captain, sir, Officer-of-the-Watch…'

Mayhew groaned and reached for the microphone beside his bed. He'd turned in after midnight when the ship reverted to defence watches and he'd been called twice in that time to be informed of unfolding events. He showered and pulled on a clean white overall that his steward had laid out for him. He hated those overalls with every fibre of his being, but they were mandatory at action stations or defence watches – white for officers and blue for ratings – and the thick cotton offered good protection from flash. In fifteen minutes he was on the bridge and groping his way to the starboard wing to take a look at the world. It was one of those rare Arabian Gulf nights with no haze, and the waning crescent moon had risen only a handsbreadth above the western horizon, casting a long, narrow moon-glade upon the water but without enough light to dim the stars. To the east, almost in line with the rising moon, the glow from the great port cities of Sharjah and Dubai broke the darkness, and over to the south and west the horizon was picked out by the flares of the oil and gas heads and the lights of the rigs. There was no wind and to the north, to *Winchester's* starboard side, there were no lights. The inky black sea reflected the twinkling stars, making it difficult to determine where the boundary lay between the water and the sky. He breathed deeply and noticed that there was not a hint of burning petrochemicals in the air. *Winchester*, *Bellona* and *Brown Rover* were in a blessed patch of the Southern Arabian Gulf which was free from production platforms and out of the normal shipping routes, it was a broad, untroubled haven in a turbulent and increasingly industrialised sea. He heard a discreet cough behind him.

'Good morning, sir.'

Mayhew was surprised for a moment. Yesterday's action had been so intense that he'd become accustomed to having Ben Saxby on the bridge, and he wasn't expecting Tom Henshaw, the most junior of the qualified bridge watchkeeping officers.

'The ship's in station on *Brown Rover*, and *Bellona's* in her station. The guide's steering three-one-five at four knots and we're on the starboard Tyne with the port shaft trailing. Nautical twilight's at zero-four-fifty-six and sunrise at zero-five-forty-six.'

'Very well, Tom. You'll be on watch for the replenishment then?'

'Yes, sir. We're due alongside *Brown Rover* at zero-six-thirty and it's *Bellona's* turn after we've finished. The replenishment point is rigged and ready.'

Mayhew nodded as the chief yeoman offered him the signal board. *Brown Rover* was due to top up her tanks from one of the terminals off Abu Dhabi, and *Winchester* and *Bellona* were taking a last suck before they lost their tanker for twenty-four hours. Replenishments at sea were such a common activity that they'd become a part of the ship's routine, to be carried out with the minimum of fuss. *Brown Rover* was theoretically capable of fuelling from both sides simultaneously, but it was a stretch on her manpower and unless it was absolutely necessary she usually serviced one warship at a time. With the figures that the MEO had given him last evening, *Winchester* should be alongside for perhaps an hour-and-a-half, and *Bellona* for an hour. He found he was actually looking forward to a simple piece of seamanship after yesterday's stresses and strains.

'What's the latest on the MCMVs Chief,' he asked as he flipped through the signals.

'It looks like they're sailing from Bahrain tomorrow. As far as I can tell the Americans have cleared a few mines and are now going elsewhere – they're not saying where – and the multi-national group is going to clear the rest of the Shah Allum MDA. The mine countermeasures commander in *Hero* has burst into life and is sending signals to anyone who'll listen.'

'No tasking for us then, Chief?'

'No, sir. It's eerily quiet.'

Mayhew kept his face immobile. Four MCMVs, a support ship and a survey ship hastily adapted for command were hardly in a position to defend themselves against the sort of threats that were becoming a daily occurrence in the Gulf, and the Shah Allum shoal was dangerously close to bandit territory. It was some years since he'd been that far himself, it was in a previous deployment before the tanker war stepped up a few notches. However, he knew that the Iraqis regularly attacked Iranian tanker convoys sailing past Lavan Island, and the Iranians had an interest in making the passage past Qatar too dangerous for the allies of its enemies. Surely the MCMV force would have an escort, and a Type 42 with its Seadart missile was the obvious choice, particularly if the American cruisers were otherwise engaged. He wasn't due to pick up his next convoy for two days, and *Bellona* was scheduled for a port visit in Dubai in the meantime. The pieces were falling into place one-by-one and he privately thought that *Winchester* would be re-tasked as soon as SNOME woke up and read his signals.

'Good morning, sir.'

'Morning, Ops, what are you doing up and about at this ungodly hour?'

To Mayhew's certain knowledge Allenby had been active since three o'clock yesterday morning and couldn't have had more than two hours sleep last night. Yet he looked fresh as a daisy, eager to get on with the day.

'Oh, I've been looking up MCMV operations, sir, and reading the signals from the commander in *Hero*, just in case we get tasked to ride shotgun on them.'

Mayhew smiled. That was so like Allenby, always trying to get a step ahead.

'The Americans are up to something, sir. They're withdrawing all their ships from the south and seem to be concentrating north of Bahrain. Perhaps they know something about those mines that we don't. They had to CASEVAC ten men from *Cranston* but I haven't heard of any deaths. It looks like they did a good job of damage control, and it's surprising that they didn't sink. Anyway, the tone of the signals is that they're going to hand over the Shah Allum shoal to the multi-national force, and I'll bet that we've been offered up as well.'

***

Mayhew watched carefully as the navigator conned *Winchester* into position for the replenishment. *Brown Rover* was making twelve knots now, the optimum speed for this manoeuvre, but it still required great care to bring the four-thousand ton destroyer safely alongside the tanker. He could see the able seaman gunner with a line-throwing rifle on the fo'c'sle. The bright yellow plastic projectile with the orange nose was slipped over the muzzle of the rifle, ready for the special blank charge to propel it on its way. A second seaman stood beside him with the two-hundred-and-fifty yards of gunline neatly coiled into a bucket, so that the projectile would carry it to *Brown Rover* without any snags.

A young officer – a midshipman – was counting down the range using a Stuart's distance meter. It used the known height of *Brown Rover's* masthead and measured the angle between it and the ship's waterline to derive a distance from the observer. It was the best way of determining the range of the tanker and whether it was increasing or decreasing. The navigator heard the midshipman's reports and minutely conned the ship, giving exact wheel orders to the helmsman. The approach had to be done quickly with a rapid deceleration once *Winchester* was in the correct position, to avoid the ship being knocked off course by the tanker's pressure waves. *Winchester's* bow came abreast *Brown Rover's* stern and the ship moved swiftly and positively along the tanker's side. Moments before the rigs of both ships were alongside each other the navigator ordered a rapid reduction in revolutions and *Winchester* crept the last few yards into position. A quick look showed that *Brown Rover's* crew had taken cover behind the winches and cranes, and the navigator looked to Mayhew for his agreement.

'Carry on Navs.'

The navigator leaned over the bridge wing and gave the thumbs-up to the petty officer on the fo'c'sle, who took a last look at the tankers deck.

'Fire!'

The sound of the rifle was flatter than if it was a live round propelling a bullet down the barrel, and the projectile soared lazily across the short distance between the ships, to pass right over the replenishment point and drop over *Brown Rover's* port side. One of the deck hands grabbed the gunline and started heaving it in. First the gunline, then a stouter messenger then a distance line and a telephone line. The deck hand on *Brown Rover* secured the distance line to an eyebolt and passed the telephone line forward to be connected. On *Winchester's* fo'c'sle the other end of the distance line was held taut by two seamen. It was never, ever made fast, in case the ships should start to separate. Now, even though the ships were too close for the Stuart's distance meter, the exact distance between the two ships could be seen at a glance, and more importantly it was immediately obvious if the distance was increasing or decreasing. It was a deceptively difficult job keeping that distance line taut, and the petty officer would relieve the two seamen after about half-an-hour.

Now that the ships were settled, *Winchester's* crew hauled the messenger back with the heavy steel wire jackstay attached. The end of it was secured above the high point by a quick release clip and when that was done the refuelling probe could be passed. The first lieutenant cast an appraising eye over the whole thing then ordered the probe to be hauled in. There was a trick to getting the probe to connect first time, and it relied upon gravity. The Jackstay was held by the tanker at a considerably higher point than at *Winchester's* end, and when the probe was close to the destroyer it was allowed to run with a rush, and with luck it would make a positive contact at the first attempt. *Brown Rover's* crew was well practiced at this and the man at the probe line winch released it at exactly the right point. The probe ran freely down the jackstay and engaged with a satisfying clunk. The release lever sprang upwards showing that the hose was now connected directly to *Winchester's* tanks and after a brief word on the telephone that was stretched between the two ships, the dieso started flowing.

The navigator always enjoyed these occasions. He was good at handling the ship; he knew it and the captain knew it and he was invariably left to get on with it. Now, standing on the bridge wing in the sunshine before the day's heat became oppressive, he was as much in his element as he would ever be. He constantly watched the distance line and his position relative to a point on *Brown Rover's* upper deck, and with precise adjustments to the ship's speed and course he could easily keep in station. Of course he was always ready for an emergency. Once, in the English Channel, the ship had suffered an electrical generator failure while it was alongside the tanker. It was a horrible moment. Much of the background noise in a warship comes from electrically-driven machinery such as ventilation fans and various pumps, and after a few days on board nobody notices it any longer. But when the power fails and the fans start winding down, the absence of the sound is deafening. *Winchester's* rudders were powered by electricity; of course there was a backup system but that took vital seconds to come on line, and as evil fate would have it he'd just ordered the helm to steer two degrees towards the tanker when the rudders froze in that position. When the auxiliary steering kicked in he had to use more wheel than he wanted to avoid a collision, and that brought his stern close to the tanker. He'd got away with it, but only by a whisker, and he was always conscious of the danger. Now he used the very minimum of wheel that he needed to stay in station, in the hope that if he should have a steering failure he'd have more time to correct it before a collision.

***

Mayhew was enjoying the weather too. He was standing beside the signal projector talking to *Brown Rover's* captain on the telephone line and like the navigator he was watching the distance line and his ship's position fore-and-aft against the tanker.

'From the MEO, fifteen minutes until we're full, sir.'

That was Henshaw, still the officer-of-the-watch until the bridge watches changed at eight o'clock.

'Very well. Chief Yeoman, hoist the prep at the dip.'

The green-and-white preparatory pennant at half-mast would tell the tanker unequivocally to stand by for *Winchester* to disengage in fifteen minutes.

Mayhew passed that information directly to *Brown Rover's* captain, only to be sociable, really. He always had to remember when dealing with the Royal Fleet Auxiliary that they had far more experience of replenishing at sea than he would ever have. This is what they existed for and they did it four months on, three months off for most of their working lives. They'd seen destroyers and frigates and aircraft carriers come and go, they'd seen the good and the bad and occasionally the quite frankly ugly. There was no turn of events that could surprise them. To *Brown Rover*, *Winchester's* replenishment was all in a day's work and she'd be ready for *Bellona* within minutes of the destroyer breaking away.

Yes, the sun was good and he'd grab it while he could, but here was the chief yeoman with his damned signal board to spoil his day.

'Immediate from SNOME, sir, to the task unit, info MOD and CINCFLEET. *Winchester* proceed to Bahrain with all dispatch as Guardian Angel for multinational MCMV force, further orders to follow. *Bellona* and *Brown Rover* proceed as previously directed.'

So his suppositions had been correct; he'd be riding shotgun on the minehunters. Now, should he stop taking in fuel? *With all dispatch* meant that he must waste no time, but he could only save ten minutes by breaking off the replenishment and it would be a wonderful feeling to have his tanks full again. If he was right, and this new task would be essentially static, then with full tanks he could last a week or two before becoming anxious about his fuel state. On balance, he'd continue to take his fuel. He could see that some of his officers had also heard the news and they were starting to look for guidance. That was disappointing, in a way. He'd rather they kept stoically to their task until ordered otherwise. Still, as the word was getting around it would be best to kill off the rumours before they went too far.

'First Lieutenant,' he shouted.

Pearson was only a few yards away at the fuelling point, and he turned to look at the captain.

'We have new orders for Bahrain. We'll fill up the tanks but then it'll be a fast passage, so expect it to be a bit bumpy as you're securing the rig.'

There, that was heard by all the bridge crew and the replenishment team so there should be no doubt. He'd put in a quick call to the MEO to let him know.

'Officer-of-the-Watch, how far to Bahrain?'

He noticed an exchange of glances with the navigator. It was normally the navigator's task to answer questions like that, but he was busy conning the ship, keeping it at a safe and consistent distance from the tanker. Tom Henshaw did some rapid work with the dividers.

'A hundred-and-eighty miles, sir, avoiding Qatar's territorial waters and keeping well south of Shah Allum.'

Mayhew calculated rapidly. These ships were theoretically capable of thirty knots on two Olympus, but that used fuel at a ridiculous rate. One Olympus and one Tyne would give him twenty-four knots and he'd use about seven-and-a-half tons an hour, or about one-and-a-quarter percent of the total fuel every hour. Seven-and-a-half hours to Bahrain would suck up between nine and ten percent of his fuel. That didn't sound bad but in an operational situation he really should try to stay above seventy-five percent. Taking these last few drops of fuel was the right thing to do.

'Chief Yeoman, reply to SNOME, info the others, S*tirling* and *Biter*. Acknowledged, my ETA Bahrain sixteen-hundred today. Request DIPCLEAR and an alongside berth. When that's gone you can talk to the pusser and get his requirements for fresh food, and the MEO in case he needs water.'

Tom Henshaw broke in.

'The MEO reports five minutes to go, sir.'

Mayhew cupped his hands about his mouth and shouted.

'Five minutes, First Lieutenant.'

Well, at least they were heading in the right direction. *Bellona* and *Brown Rover* would have seen the signal and they'd press on with fuelling and then break away for their visits. *Bellona* would enjoy some R&R in Dubai while poor old *Brown Rover* would be at some God-forsaken fuel terminal with no possibility of a run ashore. That was the way it went, and the Fleet Auxiliary had a more generous leave entitlement after a spell at sea to compensate.

'Stop pumping, sir.'

Henshaw was glued to the pelorus from where he could reach all the bridge communications systems, and he had to shout for his captain to hear.

'Prep close up, Chief Yeoman.'

As well as the preparatory flag, there was a simple system of hand flag signals between the fuel points but Mayhew backed up the *stop pumping* call directly to *Brown Rover's* captain on the telephone. The fuel line which had been rigid when the dieso was flowing, suddenly fell slack. A chief marine engineer on the fuel point opened the valve to check that the flow had really stopped. There was only a trickle that he caught with a waste rag.

'Fuel's stopped flowing, sir.'

The first lieutenant checked that his men were standing clear.

'Release the probe.'

The probe fell away freely and immediately the winch operator in *Brown Rover* started reeling it in. The telephone line was disconnected and a deck hand on the tanker ran it in hand-over-hand. A flag signal from *Brown Rover* told them that the probe was secured and couldn't slide back down the jackstay.

'Stand back from the fuel point,' the first lieutenant roared.

One last look to check that it was all secure. A hammer against the quick release clip freed the jackstay which ran over the side to be reeled in by the tanker. The distance line was let free from the tanker's eye-bolt and the two able seamen on *Winchester's* fo'c'sle hauled it in hand-over-hand. They were free!

With infinite care the navigator edged *Winchester* away from the tanker until he was a ship's length clear, then he started piling on the power until he'd drawn so far ahead that he could safely turn across the tanker's bow and shape a course to round the peninsula of Qatar. He engaged the Olympus on the port shaft and the destroyer's stern settled into the water. It accelerated to twenty-four knots as it sped away on its new mission.

Mayhew looked astern. As he thought, as was only right and proper, *Bellona* had been lurking close to port of the tanker's wake, watching *Winchester's* flag signals. She was already moving up to take station on the other side for her turn at taking on fuel. There was never any time to waste in naval operations.

***

'What do you think, Ops?'

Mayhew, Mark Pearson the first lieutenant, and Allenby were sitting in the captain's cabin enjoying a late breakfast of bacon butties and coffee as *Winchester* charged towards the northwest with the navigator rapidly plotting the route.

'Well, first thing's first, sir,' Allenby started after he'd swallowed a few mouthfuls of sandwich. 'Navs is going to keep us in deep water until we're close to Bahrain, so we won't have any problems with mines, either the moored variety or ground mines. There's a slight risk of a mine having broken free from its mooring and drifting away, but that's a chance we always take in the Gulf.'

'Yes, I'm prepared to accept that. I can't make it *with all dispatch* if we crawl along at eight knots.'

'Then there are no particular dangers on our route to Bahrain and we should be there at fifteen or sixteen hundred – it depends on the navigator's track and he's working on that now – but in any case we'll be there well before sunset. I assume we'll go alongside at Bahrain.'

'Probably, but I haven't received DIPCLEAR yet and if I don't get it in time we'll stay underway outside territorial waters, or in Manama Bay if we're too late for a berth. I hope not because I'd really like to talk to the mine clearance boys face-to-face.'

'They'll certainly need a brief sir, and I'll work something up. We'll need some simple signals for threat warnings and some standard procedures such as getting underway for a red warning, and turning towards the threat direction. Standard stuff, but I doubt whether it's at the forefront of their minds.'

'And what's your assessment of the threat at the Shah Allum shoal?'

Mayhew already had his own ideas but it was better to ask Allenby before he revealed them.

'The shoal really is the pivot point of the Gulf, sir. It's a bit like Malta is to the Med, but without the pubs and bars.'

Mayhew and Pearson smiled at that. They were both old enough to remember when Malta was a standard run ashore port for the navy, before the island embraced its independence under their prime minister Dom Mintoff and aligned the island nation with Libya. Saxby must be too young for all that but the navy retained a corporate memory. In its heyday it was a stunningly good run ashore.

'It's close to Lavan Island where most of the Iraqi attacks on Iranian tankers have happened. They fly their Mirages and Soviet-made Badgers down the airlane from Iraq, across Kuwait and then they follow the coast of Saudi Arabia until they reach Dhahran. There's a non-directional beacon there and they turn east, fly an attack profile towards Lavan Island, and release their Exocets or Silkworms at about forty-miles from their target, or less. That's probably the limit of their operational range because they don't use air-to-air refuelling. The problem is that the Shah Allum shoal is about thirty miles from those Iranian tankers, so we'll be right underneath the missile release point. That's the air-to-surface threat, but also we'll be no great distance from the Iranian coast. There's no intelligence suggesting there are Silkworm platforms on Lavan, but they could quickly improvise something if they had a mind to. I suspect Boghammers are less of a threat, but of course if we manoeuvre near the MDA we'll have to do so at slow speed and preferably in daylight.'

There was a pause as the three men thought through the implications.

'Is that all, Charles? Can't you throw in a handful of submarines to keep us entertained?'

Allenby opened his mouth to reply. The Iranians had a few Soviet Foxtrot class diesel submarines but they weren't thought to be operational. He caught himself just before he fell into the trap of taking the first lieutenant too literally. The problem was that Pearson was very much his senior on the navy list. He'd been a lieutenant commander when Allenby was still a sub lieutenant in his first ship, and now he was almost out of the promotion zone. He'd even been senior to Mayhew as a lieutenant commander but Mayhew had leapfrogged him to become an early promotion commander. Allenby had a tendency to treat the first lieutenant with too much deference.

'Yes, well, I think we can discount submarines.'

Mayhew had to laugh, but he had nothing more to add; Allenby had thought it all through.

'The AAWO can cover the ops room watches for the rest of the day, Ops. I'd like to see your brief to the MCMVs before we get to Bahrain, so concentrate on that, please.

***

Chapter Twelve

Thursday, 0100
HMS Winchester, at Anchor, Manama Bay, Bahrain
Operation Armilla Daily Sitrep: Iraqi Silkworm strike north of Lavan Island...

Diplomatic clearance had been late in arriving and *Winchester* missed her opportunity for an alongside berth. She lay uneasily to her anchor that night with the ship at defence watches and with all the main systems ready for action. After a few hours of sleep Allenby had the long morning watch in the AAWO's seat from midnight to six-o'clock. It should have been very quiet but the Americans were on edge and the US Air Force AWACS – callsign *Magic* – that circled over the northeastern corner of Saudi Arabia was reporting the picture with unusual diligence. The airlanes were quieter than they were in the day, but the data link picture that was being transmitted showed an unusual number of contacts in the northern part of the Gulf. Allenby reported his air picture to *USS Havelock* along with all the US Navy units, and there seemed to be a great number of them. Like all the team in the ops room, Allenby was alert and waiting for a particular event. It was well known that two or three nights a week the Iraqi air force launched a strike against the Iranian tankers that were staying close to the eastern shore of the Gulf on their way to the oil ports around Bushehr, or heading south having already taken on their cargo. Allenby wanted very much to see this in action, not merely for the thrill of it, but because he could easily see the potential for the Iraqis to attack the wrong target. As far as he could tell there was no attempt to identify their target beyond it being in Iranian territorial waters and therefore assumed to be a legitimate victim.

'Anything happening, FC?'

He'd tasked Beresford to watch Kuwait and the area to its south. The air picture supervisor and his team of trackers were quite capable of spotting potential threats in the open ocean, but they didn't have Beresford's training in dealing with crowded civilian airspace. Allenby trusted Beresford to spot something that didn't look quite right or that breached the normal patterns of activity.

'Nothing, AAWO, it all looks normal. Oh, wait, *Magic* is transmitting an unknown track four-two-three-zero bearing three-two-zero at two-hundred-and-seventy miles from us, heading southeast fast. That's slightly west of Kuwait city. It's more-or-less in the airlane, but it could be…'

'Roger, FC. Watch track four-two-three-zero. APS, do you see it?'

'Affirmative, AAWO. I'll establish a local track as soon as it shows on our radar.'

'Roger, APS.'

Winchester's 1022 long range air search radar wouldn't be likely to pick up the target until it was about a hundred-and-forty miles away, until then they'd have to rely upon the data link track from *Magic*.

Allenby's assistant expanded the range on the tactical display. The airspace over Kuwait was only moderately busy and it took just a few seconds to find alligator track four-two-three-zero. He hooked the track and displayed it on his vertical tote display so he could see it in detail. Course one-six-zero, speed five-hundred-and-twenty knots, no height displayed. It was marked as unknown, pending identification, which suggested that *Magic* either couldn't pick up a squawk, or didn't recognise it.

'AAWO, FC. If that speed's correct it's travelling too fast to be a commercial airliner.'

'Roger, FC.'

Allenby thought quickly. If it held its course and speed the unknown aircraft would be to the west of Bahrain in twenty-five minutes, and if it was an Iraqi B-6D – a *Badger* jet attack aircraft – then it would make its turn over the Dhahran beacon and start its attack run to the Iranian coast. It was strictly nothing to do with him. In this anchorage the

Badger would never be able to isolate *Winchester* as a target among all the other ships and the islands, even if *Winchester* was its intended target, which he very much doubted. Iraq had no interest in attacking the western alliance; after all, it exported much of its oil through Kuwait and that was only made possible by the Americans. Nevertheless, Saddam Hussein and his Ba'ath party were unpredictable; they'd been hardened by seven years of bitter warfare and had grown cynical and manipulative, capable of anything if it was in their narrow interest. Still, there was no cause for alarm in Manama Bay, but Allenby was certain that the captain would like to see this. He'd wait until it showed on 1022 and if it still looked promising he'd call the captain.

'AAWO, FC. Track four-two-three-zero is clear of Kuwait airspace now and is directly in the airlane. Still going too fast to be commercial air.'

'EWD, AAWO. Do you have any racket from track four-two-three-zero?'

'Nothing specific, sir. I have half a dozen civilian aircraft navigational radars on that bearing and any of them could be coming from that track.'

'You know what you're looking for?'

'Affirmative, sir.'

Allenby had a moment to look up from his tactical display. The whole ops room was tense and focussed. A quick glance told him that the air picture team was still looking through three-hundred-and-sixty degrees, and that was good. So far this track to the northwest was merely interesting and a real attack could come from any direction. He was pleased to see that they still took things seriously even when their ship was in a friendly anchorage.

'AAWO, FC. Track four-two-three-zero has changed to neutral. Still no height shown.'

That suggested that *Magic* knew the identity of the track and wasn't concerned, it was just a routine event to them.

'What's the range now, FC?'

'A hundred-and-eighty miles, sir.'

He could see the APS adjusting his display so that he'd see the contact the moment it showed on his radar.

'Are you copying *Magic's* co-ordination frequency, FC?'

'Affirmative. It's all quiet except for the occasional check calls. No foreign accents.'

'AAWO, APS. Contact sir, three-one-zero at a hundred-and-forty-five miles. No height information from 1022 yet. Local track number three-five-zero-one, not released to alligator.'

Allenby took a look at his own tactical display. There it was, a wide eyebrow of a radar return. With a beamwidth of over two degrees any target at that range would appear grotesquely distorted in width. It would get smaller as it came closer and the angle narrowed.

'Officer-of-the-Watch, AAWO. Call the captain and tell him that I believe there's an Iraqi Badger raid in progress now a hundred-and-forty miles from its turning point.'

'Will do, AAWO.'

Now, with *Winchester's* own local track on the presumed Badger, Allenby could follow it easily. Yes, it was certainly traveling too fast for a normal airliner but it looked to be firmly in the airlane.

'AAWO, APS. Track three-five-zero-one is showing at ten thousand feet now. That'll be correct within two thousand. No mode three squawk showing.'

'AAWO, FC. That's well below the lower height of the airlane.'

Allenby was becoming more and more certain.

'What have you got, Ops?'

Mayhew had come silently into the ops room, or was it that everyone was too engrossed to notice him?

'There, sir,' Allenby pointed to the track. 'There's no ESM intercept yet but that's exactly the right flight profile.'

'Where's the Dhahran beacon?'

'About here, sir.'

Allenby's assistant was keeping a chinagraph mark at the

point where two airlanes met and the presumed Badger was tracking right towards it.

Mayhew turned around to the EWD.

'Any indications, Petty Officer Dickens?'

'Well, sir, I think I've isolated a radar that I can correlate with the track, but it's a normal navigation and weather avoidance radar. No sign of any kind of targeting yet.'

'AAWO, FC. Track three-five-zero-one has ten miles to run to the Dhahran beacon.'

Ten miles at a little over five hundred knots. Then if it's a Badger it will make its turn in a minute, more-or-less.

The ops room was hushed again. Everyone whose duty didn't commit them to anything else was watching the track. The missile gun director blind broke the spell.

'It'll be a great Seadart target, sir.'

'Not our target, Chief, not today.'

'Overhead the beacon now. Ah, he's turning to port, sir,' Allenby said softly.

Mayhew leaned in closer. Yes, it was certainly turning.

'Switching to 992, sir.'

Allenby nudged his assistant who punched an illuminated button to switch to the target acquisition radar. Suddenly the wide, curved blob became a dot, and its progress could be detected with the naked eye as each rapid sweep of the radar antenna passed over it.

Allenby looked up at his tote display. The aircraft had settled on a course of zero-seven-five, fifteen degrees north of east. That would take him ten or fifteen miles north of Lavan Island, if he should dare to penetrate Iranian airspace so boldly.

'Still nothing, EWD?' the captain asked.

'No, sir, but I'm confident of his navigation radar.'

'AAWO, APS. He's descending, showing five-thousand feet now.'

'That's an air-launched Silkworm attack profile, sir,' Allenby commented. 'He's definitely not interested in us though, we'd have seen his Puffball radar otherwise. We might still detect it though, it's omni-directional in its surveillance mode.'

They watched in silence as the track passed over the northern tip of Bahrain Island.

'AAWO, Officer-of-the-Watch. I think I see him, bearing three-five-zero, tracking left to right. He's showing the normal aircraft navigation lights and looks to be about five-thousand feet.'

'AAWO, Visual. Port LAS is tracking the target, elevation five degrees.'

'AAWO, EWD. Puffball, surveillance mode, correlates alligator track four-two-three-zero and local track three-five-zero-one.'

Allenby winced. He hadn't thought to tell Dickens to hold the whistle unless he detected the Puffball in acquisition or locked-on mode. Normally any Puffball mode was worth the whistle, and it would alert everyone to the threat. However, today the Puffball was no threat, and Dickens was switched-on enough to realise that.

'EWD, AAWO. Make the correlation on the AAW circuit and alligator.'

That would alert the anti-air-warfare commander in *USS Havelock* that there was a confirmed Iraqi air raid in progress, unless he already knew.

'How far does he have to run, AAWO?'

'They generally launch at thirty or forty miles range, so about seventy or eighty miles if he sees a target just north of Lavan Island.'

'And if he doesn't?'

Mayhew already knew the answer to that but it would be good for the command team to hear it.

'He won't spend much time loitering, he doesn't have enough fuel after that run from his home base. In any case, those Iraqi pilots are nervous of Iranian air defences. They still have F-4s and a few F-14s from the Shah's days, and an old Soviet Badger's no match for either of those. If there's nothing there he'll head back pretty damned quickly.'

'AAWO, FC. He's accelerating, Mach 0.85 now, that's about his buster speed.'

Buster was the codeword for combat speed and most aircraft could only hold it for a limited time before they started to run out of fuel. It was generally used for the final stages of an attack profile.

They watched the radar contact continue east until at twenty miles from Lavan Island it abruptly turned and retraced its path towards the Dhahran beacon. It was an anti-climax, and the team in *Winchester* had no idea whether the Badger had found a target, whether it had launched a missile and if so, whether it had been successful. There could be a burning tanker over there towards the Iranian coast, seamen could be fighting for their lives in the water with fuel oil filling their lungs, and given the secrecy that surrounded both the Iranian and Iraqi regimes, *Winchester* would never know.

'AAWO, FC. He's climbing now and throttling back, conserving his fuel for the trip home.'

'AAWO, EWD. Puffball ceased, track three-five-zero-one.'

'Roger, EWD. Let Golf Whiskey know.'

The Badger passed five miles to the north of *Winchester*, but a haze had fallen over the sea and he'd climbed too far to be seen from the bridge or by the LAS operator. Allenby sensed the ops room relaxing. They'd done well; there was no panic and they all remembered their drills, he was proud of them.

'Well, Ops, that was educational, wouldn't you say?'

'It certainly was, sir. I think that's made true believers of them all.'

Mayhew walked over to the GOP, beckoning Allenby to follow him. The GOP operator saw that they wanted privacy and retreated towards the MCO to check on the latest intelligence signals.

'We should have a talk about Petty Officer Dickens when we have a quiet moment, Ops. He's far too good for the EWD's seat.'

Mayhew looked significantly at Allenby and nodded towards where the EWD was still following the retreating Badger and watching for any change in its transmissions.

'You're thinking of starting his papers for a commission, sir?'

'I'd like to discuss it. He has a certain presence about him, don't you think? I can see him as an outstanding PWO.'

'I'll dig out his docs and bring them along, and I'll talk to the first lieutenant about it, sir.'

***

Winchester's cable rattled and grumbled as it snaked grudgingly through the hawse, over the fo'c'sle, around the capstan and down through the navel pipe to the cable locker, hauling the reluctant anchor from the sea bed. A party of seamen held a fire hose over the guardrail to remove the mud, but unlike Spithead and Portland, the bottom of Manama Bay was composed of fine white sand and crushed coral that had no power to stick to the cable or the anchor, so there was little for them to do but try to loosen the few grains that always clung to the angles and crevices of the joining shackle.

Gavin Beresford was the fo'c'sle officer as well as being a fighter controller and an officer-of-the-watch and any other jobs the first lieutenant felt would improve his general education and moral fibre. He was also leaning over the guardrail waiting for the telltale sign that the anchor had broken free from the bottom. Ah, there it was. The cable suddenly quivered, surged aft and swung freely from the hawse hole, hanging vertically rather than stretching forward.

'Anchor's aweigh,' he reported through his microphone.

He felt the vibration as *Winchester* started to move slowly forward to counteract the wind that was pushing them astern, and he continued to watch as the cable came home.

There was still one more critical report to be made before the ship could move confidently out of the anchorage.

This was so unlike the turgid waters of the south coast of England. Here, he could see far into the crystal-clear water, and the great mass of the anchor became visible while it was still ten yards below the surface. He studied it carefully looking for any sign that it had picked up a stray cable, an old anchor or even a discarded oil drum. He couldn't see anything of that sort, and now the anchor was plainly visible.

'Anchor's clear.'

If there had been anything amiss he'd have reported that the anchor was foul, and then there would have been the painful task of freeing whatever it was that they'd picked up. At least with all these minehunters around they wouldn't be short of divers to help them out. This class of ship had only one hawse pipe, a single cable and only one set of deck gear; consequently a foul anchor was much more of an issue than it was with any other ship in the navy. Beresford had heard that the deficiency was to reduce the weight in the forward part of the ship, but he privately suspected that it was really for economy's sake. He'd hear nothing said against the Type 42s – he loved them dearly – but they had certainly been designed to cost, and sometimes it showed. There was a spare anchor but no spare cable. It was clamped to the bulkhead below the bridge and was a distinguishing feature of the class of ship that nobody ever forgot. He'd even practiced using the spare anchor while they were at Portland before deploying. It was a monstrous task to break it away and bring it to the ship's side, and he sincerely hoped that he wouldn't be called upon to do it again.

Before the anchor was even clear of the water Beresford felt the rumble as the engines increased their power, and the heel of the deck as *Winchester* turned and headed out to sea. He'd need to be on the fo'c'sle for another hour yet, until the anchor was properly secured with the whole arcane catalogue of brake, guillotine, screw slip, blake slip, and the final handful of rags stuffed into the mouth of the navel pipe to keep the water out. Then, in this fine weather, a quick lick of grey paint to cover the bare metal where the cable had ground out a fresh groove in the hawse pipe's steel lip. He didn't mind really, but he'd much rather be in the ops room. He shared the defence watch and action stations with the ops officer and he felt they worked well as a team. His knowledge of the patterns of air movements helped Allenby sort out the picture so that they knew at a glance what was innocent civilian traffic, what was allied military air, and what was a potential threat. He'd been in his element last night when the Iraqi Badger came through, all that could have improved it was a pair of Sea Harrier jump-jet fighters under his control, and the rules of engagement to allow him to intercept the bomber. He licked his lips at the thought.

'Anchor's home, sir.'

The fo'c'sle petty officer made his report to Beresford, but he didn't wait for a response. He reckoned that he knew far more about cable work than the lieutenant who was rarely seen outside the ops room, and he turned away and started throwing orders at his team.

'Right, screw that brake down tight, get the blake slip on. Come on, let's get on with it, the sooner it's done the sooner you can get below for a cup of tea before your defence watch.'

Mayhew watched from the bridge. Beresford was like most of the fighter controllers that he'd known, only happy in the gloom of the ops room with their intercept widger in hand and a headset clamped over their ears. Well, they all had to learn that they were seamen first and foremost, and their future careers depended upon them being proficient on the bridge and in the seamanship tasks about the ship. If Beresford had wanted to do nothing but talk to fighter aircraft he should have joined the air force. He could expect no more than two appointments as a fighter controller – as his first was to a destroyer, the second would probably be to an aircraft carrier – and then he'd be sent to a destroyer or frigate as a navigating officer, and then to the PWO's course. It was positively harmful to allow him to lock himself below with his radar display, however fascinating he found it.

***

The wind had picked up from the north overnight and the low morning sun picked out the crests of the little waves that romped across Manama Bay. *Winchester* steered for the deep water channel just as the first of the minehunter squadron started moving away from its alongside berth in the harbour. *HMS Hero* was first, looking out of place in her white survey ship livery with her buff-coloured funnel and mast, as though she was trying to keep her distance from these warlike events. Yet a closer look showed that she was festooned in light grey squares of radar absorbent material to reduce her radar cross-section, and the black muzzles of GPMGs poked incongruously from her railings. She was followed by *HMS Exmoor* and *HMS Hambledon*, two sturdy Hunt class minehunters, looking solid and reliable and workmanlike. *Aconite*, the Belgian support ship followed and then two Tripartite minehunters, one each from Holland and Belgium. It was a truly international affair. It seemed strange to Mayhew that *Hero* wasn't painted grey, but there was a significant cost to repainting an entire ship, and minehunter command ships weren't meant to go into harm's way. In fact it had been one of the topics of discussion yesterday, whether the MCMV staffs could carry out their duties from Manama Bay, rather than actually being present in the MDA. There was something to be said for that: the communications with the outside world were easier if the ship was hooked up to telephone lines, and the fewer ships in the MDA the better. Yet it was undoubtedly true that command was easier on the spot. Only by being at the Shah Allum shoal could informed decisions be made about weather, about enemy activity, and about the real dangers of sending ships into known mined waters. And then, of course, both *Hero* and *Aconite* carried specialised spare parts to keep the minehunters on task.

Silkworm

The minehunters and *Aconite* were slow, but *Hero* was even slower, and with her comfortable cruising speed of twelve knots, the hundred mile passage to the shoal took up the whole day. By the time they reached the anchorage just outside the MDA, the sun was already dipping towards the horizon, and the two American minehunters were eager to be relieved and away to the north. In a brief meeting on board *Hero*, they handed over a chart of the area that they had already cleared and the details of the two mines that they found, ominously carrying serial numbers in the same sequence that had been found on *Iran Ajr*, the Iranian minelayer, the year before. They knew nothing certain about their future tasking, but putting two-and-two together it appeared that the Iranians were in for a short, sharp shock.

***

'Well, Ops, what's your assessment of the threat direction?'

Mayhew had a hundred things on his mind but first and foremost was to set up a proper defence for this squadron of Minnows under his protection. The American minehunters had started clearing from the north of the shoal, and that determined where the MCMVs could safely anchor.

'We're further offshore than the Boghammers have been seen, sir, but *Sabalan* or another frigate could try their luck. They can't approach from the south, it's too shallow, there's less than three metres over the highest point on the shoal, so to guard against a surface attack we should be to the north, looking east and west.'

'And for air attack?'

Allenby thought for a moment.

'The Iranians haven't staged air attacks this far south, and with so many American units moving north I think we can discount that. It's the Iraqis that worry me. One of those Badgers wouldn't need to be far off in its navigation to mistake us for a convoy of tankers. We assume that they use the beacon at Dhahran to make their turn, but that's only an assumption. They could be running on dead reckoning, and a small compass or airspeed error would easily put them twenty or forty miles out in their reckoning.'

'Then we should be to the north; we'll need room to manoeuvre for weapon arcs. How close do you think?'

'We can only really cover them with Seadart if we're within four miles of the Minnows, but the closer the better. I suggest a four-mile east-west patrol line two miles to the north of the anchorage. That'll also keep us in good VHF range.'

Mayhew stared at the chart, measuring the distances with his outstretched fingers. He really didn't like the look of this shoal with its uncertain soundings and half-collapsed beacon, yet the Minnows must anchor in shallow water and preferably close to the MDA, and he must therefore be close to them.

'What do you think, Mark?'

The first lieutenant smiled ruefully. Warfare wasn't really his thing, he was more interested in seamanship and managing the destroyer, that's what he was good at.

'I'll go along with Charles, sir, I'm not sure I can offer anything more.'

Mayhew smiled and slapped his first lieutenant on the back.

'Very generous of you, Mark. Then that's what we'll do. Make it so, Ops, and draft my night order book would you?'

***

Chapter Thirteen

Thursday, 0700
HMS Winchester, at Sea, Shah Allum Shoal
Operation Armilla Daily Sitrep: Guardian Angel for multinational MCMV force…

The Lynx rotor blades were already turning when two burly members of the flight deck crew ushered Allenby out of the hangar and into a passenger seat in the back of the helicopter. The flight observer twisted his body and leaned to the rear to plug in his helmet – his bone-dome, as it was usually called – and he instantly heard the internal talk between the pilot and the observer, and the helicopter control radio circuit. He was intensely interested in all this and tried to follow the actions of the two officers in the front seats, but they were far too fast for him, flicking switches and checking indicators and dials with a practiced ease. He saw the flight deck crew taking off the lashings and running forward to the hangar. They were holding up the webbing straps to show the pilot that they had all been removed, with none left behind; it was a poor way to end a promising career in an upturned Lynx that tried to launch with one strap still holding it down. Now the Lynx was held on the deck by its harpoon engaged in the grid, and by the downward thrust imparted by the reversed rotors. He felt the ship's deck heel as it turned for a flying course and sensed the increased beat of the whizzing blades above his head. By sitting tall he could see the flight deck officer leaning forward against the wind that the Lynx created, with his hands crossed in front of his body, telling the pilot to keep his harpoon engaged. The beat increased, the ship's deck steadied at the horizontal, and the flight deck officer saw the permission to fly light turn green. He lifted his hands up and down then pointed his right hand diagonally upwards to the port side of the ship; suddenly, with a jerk, the Lynx was free and flying. The pilot pulled up gently on his collective lever, pushed the cyclic stick to the left and with a deft touch on the pedal the Lynx banked away to port and cleared the ship.

'We'll get some height so you can see what's going on before I take you to *Hero*. Funny name for a survey ship, don't you think?'

Allenby would have liked nothing better than a prolonged flight in the Lynx. There was so much more to see from here and he pulled his camera out of his pocket and started snapping. It would be weeks before he saw his results because he'd have to send the film off to be developed and then it would have to be sent back in the mail, to be picked up from Dubai, probably. By then he'd hardly be able to remember what he'd photographed.

Winchester looked quite different from this angle, and festooned as she was with panels of radar absorbent material on every vertical surface, she looked quite scruffy. Nevertheless with her Seadart launcher and her gun and close range weapons she looked like what she was, an efficient fighting machine. Enough of his own ship, there were new and intriguing sights, for the sea below him was littered with vessels. Over to the east he could see *Hero's* white bulk lying quietly at anchor. Her two charges, the minehunters *Exmoor* and *Hambledon* had moved away having spent the night rafted up to their mother ship. Further west the minehunters from Holland and Belgian were still rafted against their support ship, but he could see signs that they too were on the move.

The Lynx made a low pass on *Hero* so that Allenby could get his photos. White she was, white all over, while all the other ships were painted a uniform battleship-grey, but the signs of her conversion from an inoffensive survey ship to a minehunter support role were easy to see. Before she'd left Plymouth her tiny flight deck – sized for the now-obsolete Wasp helicopter – had been extended to take a Lynx and Allenby could clearly see the flight deck crew waiting expectantly for him to arrive. Like all the other British warships in the Gulf, she sported her own selection of radar absorbent materials, and in her case the grey panels against the white hull gave her a purposeful working-day air, like a fashionable lady donning an apron before entering the kitchen. Yet these panels weren't there to catch stray drops of grease, but to make *Hero* less visible to low-angle missile attacks. The panels had never been tested in action but the trials against sea-skimming missiles had been encouraging. They reduced a ship's radar return sufficiently to make it a less attractive target for the missile's homing head than the chaff that was launched to lure it away from its true target. *Hero* had even been given her own rudimentary radar warning receiver and chaff launchers to give her a better chance against Silkworms and Exocets. Well, that was the theory, but Allenby had more faith in his Seadart and his Vulcan Phalanx than in any passive defence measures. Nevertheless, he was pleased that the navy was innovating in this way, and it was noticeable that the Dutch and Belgian ships had no RAM panels. Twenty-millimetre guns and smaller machine guns completed *Hero's* transformation. She was still no combat ship, but at least she wasn't entirely defenceless.

The two minehunters were moving slowly towards their allocated start points in the MDA, staying close together. To Allenby's untutored eye it wasn't immediately apparent what they were doing, but that was the point of this visit to *Hero*. Yesterday's meeting had established some general principles, but now they were on the spot and had taken the handover, things might look quite different.

'Seen enough?' the pilot asked.

'Yes, thanks.'

'Well, I'd better get you onto *Hero's* deck then.'

The pilot made a cautious approach. He'd never landed on a survey ship's deck before and he was well aware that its operating limits had been tested very rapidly – perhaps too rapidly – before it deployed to the Gulf. To make matters worse, *Hero* was at anchor, and that always added complexity as the wind over the deck would be oscillating either side of the bows rather than blowing steadily from twenty or so degrees off the port bow as the Lynx preferred. It was a bumpy landing. Allenby was glad to be hustled forward away from the Lynx, and relieved to see it climb away safely and bank towards the east where it would conduct a surface search for an hour.

***

'Morning, sir, Morning, sir.'

Allenby shook hands with the two commanders, one of whom captained *Hero*, while the other commanded the MCMV squadron as a tenant on board the survey ship.

The MCMV squadron commander was a short, powerfully-built, brisk man who had been a mine clearance diver in his younger days, and who intensely disliked being called an *ex*-mine clearance diver. Now he controlled the navy's mine countermeasures effort in the Gulf. If his appointment as a squadron commander was the pinnacle of his career, then this deployment of his ships into an active mine danger area was the shining, golden point of the pinnacle; he was prepared to thoroughly enjoy himself. So far he'd been no closer to a mine than examining the photographs that his ships brought back while he was tied to his operations room on board *Hero*, strapped alongside in some Gulf port. He was itching to deploy his ships, to find mines, to hear the technical reports of what they'd found and to witness the satisfying bulge in the sea's surface as a mine was detonated underwater. Allenby was always cautious in his dealings with these men who willingly dived into the depths to confront the lurking menace that lay beneath. He thought them odd at best, and was concerned that they could become dangerously unhinged after too long in the profession. *Hero's* captain was an equally unusual type of officer as far as Allenby was concerned. He'd spent his career in survey ships, mapping the bottom of the sea and fixing the positions of headlands and bays, and was rather old to be in command of a ship of this size. Little did he know about any kind of warfare, yet he looked competent and he'd brought his ship this far unscathed. Presumably he and his officers had been given some instruction on the ship's close range weapons and chaff launchers. It was *Hero's* captain that took the lead.

'Morning, Charles. How long do you have?'

'The Lynx will come back for me at zero-eight-ten, sir, after it's had a look towards the Iranian coast.'

Hero's captain nodded and appeared satisfied. He looked to the more junior commander to continue the conversation, although he made no move to leave them to it.

The MCM commander had qualified as a PWO many years ago but had spent only a very short time in an ancient frigate as the anti-submarine warfare officer with never a computer nor modern missile system to bother him, before he was whisked away to take command of an equally ancient wooden minesweeper. He certainly knew about mines but it soon became clear that he had only the vaguest idea of the overall tactical situation. This was what concerned him, this oval-shaped patch of shallow water in the middle of the Gulf that some obliging Iranian had scattered with obsolete Chinese mines so that he could have the pleasure of removing them.

'Well, we'd better get cracking then. I gather you want to be sure that we know what to do if we're attacked.'

'Yes, there'll be no time to give you instructions when it all kicks off.'

'What are you particularly looking out for then?'

'That's a good question. It could be anything, but we've done our threat reduction exercise and the most likely is an accidental strike by an Iraqi Silkworm. Their targets are only forty miles or so to the east of us and they have no real strike support to make sure they fire at the Iranians and not at anyone else in their line of sight. Of course the Iranians might try the same thing but they're fully occupied, with the Americans lusting for blood after *Cranston* hit that mine.

Other than that, it could be an Iranian frigate or at a stretch Boghammers. That's why the Lynx is heading east now, to see if there's any trouble brewing.'

'Well, we've got your instructions. At air warning red we weigh anchor, the MCMVs haul in their sweeps and we disperse unless you tell us otherwise. You'll tell us the threat direction and we put that fifteen degrees on either bow for the smallest radar signature and we fire chaff when you say. If you order *weapons free* then we let fly at anything that we're not sure is friendly. Fair enough?'

Allenby nodded. That was about as succinct as it was possible to make it, and if they all followed those instructions they'd be as safe as they ever could be, given the situation. Just as importantly, friendly and neutral units would be safe too.

'That's about it, sir, and if it's a surface warning red, close on *Winchester* as fast as possible. Again, wait for the *weapons free* before blasting anyone. There are a lot of dhows and other tiddlers in this pond, and it would be easy to get this wrong at night.'

Hero's captain cleared his throat.

'This radio circuit that we'll be using, who'll be on the other end?'

'One of the PWOs or a fighter controller, sir, depending on what we're up against. He'll be in the ops room and he'll be fully up-to-speed with the situation. We'll do a radio check every fifteen minutes to avoid having to establish communications in the heat of an action. You'll have your operator on the bridge, I assume.'

'Yes, it will be one of my officers-of-the-watch and he'll be able to shout to the gun crews and the chaff launchers.'

'It'll be the same in the minehunters,' said the MCM commander. 'Now, let's go to my ops room and I'll show you what we'll be doing.'

***

Silkworm

The MCM commander and his tiny staff had taken over the survey chart room for their operations centre, and the space was dominated by a large table bearing an admiralty chart of the central Arabian Gulf, and a number of detailed plans of the Shah Allum shoal.

'Here's the MDA. You can see that it's shaped like a lozenge and it contains all of the shoal that we believe the Iranians are capable of mining; the Goldilocks zone you might say, not too deep and not too shallow but just right. I say the Iranians because our American cousins are quite certain that they laid the mines, and not the Iraqis or a third party. Apart from anything else they've traced the serial number of one that they recovered back to a shipment that went from China to Iran a few years ago. They swept six of the mines before they were pulled out last night, but they kindly left us the coordinates.'

He pointed to a neat row of crosses that lay in a slightly curved line from northeast to southwest passing south of the shoal's decrepit beacon.

'You can see the pattern here on this chart; anything strike you about it?'

Allenby looked again. What could he say, the mines weren't quite in a straight line but they curved very slightly as though they minelayer had been drifting, but there wasn't enough current here to cause that, nor had there been enough wind, and in any case the curve was too regular. They weren't evenly spaced either, leaving gaps that might indicate where more mines were to be found. The commander was evidently testing him – he was grinning now – and Allenby didn't want to appear dim. He squinted and looked again at the curved line, there was something about it…

'Could that be following a Decca Navigator line?'

'Oh, well done Charles. None of my people spotted it but the Droggies got it in a flash. That's the Gulf Main Decca chain, the red component. Whoever was laying those mines took the easy option and followed his Decca navigator and it naturally took him on that curve. It's a good way of covering a shipping route, if the Decca lines happen to lie perpendicular to the traffic flow. Fishermen in the North Sea have been doing it for years, setting their autopilots to follow a Decca lane. It gives us a really good clue as to where we should look.'

Allenby glanced at *Hero's* captain, but he didn't seem to mind the use of the common slang for hydrographic survey officers, *Droggies*. It would hardly have done him any good if he did object, the nickname was so deeply ingrained in the navy that it couldn't be eradicated by a mere commander's dislike of it.

'We've split the MDA into two rectangles; the Dutch and the Belgians will take the west and we'll take the east. They don't have any sweep gear so they'll go straight into sonar mine hunting. It's a bit more dangerous as they'll have to put their ships into unswept waters, but they seem happy enough. We'll do a team sweep of our whole area, then a sonar search and then put the divers down if we see anything. You probably saw *Exmoor* and *Hambledon* on their way to their first lane as you flew in. They'll be team sweeping by now.'

'Any idea how long it'll take, sir?'

The MCM commander stroked his chin.

'Hard to say until we've done the complete team sweep. Even if there's only this single line of mines we'll still have to examine the whole area, to be certain that it's clear. I'd say a week, perhaps two. Of course it will be less if the Americans come back.'

A week or two! That would knock a hole in the schedule of escorted convoys. Could *Winchester* really be spared for so long? Well, that was for SNOME and the ministry to sort out.

'Presumably you'll only operate in the daylight, sir.'

'Oh yes. We can sweep and hunt at night but it's too risky and too uncertain. Apart from running into one, the easiest way to find a mine is to get a visual on it, and we can't do that in the dark. No, the hunters will be tucked up alongside *Hero* by sunset.'

***

There was one more thing that Allenby wanted to do before he left. He was very conscious that the co-ordination of the defence in the MDA was reliant upon a single communications circuit, and he wanted to test it. *Hero's* captain took him up to the bridge where he found the officer-of-the-watch with the communications console in easy reach; he was properly dressed in action overalls and with his steel helmet by his side.

'May I?' Allenby asked.

He picked up the microphone and tested the press-to-transmit button. He'd deliberately kept this all simple, giving each of the units a two-letter callsign starting with November. There were no encrypted callsigns and no confusing codewords. This circuit was for use only in an emergency, when the force was under attack, and in that situation speed and simplicity overrode the niceties of operational security.

'Alfa November this is Bravo November, Allenby, radio check, over.'

A pause, he could sense Paul Buckley hurrying to the GOP where this circuit terminated and the voice that answered was slightly breathless.

'Bravo November this is Alfa November, loud and clear, over.'

'Alfa November this is Bravo November, loud and clear also. Alfa November carry out a radio check with all units on this circuit, over.'

He listened as each of the ships responded in turn, some faster than others. These MCM specialists had other things on their minds but it was vitally important that they listened to this circuit; it could save their ships and their lives. By constant radio checks he could train them all to keep a good listening watch twenty-four-hours a day. When he was back in *Winchester* he'd tell the PWO to name-and-shame those who were slow in responding.

The MCM commander knew what Allenby was doing, and why, and he wanted to make the point that his ships really were unable to defend themselves; that they depended entirely on *Winchester* for the technical capability to defeat the enemy's best efforts to sink them.

'We can clear the mines, Charles, if you can keep the Iranians and the Iraqis off our back. I'm warfare trained too, and I can assure you that a minehunter is really very focussed on a single task. This is the only real automation that we have,' he said pointing to a dark grey cube mounted at the back of the bridge.

Allenby looked at it critically. But for the rows of buttons surrounding the square screen at its centre, it could have been an old television set from the nineteen-sixties. It would have looked downright antiquated in *Winchester's* ops room.

'It's a hyperfix positioning system and it's about the only nod to modernity in the whole of the MCM world. It's funny how things turn out, because we'd barely been using its full potential until we hitched up with the Droggies. Apparently it's a two megahertz hyperbolic positioning system – or something of that nature – and it needs special care and feeding. We were doing it all wrong, it seems, and now we know what we're doing it's a real force multiplier. We can run our sweep lanes much more accurately and reduce the overlap for navigation errors. I reckon we'd need fifty percent longer to clear the MDA without that. Anyway, I'm showing it to you so that you know that we're doing everything we can to clear the Shah Allum MDA quickly. We have no desire to stay here, and from the sound of your threat assessment it could become unhealthy very quickly.'

Allenby had almost seen enough. He took a quick look around the upper deck to see that the close range weapons were properly manned and then it was time to go to the flight deck for the Lynx. Next stop was to be the Belgian support ship, *Aconite*, which he wasn't looking forward to. The Belgian ship had a flight deck and its own helicopter, an Alouette, but the Lynx wasn't cleared to land on *Aconite's* deck and he'd have to be winched down. There was no less dignified way to arrive on a foreign ship than dangling on the end of a wire with your overalls flapping in the downdraft. But he couldn't avoid it, and only after he'd briefed the Belgian and Dutch team could he return to *Winchester* and have a shower and a short sleep before his watch.

***

Allenby was shaken abruptly from his sleep. Kesteven had given him an extra couple of hours in his bunk, but now it was two o'clock and time for him to take over the watch in the AAWO's seat.

'I'd like to say that it's all quiet,' Kesteven said, 'but it looks like the Americans are teaching the Iranians a lesson in naval power. You can hear it all kicking off on Navy Red and on the AAW circuit. It's a long way north of here but I haven't relaxed defence watches at all. All systems are operating, and we did a full set of checks an hour ago. The Lynx is at alert fifteen. There's no news of any finds by the minehunters.'

'Are they responding to the radio checks?'

'Oh yes. The FC has been varying the intervals to make sure they don't only man the set every fifteen minutes.'

'Great. Get some rest yourself, I have the watch. Yeoman, bring the signals over will you?'

Allenby settled into his chair and listened to the AAW circuit for a few minutes, then to Navy Red. He could hear all the commotion to the north and he could see on the data link that most of the US Navy units were far up in the northern Gulf. Otherwise it was eerily quiet. There were no tankers on the plot except those at the oil terminals in the south, and the normal dhow traffic had entirely ceased. Probably they'd got wind that it was dangerous to be at sea today.

Allenby took a last look at the air picture and settled down to read the signals. Most of it was the usual admin that he could read and discard, but one signal from SNOME caught his eye. It was to *Stirling* and because he hadn't seen the original signal, it was quite difficult to understand its meaning. *Stirling* was the other Type 42 in the area, and they'd just come back from a port visit to Mombasa. It seemed that they'd reported that their port Olympus was unusable, and were questioning whether they were fit to lead a convoy through the Straits. All that was merely supposition, for all that Allenby could see was SNOME's response that told *Stirling* to continue as previously ordered. To Allenby that looked like a holding reply if he'd ever seen one. Certainly an escort through the Straits should have its full manoeuvrability; *Winchester's* passage two days ago showed that. A GTU change was achievable, but the navy's heavy repair ship was at Mina Raysut far to the west of Muscat, almost at the border of Yemen. To gather up the new unit and the Fleet Maintenance Group and fly them from UK would take a couple of days at least, and that assumed there was a spare unit available. However, this task at the Shah Allum shoal was essentially static. Perhaps he was jumping to conclusions, but it did seem that sending *Stirling* to relieve *Winchester*, and having *Winchester* and *Bellona* take the next outbound convoy was a potential answer to the problem. He selected the communications office on his intercom panel and heard the buzz as he waited for a reply.

'MCO, Chief Yeoman.'

'Ops here. I've got a signal from SNOME to *Stirling*,' he gave the date-time group, 'and I'd be interested to see the signals that led up to it. Could you look at the back-roll and dig them out?'

'Aye-aye sir. It'll take me twenty minutes because they're quite old now.'

'Well, do your best.'

It was a kind of eavesdropping. Those signals would have come into the MCO and they'd have been discarded because they weren't addressed to *Winchester*. However, they'd still be on the paper roll with all the other traffic, and with a bit of ferreting the chief yeoman could retrieve them.

Allenby hoped that they'd give him a better idea of *Stirling's* problems.

'GOP,' he called over his shoulder, 'where's *Stirling* now?'

'Last report was six hours ago, sir, passing Fujairah inbound. *Biter's* still in the Indian Ocean, they left Mombasa four days behind *Stirling*.'

'Thanks, GOP,' he replied thoughtfully, 'that's very interesting.'

'What's very interesting, Ops?'

The captain had come unnoticed into the ops room from the passageway on the port side rather than his normal starboard side route from the bridge or his cabin.

'Ah, I was about to call you, sir. Have you seen the signal from SNOME telling *Stirling* to continue into the Gulf?'

'Yes, I did, but I only skimmed it.'

'Well, it looks like *Stirling* needs an Olympus GTU change. He'll be OK for a solo inbound passage but I think we proved that nowadays you need all your speed and manoeuvrability to escort through the Straits. I'm wondering whether that's a holding order while SNOME juggles GTU change availability and his need for escorts. Having *Stirling* relieve us is a glaringly obvious solution; they could be here tomorrow morning and if we hustle we could pick up the next outbound convoy.'

Mayhew read the signal through carefully, mentally kicking himself for not having studied it more closely before. It had looked so ordinary and *Winchester* wasn't even an action addressee. It was just a ship being told to proceed as previously ordered, but in fact it could be most important. What would he do if he was SNOME? His train of thought was interrupted by the chief yeoman.

'Here's the signal from *Stirling* to SNOME, sir.'

Allenby noticed that the chief yeoman only had a loose sheet from the back roll. He evidently wasn't expecting to find the captain in the ops room, otherwise he'd have had his signal board. He started to reach out his hand but the chief yeoman pointedly gave the signal to the captain and retreated to the MCO.

Mayhew read it and handed it over to Allenby.

'You were right, Ops. Well spotted. Now let's see if your prediction comes true. I must say that I'd rather have a break before we run the Straits again. It's *Stirling's* turn, surely. Oh-oh, here's bad news.'

The chief yeoman again, that unfailing harbinger of evil tidings, and this time he had his damned varnished signal board.

'Captain, sir. Immediate from SNOME to *Stirling* and *Winchester*.'

So there it was, exactly as Ops had predicted. He read the signal through twice then handed it to Allenby without a word.

From SNOME to *Stirling, Winchester, Bellona. Stirling* proceed best speed to relieve *Winchester* at Shah Allum shoal, fuelling from *Brown Rover* on passage. When relieved *Winchester* RV *Bellona* and MERSHIPs – it reeled off three familiar tanker names – Friday 1800D off Dubai, outside TW, and escort outbound. Intentions for *Stirling* GTU change to follow.

'Well done, Ops. If I may attempt to beat your crystal ball gazing, we'll escort one convoy outbound then the next inbound and that will be about the right time to relieve *Stirling* again so that they can transit outbound to reach Mina Raysut when their new GTU arrives.'

'It's a wonderful world isn't it sir, when it's all so predictable.'

Mayhew laughed. There was nothing predictable about naval operations.

'Indeed, now let's get our Minnows safely through the rest of today and tonight and hand them over intact to *Stirling*.'

***

Chapter Fourteen

Thursday, 1730
HMS Winchester, at Sea, Shah Allum Shoal
Operation Armilla Daily Sitrep: Boghammers detected off Lavan Island...

Early in Allenby's career he'd learned to listen to two radio circuits at once and pick the essentials from each, but now he needed to be on the internal command open line and that left only one other ear for the external circuits. He glanced across the ops room to confirm that Beresford was in his seat.

'FC, listen to the AAW circuit for me, I'm going onto Navy Red.'

The ops room was quiet, with only the soft murmurs of trackers and supervisors speaking into their boom microphones. A Type 42's ops room was an ergonomic slum at the best of times, with consoles and seats so close together that it was difficult for the ops room supervisor to get from one place to another. At defence watches all but a handful of seats were filled and the trackers cursed silently as the petty officer in charge pushed through the narrow gap behind their seats making them swivel unexpectedly. Allenby cast an experienced eye over it all, noting the operators' relaxed posture while they still scanned their radar displays and their flashing lights and data readouts. That was good, because at any moment he or the PWO might have to bring the ship to action stations and nobody could tell how long that heightened state of readiness would last. These young men – boys really – might be in their seats for twelve hours or more, with a break only to run quickly to the heads to relieve themselves. Allenby was lucky in a way, being able to delegate some of his duties while it was quiet, and he dearly wanted to listen to the Navy Red circuit to learn what mayhem the Americans were unleashing to the north.

He was quiet for perhaps ten minutes. An observer would conclude from his downcast gaze that there was something deeply interesting happening on his tactical display, but really his concentration was on what he was hearing on Navy Red. It was a UHF circuit which meant that under normal circumstances it could only be received at horizon ranges, about twenty miles between ships or much more when an aircraft was involved, depending on its height. However, the Arabian Gulf was famous for its atmospheric temperature layers that trapped the signals in ducts near the surface and allowed them to travel much greater distances. Today he could hear scraps of conversation more than two-hundred miles away. Sometimes he could only pick out parts of the rapidly delivered orders and reports – it was like listening to half a conversation – but his practiced ear extracted the essentials. There was a major battle raging around the oil terminals in the northern Gulf where the great rivers of antiquity, Tigris and Euphrates, flowed to the sea. Iran, Iraq and Kuwait were close but nervous neighbours around the estuaries, and it was here that most of the fighting at sea had taken place during the long Iran Iraq war. The fighting involved sea and air forces and unsurprisingly the Americans were having the best of it. He could hear strikes being called in against Iranian warships – he wondered briefly whether *Sabalan* was up there – and against the small boats of the IRGC. Oil platforms were being hit and he could hear second-hand accounts of Iranian civilian rig managers negotiating for more time to evacuate their men before their rig was destroyed. Kharg Island, just off the Iranian coast near Bushehr, was getting a lot of unwelcome attention, and it appeared that its refineries and terminals were being hit hard. So this was America's revenge for the near-sinking of *USS Cranston*. All that they had needed was confirmation that the serial numbers of the mines matched known Iranian stocks, and they'd unleashed a shocking retribution.

Allenby swapped back to the AAW circuit for a moment.

Silkworm

He could hear *Magic* making its routine reports of air traffic. The Saudis were active too and the data link picture showed two Saudi Airforce F-15 combat air patrols over their territory, inland from Dhahran and up towards the Kuwait border. They were sensibly keeping their aircraft feet dry while there was so many American combat aircraft in the area. There was a carrier battle group out in the Gulf of Oman and it was flying A-6 strikes against Iranian targets, with air-to-air refuelling and their own fighter cover. It was good to see that they were keeping clear of *Winchester's* missile engagement zone and flying over Qatar on their way north. The EWD was having a grand time identifying all the aircraft passing through. There was nothing to worry about then, not yet at least. He listened again to Navy Red then expanded his radar display range to see the mass of contacts to the north. Surely that huge concentration of American sea power would elicit some sort of reaction from the Iranians in the central and southern Gulf, but he could see no sign of anything. He stretched and rolled his shoulders to keep the cramps away, then he heard the EWD break in on the command open line.

'PWO, AAWO, EWD. I'm detecting a number of civilian navigation radars in the direction of Lavan Island. They're like the Boghammers we saw in the Straits, I'm analysing the PRFs now.'

Allenby glanced at Petty Officer Dickens. He was flicking switches and running his fingers over lines of numbers on his display totes.

'Get Chief Quinn out of his bunk if you need him, EWD.'

'He's on his way, sir. He has a sixth sense for a good PRF analysis.'

Lavan Island was over forty miles away from the Shah Allum shoal, and that was long range for Boghammers, they normally stayed much closer to shore. Nevertheless, this could be the Iranian reaction to the hammering they were taking in the north. A Boghammer could cover that distance in little more than an hour, and the minehunters spread over twenty square miles would be a tempting target. Should he call the captain for his advice? No, this was a time for instant, decisive action, and he needed to bring his most effective weapons to immediate readiness.

'PWO, AAWO. Bring the Lynx to alert five in the surface action role. Sea Skuas and fifty calibre gun. Officer-of-the-Watch, call the captain and tell him we have a possible surface threat building from the east, probable Boghammers. PWO, keep the surface threat warning yellow.'

Allenby knew he was trampling right over the PWO's turf, but Buckley looked like a rabbit caught in the headlights. Even though the threat didn't look imminent, the sooner they got the Lynx airborne the better, and if it was properly armed it could deter and if necessary engage the Iranian small boats.

He heard the main broadcast: *Lynx to Alert five, Lynx to alert five, surface action*, and heard the running feet as the flight deck crew rushed to their stations.

'What's happening, Ops?'

The captain was at his shoulder looking calm and collected, but nevertheless his eyes moved swiftly between the tactical display to the EWD's desk.

'I believe we have a concentration of small craft around Lavan Island, sir. I suggest we launch the Lynx to investigate.'

Mayhew pulled his headset over his ears and moved over to the GOP where he could better see the geography of this middle section of the Gulf. Forty miles might be a long distance for a Boghammer, but it was too close for Mayhew's peace of mind. That was the problem in the Gulf, there was no strategic depth, there was no time to decide whether a threat was building, and Allenby was right to act fast.

'What's the bearing of those radars EWD?'

'Between zero-six-six and zero-seven-two, sir.'

Silkworm

There was a heavy brass rolling ruler on the GOP. The operator, anticipating Mayhew's needs, used it to run a line from the ship's present position to the centre of the concentration of intercepts; it passed a mile to the west of Lavan Island.

Buckley had snapped out of his stupor and had moved to the GOP.

'It could be an Iranian convoy, sir.'

Mayhew grimaced and glanced at Allenby for his opinion. The ops officer shook his head emphatically.

'The Iranians won't be running a convoy up the coast today, nor for the foreseeable future, it would be too tempting a target for the A-6s. The Americans might balk at hitting a tanker in its anchorage, but if it's on the move they'll probably call it fair game.'

Mayhew nodded, looking thoughtful.

'Well, the best way to find out is to launch the Lynx. What's its state now?'

Buckley knew the answer to that.

'Two Sea Skua and a fifty-calibre pod, sir, and it'll be at alert five in five minutes.'

As a matter of policy *Winchester* was at flying stations whenever the ship was at defence or action stations. The flight deck nets would be already lowered and all preparations for flying would be complete. At alert fifteen the pilot and the observer would have been briefed on the weather and the ship's position but they'd be resting in their cabins, fully dressed. Now that they'd been brought to alert five they'd soon be climbing into the cab, where they'd stay until the aircraft was launched or until it reverted to a lower state of readiness.

'Right, hold the Lynx at alert five and have the observer report to the ops room for a tactical brief.'

***

Joe Flanagan had only completed his training six months ago, and this was his first operational deployment. While he didn't fly the Lynx helicopter – that was the pilot's job – he did control its bewildering array of sensors and weapons. It was Joe who operated the radar and the electronic warfare equipment and prepared the weapons for firing while his boss, the flight commander, kept the beast in the sky and pointing in the right direction. Usually – in fact, always, so far – there'd been time for Carl Stevens to be briefed before a mission, so Joe was still not used to dealing directly with the captain.

'You see the situation? The EWD's intercepted a lot of I-band radars here to the west of Lavan Island and we believe it might be a concentration of Boghammers preparing to pounce on us; they're probably waiting for the sun to set. You'll need to stay outside Iranian waters, so you're unlikely to get a visual identification. Can your radar make out targets like that?'

'Yes, sir. Seaspray should be able to tell us something and Orange Crop can give us a cross-fix against the UAA-1. Have we got the radar frequencies and PRFs sir?'

Chief Quinn was in his seat now, and he'd already carried out the first stage of the analysis. He thrust a loose note into the observer's hand and turned back to his work. Orange Crop wasn't as good at electronic surveillance as his own UAA-1, it was too automated and it was best at looking for known threat radars. However, if the observer knew what he was looking for, between the two of them they should be able to get an identity for the vessels that carried the radars and fix their positions.

'It would be best if the Boghammers, or whatever they are, don't see you, but that shouldn't be any problem at that range.'

'No, sir, we can certainly keep out of sight. Is that all you want, just a radar contact and a cross-fix?'

'For now, yes. As soon as we know what we're dealing with, and unless they're coming this way, I'll probably bring you back for refuel and to hold at alert five until they disperse.'

Flanagan nodded.

'Got it, sir. If that's all I'll get moving.'

'Yes, that's all. Remember, I want a location. I don't expect a positive visual identification, we can infer that from their radar characteristics. And whatever happens, keep outside Iranian territorial waters unless I give you clearance to enter. If I do, you'll probably be going in hot.'

***

Going in hot! It sounded like a scene from *Top Gun*, and Joe Flanagan was happy with that. Joe was a Southern Irishman from County Clare in the far west and he'd joined the Royal Navy through a sense of frustration at his own country's refusal to play its part in the alliance of western nations. He'd left his home to spend years in England studying his trade, scraping through exams and surviving unnumbered check flights, and now he wanted some action. He'd learned to be a navigator, a radar operator, an electronic warfare operator, a gunner, a missileman an anti-submarine specialist, and that only scratched the surface of the skills necessary to be a Lynx observer. It was all very well, but in his heart Joe was a fighter, he even looked like one with his pugnacious jaw and his crooked nose. Joe was probably the most frequent user of the ship's gym and despite his outward friendliness, those close to him had learned not to push him too far. Most men went into combat reluctantly, out of a sense of duty or loyalty, but not Joe. He yearned for a scrap and he watched with growing excitement as the feeling of danger increased with every day that *Winchester* spent in the Gulf. For he could sense that trouble was brewing, with the Iranians certainly and possibly also with the Iraqis. When the Ayatollah Khomeini branded America *The Great Satan*, it was quite clear that he encompassed all the western nations in that sweeping denouncement, and most of all – most passionately – the British. Surveillance, probes, provocations, armed confrontations; Iran had already done all these things in the last few days, and all under *Winchester's* nose. Any fool could see that they were the classic escalations before a deadly attack. It was with a growing sense of mission that Joe Flanagan made his way back to the flight deck, to his beloved *Snarling Warthog*.

***

'Action Lynx, Action Lynx.'

The main broadcast reached into every part of the ship declaring that *Winchester* was about to embark on one of the most hazardous routine operations possible, and it was necessary that every man on board the destroyer knew it.

'What's the flying course, Officer-of-the-Watch?'

Mayhew had settled himself in the ops room again. Many captains wouldn't be anywhere but the bridge when their helicopter was to be launched, but Mayhew suspected that was because they didn't trust their bridge team. It was true that his officers-of-the-watch and even his navigator were very junior officers, all in their first, second or third appointment at sea, whereas the PWOs and AAWOs in the ops room had already passed through that stage of their careers. There was good reason to keep them under supervision, but at the same time they would learn much faster if they were given responsibility. Mayhew couldn't monitor them from his seat in the ops room, but he could see the course the ship was steering, he could see the relative wind, he could feel the pitch and roll and on his radar display he could watch the glowing dots that represented other ships close by. Privately he thought it was the captains who needed the professional development not the young men on the bridge. Too many of them felt uneasy in ops rooms, while he felt perfectly comfortable managing things from his seat three decks below.

'Zero-four-zero, sir. Coming right now and increasing twenty knots.'

Mayhew didn't need to be on the bridge to envisage what was happening. The Lynx would be heavy with topped-up fuel tanks, two Sea Skua missiles and a fully loaded fifty-calibre machine-gun pod; it needed a good wind over the deck to become airborne. Saxby would already have taken a look at the radar to ensure his new course was clear. He'd have checked the flight deck camera in case there were any dramas developing, and he'd have declared in a loud voice: *Check Starboard*. That was the cue for the second officer-of-the-watch – a sub lieutenant working towards his own bridge watchkeeping certificate or a midshipman under training – to walk deliberately to the bridge wing, sweep the stern quarters with his eye, and to declare: *Clear Starboard*. Then, and only then, he'd give the orders to the quartermaster to turn the destroyer onto the flying course.

The beat of the helicopter's rotor blades came through to the ops room as more of a vibration than a sound. Mayhew saw the *request permission to fly* light burning and flicked his permission switch. There was a pause – half-a-dozen seconds as the heavily-laden Lynx left the deck – and the vibration stopped. With the Lynx airborne he made the *do not fly button* and felt the ship returning to its original course. Yes, his policy of delegation was paying off and he really felt that he could rely on these junior officers.

He pressed the button that would show the helicopter's transponder – its *chirp* – and settled back to watch its progress towards the Iranian shore.

***

Flanagan's practiced fingers flew from button to switch to cursor as he prepared his sensors to make the first possible contact with the enemy. He understood his captain's preference that his officers shouldn't describe either the Iranians or the Iraqis as *enemy*, in an attempt to prevent his people over-reacting, yet he was certain of what they were, the Iranians particularly. With a small part of his attention he watched the green dots on his Seaspray radar, but most of his attention was on his Orange Crop electronic surveillance kit. The radar merely showed that something was there – a contact, unidentified, it could be anything – but by detecting and analysing their radar emissions he could determine who they were, and sometimes their intentions. All the instructors at the training squadron emphasised that Orange Crop was a threat warning receiver, with a limited capacity for surveillance, but Joe knew better. He didn't have the same capability as Chief Quinn or Petty Officer Dickens with their UAA-1 but if he was given a cue – and the paper that was thrust into his hand in the ops room was exactly that – he could do almost as well.

Ah, there they were, I-band navigation radars right on the nose. He glanced at the radar display but the intercept bearing was too close to the western tip of Lavan Island to make out any details.

'Multiple surface rackets bearing zero-seven-five,' he said on the helicopter's internal circuit. 'I can't correlate them with the surface contacts yet. Come left zero-two-zero to set up a cross-fix.'

'Roger.'

Stevens banked left and pulled gently on his collective to climb to a thousand feet. There was no need to stay low today, Boghammers had no air search radar and a Lynx was a notoriously difficult target for an I-band navigation radar unless it could read the helicopter's transponder.

This was one of the great things about a small helicopter, there were only two crew on board so there was no need to declare either who was speaking or who was being addressed. In fact, in a good crew there was little need to talk at all; the pilot and the observer knew what the other would be doing almost before they thought of it; and *Winchester's* Lynx had a very good crew.

Flanagan unplugged his headset from his normal radio box and plugged it into the new secure speech equipment. He called *Winchester* and after an acknowledgement from the helicopter controller he heard Petty Officer Dickens. Both of them were now certain that the IRGC Boghammers were concentrating close to the western tip of Lavan Island. Flanagan had heard about the American actions at the other end of the Gulf and it seemed that they were busy destroying the Iranian navy's offensive capability as swiftly as possible. He wished he was there with them, but for now he had a job to do, and not even the Americans with all their reconnaissance assets could keep tabs on these little boats.

Flanagan went back to the Orange Crop and studied the intercepts as the Lynx banked to the right and headed to the northeast. That would do until he had a bit more to go on. It was difficult to isolate the PRFs on Orange Crop but he'd nailed down at least one of them and it matched one of the numbers that Dickens had given him. He made the report on the covered circuit: track number, frequency, PRF and bearing and heard Dickens reply with another bearing. They crossed a little to the west of the island, but the Lynx wasn't yet in the optimum position to provide an accurate cross-fix. The ideal situation was for the two receiving units and the target – *Winchester*, the Lynx and the Boghammers in this case – to form a right-angle triangle, with the target at the right angle and the line between the two receiving units forming the hypotenuse. Of course the adjacent and the opposite sides of the triangle should be as short as possible so that the characteristics of the intercepted radar should be clear and undistorted when they reached the two receivers. Flanagan's whole focus now was to create a geometrical shape as close to a perfect right-angle triangle as possible. Then he would reduce the length of the adjacent side – the shorter of the two sides, between the Lynx and the target – by flying directly towards the Boghammers, so that both his Orange Crop and his Seaspray radar could have a chance to sort out the identity and disposition of the targets. Meanwhile, he had a better handle on the situation since the first snap heading that he'd given to the flight commander.

'Right zero-two-five. When we get to the twelve-mile limit we'll turn southeast to close them.'

'Right zero-two-five,' Stevens acknowledged the new heading.

Every moment that the Lynx headed towards the Iranian shore gave Flanagan more information. He was confident now that there were six Boghammers with their radars turning and burning. That didn't mean that there weren't more, there could be other boats that either didn't have radar or weren't transmitting. He switched his attention to his own Seaspray. The heading he'd given to Stevens wasn't only the best way to set up a cross-fix, it also allowed him to keep the Boghammers on his radar screen. The Seaspray's field of view was ninety-degrees either side of the nose, and as soon as the Lynx turned more than ninety degrees away from the target, it was lost. The Boghammers were still ten degrees within his field of view, but inching towards the edge.

'Come right ten degrees.'

The Lynx shuddered slightly as it responded to Stevens' touches on the controls, and it sped on as the sun sunk slowly astern. While Flanagan had his nose in his instruments, Stevens could look out of the window. There was no doubt that the Gulf was quieter than usual. They were cutting across the main route from the Straits to the oil producing platforms to the north, and yet there wasn't a tanker in sight, nor any of the smaller craft that criss-crossed the Gulf in normal times. Air traffic seemed to have ceased too and the few contrails were high and far away to the south and east. He could vaguely see the low lying Iranian coast ahead, and with a bit of imagination he could persuade himself that he could see the far mountains climbing away to be lost in the distance. Stevens didn't have Flanagan's warlike instincts, he was more of a thinker, and if he'd been asked he'd have said that they made the perfect aeronautical couple. While Flanagan plotted the downfall of the Queen's enemies he could keep a cool head to ensure that every launch of his Lynx was followed by a successful recovery, with no accidents and the minimum of incidents. He'd often wondered about Joe's motivation, Elizabeth wasn't his Queen after all, but the subject was sensitive, like anything to do with Irish nationhood, and he left it well alone. He checked his gauges and dials, running his eyes across them in the same sequence that he always used. He could do it in his sleep, and many was the night that he'd woken in his bunk to find himself questioning his airspeed indicator or the reading on a torque gauge. When he was flying he made that survey every minute or so, more often if he suspected that a problem might be brewing.

'Approaching the twelve mile limit, come right one-three-five.'

Stevens moved his cyclic to the right, applied a little upwards pressure on the collective, nudged the pedal and the Lynx banked to the right. Unlike a fixed-wing aircraft, a rotorcraft was inherently unstable and every action had to be counteracted when the new heading or height or attitude had been achieved. It came as second nature to Stevens but still, if he analysed it he was surprised that it was possible for a human to make those fine calculations and back them up with such precise movement.

'They're on the move, heading southwest.'

Flanagan was certain now. Six targets had detached themselves from the western tip of the island and they were moving into the open waters of the gulf, towards the Shah Allum shoal. Another glance at his Orange Crop confirmed that the radar targets correlated with the intercepted bearings.

'Contacts one-zero-five twenty miles. Six of them and they have the same radars as the Boghammers. Chopping to secure to speak to Mum.'

Stevens glanced to his left but he wouldn't be able to see a forty-foot speedboat at this range. However, he was starting to be certain that he could distinguish the barren western end of Lavan Island. The refineries were all at the other end, and that was some fifteen miles further east. There was an airfield there too, but it was this deserted western end that was his concern. The sun was setting fast now and soon there wouldn't be enough light for him to see the targets, even if they came out from the twelve-mile limit. He kept the Lynx level and steady to give the radar the best chance of seeing them as his eyes moved ceaselessly from his instruments to the dark mass that he was now certain was Lavan Island.

***

Chapter Fifteen

Thursday, 1830
HMS Winchester, at Sea, Shah Allum Shoal
Operation Armilla Daily Sitrep: Boghammer attack on MCMV force...

'Captain, PWO. Lynx reports the six probable Boghammers are moving away from Lavan Island and heading southwest. That will put them forty miles bearing zero-seven-zero.'

'EWD, sir. That correlates with their rackets. Six I-band navigation radars with the right PRFs. They're the same ones that we saw on Tuesday, sir, and they're all radiating non-stop this time.'

Mayhew looked at the clock. The sun had set four minutes ago and it would be completely dark in forty-five, about the time that the Boghammers would arrive. That would make things awkward, and with only one helicopter – he discounted the Belgian Alouette as being more of a liability than a help – he could soon be in a tricky position.

'AAWO, is there any sign of enemy airborne surveillance?'

'Nothing, sir. They'll know where we are and it's just a matter of navigation to find us.'

'What speed will they use to transit here?'

'Well, they're said to be capable of forty knots, but they won't be able to keep that up for long. I'd say twenty-five knots and they'll come up to combat speed when they identify us.'

'Captain, PWO. The Lynx reports the Boghammers' speed at ten knots.'

Buckley was belatedly asserting his relevance to this impending action.

'Thank you, PWO.'

Ten knots, that would be the speed they'd make while they found their proper places in the formation. They would certainly increase speed when they had their ducks in a row.

'We'll have them on radar before they see us, sir, with their masthead being so much lower than ours. We could try to confuse them with chaff rounds from the gun. If we wait until they're fifteen miles away then start firing shells five miles to the northeast, they'll see the chaff before they see us. It'll give them something to think about. We could have the Lynx drop chaff, but really it's better if they keep theirs for a surface attack, if it comes to that. We should bring the Lynx back for a rotors-running refuel so that it's available.'

'Remind me, what's it armed with?'

'Two Sea Skuas and the fifty-calibre, sir.'

'Very well, recover the Lynx for rotors-running refuel and relaunch for surface action. PWO, we'll be blind as soon as the Lynx turns towards us. Keep a very close watch to the northeast. Is there anything on the data link?'

'No, sir. *Magic* won't pick them up at that range even if he hasn't filtered out surface contacts. Everything else is up in the north.'

'Then we're on our own. Officer-of-the-Watch, pipe hands to action stations, state one condition zulu, surface threat yellow for the time being. Who's talking to the Minnows?'

'Fighter controller, sir,' Beresford responded, 'until the off-watch PWO closes up.'

'Very well, FC. Tell them the situation. They've all anchored or rafted-up for the night by now but they are to get underway immediately and take stations to the west of *Winchester* within two miles. All ships are to be darkened. I don't expect the Belgians or Dutch will object, but if they do you may insist upon it.'

The main broadcast sprang abruptly into life.

'Hands to action stations, hands to action stations. Assume state one condition zulu.'

The sound of running feet and slamming hatches reached even into the ops room as off-watch members of

Silkworm

the crew hurried to their stations.

'Navigator, Captain. Six short blasts for the Minnows. As soon as the ship is at action stations make another pipe to tell everyone the situation. We have half-a-dozen Boghammers heading our way; we believe they're the same ones that we met on Tuesday night but we don't know their intentions. If they want a fight we're ready for them. You know what to say.'

'Aye-aye sir.'

***

Mayhew stepped over to the GOP where the operator was busy plotting the position of the Boghammers. He tried to imagine what they would be doing. They should have formed up by now and would be doing twenty or twenty-five knots towards *Winchester* and the Minnows. They'd surely reserve their full forty knots for the final attack, rather than risk the stresses of that speed causing breakdowns on the way here, and the very real risk of losing their formation. There was enough time to refuel the Lynx and send it away again, yet he still didn't know their intentions. This could be nothing more than another probe like they'd tried two days ago, but it felt different this time. The Iranians must be frustrated by their inability to defend themselves against the American attacks on their navy – Mayhew could well imagine how that was going, they'd be fortunate if they had a navy left by tomorrow – and perhaps this was their way of hitting back. They'd see this group of Brits, Dutch and Belgians as an easy target. In any case he must be prepared for the worst, and the first thing was to disrupt their ability to find *Winchester* and the MCMVs.

'Captain, FC. The two Hunts have slipped from *Hero* and she's weighing anchor now. The others are doing the same.'

'Thanks, FC. Officer-of-the-Watch, can you see the Minnows?'

'Yes, sir, there's plenty of light.'

'Captain, HC. Lynx inbound at ten miles.'

'Officer-of-the-Watch, Captain. Turn to the flying

course. AAWO, PWO. Weapons tight for the returning Lynx.'

'Captain, Officer-of-the-Watch. Lynx visual bearing zero-seven-five.'

Mayhew looked around but it was difficult to see anyone through the great press of people that the pipe for action stations had brought hurrying into the ops room.

'Where's the ops room supervisor? Ah there you are, Chief. As soon as the Lynx is on deck, patch me through on the flight deck intercom.'

Mayhew felt his ship turn, and he made the *permission to fly* switch. He felt the deep vibration of the rotor blades as the Lynx landed, then the lesser trembling as the harpoon held it on deck and it started to take on fuel. He heard his internal circuit being switched, then Carl Stevens' voice came magically into his ear. It was quite recognisable even against the background noise of the helicopter's roaring turbines and whirring blades.

'Ah, Flight Commander, welcome back. Did you get a sight of them?'

'No, sir, they were too far away and we couldn't cross the twelve-mile line. We had them loud and clear on radar and Orange Crop though, and they were heading this way at about twelve knots in a loose formation when we turned away.'

'Good. I don't know their plans but we must be prepared for the worst. I'm going to fire chaff charlie to the northwest to confuse them and I'll keep *Winchester* between them and the Minnows. I want you to stay to the southeast of them and keep them under surveillance, but stay clear of my line of fire and watch out for SAMs.'

'I'm not too worried about them at night, sir. They'll have to see us to launch a SAM and it'll be pitch dark before they arrive. I didn't take note of moonrise though.'

Mayhew rapped his knuckles on his radar display. He should have thought of that but so too should Stevens.

'PWO, when's moonrise?'

Silkworm

There was a pause as Buckley looked appealingly at the FC. Beresford realised that the captain wouldn't hear him on command open line so he dropped his headset and moved to the captain's side.

'Zero-four-zero-nine, almost dead east. It'll be nothing more than a thin crescent though.'

'Thank you FC. Did you hear that Flight Commander?'

'No, sir.'

'There's no moon until four o'clock, so you'll be in the dark.'

'Very happy with that, sir.'

'Very well. Remember, we're not at war and the rules of engagement still apply. In this case, if they approach within two miles of *Winchester* or the Minnows, travelling fast in formation, I'll take that as hostile intent. Naturally if they fire that'll be a hostile act. In either case you'll then be weapons free.'

'Understood, sir. We'll be ready for relaunch in five minutes.'

'Any questions, Flight Commander?'

'No, sir.'

'Very well. Captain off.'

Mayhew stopped for a moment as the Chief switched him off the flight deck intercom and onto command open line. Should he have said more to these two men about to launch themselves into a dark night against an enemy with unknown intentions? What would he say? Good luck? No, that would be banal. Stevens and Flanagan knew well enough what they should do and it was better to leave it at that.

'Captain, Officer-of-the-Watch. The ship's on the flying course. I'm waiting for the flight deck to request permission to launch.'

'Very well. Is *Hero* underway?'

'Yes, sir. She's doused her anchor light and she's turning to the west. The two Hunts are staying close, very close, on her down-threat side.'

Good, Mayhew thought, then *Hero* was doing exactly what she was supposed to do, and living up to her name. She was far bigger than the minehunters, she could take more punishment and was much more likely to survive a Boghammer attack. She wasn't entirely defenceless either, and her twenty-millimetre guns and smaller machine-guns could rip apart a Boghammer in short order. It would be interesting at another time to study how great a difference it made to be firing from a relatively stable platform like a two-thousand-ton support ship rather than from a forty-foot Boghammer bouncing on its own wash as it twisted and turned.

Mayhew saw the familiar sequence of lights and flicked the *permission to fly* switch. The vibration from the rotor blades increased and then suddenly stopped as the Lynx sprang clear of the flight deck and climbed away to its task.

'Captain, PWO. I estimate the Boghammers should be twenty-five miles away now.'

'Thanks PWO. The Lynx will give us a cross-fix soon.'

'Captain, EWD. The bearing is drawing left slowly.'

Drawing left; that was odd, but of course their navigation wouldn't be too good. They'd have lost any contact with the land on their radar by now, and they'd be reliant on a magnetic compass to find their way to the Shah Allum shoal, for he was certain that was their intended destination. If they were heading too far north, then *Winchester's* chaff would add to their misconception.

'Captain, PWO. We have a cross-fix and the Lynx has radar contact. They're twenty miles away heading to pass four miles north at twenty knots.'

'Very well, PWO. Stand by with chaff charlie.'

Mayhew could hear the sequence of orders between the missile gun director blind and the gun controller and clearly heard the firm command: 'With chaff charlie India-band, load, load, load.'

Very well. There was no need to ask if the close range weapons were ready. There was just one more thing that he could do to persuade the Boghammers that this was no easy target. The 4.5 inch gun could fire starshell rounds that released a parachute flare high above a target. The flare burned with the light of forty-thousand candles for forty seconds, falling at four yards per second until it fell into the sea and extinguished. All the fours – forty thousand, forty, four – it was easy to remember, and the flare could be refreshed with a new starshell as often as was required. An attacker believing themselves concealed by the darkness would suddenly find themselves exposed under a ghastly white light; it was one of the best deterrents against something like a Boghammer.

'PWO. I might call for starshell after the chaff charlie.'

'Yes, sir.'

'PWO, Visual. Possibility of starshell after the chaff charlie, roger.'

'Seventeen miles, sir.'

'Very well, PWO. Use the range safety checks for the first then fire seven rounds at thirty-second intervals.'

Buckley took a deep breath.

'Check safety chaff charlie bearing three-three-zero.'

'Clear visual.'

'Clear blind.'

'Turret correct.'

'Helicopter correct.'

Another deep breath from Buckley. What was he waiting for? Mayhew resisted the temptation to shake his head in despair, or to shake Buckley.

'Four-Five, engage.'

'Shoot!'

Mayhew distinctly heard the gun controller press down on the foot trigger then the crack of the gun and the slight shake of his seat as the first chaff round sped away. He looked at his radar display hoping to see the bloom of chaff. His console was switched to the I-band radar so the chaff should be easy to see. Ah, there, five miles to the northwest, a very creditable fake target. He heard the second round fired and a few seconds later another load of chaff bloomed. The missile gun director visual was shifting the target a few degrees each time so that the chaff blooms would look like a group of ships. The first bloom was still spreading as the third round fired. Seven rounds would be enough, one for each of the allied ships, and he'd leave it at that. He tried to imagine the Iranian commander staring at his radar display as his boat bucked and rolled across the swell. It would be hard enough to see a contact at all, and surely he'd believe that the first group of big, fat blips that he saw on his radar was his target. He heard the reports again.

'Seven rounds chaff charlie fired. Gun clear.'

'Captain, PWO. Contact sir. Zero-five-zero, ten miles. They've turned towards the chaff charlie blooms. Cover with gun, sir?'

If those Boghammers had any sort of radar warning receiver then they would pick up a fire control radar in a flash. However, he needed the 909s to be locked on for the starshell to be placed accurately and in any case, it would probably add to the Boghammer squadron commander's uncertainty.

'Cover with gun, PWO. Standby to fire starshell.'

Again, the litany of orders from behind Mayhew.

'With starshell, load, load, load.'

'PWO, Captain. Keep us between the Minnows and the Boghammers.'

'Officer-of-the-Watch, PWO. Come left three-three-zero.'

Mayhew could see the whole situation now on his console. There were six Boghammers, as the Lynx and the EWD had reported. They were in a loose vee-formation and were heading fast towards the chaff blooms, which were five miles north of *Winchester*. Any moment now they'd detect the fire control radar and uncertainty would start to creep in.

'Captain, PWO. They're slowing down.'

The PWO had the benefit of a tactical display and could

Silkworm

see the computer-generated speed of the targets. Any moment now…

'PWO. Stand by starshell.'

'Captain, Officer-of-the-Watch. It's all dark to the north of us, they must have their lights out.'

Well, so did *Winchester* and the Minnows, and the Lynx too. This was a game of blind-man's bluff but with electronic ears and – he was becoming certain – with deadly intent.

'Captain, AAWO. I think they're turning towards us…'

Ah, Allenby was watching the surface picture too. Good.

'…yes, they've turned towards us and they're increasing speed, six miles to run.'

'Where's the Lynx, PWO?'

'Two miles clear of the Boghammers to the east of them.'

Mayhew realised that Buckley was fine so long as he only had to answer questions, but that wasn't good enough for a PWO. Well, he'd address that another day.

'PWO, Captain. Illuminate the Boghammers with starshell. Use the lead boat as your target.'

The gun direction system would use the speed of the approaching boats, and their course, together with the time-of-flight of the shell to calculate where it should be aimed so that its light was at its maximum as it was immediately above the target.

'Shoot!'

The gun controller pressed the foot trigger and the gun fired.

Bang!

Now Mayhew wished he was on the bridge to see the starshell light up the sea, but in that case he'd be a mere spectator. This is where he should be.

'HC, Captain. Tell the Lynx to turn on his lights for twenty seconds.'

That should be enough to show the Boghammers that they were outflanked as well as facing an alert and dangerous enemy, without offering the Lynx as a target for SAMs for too long.

'Captain, AAWO. The lead boat's turning to starboard.'

'PWO, Captain. Keep the ship between the Boghammers and the Minnows.'

'Captain, Visual. LAS operator reports six boats under the starshell, range about four miles. They appear to be turning to starboard. The Lynx has turned on its lights.'

'PWO, Captain. Another starshell.'

'Shoot!'

Bang!

'Captain, Officer-of-the-Watch. The Lynx has turned off its lights, sir.'

Very wise, Mayhew thought, there was no telling whether the Boghammers had SAMs. Twenty seconds was plenty, then dive for the deck and move away before a SAM firer can react.

'Captain, AAWO. They're reversing their course and heading away to the north, fast. They're still in starshell range. The Lynx is clear to the east.'

'PWO, one more starshell to speed them on their way.'

'Shoot!'

Bang!

The Iranians must be firmly spooked by now. They wouldn't have seen *Winchester* or any of the MCMV force, but they'd have been chased by starshells that seemed to anticipate their every move. The Lynx lighting up on their flanks must have been the last straw. Probably the IRGC commander had hoped to sneak in under cover of darkness, fire a few rockets and machine-guns to make a point, then be away before anybody could react. Well, his plans had been well-and-truly foiled.

'PWO, Captain. Tell the Lynx to shadow them out of range of SAMs and to turn on his lights occasionally, to let them know that he's still there. He's to turn back before the twelve-mile limit and return to Mum. We'll remain at action stations until the Lynx is back on deck. FC, tell the Minnows

Silkworm

what's happening. As soon as we hear that the Boghammers are back inside their own waters the surface warning can go back to yellow and the Minnows can anchor and raft up again.'

Mayhew looked around and spotted the off-watch AAWO.

'Ah, Gordon. Could you take the AAWO seat while Ops comes for a chat with me?'

***

The captain's cabin was a blessed haven after so many hours in the ops room. It even smelled better, although nothing on this earth could be worse than a Type 42's ops room at action stations in the Gulf. Mayhew switched his cabin speaker to command open line and as if by magic his steward appeared. Saxby must have heard that the captain was heading for his cabin and released his steward from his action station.

'Coffee, sir? It'll be ready in five minutes.'

Mayhew nodded distractedly. It would be instant with powdered milk if it came that quickly, but it was better than nothing.

'Close the scullery door would you.'

The steward would have done that anyway; it was a certainty that whatever he had to talk to the ops officer about at actions stations would be sensitive at the least.

They settled into the chintz-covered chairs and Mayhew paused to collect his thoughts, but nothing came. Perhaps an indirect approach would be best.

'What do you think, Charles?'

'Of the action, sir…?'

'We can start with that.'

'…or of Paul Buckley?'

Mayhew grimaced painfully.

'I see we think as one.'

Allenby had grown up with the mantra that you never state a problem without offering a solution, and he wasn't going to change now. Unless the captain interrupted him he'd unload the whole plan in one go and then see what reaction he got.

'He's getting worse, sir. He was satisfactory at Portland and for the passage to the Gulf, but since we've been in contact with the enemy,' Allenby knew of no better way to describe the Iranians, 'he seems to have frozen. Oh, he obeys orders well enough, and he has good situational awareness – sometimes – and he can make reports, but he seems to have left his initiative behind somewhere in the Red Sea, I can't state it more clearly than that. I suspect it's something to do with his family, but he won't talk about it. Certainly he's worse after we get mail. I was going to ask to talk to you after tonight in any case. I'd like to swap him and Jerry around. That would put Jerry in the PWO seat at action stations and Paul as the duty staff officer.'

Mayhew looked thoughtful. It was the obvious solution and he was going to suggest it anyway, but there were implications for the management of his officers. Buckley was the above water specialist while Harling was the expert at anti-submarine warfare. In principle they were interchangeable in the PWO seat at action stations or in defence watches, and their specialist skills only became relevant for warfare planning. Nevertheless, there was no credible submarine threat in the Gulf and almost every Type 42 on the Armilla Patrol put the above water specialist in the PWO seat at action stations. Moving Buckley out would be a clear statement of the command's lack of trust.

'I obviously don't want to do this, sir, and I'll have to find a way of softening the blow, at least in public, but, well, things are definitely hotting up…'

'You're right, Charles, it's the only solution and we should do it immediately. I'll back you up of course, but it would be best for the decision to come from your level. Be firm, but I'm sure you will be without me saying anything. I didn't tell you before, but the training commander at *HMS Dryad* did warn me that Buckley might be a problem. He passed the final trainer runs of course, but there was something hesitant that they didn't quite like, a reluctance to commit to action. He must know that he's a weak link, I wonder whether he's expecting something like this.'

'Well, I'm going to give it to him straight, sir, but for public consumption I'm going to make it look like a routine swap. He and Jerry will change watches so that he's teamed with Gordon rather than with me, and that will naturally mean that Jerry will be the action PWO. I'll do it at the change of the watch at midnight, and I'll speak to them both beforehand.'

'Good, let me know how it goes. Ah here's the coffee. Stay a while as I really would like to hear your view of tonight's little action. What do you think they were up to?'

Allenby sipped the scalding hot coffee. It seemed like days since he'd last had food or drink and when the steward brought a plate of biscuits – the captain's personal hobnobs, no less – he wolfed two down with hardly a pause for breath.

'It was more than a harmless provocation this time, sir. Those Boghammers meant business and they were going to work us over like *Sabalan* did to that Panamanian tanker. I think they were entirely fooled by the chaff and they're probably still wondering what they were chasing. They were completely unprepared for the starshell – they'd probably never seen anything like it before – and that must have had a huge psychological impact. I wouldn't want to be lit up like that. When they saw the Lynx lights to the east of them, cutting them off from their base, they must have realised that the game was up. I did wonder why they kept their radars on so conveniently for us, they must know that we can intercept them, but it's probably because at night they have no other way of finding their target and keeping formation.'

'My thoughts entirely, Charles. But there's something else. Every contact we've had with the Iranians these past three days has been a step up from the previous one. It's not only the mauling they're taking from the Americans, there seems to be a deliberate policy to escalate matters. They seem to be testing our resolve to hold fast to our orders, it's almost as though they know our rules of engagement as well as we do. I don't know whether they want a conflict or whether they just want us to make a slip that they can take to an international court. Holding our nerve is one thing when it's a bunch of Boghammers that might hurt us but are unlikely to sink our ships, but one wrong calculation when we're under surveillance from a Silkworm shore station, and we could all be joining the Arabian Gulf swimming club. That's partly what made me talk to you about Paul Buckley, I can't afford to have you covering for the PWO at action stations when there's a more deadly air battle to be fought.'

'Well, I expect it will all become clear before long, sir. Now, may I go and make that swap before we close down from action stations?'

***

Silkworm

Chapter Sixteen

Friday, 0100
HMS Winchester, at Sea, Shah Allum Shoal
Operation Armilla Daily Sitrep: Iraqi Silkworm strike on MCMV force...

Allenby was back on watch feeling refreshed after nearly four hours in his bunk. In the Gulf, everybody slept fully clothed but he'd long ago become used to that and it didn't interrupt his sleep at all. His meeting with Buckley had been as bad as he'd expected. He'd tried to sweeten the pill by telling him – quite truthfully – that he'd review the situation in a few weeks after both the PWOs had settled into their new roles – and less truthfully – that he was sure Buckley could step up to the challenge. Yet it left a sour taste in everybody's mouth and it would likely affect the relationship between the officers of the operations department, particularly as they shared the close confines of a small wardroom on a long deployment. Whatever Allenby could say, it was clear to Buckley that he had a black mark against his name, and that his annual report would suffer for it. Perhaps it was the sharp shock that Buckley needed, but Allenby doubted it, his problem was too deep-seated for that. Still, it hadn't affected Allenby's sleep and he and Buckley were in opposite defence watches now. He looked across to where Jerry Harling was in conversation with the surface picture supervisor and had a moment to wonder how Gordon would get on with Buckley in his watch.

Allenby sighed and looked down at his tactical display. The northern Gulf had gone quiet at midnight; it looked like the Americans had made their point and had stopped their attacks on Iranian ships and oil installations, or perhaps they had only paused. The link picture from *Magic* showed the normal patterns of activity, and the Golf Whiskey ship – *USS Havelock* – didn't seem to have much to say.

'PWO, AAWO. Is there any sign of movement around

Lavan Island?'

'Nothing, the Boghammers have disappeared, probably gone to the north side of the island or the mainland. I can't see any tankers on the move, but we have no sensors that can detect shipping inside the island. *Magic* doesn't seem to be able to see anything either and it's too far inside Iranian waters for any reconnaissance.'

In that one conversation he'd had more information from Jerry Harling than he usually had from Buckley in a whole watch.

'FC, AAWO. Are the Minnows answering your radio checks promptly.'

'Affirmative, sir, even more so after their fright from the Boghammers. They're much more proactive now, and *Hero* asked for a sitrep ten minutes ago. Oh, I've just seen one of *Magic's* alligator tracks, four-two-zero-one. It's over Kuwait and it looks the same as that Badger last night; no mode three and it's been classified as unknown, pending identification.'

Allenby expanded the range of his tactical display so that he could see the northern Gulf. Track four-two-zero-one was three hundred miles away from the Shah Allum shoal and there was no question of *Winchester's* radar holding a contact at that range. It was a good data link track though, not like some that jumped all over the place and eventually disappeared without trace or explanation.

'APS, EWD. Track four-two-zero-one is a possible Iraqi Badger, watch.'

Allenby studied the link track for a moment. It was only a symbol, identity was unknown, with the four digits of the track number beneath it. By hooking it with his tracker ball he could get a readout of the information that *Magic* was transmitting. Course one-five-two, speed five-hundred knots, height unknown. That was very similar to the data that was shown last night. The chances were that this was another Iraqi strike against Iranian targets around Lavan Island. How they organised these things was a mystery to

Allenby. Lavan Island was over three hundred miles from Iraq and there was no way that the Iraqi air planners could know what tankers were on the move; even *Winchester* at forty miles from the island didn't know. Probably they sent out a strike aircraft entirely on speculation, and if the Iraqi aircrew saw no target they would simply return to base and try again another night. To one who was used to the allied way of doing business, it seemed very hit-or-miss, and terribly open to attacking the wrong targets. That, of course, was Allenby's chief concern. *Winchester* and the MCMV force were the nearest surface units to Lavan Island, and the most likely to suffer from Iraqi targeting errors.

Not for the first time Allenby cursed the lack of a mapping facility on the tactical displays. It was all very well for Gavin Beresford to state that the track was in Kuwait's airspace – he had a paper air navigation chart to hand – but that was far too cumbersome for the tactical displays. The problem was that the ship was constantly moving, and the range scale needed to be expanded and contracted, so any attempt to mark the contours of the land using a chinagraph pencil was doomed to frustration and failure. Allenby's assistant did try his best, but he was fighting a losing battle. Allenby could guess that one day in the future a map would be projected onto the tactical display, and it would conform to the ships movements and the operator's adjustments, but not yet. For now, he could only have the vaguest idea of where track four-two-zero-one was in relation to the coastline, to international boundaries and to the airlanes; he had to rely on the fighter controller for anything more definite.

'AAWO, FC. Track four-two-zero-one is approaching Kuwait's southern border. It looks to me like it's tracking to the west of the airlane. That could be an alligator datum discrepancy between *Magic* and us, so I'll watch it carefully.'

Link datum errors; the bane of an AAWO's life. Even now that most allied warships had some sort of SATNAV, they rarely agreed; and that was reflected in the positions of their reported targets. When that was combined with all the other possible errors that the data link was prone to, it was little wonder that the position of an air contact nearly three-hundred miles away should be the matter of some speculation. Still, *Winchester's* 1022 long range radar would pick it up soon, and then they'd know for certain.

'APS, have you heard *Magic* reporting that track?'

'No, sir, nothing.'

Allenby lowered his boom microphone and pressed his transmit switch.

'*Magic*, this is *Winchester*, over.'

Nothing, only the usual crackling of static on the circuit.

'*Magic, Magic*, this is *Winchester, Winchester*, over.'

'*Winchester* this is *Magic*, go.'

The AWACS was circling over Saudi Arabia some two-hundred-and-fifty miles away from *Winchester*, so it was understandable that the reply was faint, but at least Allenby could hear him, just about, and it was an unmistakably American accent.

'*Magic* this is *Winchester*. Do you have an identity on alligator track four-two-zero-one?'

'*Winchester* this is *Magic*. Track four-two-zero-one pending, out.'

Well, that was unhelpful, but hardly surprising. However, the absence of information told Allenby that it was probably exactly what he thought, an Iraqi Badger on a strike mission. He considered his options for the space of two heartbeats.

'Officer-of-the-Watch, call the captain and tell him that we have a probable Iraqi Badger, two-hundred-and-fifty miles away, south of the Kuwait border. Could he come to the ops room?'

'Officer-of-the-Watch, roger.'

One minute. That was all it took for the captain's steps on the ops room ladder.

'What have you got, Ops?' he asked as he leaned over the air tactical display.

Silkworm

Allenby pointed to the link track.

'The data link is showing that he's out of the airlane, but that could be a datum error. Otherwise it looks very much like last night. Funny that they should come out on two consecutive nights, just when the Americans have been hammering the Iranian navy. Perhaps they're trying to tighten the screw.'

Mayhew was a specialist AAWO, like Allenby, and he could interpret an air picture as well as any other man.

'Is this possible error showing up on any other contacts?'

'We don't hold any common contacts, sir. It's very quiet, probably because of the American strikes over the past two days. The only real point of reference is *USS Havelock's* track that *Magic's* transmitting. We don't hold it on radar of course, but it's in about the normal position for Golf Whiskey.'

'Then all the indications are that the data link track is as accurate as normal. How far off the airlane is the Badger?'

'Forty miles, more-or-less, sir. About the distance as there is between us and any possible Iranian targets. On that basis I'd like to call an air threat warning red and bring the ship to action stations.'

Mayhew stared at the tactical display. That link track could be something entirely different, not an Iraqi Badger at all, and even if it was what they suspected, it could just be a re-run of last night, and not affect *Winchester* and the MCMVs at all. Yet he couldn't take the risk. The incident with *USS Stark* was too fresh in everyone's mind.

'Very well Ops, make it so, and tell the Minnows.'

Allenby swung his boom microphone down again.

'Officer-of-the Watch, pipe hands to action stations, state one condition zulu. Threat warning air, red. Sound six short blasts'

He could hear Beresford telling the MCMVs. *Hero* and *Aconite* would be sounding their sirens now and the minehunters would be flashing up their engines and separating themselves from their support ships as they worked furiously to weigh anchor. People in the ops room were sliding into the vacant seats, pulling on headsets and urgently getting to grips with the situation. He was aware that Buckley was putting on his headset and looking at the GOP.

'APS, I want a local track on alligator track four-two-zero-one as soon as possible. It should be in range of 1022 at any moment.'

'APS, roger.'

The captain's steward pushed through the throng bringing the captain's lifejacket that in his hurry he'd left in his cabin. Mayhew strapped it on, pulled on his anti-flash gloves and settled his white cotton hood around his shoulders.

'Captain on open line. Officer-of-the-Watch, let me know how the Minnows are doing.'

'They've sounded their sirens, sir, and I can see that they've flashed up their engines, but they're still all rafted up.'

'Duty Staff, PWO. Take over the MCMV co-ordination circuit from the FC. Give them a sitrep.'

'Duty Staff. Already on it.'

Allenby glanced across the ops room. That was Harling giving Buckley an order. Well, if he still resented his move from the PWO's seat, he wasn't letting it show.

'FC, AAWO. Focus on track four-two-zero-one. As soon as we have radar contact I want to know exactly where it is in relation to the airlane.'

Silence. It was as though the whole operations room was holding its breath. After the three days that they'd had there was not the slightest chance that they were underestimating this potential threat.

'AAWO, APS. Contact. Local track three-four-one-two bearing two-seven-two, one-eight-zero miles. Correlates alligator track four-two-zero-one.'

'AAWO, FC. That's exactly forty miles west of Dhahran. *Magic* was spot-on. The track's turning east now.'

Silkworm

Allenby leaned across to talk to Mayhew offline.

'I've got a bad feeling about this, sir. He thinks he's overhead Dhahran now, so when he turns on his Puffball radar he's going to see seven targets about where he expects to see Iranian tankers. I'm going to try to get *Magic* to call him off.'

'Do so, Ops.'

'*Magic, Magic*, this is *Winchester*, over.'

No response. Allenby wasn't surprised, it was long range for a UHF call and if the AWACS was turning *Winchester* could be in one of its radio antenna sectors that wasn't as good as the others.

'*Magic, Magic*, this is *Winchester, Winchester*. If you're reading this, I'm concerned that alligator track four-two-zero-one is an Iraqi strike aircraft having navigational difficulties and might misidentify his target.'

'Captain, Officer-of-the-Watch. The ship's at action stations, state one, condition zulu.'

'Thank you. Anti-flash on, hoods up and steel helmets on the bridge and upper deck. Make a short pipe telling the ship's company what's happening.'

'No response from *Magic*, sir. He could be out of range or he could have a policy of not discussing the Iraqi raids over the radio. I'll keep trying.'

'Drop it, AAWO. let's concentrate on what we can control now.'

Mayhew stood and looked at the air tactical display, trying to think like the Iraqi mission commander in that Badger – if that's what it was. Assuming he thought he was overhead Dhahran when he turned, he'd radiate his Puffball radar in surveillance mode at any moment now. He'd be looking for targets eighty miles on his nose, but would find none, because no tankers ever ploughed that patch of sea, it was too close to the Shah Allum shoal. Ten degrees to the right, however, he'd see a very tempting set of contacts; *Winchester* and her six charges. Would that be enough evidence for him to fire his Silkworms? He had to admit that everything he'd learned about the Iraqi way of doing business suggested that they'd accept those targets gladly, assuming that they were only a few miles out in their navigation, rather than forty miles out.

'AAWO, FC. The target's feet wet to the north of Bahrain.'

'Captain, AAWO. Target range ninety miles. I'd like to deploy chaff charlie to give him an alternative target right on his nose.'

'Carry on AAWO.'

'PWO, AAWO. Chaff charlie Juliet-band bearing three-four-zero.'

Allenby barely noticed the sound of the gun as it fired three rounds of chaff away to the north. The Puffball radar operated in J-band, unlike the Boghammer radars that used I-band, and it consequently needed a different length of aluminium foil to create a good radar return.

'Captain, Soft Kill. I've spoken to Golf Whiskey on Navy Red. All I can get is a *roger*.'

Mayhew nodded. Even if *Magic* or Golf Whiskey could call the Iraqi, it was unlikely that they would be in time. He almost jumped as the EWD blew his whistle.

'Puffball, two-seven-eight, Puffball!'

'Blind, AAWO. Cover track three-four-one-two with Birds. EWD, take track three-four-one-two with hooter.'

It was all happening fast now. *Winchester's* two fire control radars slewed beneath their fibreglass domes and went into a spiral search pattern on the radar bearing. Petty Officer Dickens had already set up the jammer and had only to press the button for it to start transmitting on the Puffball radar's frequency, seeking to swamp it with its powerful signals.

'AAWO, Blind. Covering track three-four-one-two with Birds. Range fifty miles.'

'Blind, AAWO. Hold fire track three-four-one-two.'

Allenby looked at the tactical display. They'd done everything they could until the Badger came within Seadart

Silkworm

range. He'd ordered *hold fire* so that he could control the engagement, if there was to be one. Allenby knew only too well the consequences of shooting down the aircraft of a nation that was at least nominally friendly to Britain, and he'd do it only as a last resort, in defence of the MCMVs and *Winchester*.

'AAWO, EWD. Ready to shift hooter to the Vampires.'

That was textbook stuff. Jam the surveillance radar until the missile was in the air then switch to the missiles. Silkworms were suspected of having a home-on-jam capability, so it was important to cease jamming while they still had some distance to run. That would force them to carry out a fresh search by which time there would be chaff blooms all over the place, and in any case the missile might be unable to re-acquire before it sped past its intended targets.

'AAWO, roger.'

'AAWO, Blind. Birds affirm track three-four-one-two.'

'AAWO, roger. Hold fire track three-four-one-two.

The Badger was within range and *Winchester's* Seadart missiles just waited the final order to streak away at Mach-two to pluck the strike aircraft out of the sky.

'Soft-Kill, deploy three-inch chaff. Phalanx to auto. FC, tell the Minnows to deploy chaff.'

Kesteven stretched up and fired a pattern of chaff rockets that sped away into the night with a short *whoosh* that could be heard in the ops room.

The Vulcan Phalanx operator made his auto switch.

'Phalanx in auto.'

Now, anything that met the weapon's engagement criteria would be subject to an aimed stream of depleted uranium shells from the six-barrelled gatling gun at the astonishing rate of three-thousand-six-hundred rounds per minute. The engagement criteria had been set up with the Silkworm particularly in mind.

'AAWO, Captain. I won't fire at the Badger, wait for the missiles.'

'AAWO roger. Holding fire track three-four-one-two.'

The captain was right, Allenby thought. The Badger's Silkworm engagement range and *Winchester's* Seadart engagement range were about the same, thirty-odd miles, so shooting down the Badger was hardly likely to stop him firing. It would be mere revenge, an empty gesture. Better to save that first Seadart salvo for the Silkworms. Still, it was a pity to miss this sitting target, such a professional opportunity might never come again in Allenby's career.

What would the Badger be seeing? That neat little group of seven targets – Iranian tankers supposedly – would have doubled or trebled by now, with all the chaff that had been deployed, that is if he could see anything through *Winchester's* jamming. His missile warning receiver would be going berserk too, with the fire control radar's J-band locked on, and that would certainly concentrate his mind. The mission commander must be wondering what he'd stumbled into at this point, he'd never have seen anything like this coming from an Iranian tanker convoy. What if it was an American force? He'd be in a decision-loop: fire and risk another *Stark* incident or withdraw and possibly miss an important Iranian convoy. His career and possibly his life depended on making the right choice. Well, he'd better decide soon because everything was ready now, just waiting.

'AAWO, Blind. Target bearing drawing right.'

'AAWO, EWD, Puffball ceased bearing two-eight-five. Strangling hooter.'

Allenby was tempted to ask the EWD to confirm that he hadn't detected a Silkworm homer, but that was entirely unnecessary. Petty Officer Dickens' whistle would have told him if that was the case, and there was no point in jamming a radar that had been switched off; it was impossible, in fact. Those two reports indicated that the Badger was turning away, aborting his mission and returning home.

'Captain, AAWO. I'd like to keep the 909s on him until he's out of range.'

'Approved, AAWO. Cover him all the way back to the

coast if you can. It should encourage him to get a move on. I really don't want to share my personal space with him any longer.'

***

You had to hand it to the Doc, nothing at all could keep him from gathering his data. He'd heard threat warning yellow called and had rushed to the ops room – scattering damage control parties and flinging open watertight doors on his way – to start taking pulse rates before they subsided too much. Allenby was talking to the captain as the doctor was pulling down his anti-flash glove to get at his arm.

'That was a close one, Ops, but we can't blame the Iranians this time. God, I was so tempted to shoot that fellow out of the sky and worry about the consequences later.'

The doctor's lips moved as he counted the beats and read the second hand on his watch.

'Would you call that hostile intent, sir?'

'Yes, I would,' Mayhew replied firmly. 'Flying an attack profile and radiating on a target acquisition radar has to meet that criteria. The next stage, releasing a Silkworm is a hostile act, and there's nothing between the two but the flick of a switch. However, I was certain that he'd misidentified us and only hoped that he'd realise his error before his finger went to that switch.'

Allenby nodded.

'We've a pretty good defence against a Silkworm; Seadart has a good probability of kill and Phalanx an excellent one. We still could have jammed the missile and fired our chaff, and even the gun would have been worth trying. The lesson for me is that what we must fear is a rapid, co-ordinated, surprise attack with multiple different weapon systems. If the enemy insists on having such a slow, methodical buildup, they'll never succeed.'

'That is until the Seadart launcher loses power, the Phalanx jams and the gun has one of its hissy fits again. Never forget the power of the gremlins, Ops.'

Mayhew and Allenby both saw the surprise on the doctor's face as he pulled the captain's glove back up.

'What is it, Doc, will I live?'

'You might yet, sir. Your heart's pumping away – if I can describe anything that lazy as *pumping* – at fifty-five beats a second. Most people's hearts are going faster than that while they sleep. Might I ask a personal question?' he glanced at Allenby who was openly listening. 'Do you ever sweat?'

Mayhew laughed; it was an unusual sound in an ops room at action stations and two dozen heads turned towards him.

'Well that is a little personal isn't it Doc? But as you ask, no, I don't much.'

'Ah! I see.'

The doctor's eyes lit up with a private intelligence as he started on Allenby's wrist, but whatever was so enlightening he chose to keep to himself. Allenby submitted to having his wrist probed without demur. It was nothing compared to the day that a sick-berth attendant, exasperated at the lieutenant commander's repeated missing of appointments for an inoculation, stabbed a needle straight through his shirt while he was defending the ship from multiple missile attacks in an air defence exercise. Naval medicine was a law unto itself.

Whatever the doctor found from Allenby's heart rate was clearly not of interest. Mayhew shook his head and smiled as the doctor moved onto other victims.

'I shan't be sorry to hand over to *Stirling* tomorrow, sir, that's for sure. I hope they know what they're doing.'

'Yes. Let's hope. Now, as soon as that clown is over the Kuwait border we can revert to defence watches. If the Minnows want to stay underway, then let them. They'll be utterly spooked by now having been through two close calls with enemies that they never even saw. I wouldn't be surprised if they accuse us of making it up. I'll be on the bridge but I'll turn in once we go to defence watches. How are you getting on with the daily sitrep?'

'I'd hardly started when this all blew up, but I'll have it ready for when I go off watch at zero-six-hundred.'

'Try to make it as concise as possible; we can save the details for the report of proceedings.'

'We should send a signal to SNOME though, to pass on to the Americans. If they do have any pre-knowledge of those Badger raids they really should share it. Better still, there should be some deconfliction.'

Mayhew shook his head slowly.

'I have no greater insight than you do, Ops, but I'm sure that any co-ordination or co-operation between the Americans and Iraq is sensitive to them, and they won't share it with us. Imagine the PR mileage that Tehran could make if they had evidence of collusion between the Americans and the Iraqis. Iran is almost entirely Shia Muslim and Iraq is split between Shia and Sunni, but Saddam Husein's Ba'ath party is almost all Sunni and they keep the Shia Muslims in their place. That's a powder keg waiting to be lit, and we don't want to be waving naked flames around it. So if there is collusion, and I can't say one way or another, we'll never hear about it. Nevertheless, I take your point and the signal should be sent, if only to give the Americans food for thought. Best make up some notes for *Stirling* as well, can you do that?'

Of course Allenby could do that, he didn't know how to say *no*. It meant that while others were winding down from the night's intense experiences, he would be juggling his duties as defence watch AAWO with writing after-action reports, and still with the command open line in one ear and the air defence circuit in the other.

***

Chapter Seventeen

Friday, 0600
HMS Winchester, at Sea, Shah Allum Shoal
Operation Armilla Daily Sitrep: Handover Guardian Angel duties to Stirling, RAS(L) Brown Rover...

'I've got *Stirling's* captain on secure UHF, sir.'

The chief yeoman offered the handset to Mayhew and stood officiously to one side with his signal board at the ready.

'*Stirling* this is *Winchester*, Charlie Oscar. Good morning sir.'

Mayhew found it impossible to talk to Jock Stewart without bringing a hint of a Scottish accent into his voice. Jock hailed from Inverness, where English pronunciations had made no inroads on the native Scots brogue, and despite a quarter-of-a-century in the Royal Navy, he'd never lost his own accent. It was so strong that others tended to pick up on it, whether they wanted to or not. Jock was a four-ring captain, and the task group commander for the two destroyers, two frigates and two auxiliaries that had sailed from Portland back in March. Allenby had flown across to *Stirling* before dawn, and would be briefing Jock's team as the two spoke.

'And a good morning to you too, David. I've had a quick chat with your ops officer, you seem to have had an exciting time of it.'

'That's one way of putting it. I hope it came over in the notes that he'll leave with you, but notwithstanding the latest attack looks like a straightforward navigation error by an Iraqi pilot, it does appear that the Iranians are deliberately provoking us. Did you have any trouble getting through the Straits, sir?'

'Very little. We saw no sign of Boghammers, but I now know that they'd all moved over to Lavan Island to amuse you. *Sabalan* didn't make an appearance either. I haven't heard whether the Americans dealt with her along with the others, but as far as I can tell they confined their attacks to the northern Gulf. We detected surveillance radars from Kuhestak, Larak and Abu Musa but nothing more. Of course, we didn't have any tankers with us so we perhaps weren't attractive enough as a target. I hope you have as quiet an outbound passage tonight, but judging by your past experience, I doubt it. *Brown Rover* is expecting you at ten-hundred, you know the rendezvous position.'

'Yes, I wouldn't want to start outbound without full tanks, sir. How's your Olympus?'

'Knackered, the MEO tells me. Not even usable in an emergency. The Fleet Maintenance Unit will fly out a new one and we'll fit it at Mina Raysut, but they don't seem to be in any hurry. If this tasking with the MCMVs continues, I won't be able to make a run through the Straits until you come back to relieve me. After what you told me about that Iraqi Badger and the Boghammers, I can't leave it to *Bellona* or *Biter* – not to any ship without a gun – and the area to be covered is too great for their Seawolfs. Still, I can do twenty-four knots if needed, so I'm not completely immobile. Look, you've got over an hour before you have to be away, can you come over for a chat? I can send my Lynx.'

There was silence as Mayhew considered Jock's proposal. Perhaps Allenby hadn't expressed quite how dangerous it was here at the Shah Allum shoal; he always had a tendency to understatement. Mayhew didn't feel comfortable leaving his ship, and he didn't sense that Jock was going to insist.

'I'd rather not, if you don't mind, sir. My Lynx is just outside territorial waters off Lavan Island and he's getting an occasional whiff of I-band radars that might or might not be from the Boghammers, and there's still a lot of air traffic up towards Kuwait. I think my place is here while my ops officer is out of the ship.'

'Fully understood, old chap. Well, I'm going to join your ops officer's briefing and I'll send him back as soon as we've finished grilling him. Good luck for the outbound.'

'And good luck to you too, sir.'

***

Winchester made a wide, sweeping turn, passing close to where *Hero* lay at anchor. The survey ship gave a single hoot of its siren, the destroyer replied, and then the Belgian *Aconite* followed with her own siren. Their association had been only thirty-six hours long, but so much had happened in that time that the two support ships seemed like old friends. He'd spoken to the British MCM commander early that morning, and he thought they'd be at the Shah Allum shoal for about another week, before they could confidently declare it free of mines. There was no question of leaving them unprotected, and as neither the Dutch nor the Belgians had a suitable destroyer or frigate available, it appeared that *Stirling* would be there to the bitter end.

'The Alouette is launching from *Stirling's* deck, sir.'

'Very well, Officer-of-the-Watch, are we on a flying course?'

'Yes, sir. Zero-nine-zero at twelve knots.'

Mayhew made the *permission to fly* switch and picked up his binoculars to watch the Belgian helicopter fly the short mile that lay between the two destroyers. The Alouette was quite different to a Lynx, laughably so, if one was feeling ungenerous. It was good for personnel transfers, for picking up the mail and for visual reconnaissance for mines, but little else. It was perfect, however, to free-up the more capable Lynx from those mundane tasks so that it could focus on what it did best, an armed surface search.

The Alouette didn't have a harpoon, but it could operate its rotors with reverse thrust, and it held itself on *Winchester's* flight deck just long enough for Allenby to jump out and be escorted by the flight deck crew to the safety of the hangar. The flight deck officer took a last look to make sure the Alouette was clear underneath, he raised and lowered his hands in an emphatic upwards motion, and the helicopter was gone, skimming low over the sea towards *Aconite*.

Silkworm

'Welcome back, Ops. How was *Stirling's* team?'

Allenby had come straight to the bridge to report to Mayhew.

'In fine form, sir, and devastated at missing all the action that we've had. Captain Stewart sent this for you,' he held out a bottle of Laphroaig whisky. 'He hopes it will bring back painful memories.'

Mayhew laughed. When they'd last been together in Gibraltar on their way to the Gulf, he and Jock and Gareth Johnson from *Bellona* had done serious damage to a bottle of eighteen-year-old Laphroaig in the Bristol Hotel while they put the world to rights. The pain wasn't only from the hangover but also from the bill that Mayhew had so casually picked up. The hotel had sold them the whisky by the glass rather than by the bottle, and he'd only discovered that the next morning when he found the credit card receipt crumpled in his pocket. He'd rushed off a quick letter to his wife to head off a self-righteous outburst when the monthly statement arrived at his home. In fact all three would have preferred the hurly-burly and the cheap beer in the Main Street bars, but that was no place for commanding officers who might – probably would – have to stand in judgement on the sailors who'd over-corrected after a spell at sea. He looked at the bottle again. Ten-year-old Laphroaig, not the eighteen-year-old good stuff; typical of Jock.

'Well, let's hope they have a quieter time on the Shah Allum shoal than we did.'

He looked appraisingly at Allenby. By rights the man should be on his knees with fatigue by now, but he looked fresh and ready for duty. Nevertheless, Mayhew knew how the effects of stress and lack of sleep could lay hidden until they suddenly appeared with dramatic effect. He'd known officers and sailors fall asleep where they stood or sat, when only moments before they'd appeared fully alert. It was no good making it a disciplinary affair, it was a failing of management and leadership, and it was invariably a man's superior officer who was really to blame when it happened.

He was Allenby's immediate superior in operational matters, and he wasn't going to let this get to the falling asleep on duty stage.

'You're off-watch now, aren't you?'

'Yes, sir, until twelve.'

'Then get some breakfast and get your head down. I don't want to see you before noon unless we have to go to action stations again,' Mayhew looked at his watch, 'that gives you a clear four hours.'

'Don't worry, sir, that's been my aim since the Alouette lifted from *Stirling's* deck. In fact they gave me a bacon roll and then pressed another on me before I left, so I'm all fixed for breakfast. By the way, I heard a good dit from the MCM commander. The Droggies have been told that *Hero* will stay in the Gulf indefinitely, and the crew can't expect reliefs any time soon. They've started calling the destroyers and frigates *bran flakes*, because we're only passing through.'

Mayhew smiled at that. It didn't take the average sailor long to find humour in any situation, even when their anticipated return home was indefinitely delayed.

'Well, have a good sleep, Ops, and we'll keep the enemy at bay for a few hours.'

***

Allenby slept through the fast passage to the rendezvous with *Brown Rover*. He snored through the hasty replenishment and he didn't wake until eleven-thirty when a bosun's mate shook him by the shoulder after he didn't respond to a loud *wakey-wakey, sir!* He had a quick shower, changed into clean white overalls and grabbed a sandwich from the wardroom on his way to the ops room.

'Ah, it's *Winchester's* own Sleeping Beauty. Glad you could honour us with your presence.'

Kesteven was older than Allenby, and he'd been promoted to lieutenant commander two years earlier. It was only because he'd been sent to the AAWO's course at *HMS Dryad* four months after Allenby that he'd arrived in *Winchester* later and had therefore taken the junior of the two

AAWO posts. It could have been a delicate matter, but both knew that they had to make the best of it. Kesteven's only sign of rebellion was that he reserved the right to speak to Allenby as an equal, and he was doing so now.

'My word, that was a good kip. I feel as though I've been asleep for days. Now what's afoot?'

'All quiet, I'm pleased to say. We're making twelve knots on two Tynes to rendezvous with the next outbound convoy off Dubai. *Magic's* occasionally readable on the Gulf AAW circuit and so is *Havelock*, and we can raise him on the satellite channel if we need to. We have a good data link picture that's only showing friendly units at the moment. You'll need to read the signals because in the big wide world there's plenty happening. There's an Earnest Will convoy gathering off Fujairah, the first since the current brawl. Speaking of which, MOD has pushed out a summary of what they think the Americans achieved against the Iranian navy and their oil platforms. It looks like they've sunk or disabled two of the Alvand class frigates and a number of Boghammers and landing craft, including the one that they suspect laid the mines. Two or three oil platforms are destroyed. It's hard to decide whether that's good news for us or bad news. There are less Iranian ships and boats to worry about but on the other hand those that are left will probably be looking for revenge, and they're not good at discriminating between Americans and Brits.'

Allenby plucked the headset from Kesteven's head and nudged him out of the AAWO's seat.

'Any word of *Sabalan*?'

'No, and I found that strange because they seem to have accounted for the others, and they're mentioned by name in the signal. I guess Captain Nasty chose discretion as the better part of valour and retreated to Bandar Abbas. We may yet meet again.'

'How about *USS Carter*?'

After *Winchester's* traumatic day and night on the Shah Allum shoal, Allenby felt a kinship for the damaged frigate.

'As far as I can tell she's alongside in Jebel Ali, probably being assessed as to whether it's worth taking her home for a rebuild. It sounds like a pretty heroic bit of damage control, her back was broken by the mine and she's leaking like a sieve. She's quite a new ship too. Anyway, we won't see her again unless she's under tow or strapped onto the deck of a heavy lift ship. I'll be off then, don't let any Silkworms inboard while I'm asleep, no matter how polite they are when they come calling.'

Allenby sat quietly for ten minutes, listening to the chatter on the AAW circuit. It was mostly American of course, as they had the greatest forces in the region. He could tell a lot from quietly listening and taking it all in. The stressed voices of the last few days had calmed down, and now it was just the routine cross-telling of air contacts, all of which were friendly or neutral. He glanced across at the PWO's seat. Harling looked back and gave him a cheerful thumbs-up. He should have asked Kesteven how he'd got on with Buckley, but as Kesteven didn't volunteer anything, perhaps that drama was over. He'd still be watching Buckley carefully, for by the end of this deployment he'd like to be in the position of giving him a decent report. If not, then they'd have to consider trying to move him out of the ship. That was a drastic step that he really would rather not take, and there was no certainty that the appointer would play ball. Then it could get messy.

***

Ben Saxby scanned the horizon through his binoculars. It was still very quiet although he could see at least one tanker to the east, heading up the Gulf, and there were two dhows chugging away with their masts and long lateen yards innocent of even a scrap of sail, going about whatever their business was. The dhows were an enigma in this wealthy, bustling part of the world, but Saxby liked to see them. They looked old as the hills, but many of them were actually very new. On the western side of the Gulf there were half-a-dozen of the stout wooden craft being built in every little creek that hadn't already been concreted over for a swanky new hotel. They scuttled backwards and forwards across the Gulf, and coasted from city to city, but for what purpose nobody could tell him. Perhaps, even in the late twentieth century, the ancient trade routes still carried the region's incidental goods from place-to-place. He'd seen the vast and colourful spice market in Muscat, and perhaps that was what they were doing, but he'd also seen a dhow with a shiny new Mercedes precariously balanced on its deck, apparently heading for the Iranian shore, in defiance of all the embargoes.

Winchester was skirting to the north of the vast oilfields that filled the area between Qatar and the UAE. A glance at the radar showed the platforms scattered across the sea to the south of the destroyer's track like a rash. The war between Iran and Iraq made it too dangerous to venture into the northern Gulf without a stronger escort than the Royal Navy could provide, and most of the tankers and gas carriers never went further than Qatar and Bahrain. It wasn't mere fear that prevented them sailing north, but the hard commercial reality of insurance rates. It was already expensive to insure a tanker to pass unaccompanied through the Straits of Hormuz, and that cost quadrupled if the destination lay beyond Bahrain. Saxby knew all this, and he also knew that the anchorages at Fujairah and Khor Fakkan were jammed with ships waiting for the Gulf to settle down after the American attacks on the Iranian navy. It wouldn't be long, for the cost of insurance had to be balanced against the cost of having ships lying idle with their crews needing to be paid. There were profits going begging too, after the fabulous rise in the price of crude oil that was caused by the refineries in Europe and the Far East being starved of shipments.

Lunch was over and the galley must have been secured because there was a group of cooks - *chefs* as they were universally known – out on the port bridge wing, taking turns to don a steel helmet and pose for a photograph at the

GPMG. That would give them something to talk about when they went home on leave. Saxby didn't mind that at all because he could see that the lookouts were still doing their jobs, scanning the sea for any sign of... well, anything. There was a mine lookout in the bows with the fo'c'sle officer's headset on a long lead, and he was being relieved every twenty minutes. On a clear day like this, and with the ship doing only twelve knots to make its rendezvous, it was entirely feasible to see a floating mine that had broken free from its mooring, and for the office-of-the-watch to react in time to avoid it. In fact, that was part of the calculation that determined the ship's speed, a compromise between the mining risk and the need to be off Dubai by eighteen hundred. That also was why Saxby hadn't left his post at the front of the bridge, not even for the time it would take to duck behind the blackout curtain and check the chart and the radar. He was relying entirely on his second officer-of-the-watch to do that while he stood at instant readiness to respond to a shout from any of the lookouts. He picked up his microphone without taking his eyes from the sea ahead.

'PWO, Officer-of-the-Watch.'

'PWO.'

'How's the mine watch at the command display doing?'

Buckley glanced to his left where an able seaman was sitting in the captain's ops room chair staring at the high resolution radar display. In this weather – high pressure, no wind and a flat-calm sea – the I-band navigation radar had a good chance of detecting a floating mine before it came in sight from the bridge. The problem was that it was prone to false alarms, even a large turtle coming up for air could look like a firm contact. Saxby remembered being on fishery patrol in the north sea off the coast of Scotland in conditions like this – much colder though, of course – and every seal that surfaced for a breath and every buoy that marked a lobster pot looked like a fishing boat on the radar screen.

'He's fine, he hasn't taken his eyes off the plot. The APS

is relieving him every twenty minutes. I'll send him to the HC's console if the captain comes down.'

'Oh, I've spoken to the captain already. He'd rather the mine watch stayed there unless we go to action stations.'

'Roger, Officer-of-the-Watch, got it.'

Saxby took another all-round scan. The visibility wasn't great, perhaps six miles. The two dhows had disappeared to the north and the tanker had passed and likewise merged into the murk astern. *Winchester* was alone in her bubble of six miles radius. The second officer-of-the-watch straightened from the chart where he'd been fixing the ship's position.

'The Decca fix shows us two cables to starboard of track and if we keep up this speed our ETA at the rendezvous is seventeen-twenty-four.'

'You've checked that you're on the right chain?'

'Yes, double checked.'

Saxby nodded. He'd normally confirm that himself. He knew from bitter experience that it was easy to be reading the wrong Decca chain and yet still achieve a plausible fix, but one that could be ten or twenty miles out. *Winchester* had a Magnavox satellite navigation system that was due for replacement by the new GPS system when the ship returned to Portsmouth. The Magnavox relied upon the Transit constellation, which had a limited number of satellites and offered fixes at long intervals. It could only be relied upon for ocean passages and in the Gulf it was only used to validate the Decca or visual fixes. Out here, with nothing in sight, he was really relying upon the Decca and he itched to check it himself. Still, his second officer-of-the-watch was reliable, and he'd have to take it on trust. In any case, the navigator came up at least once an hour during the day and when he did he always checked the ship's position.

Saxby was looking forward to another passage through the Straits. This one would be different because it would be mostly at night, and with the outbound lane of the traffic separation scheme being to the south of the inbound lane, they'd be further away from the Iranian coast. Whether that would deter the Boghammers, the frigates and the Silkworm missiles was yet to be seen. He'd heard about the American Earnest Will convoy gathering off Fujairah. The Americans didn't advertise the timings for their convoys, but there was a good chance that they'd be passing through the separation scheme at the same time as *Winchester's* convoy was outbound. If they both kept to the centre of their respective lanes they'd be five miles apart and travelling in opposite directions. The US Navy took those convoys very seriously indeed, and as well as the close escort of at least three frigates, they usually moved one of their big cruisers up to provide air defence. It would be busy in the Straits tomorrow morning.

There was a seaman waiting to speak to him.

'I'm the next fo'c'sle mine lookout, sir.'

'Excellent. You know what you're looking for?'

The seaman would have rolled his eyes, but he didn't want any trouble. Surely his title of *mine lookout* suggested what he was looking for.

Saxby smiled, he could have put that better. But still he briefed the lookout before he let him depart to take over. A few minutes passed before the speaker squawked.

'Bridge, fo'c'sle. Mine lookout relieved sir. Nothing in sight.'

The mine lookout's report came over the speaker rather than into Saxby's headset, so that it could be heard by everyone on the bridge. He picked up the microphone to reply and stepped forward so that he had a view of the fo'c'sle from the bridge window. He could see the lookout peering through his binoculars and sweeping them either side of the ship's head. Good, he had other lookouts to keep a watch for ships and aircraft, and he needed the mine lookout to focus no more than a mile ahead and no more than thirty degrees either side.

'Roger, keep a good lookout.'

That was all he could do. It was interesting to note that

the ship's defence against what had proved to be Iran's most potent maritime weapon was in the hands of two able seamen, each of whom was even younger than Saxby himself. But that was the way of the navy and always had been. The officers and senior rates could organise and plan, they could publish watch bills and instructions, but in the end it was a nineteen-year-old who had to stand that watch and carry out those instructions. A Type 42 destroyer cost thirty million pounds to build and carried the latest in sophisticated naval weaponry that could blast an enemy aircraft from the sky at forty miles. It housed and fed two-hundred-and-fifty souls who had been trained at vast expense to the very peak of efficiency. Did his family and friends at home have even the slightest idea of the responsibility that he carried so lightly on his shoulders? His schoolmates who worked in the supermarket or the bank could be told, but they would never understand.

***

Chapter Eighteen

Friday, 1800
HMS Winchester, at Sea, Southern Arabian Gulf
Operation Armilla Daily Sitrep: RV Dubai Anchorage, Bellona, World Antigua, Gas Enterprise, Highlander, Eastern Heritage…

Mayhew had rarely left his ship while it was at sea, and the few occasions that he had he'd left the first lieutenant in command. Today he had a powerful reason for wanting to go over to *World Antigua* and as there was no time for separate trips for him and the first lieutenant, they were both leaving the ship at the same time. That created a slight difficulty, for the succession of sea command was in strict order of seniority among the remaining officers of the executive branch. Kesteven was senior to Allenby so although Allenby was the head of the warfare officers it was Kesteven who commanded in the absence of the captain and first lieutenant, not Allenby. Mayhew was being too sensitive about it, he knew, and when he explained the situation Allenby had the look of a man who had expected nothing else.

The convoy rendezvous was outside UAE territorial waters, which allowed the Lynx to be used for the transfers. It was a short hop from *Winchester* to the lead tanker and it gave Mayhew little time to wonder at the spectacle of these four massive ships being escorted by the diminutive escorts. It had been ever thus, and the great Atlantic convoys that had kept Britain fed and maintained its fighting capability during the dark days before America joined the Second World War had been guarded by even smaller corvettes and frigates.

Mayhew kept his head well down and his knees bent as he moved swiftly out of the lethal arc of the spinning rotor blades, followed by his first lieutenant and the Javelin team. They gathered in a cluster on *World Antigua's* deck to watch the Lynx lift away and head back to *Winchester* to take the other Javelin units to *Highlander* and *Eastern Heritage*. It was almost the old team for this outbound convoy, except for *British Solace* which needed some repairs before taking on her cargo, and would wait for the next outbound convoy, and *Brown Rover* was staying in the Gulf to support *Stirling* and the MCMVs. The new boy was a liquid petroleum gas carrier named *Gas Enterprise*, a smart new ship on its maiden voyage and it looked out of place among the weather-worn oil tankers.

It was a long walk from the helicopter landing pad to the after end of the ship, and the bridge was so far above the deck that Mayhew and the first lieutenant had to take a lift. They emerged on the bridge deck to be greeted by Captain McKenzie.

'It's good to meet you, Captain Mayhew, and to have this opportunity to thank you for bringing us through safely on Tuesday.'

Mayhew decided this wasn't the time to explain the difference between a commander by rank and a captain by courtesy, and in any case he suspected that McKenzie knew already but was just being polite in his own way. In the merchant navy anyone who commanded a ship had both the rank and the title of captain, but in the Royal Navy it was only ships larger than destroyers or the lead ships of squadrons that were commanded by real four-ring captains.

'Well, it had its moments as I'm sure you noticed. But I have to thank you also for keeping the convoy in line. Not everyone does that you know.'

'Indeed, I can imagine.'

McKenzie was much older than Mayhew, he could have been at sea over twice as long, and would have a wealth of experience. Probably he'd been convoyed through the Straits more often than Mayhew had done the convoying. He looked solid and dependable.

'You know Mark Pearson already.'

'I do indeed, welcome back. I expect you remember where to set up your radio and where your marines should be.'

'I'll leave them to it,' Mayhew said. 'I regret that I only have half an hour before my helicopter will be back for me but I want to take this opportunity to brief you on what I think is happening. You've been watching the news, I expect.'

'Certainly, the Americans seem to have annihilated the Iranian navy in an afternoon, as far as I can tell. That's good news, I assume. Have you heard anything about that damned *Sabalan*?'

'Not directly. They have only one frigate left and it could well be *Sabalan*, the same one that attacked the Panamanian ship on the way inbound, but *Sabalan* could be at the bottom of the Gulf for all that I know. Their Boghammer fleet in the northern Gulf suffered too but whether that means they'll withdraw some from the Straits, well, you're guess is as good as mine. Is it good news for us? I'm cautious though for two reasons. First because, as you'll have noticed, that inbound transit was a lot more difficult than we've been used to…'

McKenzie nodded in agreement.

'…and since then we've had to ward off a fairly determined attack by a group of Boghammers that we think were the same ones that tried their luck in the Straits. That was at the Shah Allum shoal.'

'Ah yes, that's where the American frigate hit a mine. I'm surprised he was so close, I wouldn't take my ship within ten miles of that patch.'

'Yes, and it's being cleared by our minehunters and some Belgian and Dutch ones. I was watching over them when the attack happened. Taken along with all the alarms on Tuesday, it looks like the Iranians were prepared to raise the stakes even before *USS Cranston* hit the mine and certainly before the American attacks. I fear that it might be the start of a new way of doing business for them.'

McKenzie looked thoughtful. The shipping company that he worked for was hungry for intelligence, anything that could be used to adjust the way that they carried their cargoes through the Straits and that might mitigate the ruinous insurance bills.

'It was an Iranian mine, I gather.'

'Oh yes, the Americans recovered one before our minehunters arrived and it had a serial number in the same sequence as those that were taken from an Iranian minelayer last year. There's no doubt about it, and the Iranians don't seem to be even trying to deny it. They've never been rigorous about separating the Americans from the other western nations, and they often lump Britain in with any denunciations of America. We might be in for a rocky ride tonight.'

McKenzie stroked his beard and looked thoughtfully out of the bridge window.

'I see. How can I help with this?'

'By doing the same as you did on Tuesday. I need a steady hand at the head of the convoy to set an example for the others. It's really important that I can predict what you're going to do so that I can position *Winchester* and *Bellona* to protect you. A steady course and speed, if you will, and only divert from that if I ask you to do so. That would be only in a dire emergency of course.'

'Yes, of course, we can't have supertankers zig-zagging all over a traffic separation scheme. Lord alone knows what the insurance underwriters would say about that.'

'Indeed, and I wouldn't anticipate asking you to manoeuvre for a missile attack, you wouldn't be able to turn in time anyway. The only thing I can think of is a major attack by the Iranians causing us to turn around and go back the way we came.'

McKenzie frowned at that; it went against a lifetime of experience at sea. His ship could just about turn back upon itself in the space of the traffic separation scheme but only if there was no other shipping around.

'Then it'll be steady as she goes for me. If you do have to ask for anything radical I expect you'll come in the radio in person, Captain.'

'Yes, if I possibly can.'

'Well then, let's hope it's not necessary.'

A young third officer interrupted them.

'Excuse me, sir. Your helicopter's dropped off at *Eastern Heritage* and seems to be coming to us now.' Mayhew looked where the third officer was pointing. The Lynx was flying low and fast towards *World Antigua*, looking mean and powerful, as only a Lynx could. It would be on the deck in a few minutes.

'I see I must go now. Mark can brief you on everything else, Captain McKenzie, and let's hope for a quiet passage.'

'We might hope, Captain, but from what you've said and from what I've heard it's likely to be nothing of the sort. You and your warriors might be needed before we see the dawn tomorrow.'

***

'Eighteen-hundred on the dot, sir.'

The navigator looked impressed for he'd just seen *World Antigua's* propellor-wash break the surface and its head starting to swing ponderously towards the northeast as it started its run towards the Straits. Was McKenzie making a point about his ability to keep to a schedule? Probably so, Mayhew thought, and he was pleased to see it. That punctuality would set a good example to the other ships and impress on them that things had to be done precisely as ordered, whether that was station keeping, timing or taking cover for an attack. He didn't know what the next few hours would bring but it would all go much better if he could rely on the lead ship of the convoy to stick to the plan and the others to follow. He watched as the four ships formed their line. The second and third ships manoeuvred like old hands but the LPG carrier appeared hesitant, as though this was all new to her captain, as indeed it probably was. *Gas Enterprise* had come into the Gulf some months before under a UAE flag with no fear of being bothered by the Iranians. In Dubai she'd been fitted out for her maiden cargo voyage, and perhaps with convoying in mind, she'd been sold to a consortium with a substantial British interest. She flew the flag of Panama now, but was entitled to Royal Navy protection. Mayhew had misgivings about her and wished he'd had time to call on her captain, but as always, there was no time to be lost, and he had to make the best of the situation. *Bellona's* station was on the port beam of *Gas Enterprise* and he could see that Gareth Johnson was moving his frigate closer to the LPG carrier to encourage it into station. Mayhew didn't know the nationality of *Gas Enterprise's* captain – he certainly wasn't British – and he wondered what he made of all this. He'd probably no more than skimmed the sheaf of instructions that the MOD sent him and was playing it by ear.

'Any sign of hangers-on, Navs?'

'Nothing yet, sir.'

The officer-of-the-watch interrupted.

'Ops room reports a contact coming out of the Sharjah anchorage, sir, zero-nine-five at nine miles, heading three-zero-zero at thirteen knots. That's a good course to slot in behind the LPG carrier.'

Mayhew picked up his binoculars and trained them forty-five degrees on the starboard bow. The visibility had improved as the sun slid towards the western horizon, below the level of the ever-present murk, and the contact was just becoming visible against the darkening sky to the east. It was an oil tanker and there was something familiar about it.

'That looks like one of our Filipino friends, Navigator, what do you think?'

The navigator was already looking at the contact and had formed his own opinion.

'I'd say that's one of them, but I don't know which. I wonder where the other is.'

'Well, when he calls make him feel welcome without any obligations on our part. He should know the drill by now. I suppose we should feel flattered that he wants to join us again.'

Mayhew watched the scene unfold. This ability of ships at sea to manoeuvre so daintily, however huge and cumbersome they might look, never failed to impress him. The LPG carrier was almost in station now, and *Bellona* was moving away onto her beam. It was clear that the captain of the Filipino tanker knew what he was about, because his present course would bring him half a mile astern of *Gas Enterprise,* and if he judged the final turn just right he'd become part of the convoy as though he had every right to be there. The sun had almost set now. It would be completely dark in fifty minutes, and his convoy was already heading in the right direction. All was well with the world. And then he heard the command open line burst into life.

'EWD. Surveillance radar bearing three-five-zero. That looks like Abu Musa again.'

Mayhew picked up the open line headset in time to hear Allenby's calm voice.

'Captain, AAWO. That bearing cuts right through Abu Musa, it's the same Iranian surveillance radar that we found on Tuesday and it's sometimes associated with a Silkworm site. There's no indication that we've been identified yet but we're thirty-five miles from the island and getting closer. I'd like to go to action stations now, twenty minutes earlier than we'd planned, and keep the air threat warning at yellow until we get any other indications.'

Now that was the kind of report that Mayhew liked. There was nothing more to add and it ended with a firm and appropriate recommendation for action.

'Officer-of-the-Watch, pipe action stations, state one condition zulu. Make sure the first lieutenant knows. Javelin Commander, inform your fire units. As soon as action stations is reported you may relax anti-flash and steel helmets.'

The alarm blared and the bosun's mate's call was drowned out by the noise of steaming boots running on hard steel decks, watertight hatches slamming and heavy steel clips being closed. The ship's company had been expecting action stations in twenty minutes when *Winchester* entered the acknowledged Silkworm envelope, but it would do no harm to remind everyone that the enemy didn't always follow the same script. Mayhew waited until Saxby took over the bridge watch, saw that he had a grasp of things, then he walked calmly down the ladders to the ops room, pushing through the growing throng to reach his seat. He clamped the command open line headset over his ears then looked over the EWD's shoulder.

'There it is, sir, the same as when we passed through here on Tuesday. It's not much different to a ship's I-band navigational radar but it seems to be higher powered and by the way we're receiving it so loud and clear I would say it's mounted on some sort of tall mast.'

Mayhew had seen it before, but since the events of the last few days he had to look at everything with fresh eyes. What had been routine Iranian actions could now be the precursor to a deadly attack, and *Winchester* and the convoy were in international waters so in a way they were fair game. Ideally he'd launch the Lynx now and send it to look at Abu Musa. It was a small enough island that they'd probably see a mobile Silkworm launcher if there was one. Yet although Abu Musa's ownership was contested, it was garrisoned by Iran and had been *de facto* Iranian for fifteen years. However, the international community didn't recognise Iranian sovereignty, and therefore they had no jurisdiction over the surrounding waters and airspace. Yet this didn't seem like the time to be testing that point of law, and if the Lynx couldn't approach closer than twelve miles there was no sense in launching it.

'Watch it carefully, Petty Officer Dickens. Let me know if anything changes. AAWO, is there any sign of Iranian air activity?'

'Nothing inside the Gulf, sir. The data link was showing the P-3 on its normal patrol in the Gulf of Oman, but it's heading back to Bandar Abbas now. Judging by the number of American jets out there I'm fairly sure the carrier battle group has moved forward, probably to cover the Earnest Will convoy.'

That was the problem with the data link, it only showed the most basic of information about an air contact. Without the backup of voice reporting it was difficult to decide what sort of aircraft it was. If it was friendly it could always put its data link into receive-only mode and not advertise its position at all. The same went for ships, and any one of those contacts off Muscat could be a frigate or it could be an aircraft carrier. On balance he tended to agree with Allenby: something was brewing in the Gulf of Oman. It would be only prudent for the Americans to bring their carrier battle group closer in case of need, and it would be wise to avoid advertising its exact position. It would be helpful, however, if he knew the start time of the American convoy, then it wouldn't be a surprise when they met.

'The ship's at action stations, sir,' Saxby reported over open line. 'I've relaxed anti-flash and steel helmets.'

'Where's that Filipino tanker now?'

'Two miles to run to the rear of the convoy. It's *Sea Surge*, sir, her master has just called on VHF. The navigator is talking to him now.'

'What's the light like up there?'

'Pitch dark, sir.'

Then the convoy would be hidden by the darkness. That didn't help because he couldn't order them to douse their navigation lights, not in a traffic separations scheme, but it did mean that any Iranian surface units would have to come close to separately identify the ships. That was exactly how *Sabalan's* captain had achieved his infamy, by sailing close enough to shine his light on a tanker's stern to read its name and port of registry, then taking his pick of the targets.

'Anything new, EWD?'

'Nothing, sir, but that radar on Abu Musa is definitely more powerful than a normal navigation radar. It's steady though, it hasn't changed at all, so I don't believe it's in a targeting mode. He'll be able to say that we're a convoy though, and he'll have counted the ships.'

Yes, Mayhew thought, and they'll have seen from the disposition that there are five merchant ships and two escorts. The Iranians weren't stupid, they knew that a British convoy came inbound three days ago and that was exactly the right amount of time for a tanker to take on its cargo and be ready for an outbound run. They probably wouldn't have guessed the identity of the escort though, what with *Stirling* coming through the Straits yesterday, *Bellona* having a port visit to Dubai and *Winchester* at the Shah Allum shoal. All of those things would be known to them and each would serve to obfuscate the issue and make the Iranian decision-making more difficult.

'Navigator, what speed is *World Antigua* doing?'

'We're keeping pace at exactly thirteen knots, sir. We should be out of the traffic separation scheme at five-thirty in the morning, just before sunrise.'

Mayhew looked keenly around the ops room. It was good to see that everyone was taking the situation seriously, as was to be expected after their experiences of the last three days. The air trackers had their eyes glued to their consoles in case an inbound missile should suddenly pop up. The electronic warfare desk was alert too, for it was they who would be most likely to make the first contact. The missile and gun desk was more relaxed, they had little to do until someone else alerted them, but then they had to be ready to spring into action. The dim lighting, the multi-coloured glows from radar displays, indicator lights and switches, the quiet murmur of forty-odd voices and the gross overcrowding gave the ops room an ambience that couldn't be found anywhere else on earth. The general feeling was of a spring wound tight and ready to be released, to throw cogs and levers into action, to wreak havoc upon the designs of the enemy. Yes, it would be a long night and a testing one, but David Mayhew wouldn't wish to be anywhere else.

***

Chapter Nineteen

Friday, 2300
HMS Winchester, at Sea, Straits of Hormuz
Operation Armilla Daily Sitrep: Entered Silkworm Envelope, intercepted by IRIS Sabalan…

'AAWO, EWD. I-band surveillance radar bearing three-one-four. It's the same type as the Abu Musa radar.'

'Officer-of-the-Watch, AAWO. What's the bearing of Tunb Island now?

'Tunb Island bears three-one-three at twenty-six miles.'

Then this new radar was probably coming from Tunb. Allenby called the chart to his mind. If the islands had only radar intercept equipment providing a bearing but no range, then Abu Musa and Tunb would create an ideal baseline for triangulation. However, active radar needed no such help and a single site could provide an exact location of any targets within its range. A handover then, from one surveillance station to another as they tracked *Winchester's* convoy on its passage to the Straits.

'Do you still hold the radar on Abu Musa, EWD?'

'Very faintly, sir, bearing two-six-two. I expect we'll lose it in a few minutes.'

The AAWO's assistant pointed to two chinagraph marks where he'd plotted the positions of the islands, identified by a simple A and T. There were two further marks about forty and sixty miles ahead labelled H and L. This was the chain of islands that hemmed in the northern part of the Straits: Abu Musa, Tunb, Hengam, Larak. They pushed the Iranian territorial waters far out towards the UAE and Oman and gave Iran a stranglehold over this vital and strategic waterway.

Allenby started to raise his boom microphone to speak to the captain offline, but thought better of it. The command team would react all the more intelligently for knowing the situation, and they could all hear the command open line.

'Captain, AAWO. That's a handover from the radar on Abu Musa. Hengam will be next. They didn't light up all of these last Tuesday, so it looks like they're actively tracking our progress.'

'Yes, but it might have more to do with the Earnest Will convoy. Any sign of that EWD?'

'No, sir, but if they're still the other side of the Musandam Peninsula, we probably can't expect to detect them.'

'Captain, PWO. There's a concentration of friendly tracks on the data link, passing the Soviet anchorage, forty-three miles from the start of the inbound traffic separation scheme. A destroyer and two frigates with three other unidentified friendlies. That looks like an Earnest Will convoy to me.'

Mayhew was startled to hear this unsolicited input from the PWO's position. Jerry Harling was already proving to be a much better action stations PWO than Buckley was. He could see Buckley over in the corner at the GOP table. Now, let's see if he's properly grasped the situation.

'Have you plotted those link tracks on the chart?'

'Here they are, sir.'

Buckley pointed to the chart on the GOP which showed the Straits of Hormuz from Siri Island in the west to the Gulf of Oman in the east. The traffic separation scheme was marked in the Admiralty Hydrographic Department's favourite stand-out colour, magenta. The islands were all clearly identified and two curved pencilled arcs showed the assumed limit of the Silkworm envelope at each end of the Straits. The positions of *Winchester's* convoy was shown, a few miles past Abu Musa, and the convoy that was being reported on the data link was shown approaching the Straits from the east.

'The Earnest Will convoy has forty-three miles to run to the traffic separation scheme, sir, as the PWO said, and we have exactly the same distance to run to the start of the outbound lane. We'll meet in the middle at about zero-four-hundred, unless something changes.'

Well, well. Buckley was blossoming as the duty staff officer and anticipating the command's information needs. What a change! Perhaps he performed better when he wasn't under the pressure of real-time events.

'What time will the Americans enter the Silkworm envelope, assuming they define its limits the same way that we do?'

Buckley did some deft work with the dividers and checked the distance against the latitude scale at the side of the chart.

'Zero-one-thirty, sir, based on a possible launch site at Kuhestak.'

Mayhew pondered as he stared at the chart. He'd always wondered why there had never been any definite intelligence about Silkworm sites on the islands; they were such obvious places for the Iranians to close off the Straits, but when it was shown like this, the explanation became apparent. With the allies controlling the water of the Gulf, they could easily blockade the islands and prevent missiles, launchers and supplies from reaching them from the mainland. Furthermore, and particularly in the case of Siri, Abu Musa and Tunb, the islands were too small and barren to hide anything as substantial as a Silkworm mobile launcher. There was almost no vegetation and any excavations were immediately obvious to reconnaissance flights, and to satellite surveillance. The Iranians had a limited supply of both missiles and launchers, and in all probability they didn't want to risk them on the islands, it was as simple as that. He could imagine what would happen as soon as they launched a missile at an allied convoy. The Americans would immediately see that as a threat whether it was fired at their ships, at a British convoy or a French or Italian one. They'd react with overwhelming force by launching an air strike from the carrier battle group that prowled the Gulf of Oman, and that launcher, with its missiles, would be obliterated. A Silkworm launcher on the mainland, on the other hand, had a good chance of packing up and moving to a hidden location before it was attacked. In that case only the pre-prepared launching pad would be lost, a matter of a few hundred cubic yards of concrete and sand, and the Iranians had plenty of both. The tactic was called shoot-and-scoot and was well known and practiced by artillery batteries of all armies, if they wanted to survive in a battlefield under constant surveillance. However, if the mobile launcher was on a small, barren island like Siri, or Tunb or Abu Musa it would have nowhere to hide and would certainly be found and destroyed. The intelligence assessments that pushed the Silkworm envelope as far south and west as the anchorage off Sharjah were too pessimistic.

'Draw an arc radius forty-five miles from that Kuhestak site, would you?'

That made more sense. The arc just touched the western end of the traffic separation scheme and covered the whole of the eastern approaches. There was still a possibility of launchers on Qeshm Island which was far bigger than the other five islands. Qeshm had more places to hide a Silkworm launcher, and it was so close to the mainland that it would be difficult to blockade. Yet no site had ever been seen on Qeshm despite intensive searches. It shouldn't be discounted, but to Mayhew the immediate threat appeared to come from Kuhestak and nowhere else. A Silkworm missile battery at Kuhestak could command the critical part of the Straits – the traffic separation scheme – and was only sixty miles from the military airfield at Bandar Abbas. There was a good road that might have been built for the purpose of supplying missile batteries.

The Earnest Will convoy would enter the envelope at one-thirty and Mayhew's convoy an hour later, and they'd meet at the turning point of the separation scheme at four o'clock. Mayhew glanced up at the ops room clock. Fifty minutes to midnight, but he'd be a fool to imagine that he had two hours and twenty minutes of peaceful steaming.

'AAWO, EWD. I've lost the radar on Abu Musa now. The Tunb radar is still transmitting.'

***

Mayhew returned to his seat and watched the interaction between the different functions in the ops room. There was no doubt that it was running more smoothly since Buckley had been replaced by Harling. Why hadn't Buckley's reticence been spotted by the staff at Portland? There were two reasons that came to mind. First, the training at Portland was quite scripted and left little room for tactical thought, it was more about following well-understood procedures and reacting correctly to known threats. Buckley was perfectly capable of doing that, it was the lateral thinking that let him down. In the Gulf nothing was scripted and a warfare team must be able to create its own tactical responses on the fly. However, there was another reason that Mayhew was aware of, and he really needed to address it when things calmed down. Like many in the ship's company Buckley had left a young family behind in Portsmouth. As far as Mayhew knew his wife was coping as well as any others, but that didn't help Buckley's feelings of guilt. Mayhew knew only too well how that could prey on a man's mind to the extent of affecting his performance and endangering the team. He'd ask Allenby to have a chat with Buckley and then he could decide what to do about it. Well, that was for another day.

'Captain, PWO. We've detected a surface track coming from behind Tunb. It looks like it's heading to join the outbound traffic separation scheme. I'm releasing it to alligator as an unknown.'

Mayhew and Allenby glanced at each other and Mayhew nodded knowingly.

'Roger PWO, watch it carefully. EWD, any racket?'

'Nothing sir. There's only the Tunb surveillance radar in that direction.'

Well, it still might be innocent merchant traffic, although it was odd that it wasn't using a radar. There was another traffic separation scheme that started at Tunb island and headed east-west along the Iranian coast. It was only used by ships heading towards the oil terminals on Lavan Island and further north to Kharg Island, and inevitably they were either Iranian or belonging to nations that had friendly relations with Iran. The Iraqis loved it and used it as the identification basis for targeting their own air-launched Exocet and Silkworm strikes. As far as they were concerned, anything using that route was fair game. It was that logic that had put *Winchester* and the MCMVs in such deadly danger. Was that only last night? He glanced across at the UAA-1 to see Dickens' shoulders tense up as he stared at a particular spike on his display. He looked down at some notes then without hesitating spoke urgently into his microphone.

'Captain, EWD. I have *Sabalan's* Plessey air surveillance radar to the northwest.'

'Captain, PWO. That correlates with track three-six-two-zero on that bearing, range ten miles. It's the track that came from behind the island and it's just leaving the bulge of Iranian territorial waters off Tunb. This is about where we met *Sabalan* on Tuesday night.'

'Make the threat warning air and surface red. Officer-of-the-Watch, make sure that the tankers know. Javelin Commander, pass that to the fire units. PWO make that a hostile on alligator. On anti-flash, on steel helmets.'

'Hostile, sir?'

It wasn't normal to declare Iranian contacts as hostile, it brought a risk of over-reaction and on an electronic data link it was impossible to convey the subtleties of the situation that caused Mayhew to make that decision. Yet he felt that something had changed in the Iranian attitude.

'Yes, hostile, PWO. Cover track three-six-two-zero with Seadart in surface mode and with the gun. EWD, if you detect his Seahunter fire control radar, blow that whistle without hesitating. AAWO, we'll have the Phalanx in auto.'

Mayhew left a few seconds for his orders to be carried

out.

'Command Team, Captain. Be prepared for anything from *Sabalan*. This surveillance buildup is quite different to last Tuesday, it feels much more purposeful. You all know what to do.'

'Bring the Lynx to alert five, sir?'

Harling had a good point, and the Lynx was an effective counter to a small frigate. But still Mayhew paused. They'd be in Oman's territorial waters in a little over an hour and then they'd have to bring the Lynx back on deck, *Sabalan* or no *Sabalan*. If this became a long standoff between *Winchester* and the frigate, he didn't want it to look as though he was backing down right at the onset, and bringing the Lynx in might look like that. Nevertheless, having it at alert five kept his options open.

'Yes, PWO. Bring the Lynx to alert five in the surface action role.'

A single Sea Skua would probably destroy *Sabalan's* fighting capability out of hand and two missiles would render the frigate a floating wreck, if she didn't sink. The heavy machine gun pod gave him less drastic options, although a burst of fifty-calibre bullets into an unarmoured frigate would be deadly. Yet it was right to keep the Lynx on deck, and at alert five it was almost as useful as it was in the air. Yet he must try to de-escalate the situation without dropping his guard.

'Navigator, give me a new course to bring the convoy into Omani territorial waters earlier than planned, without being too obvious about it.'

'Fifteen degrees to starboard will do it in thirty minutes, sir, then we can come back ten degrees for the traffic separation scheme.'

Mayhew considered for a moment. There was a degree of safety in Oman's territorial waters but it mustn't look as though he was doing it deliberately. He could pass through on what was called *innocent passage*, so long as he kept a steady course, but a deliberate alteration would be seen as a violation. Probably the Omani coastal radar would pick it up, but they could ignore such a small alteration if they wished, and put it down to a navigational correction. It also meant that he'd lose the potential use of his Lynx that much earlier.

'Make it so. Call *World Antigua* on Cougar Bright and tell her to alter course and make sure the first lieutenant understands. The rest of the convoy will follow.'

'Blind, tell Visual that I'll want the signal projectors as well as all the close range weapons. PWO, what's *Sabalan's* range now?'

'Eight miles, steering an intercept course for the centre of the convoy.'

Mayhew looked left and right. His AAWO and PWO had things under control. If there was to be an engagement it would be at close range and he needed to be where he could see the action.

'Command team, Captain. I'll be on the bridge.'

He hung up his headset and ran up the three ladders, haunted by the fear that something should happen while he was absent from the command open line. Allenby and Harling had it under control, they'd act appropriately without asking his permission and without waiting for his orders, but still…

He slowed down as he reached the bridge, it would only disturb the men to see the captain running. He placed the command open line headset over his ears and adjusted the boom microphone.

'Captain on.'

'Nothing new, sir,' that was Allenby's reassuring voice. '*Sabalan* is still closing on a steady bearing and only radiating on her air surveillance radar. I'm being called by *Casablanca* on Navy Red, stand by.'

'Where is he Officer-of-the-Watch?'

Saxby pointed to a green and white light close together on the port beam. Tankers carried a single green side light on their starboard side and two white steaming lights but naval vessels could claim an exemption and carry only one white light. Its lights gave it away as a naval vessel, and it was indeed steering an intercept course.

Mayhew looked out onto the port bridge wing. The missile gun director visual was there on his long-lead headset, and gave a thumbs-up when he saw the captain. The signalman at the projector was the same man that had done so well on Tuesday and he looked around and nodded. It was difficult to do more when only his eyes were showing through his anti-flash hood.

'Has the first lieutenant acknowledged the threat warning red?'

'Yes, sir, and the navigator has briefed him over Cougar Bright. The Javelin teams are ready too. The Filipino *Sea Surge* called and asked to speak to you on Channel sixteen, so I gave him an outline of what was happening and told him you were busy. He sounded nervous.'

As well he might, Mayhew thought.

He turned his attention back to the approaching frigate. It was a dark, moonless night but the stars were bright enough to pick out its outline behind its navigation lights. It was still coming on but appeared to be in no particular hurry, about thirteen knots, Mayhew estimated, the same speed as the convoy.

'His bearing's drawing left, sir. I think he's steering for the rear of the convoy now.'

'Captain, AAWO. *Casablanca* says that they have to cover the Earnest Will convoy and that there are no US Navy assets in the western Straits. He's asked for a running commentary so I've put the FC on Navy Red, and he'll ask me before he says anything that might be sensitive.'

'*Sea Surge* is asking for you again, sir, on Channel thirteen now.'

Damn. He really didn't have time for this. Anything said on the VHF would be heard by *Sabalan*, and he already knew that the Iranian captain spoke good English. Yet whatever *Sea Surge* had said would already have given a lot away.

Sabalan would know that it was a British convoy, he'd know that *Winchester* was the escort commander and he'd know that there was an unentitled ship called *Sea Surge* and would guess that it was at the tail of the convoy. He might as well speak to the Filipino captain.

'*Sea Surge* this is *Winchester*, Captain speaking, over.'

'*Winchester*, this is *Sea Surge*, Captain speaking also. Can you tell me, are we in danger?'

A foreign accent, but it could be from anywhere to the east of the Red Sea. Filipino, perhaps, but a Philippines registration didn't mean a Filipino captain.

'*Sea Surge* this is *Winchester*. We're being approached by the same Iranian frigate that we met on Tuesday.'

There was silence at the other end. Mayhew hoped that the tanker's captain understood that he couldn't say anything more. Not only would it compromise *Winchester* and *Bellona's* ability to protect the convoy, but it would give *Sabalan* vital information about his attitude to the unentitled ship. Mayhew wanted to protect *Sea Surge*; apart from the humanitarian issues, he'd become fond of the Filipino tanker. It was well-handled, it stayed as rigidly in line as its British counterparts and… and it deserved better than to be mauled by *Sabalan*, whatever his rules of engagement said.

'*Winchester*, this is *Sea Surge*, understood, listening channels sixteen and thirteen. Out.

Perhaps he really did understand, but now that *Sabalan* had shown his hand by steering for the rear, Mayhew had to counter that move. There was just enough time.

'Officer-of-the-Watch, come hard left onto a reciprocal heading and steer for the tail of the convoy. Chief Yeoman, get *Bellona's* captain on the secure line.'

Winchester heeled sharply as the quartermaster applied twenty degrees of helm. The chief yeoman offered the secure handset to Mayhew as he felt himself slide across the smooth seat of his chair to fetch up against the armrest. No preamble was needed, the chief would have made certain that *Bellona's* captain was on the line.

'Gareth, this is David, over.'

'Gareth, over.'

'*Sabalan's* heading for the rear of the convoy and I need *Winchester's* gun back there. We'll swap stations. Increase to your best speed and we'll pass port-to-port.'

'Roger David, understood. Is that all?'

'I'll only add that I'm going to do all I can to protect our Filipino friend without doing anything foolish.'

'Understood and agreed. Out.'

What Mayhew intended was bordering on reckless and he had to take the responsibility himself.

'Officer-of-the-Watch, I have the ship.'

'Course two-two-two, thirteen knots on two Tynes. You have the ship, sir.'

'Quartermaster engage both Olympus. Officer-of-the-Watch, call the MCR and warn them that we'll be manoeuvering at high speed. Make a pipe also.'

'Engage both Olympus, sir.'

In the Royal Navy every order for manoeuvering the ship was repeated exactly as it was given so that there was no chance of misunderstanding. Saxby no longer had the con, but he was still the officer-of-the-watch and he listened to confirm that the order had been accurately received.

Mayhew heard the bosun's mate's voice in stereo, for they were standing only two yards apart and his voice was also booming over the main broadcast speaker.

'D'you hear there. The ship will be manoeuvering at high speed, the ship will be manoeuvering at high speed. That's all.'

'Starboard wheel steer two-two-five.'

'Starboard wheel steer two-two-five, sir,' the quartermaster replied.

That should give *Bellona* a little more space to pass between the convoy and the destroyer.

He heard the sound of the two mighty Olympus gas turbines and didn't wait for the quartermaster at the wheel to report.

'Revolutions for twenty-five knots.'

'Revolutions for twenty-five knots, sir.'

The quartermaster pushed forward on the two machinery control levers and Mayhew felt the pressure in his back as the ship accelerated.

'What's *Sabalan's* bearing doing now, Navigator?'

'Drawing right, sir.'

Then *Winchester* would reach the rear of the line before *Sabalan*.

'*Bellona's* bearing is drawing left, sir.'

He'd momentarily forgotten about *Bellona*. The bearing drawing left meant that the frigate would pass to the southeast of him, port-to-port as he'd ordered. It looked like *Bellona* had piled on the power as rapidly as *Winchester* had, and the two ships were approaching each other at a combined speed of fifty knots. This is no time for a steering gear failure, Mayhew thought.

A flash of racing navigation lights and *Bellona* was past and gone, speeding for her new station at the head of the line. Now, this next manoeuvre was the tricky one. Mayhew looked out of the starboard bridge wing to see that *Sabalan* was two miles on his quarter. There was just enough time for what he intended.

'Starboard twenty.'

'Starboard twenty, sir.'

At twenty-five knots, *Winchester* heeled extravagantly as she turned. From far away he heard the crash of unsecured gear slipping from its stowage.

'Reduce twelve knots.'

'Reduce twelve knots, sir.'

'Steer zero-five-zero.'

'Steer zero-five-zero, sir.'

The effect on the ship was extraordinary as it rode over its own bow wave and water leapt in great disorganised spouts to fall on the gun crews on the upper deck. But it had its effect and now *Winchester* was half a mile on *Sea Surge's* beam with her bows pointing ten degrees to the right of the advancing Iranian frigate.

'Course zero-five-zero, twelve knots on two Olympus. Officer-of-the-Watch, you have the ship.'

'Course zero-five-zero, twelve knots on two Olympus. I have the ship, sir.'

'Close *Sea Surge* to three cables on her port beam then match her course and speed.'

'Aye-aye sir. Close *Sea Surge* to three cables on her port beam then match her course and speed.'

'Visual, Captain. Cover Sabalan with close range weapons. Stand by the port signal lantern, at my word.'

***

Mayhew watched *Sabalan* carefully. It appeared that his manoeuvre had rattled the Iranian captain and he'd sheered off to starboard in alarm when he saw *Winchester's* high speed turn. That was good, he wanted his opponent to know that he wasn't going to act in a conventional manner and he wasn't afraid to be bold. *Sabalan* made the best of her unintended turn and reversed her wheel to make a wide sweep to port, with the clear intention of coming up on the rear of the convoy. Well, Mayhew wasn't going to make it easy for him.

'Officer-of-the-Watch, reduce eight knots.'

That would keep *Winchester* between *Sabalan* and *Sea Surge*, and this time the rule of the road favoured *Winchester*, for *Sabalan* was both astern and to port. If there was a collision, it would be *Sabalan's* captain that would have the questions to answer.

It was a game again, but a game with potentially deadly consequences. Mayhew adjusted course and speed to frustrate the Iranian's clear intention to get close to the Filipino tanker. A beam of light stabbed into the darkness from *Sabalan*, it was aiming a signal projector towards the tankers stern, where her name and port of registry could be read. *Winchester's* twenty-inch projector replied, shining right into the frigate's bridge, and all the time *Winchester's* weapons followed the Iranian's every move, threatening instant retribution for any hostile act. After a few seconds *Sabalan* turned its signal projector off.

'Turn off the twenty-inch, Chief.'

It was like training a pet dog, rewarding good behaviour with treats.

'British warship *Winchester*, this is Iranian frigate, over.'

Ah, that was what Mayhew was hoping for. He shook his head at the chief yeoman who was offering the handset. He was prepared to talk all night if it protected his convoy, but he'd let *Sabalan* do all the running. It was funny how he thought of *Sea Surge* as being under his protection, even though his government would disavow him entirely. He hadn't felt so strongly when he came into the Gulf, perhaps it was because this was the second time *Sea Surge* had joined him.

'British warship *Winchester*, British warship *Winchester*, this is Iranian frigate, over.'

'I'll have that handset now, Chief Yeoman.'

Mayhew waited a few more seconds then pressed the transmit button.

'Iranian warship *Sabalan*, this is British warship. You are manoeuvering dangerously in the approaches to an international traffic separation scheme, I request that you move away to the west, over.'

Now the Iranian knew that his identity was known and Mayhew had established a legal framework for his actions. *Sabalan's* turn.

'*Winchester*, this is *Sabalan*. We are in the high seas and I have the right of stop and search as a representative of a belligerent nation. I intend to board the ship on your starboard side and I insist that you stand clear.'

'Visual. Stand by the port signal projector.'

'Ready, sir.'

'When I give the word, light up his bridge again.'

'*Sabalan*, this is *Winchester*. You should make your protest through the normal channels. For now you are endangering life at sea. Move away immediately.'

'Stand by, Visual.'
'*Winchester*, this is...'
'Light him up, Visual.'

Mayhew leapt out onto the port bridge wing and looked aft onto the quarter. *Sabalan* appeared very close, but that was an illusion caused by the twenty-inch signal projector shining right at her. In fact she was two cables away which under any other circumstances would be foolishly close to another ship at sea. He looked through his binoculars and thought he could see the officers on the bridge shielding their eyes. Again *Sabalan* shone her own puny version of a signal projector, but it was playing on *Winchester's* flight deck, not on her bridge. All they would see was a Lynx helicopter armed and ready to take to the air from where it could punch a pair of sea-skimming missiles into the frigate's hull.

'Officer-of-the-Watch, I want you to drop back slowly, keeping the same relative bearing on *Sea Surge*, but two knots slower.'

He had to hand it to *Sabalan's* captain, he didn't give in easily, but soon the convoy would be in Omani territorial waters and he almost certainly had orders not to operate inside their twelve-mile limit. In any case, after following mutely for twenty minutes, and right on the twelve-mile line, he hauled off to port, and this time there was no sarcastic farewell on VHF.

***

Chapter Twenty

Saturday, 0300
HMS Winchester, at Sea, Straits of Hormuz
Operation Armilla Daily Sitrep: Detected Iranian F-14 over Bandar Abbas...

'Captain, Officer-of-the-Watch. There's a bit of haze gathering overhead. The surface visibility is still good but there's not much starlight getting through and the sun won't rise until five-twenty-two local time. I can see the tanker lights quite easily but I won't see an unlit vessel until it's very close.'

'Thank you, Officer-of-the-Watch.'

There was a feeling of brooding menace in the Straits tonight. *Sabalan's* attempt at the convoy had been beaten by strategy and by dogged determination, but Mayhew knew that in the end it was Oman's territorial waters that persuaded the Iranian captain to withdraw. A frigate might be small in relation to the huge oil tankers that plied these waters, but it was large enough to be easily detected by the Omani coastal radars on the Musandam Peninsula, and the naval headquarters at Goat Island would have intervened. Iran had enough enemies in the Gulf without adding Oman to the list. It would be easy to conclude that the convoy was safe until it left Oman's territorial waters at about five-thirty in the morning, but that would be a dangerous assumption. A frigate could be tracked, photographed and the evidence used to back up a strong diplomatic protest from Oman to Iran, but missiles and small boats were another matter, particularly on a dark, moonless night when even the stars hid behind the haze.

'PWO, what's the latest on the Earnest Will convoy?'

'One-zero-zero at twenty-eight miles, sir, entering the traffic separation scheme. Three merchantmen, presumably tankers. *Casablanca's* in close escort now and there's a destroyer and two frigates. The cruiser and the destroyer are stationed on the northern side of the convoy and the frigates are at the head and the rear. We know about *Casablanca*, and the radar emissions suggest that the destroyer's a Kidd class and the other two are Fig-Sevens.'

Then the two convoys would be passing in a little over an hour. *Winchester* was back at the head and *Bellona* at the rear, so it was *Winchester* that would see them first.

The Americans had a strong escort, much more able to fend off a serious attack than Mayhew's force. *Casablanca* was a Ticonderoga-class cruiser with the formidable Aegis combat system; it was arguably too capable for the enclosed waters of the Gulf but a sledgehammer always was the perfect implement to crack a nut. The four ships of the Kidd class were enormous destroyers that were being built for Iran before the revolution and were never delivered. Instead they were completed for the United States Navy and forever after were affectionately called the *Ayatollah* class. The FFG-7s, Oliver Hazard Perry class frigates, or Fig-Sevens to all and sundry, were the workhorses of the American fleet, the same class of ships as the ill-fated *Cranston* that hit a mine on the Shah Allum shoal. Each of the four American warships carried medium range surface-to-air missiles at least as capable as *Winchester's* Seadart. They also carried Harpoon surface-to-surface missiles, and each had a gun that could be used for closer range surface engagements, and a multi-role Seahawk helicopter. It was a strong escort for just three tankers bound for Kuwait, but then there was a particular rivalry – a grudge even – between America and Iran that dated back to the hostage crisis in nineteen-seventy-nine. Given an equal choice of targets, the Iranians would choose the Americans over the British. However, with the huge American presence in the Gulf, and their proven ability to punish Iran quickly and decisively, Iran might be tempted to take the easier option, and tonight that was the British convoy.

'Oh for a couple of Lynx or Seahawks on surface search now, sir. *Sabalan* might be deterred from doing mischief so close to Oman, but I doubt whether the IRGC will be so shy about it.'

Allenby could have been reading his mind, so closely did their thoughts align. To know one's enemy had always been the wise naval commander's aim, and in this case Mayhew had to remember that the regular Iranian forces and the Islamic Revolutionary Guard Corps were two separate organisations. They had different command structures, different aims and different ideologies. The IRGC was perfectly capable of ignoring the principles of international law, and their fleet of Boghammers gave them the means to do so in a way that could be later denied. Helicopters armed with air-to-surface missiles were the best means of defeating them, but neither of the two convoy commanders could fly their helicopters while their ships were in Oman's territorial waters, and that meant the whole of the passage of the traffic separation scheme was a no-fly zone.

'What would you do, Ops, if you commanded that Boghammer squadron – let's assume they've moved from Lavan Island down to the Straits – and you had your eye on one of these convoys?'

Allenby tapped his assistant on the shoulder and motioned that he was taking off his headset.

'We've been under surveillance from the Iranian shore stations since we left the anchorage at Dubai, sir. They'll have no doubt about who we are, where we are and where we're going, so finding us or the Americans will be no trouble to them at all. I doubt whether their command-and-control is very sophisticated but they can surely plot our location, establish a dead reckoning future position and head for that point. They'll know that we can't turn off our nav lights, not in the Straits and not with so many ships in close company; but they can, and I'm sure they will, if they come out at all. If I commanded those boats, I'd strangle all my radars, turn off all the lights and order a close formation so that the boats don't lose touch with each other, and I'd go full blast for us. Once I spotted the convoy I'd stay so close that none of the British or American missiles or the medium guns can get a firing solution. Then I'd run up and down the convoy firing at anything I saw, but particularly at the warships, that will give me the biggest bang for my buck. I'd give it perhaps ten minutes then full speed back to Hengam or Qeshm or wherever they've established their forward base. The greatest danger will be when I'm withdrawing, but if I lose half my boats in humbling the Great Satan, it's not a problem. At full speed I can leave the shelter of Larak Island and be beating up the convoy in half an hour.'

'You don't think *Casablanca* will engage them on the way in?'

'He can't, sir. I don't know the American rules of engagement but I expect they're probably not much more liberal than ours, and I expect they're no more keen than we are to fight inside Omani waters. Firing missiles and guns certainly doesn't come within the definition of *innocent passage*. I expect they'll need the Iranians to carry out an obvious, provable action of hostile intent before they can fire, and a fleeting radar contact of a squadron of fast boats coming their way probably doesn't cut it. They could turn out to be a flock of seagulls or a gang of smugglers in their dhows. No, the Americans have as much of a problem as we have. I hope they've been reading the enemy contact reports that we sent.'

'And the Americans are five miles nearer to the Iranians than we are, of course, being in the inbound lane.'

'Yes, sir, but I wouldn't want to rely upon that for our safe passage. If we can see that most of the American defence is to the north, then so can the radars on Hengam and Larak. A flanking attack around the head or the tail of the American convoy would bring the Boghammers onto their unprotected side.'

Mayhew nodded and lapsed into thought. He wasn't alone in feeling that this night held a particular menace, he could see that everyone in the ops room felt the same. There was a nervousness about his men that he hadn't seen before, and he could understand its cause. Over the past four days they'd been menaced from the air, the land, the sea and the sub-sea. They'd seen the whites of the enemy's eyes and they'd seen them as anonymous blips on a radar screen and flickering numbers on an electronic tote. Soon, in about three hours, they'd put all that behind them as they moved out of the Straits and into the Gulf of Oman, and they couldn't believe that the enemy would allow them to do that without one last attempt against them.

And yet, was he making too much of this? Would the IRGC really take on two well-protected convoys in a third-party country's territorial waters? It sounded unlikely and yet…

'EWD, Captain. What coastal surveillance radars are operating at the moment?'

'Hengam and Qeshm, sir, on the Iranian side, and Goat Island on the Oman side. Tunb's out of range and I've got nothing from Kuhestak yet.'

'Would you expect to detect Kuhestak at this range?'

'Forty-eight miles; yes, we should detect it if it's radiating.'

'Thank you, EWD. AAWO, what are the threat warnings?'

'Air is red, sir, based on those surveillance radars and the possibility of Silkworms on Hengam and Larak. Surface is yellow because we have no indications at present.'

Mayhew walked over to the GOP and studied the chart. He was convinced that the Iranians hadn't deployed Silkworms to Hengam and Larak, and Qeshm was now abaft the beam. He'd gone over the reasoning in his own mind time and time again. It was Kuhestak or nothing, he was sure, and Kuhestak wasn't radiating. The surface threat was only a hunch, but the circumstantial evidence had been growing these past four days. For whatever reason the Iranians seemed to have picked out *Winchester* for special treatment. It could be because he intervened when *Sabalan* was attacking the Panamanian ship on Tuesday, or it could be something else entirely. He felt in his bones that he was the target tonight and not the Americans, and for the next few hours it was a surface attack that was to be feared.

'AAWO, PWO, Captain. I want to turn those warnings around. There's no evidence of Silkworm activity so Air threat yellow, but I don't like this dark night and being only twenty miles from the Iranian islands, so surface threat warning red. Make it so please.'

He heard the AAWO and the PWO transmitting this change on their respective circuits, and saw the yeoman formalising it on his radio. Perhaps he should have discussed it with his warfare officers before making these changes, but he could only rationalise them up to a point, and the rest was just a gut feeling. He could have left the air threat warning at red, but that would keep his command team unnecessarily keyed up. He wanted the air team's attention to peak as *Winchester* came within Silkworm range of Kuhestak.

'Visual, are the close range batteries ready for a surface engagement.'

'Yes, sir. They're ready.'

'Captain, EWD. Hengam radar has ceased transmitting. Last bearing two-eight-five. I've only got Larak now, bearing zero-zero-six, and Goat Island to the south.'

'Did Hengam go out of range?'

'No sir, I had a big, fat signal when it suddenly ceased. It was switched off, I'm sure.'

'Why, Ops, why? Why turn off Hengam radar right now? The Earnest Will convoy is going that way even if we're heading the other way.'

Allenby thought for a moment.

'They must be getting all the information they need from the Larak radar so they don't need the Hengam radar any more. Are they trying to draw our attention away from the west?'

'That's what I suspect. PWO, tell *Bellona* that the threat

direction is two-eight-five and they're to keep a good surface watch to the west and northwest. Report any contacts immediately, however fleeting, and release them to the link as soon as they have a firm track.'

Bellona had a better surface search radar than *Winchester*, it was optimised to pick up sea-skimming targets for its Seawolf missile system. If there were any Boghammers lurking out there *Bellona* was the best unit to spot them, in the absence of the Lynx. Now, should he move *Winchester* back to the rear of the convoy? No, not yet, after all there was still a Silkworm threat, although it was low, and a Silkworm trumped a Boghammer any day.

'Captain, PWO. The lead ship of the Earnest Will convoy is ten miles away now.'

'EWD. F-14 Tomcat radar bearing three-five-five. That's the same bearing as Bandar Abbas airfield, sir.'

For a moment Mayhew was confused. The US Navy operated F-14 Tomcats off their carriers, so what on earth was one doing at Bandar Abbas?

'Captain, AAWO. That'll be one of the Iranian F-14s that they bought before the revolution. They've kept two aircraft operational by robbing the others for spares.'

'Ah, thanks, AAWO. Not a threat then, they're strictly fighter aircraft, air-to-air missiles only.'

'Maybe, sir, but there was talk of them being fitted with Maverick missiles. That would give them some sort of an anti-ship capability. Nobody really believes it though. Ah, *Casablanca* is calling air threat warning red based on the F-14 radar, they must have detected it too. I recommend we stay at air threat warning yellow. There'll be plenty of time to react if the F-14 starts coming this way.'

'Do we have it on radar, AAWO?'

'Captain, AAWO, APS. It's hostile three-six-five-one, bearing three-five-five range thirty-nine miles.'

'Captain, FC. That track's in the airlane from Bandar Abbas to Dubai, it's squawking civilian.'

Mayhew banged his fist on his radar display.

'Is it military or civilian. Sort it out air team.'

Mayhew had never lost his temper before in the ops room, but this was ridiculous. He had the most sophisticated equipment that the Royal Navy could provide, and still he couldn't tell friend from neutral from hostile at less than forty miles. Allenby was still cool, though.

'Captain, AAWO. There are two aircraft near Bandar Abbas. Track three-six-five-one is diverging from the EWD's racket and 1022 shows it climbing. That's a civilian airliner joining the airlane and I've called weapons tight on it internally. There's also an F-14 on the ground or in a tight circuit over Bandar Abbas, and we don't hold a radar contact on that one.'

Mayhew glanced at the fighter controller who was looking over his shoulder and nodding vigorously. He dropped his boom microphone and burst in on command open line.

'FC concurs, sir.'

Beresford had the air map in front of him and was in the best position to tell exactly where the target was in relation to the complex web of air routes and zones.

'Captain, AAWO. I'd like to cover track three-six-five-one – the probable airliner – with the 909's I-band and get an accurate height and be ready to engage if it turns out hostile.'

'Will *Casablanca* see our 909 emissions?'

'No sir, we've got a clear range to the target.'

'Very well, AAWO.'

That was important. He didn't want to squirt his fire control radar at an American ship that was armed with harpoon missiles, particularly as they were probably feeling jittery by now. The 909s had a pencil beam and couldn't be detected by anything not directly in its line of sight.

'Blind, AAWO. Cover track three-six-five-one with birds. Do not load the launcher. Hold fire track three-six-five-one.'

Mayhew looked over Allenby's shoulder. There it was,

an innocuous orange blip moving across the screen. Allenby's tote showed that it was doing four-hundred-and-fifty knots and that it was climbing through ten thousand feet. He could see the mode three response that suggested that it was a civilian aircraft. If that was an attack profile then it was a mighty strange one.

'Captain, AAWO, FC. I'm on Navy Red, sir. *Casablanca* is still convinced that it's a hostile F-14. I can hear him on aeronautical distress as well, but the airliner isn't answering.'

'Captain, AAWO. *Casablanca's* covering track three-six-five-one with birds. I'm switching to Navy Red to talk him out of it. Soft Kill switch to the AAW circuit.'

Mayhew felt that he was living in a nightmare, trapped by fast-moving circumstances that he had no means of controlling. *Casablanca* was the anti-air-warfare commander for the southern Gulf, and in matters of air defence his word was law. Yet Mayhew was convinced that he was making a mistake, and that if he went through with an engagement it would be a fatal error with far-reaching consequences. He heard Allenby slowly explaining his rationale but time was running out. The target – the civilian airliner, he was certain of that now – was only thirteen miles from the cruiser. If *Casablanca* fired, the chances of its missiles failing to hit the airliner were vanishingly small.

'Captain, Soft Kill, Golf Whiskey has ordered *Casablanca* to take track three-six-five-one with birds.'

Mayhew felt dizzy. Golf Whiskey was in *Casablanca*; the cruiser was effectively ordering itself to shoot down the airliner. That was absolutely the correct procedure but it sounded bizarre under these circumstances, like the checks and balances had been swept away. He could see that Allenby was using all his persuasive power, but not winning. Another look showed the target climbing through twelve-thousand feet to get to the correct cruising altitude for the short hop to Dubai. Any moment now *Casablanca's* vertical launch system would fire a pair of standard missiles. They would climb straight up, then they'd bunt over and streak towards the target. Any moment now…

He saw Allenby raise his hand with his thumb upright.

'Captain, Soft Kill. Golf Whiskey has ordered hold fire on track three-six-five-one. Assessed neutral, covering with birds.'

Mayhew exhaled the breath that he'd been holding and realised that he felt dizzy. He grabbed his chair to steady himself but it was a revolving chair and he lurched against the missile gun director blind's broad back.

'Sorry Chief.'

'No problem, sir. The ship must have rolled.'

'Blind, AAWO. Cease covering track three-six-five-one.'

'EWD. F-14 Tomcat racket ceased, last bearing three-four-seven.'

Allenby was aware of a sigh of relief in the ops room. That would never do, the most dangerous enemy is the one that you can't see. He had a flashback memory of telling his little sister that out-of-sight was out-of-mind, and her rapier fast response: *really? when I've just seen a spider disappear behind my headboard?*

And she was right. He brought his command open line microphone close to his mouth and spoke deliberately.

'This is the AAWO. Stay focussed and look out for bogies bearing three-five-five. That F-14 could have gone silent for an attack, it isn't over yet.'

He switched to AAW circuit, the rest of his force needed to be equally alert, and *Bellona* had the better radar to detect a low, fast aircraft.

'*Bellona* this is *Winchester*. Threat direction three-five-five, Bandar Abbas airport, based on faded F-14 racket. Look out for low and fast popup bogies. Threat warning air red.'

That got everyone's attention. He could see the air picture team leaning into their radar displays. The APS reached over to one of them and offset his screen so that he could see the area around Bandar Abbas in detail. It was as though the ship itself was holding its breath.

Thirty seconds passed. If an F-14 was powering towards

them at low level it would have travelled five miles already, and that was without going supersonic. A minute, still nothing.

'EWD, AAWO. Any rackets towards Bandar Abbas?'

'Negative, sir, not even the air traffic radar. It looks like they've closed down for the night.'

'Keep looking.'

Five minutes passed and Allenby started to relax. He rolled his shoulders to ease the tension.

'Captain, AAWO. I assess that the air threat from the north has eased. We should go to air threat warning yellow.'

Mayhew looked again at his radar display. Allenby had called it correctly; he was right to have kept the ops room alert and now he was right to let them relax a little.

'Make it so AAWO.'

***

Mayhew sat back in his chair and tried to control his breathing. The doc should be here now, testing his pulse. On the other had he'd probably declare him unfit for duty, but at least he wasn't sweating. He could feel his racing heart starting to fall back towards its normal rate.

'What the hell was all that Ops?'

Allenby smiled broadly. To him it was all in a day's work; he'd felt in control from the beginning to the end, and if the Americans didn't take his firm advice, well, there was nothing more that he could do. He didn't have the empathy to see that his captain had responsibility without authority, and was tearing himself apart.

'It was a close run thing, sir, but all's well that ends well. I visited one of those Aegis cruisers in Norfolk last year and I can see where they might have more difficulty than us in sorting out the air picture. They're built for the open ocean, not for tight spaces like this, and there's so much information flying around their combat information centre that it can take a while to come to a definite identification. That airliner was lucky and it should have responded on the aeronautical call-up frequency. They'll never know how close they came to disaster.'

'Yes, I'm sure you're right, Ops. Our system might not be as capable but at least it's manageable.'

Allenby tapped his console affectionately.

'No doubt about that, sir. I'd love to have that Spy-One radar and their extended range missiles, but I'm not sure I'd like to bring an Aegis system into the Straits of Hormuz. I wonder what the Kidd class and the Fig-Sevens thought about it.'

'The same as us, sir,' Beresford chipped in. 'The destroyer was almost screaming at *Casablanca* on Navy Red. It wasn't only us telling him that he'd got it wrong. In fact, I suspect if it was just us things would have gone very badly indeed. Ah, *Casablanca's* calling air threat warning yellow, weapons tight.'

'Right,' Mayhew looked quickly around, 'everyone seems a bit jumpy, let's try to settle things down. We're still surface warning red.'

***

Chapter Twenty-One

Saturday, 0330
HMS Winchester, at Sea, Straits of Hormuz
Operation Armilla Daily Sitrep: Passed Earnest Will Convoy in TSS, detected Boghammers south of Larak...

Mayhew stood up and stretched. He didn't know how these young men did it, sitting for hours on end staring at a radar display against the chance that something would pop up. How did they maintain their concentration? The answer of course was in their supervisors and their directors; petty officers and chief petty officers who had passed through the operator and tracker stage to be lords of all they surveyed within their own domains. The chief ops room supervisor, for example, could see a man who wasn't concentrating from far across a crowded ops room, and was on him like a ton of bricks. Perhaps that was what he needed, a supervisor to keep him focussed.

'Captain, PWO. Surface sitrep...'

Ah, that was what he needed to bring him back to reality; he'd almost forgotten that Boghammers were the principal danger, by his own assessment.

'...the Earnest Will convoy is on our port bow at eight miles with a CPA of five miles to port. Our convoy remains under surveillance from Larak Island and we're holding the Omani's Goat Island radar also. *Bellona* is watching the direction of Hengam Island. Surface threat warning red based on the Larak Island radar. Weapons tight.'

'Thank you, PWO.'

'We'll be covered from the north by the Earnest Will convoy soon. I suggest our threat direction should shift to north and northeast, sir.'

Mayhew looked over at the PWO's tactical display. Harling was right and he should have thought of that himself. With the rapidly changing relative positions of the convoys, the Boghammers – if they were about tonight –

would soon have to come through the American convoy to reach the British convoy's rear. They would have to make a very wide sweep to the west, for which they probably didn't have enough fuel. They'd want to spend the minimum amount of time in Oman's territorial waters, too, and as Mayhew's ships were moving quickly east, it suggested an attack from the north or northeast. Those four American warships were an effective protection now, but the two convoys were opening from each other at a combined speed of twenty-six knots. Soon there'd be nothing between *Winchester* and the two islands of Larak and Hormuz that hemmed in the approaches to Bandar Abbas. Surely that's where the Boghammers would have set up their forward base, where they had easy access to the road and air connections at Bandar Abbas.

'The lead escort of the Earnest Will convoy is passing us now, sir. I exchanged identities by light and he replied. I can see three big tankers and four warships.'

'Very well, Officer-of-the-Watch. Make by light: from Charlie Oscar, fair winds and following seas.'

'Aye-aye sir. They'll all be past and gone in three minutes.'

So fast! But at twenty-six knots opening speed there was little time to get acquainted. Then in five minutes maximum the British convoy would be completely exposed to the north. If the IRGC Boghammer commander thought along those lines – if he was even here and not still off Lavan Island waiting to pounce upon *Stirling* and the MCMVs – he'd know that the Americans could offer no help to the British convoy once they were past and clear and on their way into the Gulf. They'd never turn back and abandon their convoy, and those tankers were going nowhere but west and then north towards Kuwait. And yet, every minute that passed reduced the chance of a Boghammer attack as *Winchester*'s convoy moved inexorably eastward.

Twenty minutes passed and there was no sign of an attack. Perhaps the Boghammers were at this moment roaring in towards the Shah Allum shoal. Well, that was Jock Stewart's business.

'Now, PWO. What's next?' Mayhew asked offline.

'A quiet passage, I hope, sir. There's nothing suspicious on the plot and no rackets to be concerned about. Larak Island is twenty miles away.'

'Well, we'd expect to detect any small surface craft on the target indication radar at about fifteen miles in this weather, maybe a mile or two less on the nav radar.'

'Yes, sir, but we're moving away from Larak now and when the traffic separation scheme turns south the range will open rapidly. If they're going to come they'd better get a move on.'

Mayhew took another look at the chart. Boghammers by necessity operated close to a forward base and if that was Larak Island then the convoy was already beyond the range that they'd typically been seen operating.

'You're right, PWO, we're past the optimum point now. You can go to threat warning surface yellow, off anti-flash, off steel helmets.'

The PWO swung down his boom microphone to make an announcement on command open line…

'Contact!' shouted the surface picture supervisor, 'fast moving contacts bearing three-four-zero, twelve miles. Stand by for course and speed.'

'Threat warning surface red, PWO. Belay my order about anti-flash and steel helmets. Officer-of-the-Watch, engage both Olympus. Chief Yeoman patch me through to *Bellona* on secure.'

The change in the ops room was dramatic. There was no running around or shouting, but everyone suddenly had a new sense of purpose. He could see the concentration in the set of the trackers' shoulders and in the way that the equipment operators glanced rapidly along their rows of buttons and switches. They were old hands at Boghammers now and knew that speed was essential to counter these agile craft. And they were confident, they'd seen off that particular threat twice already. Nevertheless, it wasn't the ops room that was going to determine how this encounter would turn out, it was the upper deck weapon crews.

Mayhew stared at his own display. Ah, there they were, about six of them again, almost certainly the ones, and they were ignoring the Earnest Will convoy and clearly and unequivocally heading to intercept the British convoy.

'Duty Staff, call Goat Island and tell them that there are six fast-moving boats entering the traffic separation scheme from the north in radar silence... what speed SPS?'

Sharkey Ward moved his tracker ball and hooked the contact.

'Thirty-four knots, sir.'

'... thirty-four knots, Duty Staff.'

The Omanis couldn't do anything about this situation. By the time they scrambled a patrol boat from Goat Island it would all be over, but informing them established that the British convoy escort wasn't being underhand.

'*Bellona's* captain, sir,' the chief yeoman said, flicking the switches to put the secure circuit onto Mayhew's headset.

'*Bellona*, *Winchester*.'

'*Bellona*, Charlie-Oscar.'

'It's the Boghammers again, Gareth, coming from the north. They must have waited for the Earnest Will convoy to clear to the west. That says to me that we're their target for tonight. Bring *Bellona* up to cover the middle of the convoy, I'll take the head. Lynx to alert five.'

The line was silent for a few seconds.

'You'll launch the helicopters in Omani territorial waters?'

'Yes, if we see a hostile act from the Boghammers. Hostile act, not hostile intent. You can still defend yourself and the convoy with your own ship's weapons under the ROE, but I'll want to see weapons fired before I'll launch the helicopters.'

'Understood.'

'Good luck, Gareth. Out.'

Silkworm

Mayhew took a last look at the PWO's tactical console. The Boghammers were only nine miles away now.

'PWO, cover the Boghammers with Seadart in surface mode and with the gun. There's no point in firing chaff, they're not using radar and they can surely see us by now. Tell *Bellona* to cover with bulldogs. Bring the Lynx to alert five for surface action. I'll be on the bridge on open line, I want a countdown as they close the convoy, you can use the FC for that.'

***

'Your helmet, sir.'

The bosun's mate kept Mayhew's helmet on a hook below the engine controls and he held it out as soon as he saw Mayhew walk onto the bridge.

The convoy's navigation lights burned obscenely bright in the blackness of this pitch-dark night. Mayhew had already considered telling the tankers to turn off their lights, but it would be contravening the laws of the sea and would expose them to a danger of collision which could be greater than any damage that a Boghammer could achieve. No, the tankers must stay lit, but the same rules didn't apply to warships, at least not to the same extent. It could be done quickly too. Both *Winchester* and *Bellona* had already gone through the exhaustive process of checking that nothing except the navigation lights showed on the upper deck, so it was a matter of seconds to fully darken.

'Chief Yeoman, make to *Bellona*: darken ship. Back it up by telling him to turn off his nav lights, so that there's no doubt what I mean.'

'Officer-of-the-Watch, turn off our nav lights and send someone around at full speed to check on the darken ship.'

Now he felt better. The Boghammers could find the convoy but they'd be uncertain of the position of the escorts.

'Officer-of-the-Watch, increase twenty-four knots, turn towards the Boghammers. PWO, continue to cover with the gun but I don't intend to use it unless things get really nasty.

Tell the flight commander the situation. I don't expect to launch him but he's to remain at alert five until this is all over.'

Mayhew was still hoping to keep this action out of sight of the Omanis. He could do that, perhaps, if he only used close range weapons, but if he started lighting up the sky with the muzzle flash of his 4.5 inch gun and flying his helicopters, it would rapidly become a diplomatic issue. By looking over the bridge wing screen, he could make out the Seadart launcher and the gun moving in unison as they followed the advancing Boghammers. The close-range weapons were ready too, with steel-helmeted sailors at every post, waiting to get to grips with the enemy. Were they feeling nervous? They should be, because Mayhew was convinced that this time the Boghammers meant business. He was certain that they were the same boats that had probed them on the inbound run, and the same that tried to attack the minehunters at the Shah Allum shoal. They'd failed both times, but surely that would make them all the more determined now. He was convinced that for the first time his ship was going to come under fire.

'Six miles, sir, look left twenty degrees in the turn.'

Mayhew allowed himself a brief smile. Beresford was reading off the target range and bearing using the same calls as he would to a fighter aircraft. It was a much more useful way of presenting the data while *Winchester* heeled sharply and the Boghammers approached at speed.

'They're still not visual, keep reporting FC.'

If he couldn't see the Boghammers they almost certainly couldn't see the destroyer rushing towards them. Well, they were about to get a rude awakening. He shouted over his shoulder to the missile gun director visual.

'Chief!'

'Yes, sir.'

'I'm not going to wait for them to fire first. Weapons are tight but as soon as I'm satisfied that they're Boghammers I'm going to call weapons free. Wait for my command though. Where's the night vision aid?'

'Right here, sir. I can't see anything yet.'

Mayhew hadn't even noticed the petty officer only a few yards away from him, but now he looked he could see that he had the bulky night vision aid trained in the direction of the Boghammers.

'You know what a Boghammer looks like, Petty Officer White?'

'Yes, sir. I got a good look at them as we came through on Tuesday. Nothing yet, sir… Oh, contact! Two fast boats coming straight at us, no, three. At least three, sir. No ID yet.'

Mayhew itched to grab the night vision aid from the petty officer and see for himself, but he'd waste precious seconds adjusting to the ghostly green images, and the positive identification would be delayed. Better to leave it to the expert.

'I have six of them now, sir, spread out in a sort-of vee formation, and heading just to the left of us, towards the convoy.'

'Two miles, sir. Look left ten degrees.'

Beresford's call came through clearly and now Mayhew could mentally correlate that with the visual sighting.

'What's your course Officer-of-the-Watch?'

'Three-four-zero, sir.'

'Come twenty degrees to port. Reduce eighteen knots.'

'That should give you a stable platform, Chief.'

'Aye, thanks, sir.'

'They're Boghammers, sir, I'm certain.'

Mayhew glanced at Petty Officer White. This was important, for if they turned out to be nothing more than smugglers, and *Winchester* fired at them, perhaps killing or injuring some of the crew, even sinking one of the boats, there'd be hell to pay.

'Definitely Boghammers, sir. I can see the radars on the cabin tops and one of them is flying a big flag from that stumpy mast, just like the lead ship did before. I can't see what sort of flag.'

Mayhew drew a breath and spoke calmly and clearly on command open line.

'Weapons free on the approaching Boghammers.'

Weapons Free, that phrase beloved of Hollywood and always, always misused. It didn't mean commence firing, it meant that weapons may be fired at targets that are not positively identified as friendly. The missile gun director visual still had to confirm that they weren't obviously friendly, but he didn't have to be certain that they were enemies; there was a not-so-subtle difference. Mayhew had control of the guns until now, but when he called weapons free, he gave the responsibility to the missile gun director visual. It was a momentous decision when Britain was not at war, but his rules of engagement allowed it. Those six boats were clearly showing hostile intent and he was determined that he wouldn't wait for them to start firing their rockets at his convoy. He was going to hit first and hit hard.

Mayhew trained his binoculars towards the targets. They had excellent optics that even without night vision technology allowed him to see things better in the dark than he could have done with his naked eye. And there they were. Yes, Boghammers without a doubt, and they were in an attack formation. Had they seen *Winchester* bearing down upon them? If they had they were ignoring the destroyer and making for the tankers. *Winchester* would be difficult to see on this dark night, and when their attention was focussed on the tankers, it would be doubly difficult. Even if the squadron commander had realised that the convoy escorts had disappeared, he probably couldn't do anything to control the engagement when his boats were speeding over the sea. Most likely the other skippers couldn't hear him over the roar of their engines, even if he did try to call them. They were right on his ship's head at less than a mile and unless they turned they would pass either side of *Winchester*. He gulped when he realised that there was even a risk of collision. The missile gun director visual's call put all of his doubts behind him.

'Close range batteries, targets to port and starboard, engage!'

The dark night was split open by the muzzle flashes from the two belt-fed BMARC twenty-millimetres and the GPMGs. In the infernal light Mayhew could see the BMARC aimer leaning back in his retaining strap while he fired short, aimed bursts at the passing boats. They were taken entirely by surprise but still they were very difficult targets as they flashed past at over thirty knots. Nevertheless, in the precious few seconds that they were within range, he could see that some of the BMARC explosive shells were hitting their targets, and the tracer rounds from the GPMGs were heading in the right direction. He watched the port side BMARC as it trained further and further aft.

'Officer-of-the-Watch, come hard left, increase twenty-four knots. Follow the Boghammers. Where's *Bellona*? Oh, I see her.'

Bellona had opened fire too. It looked like Gareth had put his ship in exactly the right place to engage the Boghammers as they passed out of range of *Winchester's* weapons.

'Pass *Bellona* port-to-port. Make that clear on VHF.'

'Visual. You can see *Bellona*? Make sure your aimers know she's there.'

The Boghammers had started firing now but they weren't pressing home their attack, not in the face of the fire from the two warships. The lead boat launched two rockets, but it was hopeless to try to aim as the frail craft pitched and rolled over *Winchester's* wake. Mayhew couldn't tell who the rockets had been fired at but they flew far high and wide of any possible targets. One of the Boghammers was dead in the water with smoke pouring from its cabin and a dull glow where a fire had started. It was already starting to settle in the water, and only an improbable succession of miracles would see it safely home to Iran. It must have been hit in its engine room; the crew were lucky that the Boghammers had diesel engines rather than petrol, for by now a petrol engine would be burning furiously and close to a catastrophic explosion. By the orange light from the fire below decks, he could see that nobody was making any attempt to man the gun or the rocket launcher, they were all busy trying to launch an inflatable life raft. It crossed Mayhew's mind that it would be better if there was no debris left to be found in the morning, and probably the IRGC commander was of the same mind. In any case it was unlikely that the stricken Boghammer would stay afloat that long, and the others could pick up the survivors.

The missile gun director visual quite properly ignored the sinking Boghammer as *Winchester* sped past in pursuit of the rest. The Iranians were firing at anything they could see now; it was like a child petulantly lashing out after being sent to bed for bad behaviour. Nevertheless, they'd learned their lesson and were clearly on the lookout for *Bellona* as they raced away to the northwest.

'Two miles, sir. On the centreline.'

Beresford was still reporting and Mayhew realised that he'd missed his last few calls. But now the Boghammers had disappeared into the night again. Had they given up?

'Two-point-five miles on the centreline, in a left turn.'

Mayhew gripped the signal projector to stop himself smashing it with his fist. They were trying to get around the rear of the convoy to attack it from the south!

He dashed into the bridge.

'I have the ship.'

'Course two-seven-five, twenty-four knots on two Olympus. You have the ship, sir.'

Saxby stepped back from the pelorus to allow the captain to stand on the ship's centreline.

'Port thirty.'

'Port thirty,' the quartermaster tilted his wheel, 'thirty of port wheel on, sir.'

'Officer-of-the-Watch, I'm going to pass between the

second and third tanker. I want you to watch the bearing of the third one, let me know if it's not drawing right. Navigator, call him on Channel sixteen to tell him what I'm doing. He's to hold his course.'

Mayhew could imagine how this looked from *Highlander's* bridge. With *Winchester* darkened, they'd only be able to see where it was by looking at the radar, and the ships were so close to each other that the destroyer would be lost in the radar's clutter. Probably *Highlander's* master had never experienced anything like this in his long career. Certainly he'd fervently hope that he never would again.

'Steer one-eight-zero.'

'Steer one-eight-zero, sir.'

Mayhew looked at *Gas Enterprise* on his port side. It was past and clear, there was no need to concern himself. However, the picture to starboard was another thing entirely. The great bulk of the oil tanker filled his field of vision, it looked impossible that they'd avoid a collision.

'*Highlander's* bow is drawing slowly right, sir. He might collide with our stern.'

The navigator's voice, usually so calm and measured, betrayed his concern.

'Port fifteen.'

'Port fifteen. Fifteen of port wheel on, sir.'

Mayhew saw the navigator and Saxby exchanging glances. By coming to port the destroyer's bows would start to steer away from danger, but its stern would swing in towards the tanker. It would be a close thing.

A corner of his mind, the part that wasn't making rapid calculations of course and speed and relative closing rates, recognised this situation. He'd never done anything as reckless as this before, so why did he have this sense of *déjà vu?*

'I'm still taking a bearing on her bows, sir. They're drawing right slowly. We might make it.'

Mayhew was utterly calm now. The navigator was wrong, they were turning too slowly and if he left it at that a collision was inevitable.

'Full ahead both.'

'Full ahead both.'

He saw the bosun's mate push the engine control levers tight to their stops. Full ahead was only used in response to an emergency, and Mayhew had never ordered it before. Nobody on the bridge had ever heard it either.

'Both engines full ahead, sir.'

Winchester's stern dug deep into the water and the acceleration could be felt as the two mighty gas turbines thrust the four-thousand tons of steel forward. They were under the tanker's bows now and powering forward.

Mayhew stepped as casually as he could out onto the bridge wing and looked up at the awful sight. He should be terrified, but one glance was enough to show him that his ship was safe. If that was another warship and not a vast oil tanker he'd be more concerned, because a warship could turn at the wrong moment, but *Highlander* took minutes to respond to a helm order. The tanker would plough on while its captain held his breath and *Winchester* would pass unharmed to the other side of the convoy.

That corner of his mind had its say again and now he realized why he recognised this situation. It was from his teenage reading: C.S. Forester, *A Ship of the Line*. He couldn't remember the chapter, but Captain Horatio Hornblower in his third-rate *Sutherland* was protecting an East India convoy off Ushant, and he too passed between two ships of the convoy at high speed to fend off a pair of French privateers intent on capturing one of the richest prizes on the ocean. He felt a surge of pride at being part of that great tradition, then he shook himself back into the here-and-now.

'*Highlander's* bows are passing our midships, sir.'

'Starboard thirty,' Mayhew called as calmly as he could while his heart was racing.

The quartermaster's voice was unconcerned, as though he had no stake in the game.

'Starboard thirty.'

Mayhew watched the helmsman's every move. They were so close to the tanker that a misjudged use of the wheel could yet lead to a collision. That was why he was giving precise wheel orders rather than let the quartermaster find his own way onto the new course.

Was it working? Yes! He could feel *Winchester* turning to starboard and the stern was being kicked away from the tanker's bows. The urge to look aft was overwhelming, but it would achieve nothing. He needed to be looking ahead, hoping for the fleeting glimpse of the night-hunting Boghammers.

'Thirty of starboard wheel on.'

Mayhew waited until *Winchester's* bows were swinging towards the west.

'Midships, port fifteen.'

'Midships, port fifteen. Fifteen of port wheel on.'

Winchester's bows were almost steady now and only five degrees off course.

'Steer two-seven-zero.'

'Steer two-seven-zero, sir.'

'Four bogeys, centreline, one-point-five miles.'

Beresford had completely lapsed into fighter-control speak, but Mayhew understood. The remaining Boghammers had passed right around *Bellona* and *Sea Surge* and were racing up the starboard side of the convoy. But two were missing.

'*Bellona* reports that they hit one Boghammer and it's disabled and drifting astern a mile to the west of the one that we hit.'

'Thanks PWO. The other four have come around the convoy's stern.'

'Contact, sir. Green two-zero'

That was Petty Officer Wright with his night vision aid. The Boghammers were slightly on the starboard bow and trying to get between the destroyer and the convoy. He ordered an adjustment of course to starboard to head them off. That course alteration opened the port BMARC's

289

weapon arcs. At a command from Visual it started firing and bright green tracer rounds whizzed past the bridge wing. If the Boghammers had held their fire they'd be invisible, but they were launching rockets seemingly at random and it would only be by gross misfortune that any of them hit their target.

'One mile on the nose, sir.'

The BMARC was finding its target now. He could see its tracer hitting at the point where the Boghammers' tracer originated. It occurred to Mayhew that he should be afraid, that at any moment one of those bullets or a rocket might burst through the bridge window or the thin steel sheet below and find his own soft tissue. Yet he found that he was strangely detached from it all, as though his decisions had no bearing on his own survival.

He saw a different colour of flame that seemed to come from the last entitled tanker. That would be *Eastern Heritage*, and his heart missed a beat as he imagined one of the ships entrusted to his care being destroyed by an unlucky shot from a Boghammer's rocket. Yet it seemed too brief and too dull, and there was no sound of an explosion.

He heard a voice from the corner of the bridge.

'The Javelin's are engaging from *Eastern Heritage*, sir.'

Mayhew had entirely forgotten about the Javelin fire units. Lieutenant Hook had sat quietly in his corner through all of the actions, waiting patiently for a chance to bring his weapons into action. He'd heard the words of command – weapons free – and bided his time. Javelins were air defence weapons, but with good aiming they could – just possibly – hit a surface target, and when the range was clear of other ships he gave the order to his fire unit on the rear tanker. Whether his two missiles had hit a Boghammer, he would never know, but still, it was a glorious moment.

'Thank you Lieutenant. They may engage any Boghammer they see, so long as the range is clear.'

'Captain, FC. They're lost in the ground clutter sir.'

'Captain, Officer-of-the-Watch. *World Antigua* is making

the turn forty-five degrees to starboard to follow the separation scheme.'

Mayhew looked astern. Yes, the tanker's aspect had changed, it was in the turn. All of the ships would follow in its wake.

'The Boghammers are turning, sir, turning to starboard.'

'Thank you Petty Officer White.'

'PWO, tell *Bellona* to protect the port rear of the convoy.'

One more burst from a machine gun from the Boghammers and the firing stopped.

'Contact, sir, they're out of the ground wave and moving towards the rear.'

'Thanks, FC.'

Much good would that do them. *Bellona* was back there and every five minutes that they stayed near the convoy was another mile to home. If two of the Boghammers were disabled and probably sinking, then it was likely that others were damaged. They might have engines that threatened to fail at any moment, and casualties that needed more care than was possible at sea. Surely they'd give up now. And yet the game must be played through to its end.

'Reduce eighteen knots.'

'Reduce eighteen knots, sir.'

'PWO, is there any sign of activity other than the Boghammers. I'm particularly interested in anything to the east of us.'

'Nothing, sir. It's all quiet.'

'In that case I'm going to circle around to the rear of the convoy. PWO, tell *Bellona*, and as soon as they are disengaged from the Boghammers they're to move up to the head of the convoy on its port side.'

Mayhew tried to envisage the traffic separation scheme in relation to the land masses on either side, and particularly in relation to Larak Island and Kuhestak. The Boghammers might have a few parting shots, but they were no longer a real threat. It was the Silkworm site at Kuhestak that concerned him and he must bring *Winchester* onto the up-threat side of the convoy without leaving any gaps in the defence to tempt the Boghammer commander. *Bellona* could take the lead now while *Winchester* took the station nearest to the new threat direction.

'Officer-of-the-Watch, take the ship.'

'I have the ship, sir. Course two-seven-zero, eighteen knots on two Olympus.'

'Very well. Take us tight around *Sea Surge's* stern and run up onto the port side of *Eastern Heritage* at half a mile. I think we've had enough of seeing a tanker's bow overhead for one night.'

***

The Boghammers fired a couple of futile bursts at *Bellona* and then dropped astern, presumably to seek their less fortunate friends in the life rafts. Mayhew looked at the time and then looked again. Could it be only four o'clock? It seemed like days since they'd picked up the convoy off Dubai, and surely that action with the Boghammers had taken more than half-an-hour?

'Chief Yeoman, I want a damage report from the convoy and you can call *Sea Surge* and ask them as well.'

Mayhew realised with a guilty shock that he cared more for the Filipino tanker than he did for the four British ships. It seemed to him that *Sea Surge* embodied the best of the seafaring spirit, the determination to keep going even when the odds were stacked against them, to quietly assert the right of the freedom of the seas even when no government cared enough to offer protection. He heard the reports coming in. A few bullet holes – the captain of *Gas Enterprise* had even picked up a spent round that had shattered one of the windows on the bridge wing – but no casualties and no damage that couldn't wait until they came safely into port at the end of their voyage. Mayhew found himself most anxious in waiting to hear from *Sea Surge*, and when his steward brought him a cup of coffee just as the familiar voice declared that they were undamaged, he felt he needed to sit down for a moment and was glad of the excuse that he was holding a cup and saucer.

'Chief Yeoman, I'd better draft a Form Red.'

Mayhew paused with his pen over the signal pad. This would go to the Ministry of Defence and to the Senior Naval Officer Middle East. They would decide how much to tell the government of Oman in whose territorial waters the action had taken place, and he was glad that it wasn't his decision. He didn't know whether any Iranian lives had been lost but it appeared highly likely that two Boghammers had been sunk or at least badly damaged. Others might have been hit, it was difficult to say, and the morning might reveal a wreckage-strewn sea. Probably the Omanis would prefer to be in ignorance of the whole affair; he rather hoped so.

***

Chapter Twenty-Two

Saturday, 0400
HMS Winchester, at Sea, Straits of Hormuz
Operation Armilla Daily Sitrep: Iranian Silkworm strike on convoy from Kuhestak site…

Mayhew dashed off a quick signature at the bottom of his signal pad and handed the board back to the chief yeoman. Like most naval officers who'd been the custodian of classified information and had signed for dozens of documents every day – hundreds sometimes – he'd developed a pared-down signature that was little more than two curved diagonal lines and a sweeping horizontal.

'Navigator, what time's nautical twilight?'

'Zero-four-fifty-three, sir. Nearly an hour yet. Sunrise is at zero-five-forty-four.'

He stepped forward to the bridge window and looked out. The haze had dissipated a little and he could make out the vast bulk of *Eastern Heritage* half a mile to starboard. Further forward he could dimly see the shapes of the other three tankers with their white stern lights gleaming brightly. *Bellona* was still darkened and her flat grey paint made her completely invisible; it was a perfect demonstration of the benefits of darkening a ship. He walked out onto the bridge wing to look astern. Yes, there was *Sea Surge* keeping station as rigidly as any warship on manoeuvres. Mayhew wasn't a superstitious man – save for that touching wood thing – but the sight of the Filipino tanker gave him new strength. He had the feeling that the convoy was invulnerable as long as *Sea Surge* was tagging along at the back. He smiled at his own foolishness but still he nodded in greeting to his unknown friends. He looked around, beyond the convoy. The horizon was more to be imagined than seen and there was no sign of land or of any other shipping. The convoy might as well be in the centre of the ocean rather than in one of the world's strategic and usually busy waterways.

'Where will we be at nautical twilight, in relation to the separation scheme?'

'Half way down the last leg, sir. We'll leave Omani waters at sunrise and exit the Silkworm envelope at zero-seven-hundred.'

Three more hours then. At seven o'clock the ship could revert to defence watches and he could launch the Lynx to recover the first lieutenant and the Javelin teams. The entitled tankers would start to break away soon after and then it would be a slow passage for the rest of the day and into the night to meet *Fort Brockhurst* tomorrow to take on stores and ammunition. That would be another lost Sunday as the entire ships' company was needed to get the stores on board and strike them down below, for *Winchester* had no automation to help with that task. From the replenishment point to the cold rooms and the store rooms, every box and bundle had to be passed from hand-to-hand and nobody was spared the hard labour. Then, when that was finished, they'd be back to Fujairah to pick up the next inbound convoy and probably to relieve *Stirling* at the Shah Allum shoal so that she could transit out to have a new gas turbine unit fitted at Mina Raysut. It was a hard, unrelenting life on the Armilla Patrol.

'I'll be in the ops room, Officer-of-the-Watch.'

***

'Captain, Officer-of-the-Watch. *World Antigua* is altering course to starboard to follow the separation scheme. That's the last leg before we leave it, sir.'

'Very well. Maintain station on *Eastern Heritage*.'

Perhaps it was all over. In a few minutes when *Winchester* followed the convoy around the last bend of the separation scheme, he'd no longer be closing on the Silkworm launchers at Kuhestak – if they were even there – and the range would be opening with every mile that the convoy made towards the open waters of the Gulf of Oman. The moment of greatest danger was about to pass. He caught himself settling into complacency; this wasn't the moment to relax his guard.

'AAWO, where's *Casablanca* now?'

'Still with the Earnest Will convoy, sir. Just leaving the separation scheme westbound. They'll be in international waters in an hour and I expect *Casablanca* will take up her normal station off Hengam Island.'

'Thanks, AAWO. Is the air threat warning still yellow?'

'Yes, sir. Based on the Kuhestak radar bearing zero-five-zero.'

He should have known that, but he absolved himself, he'd had a lot on his mind in the past hour. Then his convoy was on its own. Not even an Aegis cruiser could effectively cover the eastern part of the Straits from its station to the west, not unless the enemy was flying at thirty-thousand feet. Perhaps he should relax. There was no particular indication of an attack, the Kuhestak radar was transmitting, but there was nothing new in that, it probably transmitted twenty-four hours a day to monitor the traffic in the Straits. He looked over Allenby's shoulder to see the wider picture. There was the Earnest Will convoy transmitting its position on the data link. The Americans still had to be concerned about possible mobile Silkworm sites on Hengam, Tunb, Abu Musa and Siri – although Mayhew was now convinced that the islands were innocent of missiles – but there was little else that could seriously threaten the American convoy's progress towards Kuwait. He couldn't see the US carrier battle group's location, it was using a different data link frequency and was either in the Gulf of Oman or perhaps it had moved further out into the Indian Ocean. There was only a single air contact that looked out of place, and Allenby was tracking it with his chinagraph pencil. It was to the east of Bandar Abbas, feet dry over the Iranian coast, and it apparently wasn't squawking. The air picture supervisor had classified it unknown, pending. It was probably a civilian aircraft on its way to Pakistan or India. He'd never seen things so quiet as this in the Straits of Hormuz, and it was hard to believe that he'd been in a desperate fight against fast, agile, well-armed Boghammers less than an hour ago. He wondered briefly what had happened to the two damaged Boghammers. Had they sunk by now? Had the crews been rescued? He found that he didn't care much.

'AAWO, EWD. P-3 Orion racket bearing zero-one-five. Correlates track three-five-two-one.'

Allenby stabbed his finger at the previously unknown contact to the east of Bandar Abbas.

'That's him, sir, and he's in the turn towards us at thirty-eight miles. We've never seen a P-3 come out before dawn. I'd like to call air threat warning red.'

Mayhew thought for a moment. He didn't want to overreact and a change of threat warning would be automatically transmitted to *Bellona*, the convoy, and to the Javelin fire units. He'd ordered that it should be transmitted on VHF channel thirteen too, so *Sea Surge* would hear it, and that meant that the Omani station at Goat Island would hear it too. This could be nothing more than an early morning training flight or a test flight after a repair. And yet... there was something in the air this morning. Like the weird sisters around the bubbling cauldron, he felt it by a pricking of his thumbs. Something wicked this way was coming and it wasn't Macbeth. He had no wooden binocular case to touch in the ops room.

'Yes, air threat warning red. Navigator, make sure the first lieutenant knows. Javelin Commander, are you copying?'

'Yes, sir. The fire units are standing to.'

'Captain, PWO. *Bellona's* in goalkeeping station between *World Antigua* and *Gas Enterprise*.'

'Thank you, PWO.'

'Blind, AAWO. Height-find track three-five-two-one.'

'What's your assessment, AAWO.'

'It's too much of a coincidence, sir. I believe that P-3 is on a mission to identify the convoy.'

'You don't think the Boghammers did that?'

'They could have, sir, but they report to the IRGC command, or that's our assumption. The Silkworms are controlled by the regular Iranian forces and they have a clear chain of command to the P-3. In any case, the Boghammer's information will be imprecise, at best. The shore stations will see our contacts well enough on their radar, but at thirty miles they won't be certain of our identity. The P-3 has a higher definition radar and it has ESM kit. I'm getting the feeling that we're the target of the month, not the Americans.'

Mayhew looked again at the P-3. He'd been thinking the same thing. It was plausible. For all sorts of reasons, political, strategic and even religious, they might feel that they have to strike back after they were so badly mauled a few nights ago. They'd be wary of the Americans, and they didn't have the same ingrained antipathy towards the French, Italians and the Soviets. The British made a good compromise.

'AAWO, Blind. Track three-five-two-one height eight-thousand-five-hundred feet, holding steady. It's at twenty-eight miles now, it'll soon be a good Seadart target.'

Allenby swivelled his seat to face Mayhew.

'I think we can assume that we've been identified, sir. I'd like to cover him with birds. It might at least make him keep his distance when he detects our J-band.'

'Yes, we're past tiptoeing around each other, AAWO. Cover the P-3 with birds.'

The sound of the Seadart missiles being loaded onto the launcher filtered through to the ops room. Everyone heard the hydraulic motors and the thump as heavy metal rams hit solid buffers; for the ops room team it was a definite statement of intent. Now, with a few words, Mayhew could cause that P-3 to be plucked out of the sky, inevitably killing everyone on board. It was tempting, but he couldn't honestly say that it was displaying hostile intent. When it did – if it did – *Winchester* would be so busy dealing with the immediate threat of inbound missiles that the P-3 would be able to sidle away back to Bandar Abbas without any hindrance.

'Captain, AAWO. The P-3 is turning away. It must have detected our fire control radar.'

Mayhew looked at the tactical display again. At that height the P-3 was safe so long as it stayed outside thirty miles or so. Did the aircraft's mission commander know that? It certainly seemed as though he did. He felt *Winchester* heel slightly as it took the final turn in the traffic separation scheme. Everyone was keyed-up; they understood exactly what the threat was and they knew their part in defeating it. It was exactly like the training exercises at Portland: the surveillance came first – an anticlimax – then the identification – *Winchester's* convoy in this case – then the targeting and then the attack. The first two phases were complete, now they were just waiting for the last two.

'AAWO. Give a warning to the P-3. I know it's further away than would normally warrant it, but I want to hear his reaction.'

'Roger, sir. FC, read warning one on aeronautical distress.'

The ops room was hushed as Beresford read from his script and listened for a response.

'No reply, sir. I read the warning twice and called for a response but he's either not listening or has chosen to ignore us.'

Mayhew and Allenby exchanged glances; the P-3s always replied to their calls. Their business was to keep track of the traffic in the outer approaches to the Straits and that could only be done with the tacit agreement of the American and British air defence ships that he so often found there. By not replying he was increasing the danger to his aircraft, and making his future missions that much more difficult. His silence was more eloquent than mere words.

'Blind, AAWO. Look out for popups zero-four-zero to zero-five-zero.'

'Captain, AAWO, I'd like to deploy our chaff charlie, sir.'

'Navigator, Captain. How far are we from Goat Island?'

'Sixteen miles, sir, and the edge of the peninsula is just obscuring the line-of-sight.'

'They won't see the flash, but their radar might pick up the chaff bloom,' Allenby added.

'Very well, AAWO. Two rounds chaff charlie to the northeast.'

'Blind, AAWO. Two rounds chaff charlie zero-three-zero, eight thousand yards.'

They heard the gun fire twice and felt the slight shudder of its recoil.

'AAWO, Blind. Good blooms. I can see them loud and clear on both radars.'

'That might give them a targeting problem, sir.'

Mayhew had seen the two blooms of chaff for himself. They always looked unconvincing at this close range, but he had to bear in mind that the radar operator at Kuhestak was seeing them over thirty miles away from where he was sitting. At that range they might do their job.

'Let's hope AAWO, let's hope.'

The EWD's whistle shattered the silence.

'Targeting radar zero-four-five! Targeting radar zero-four-five!'

'That's the Kuhestak site, sir,' Allenby said.

'Captain, AAWO, EWD. The Kuhestak radar has shifted frequency and PRF. That indicates it's in targeting mode.'

The third phase. Mayhew knew what was coming next. He could hear Allenby giving a sitrep on the AAW circuit. That would elicit a response from *Bellona* without him saying anything further.

'PWO, Captain. Maintain this heading, we need to stay in station on the convoy as long as we can.'

If they turned too early, by the time the missiles were on their way the convoy could be too far away to benefit from Winchester's protection.

'Aye-aye sir.'

Silkworm

Silence again. All eyes were glued to radar screens and the UAA-1.

'Contact! Zero-four-five at thirty miles, sir. Two fleeting contacts, fast-moving, they've gone now.'

The APS knew what he'd seen, everyone in the ops room knew, it was like the Portland air defence exercises. *Winchester's* target indication radar had detected two Silkworm missiles as they climbed away from their launchers, and had then lost them as they descended to their cruising height.

Whoosh, whoosh!

'Three-inch chaff launched, sir.'

Kesteven knew that he didn't ask permission at this stage of an engagement, and he'd fired his chaff to try to disrupt the missile's homing head when it was in the search phase.

'PWO, Captain. Manoeuvre for anti-ship-missile defence.'

'Officer-of-the-Watch, PWO. Come hard left zero-six-five.'

That would put the threat twenty degrees on the bow, offering the smallest radar cross-section for the missiles, and if the missile should find its target at that acute angle there was a decent chance that it would glance off the ship's side and explode outboard or just inside the ship's hull, doing much less damage than a penetrating hit. It had happened before to *HMS Glamorgan* in the Falklands, and she survived to see Portsmouth again.

Another blast on the EWD's whistle.

'Silkworm! Zero-four-zero, Silkworm!'

'Got him,' Mayhew heard from the Seadart controller. He'd been staring at that bearing waiting for the Silkworms to show.

'Blind, AAWO. Take the vampires with birds and gun. APS, release them to alligator.'

Kesteven fired a salvo of Seagnat chaff. It was designed to bloom rapidly and close to the ship so that the missile's homing radar saw the chaff and the ship as one target, then the missile would stay locked on to the chaff as the ship moved away. That was the theory in any case. It mustn't be fired too soon because it bloomed low, about where the missile's homing head expected a target to be, and it fell quickly to the sea. On deck the crews would be reloading as fast as ever they could.

Allenby rattled off a quick sitrep on the AAW circuit. *Bellona* knew what to do and would engage any targets that came within its Seawolf's engagement criteria. That would cover the head of the convoy, but only *Winchester's* Seadarts could cover the entire convoy.

'Phalanx to auto,' Allenby called.

'Captain, AAWO. Two Silkworm inbound zero-four-zero, fifteen miles. Engaging with birds and gun.'

'Look out for the second salvo, AAWO.'

'Phalanx in auto, sir.'

The standard Silkworm launcher could fire four missiles, so it was a near certainty that another salvo would follow. There could be two launchers but probably only one, and the reload time was so long that this might be their only shot before the convoy was out of range. The missiles would cover those fifteen miles in a minute-and-a-half.

'AAWO, APS. Second pair of contacts just like the first two. They've gone again.'

'AAWO, Blind. First wave of vampires at ten miles.'

Allenby glanced at the missile desk. He could see that they were poised, waiting for the low-flying Silkworms to come within range, but they knew that a second pair was on the way. They must wait. The Seadart might be able to hit a bomber at high altitude at nearly forty miles, but a sea-skimming missile didn't become a valid target until less than ten miles, often very much less.

'This pair is heading towards the rear of the convoy, sir.'

Whoosh! whoosh! A far greater volume of sound than the three-inch rockets.

'AAWO, Blind. Birds away, first pair of vampires.'

The Seadarts had left the launcher.

Silkworm

***

Saxby flinched as the two Seadarts zoomed skywards, trailing a jet of flame from their booster motors. They destroyed his night vision, and left a bank of smoke that quickly cleared as *Winchester* powered through. He'd manoeuvred the ship as the PWO had ordered and now he had to watch on the bearing that the Silkworms were expected. He could follow the track of the Seadarts by the bright efflux as they sped skywards at Mach 2. He saw the flash as the booster motors dropped away then the missiles dived steeply towards the sea, powered now by their ramjet cruise motors. He still couldn't see the Silkworms but they must be out there, streaking towards his ship. There was no radar display at the front of the bridge, but he was following the action on the command open line and he'd heard the threat direction. He saw a flash on the horizon. And after a pause he heard the missile gun director blind on the command open line.

'Splashed one vampire. Heads up one leaker.'

He stared hard down the bearing, searching for the one that had got through, the *leaker*. Was that it? That tiny, blurred dot of light? He looked again and suddenly it was obvious.

'Vampire visual,' he shouted, 'bearing...' he squinted across the azimuth circle on the pelorus, '... bearing two-three-nine.'

Saxby ran for the port bridge wing and jumped as another salvo of Seagnat shot out of the launchers. The gun was firing in its regular thump-thump-thump rhythm but he heard an authoritative voice, the PWO, calling *Four-Five check, check, check*, and it fell silent. There was little chance of hitting a sea-skimming missile with the gun and there was a greater chance of the Phalanx detecting the outgoing shells and becoming confused. But he saw what he was looking for, the Phalanx was pointing in the right direction and juddering slightly as it followed its target. It looked like a sentient being in deep thought, pondering its next move.

Then, without warning, it fired a long, rapid burst, with that same sound of a supersonic chainsaw that he'd last heard at Portland. It ripped apart the darkness with its orange-and-red glow. There was no explosion, and he didn't hear the impact of the depleted uranium shells nor the splashes as the constituent parts of the Silkworm smashed into the sea. The Vulcan Phalanx simply jerked upwards, as though it was shrugging; *that was nothing*, it seemed to be saying. Then it slewed back to its ready position and awaited the next target. It appeared to be lost in thought as its surveillance radar whirred away under its domed head.

***

Down below in the ops room they were waiting for the next wave. Any moment now…

The EWD blew his whistle.

'Silkworm! Zero-four-five, Silkworm!'

Chaff, manoeuvre, confirm the Phalanx is in auto, fresh Seadart missiles on the launcher. Ready.

'Blind, AAWO. Look out for popups zero-four-five.'

The atmosphere could be cut with a knife, but now they knew; all that training, all those weeks and months at sea away from their families, every moment was worth it. Seadart worked, it could shoot down a missile in flight. Bring on the next one.

'Contact. Vampires zero-four-five, fourteen miles.'

'Blind, AAWO. Take the vampires with birds.'

There was that slight juddering again as the fire control radar searched for its target.

'Birds affirm, inbound vampires.'

***

Saxby knew what to expect this time and he turned away to preserve his night vision before the pair of Seadarts left the launcher within two seconds of each other. He knew what to look for this time, too. Once again there was a flash on the horizon: a hit, he hoped. Then the careful search for the second one. He saw it, a hint of a dot of light, that was all, and its bearing was decidedly moving right. It was aimed at the head of the convoy this time.

'Vampire visual, bearing two-four-three, bearing drawing right.'

***

Allenby burst straight in on the AAW circuit.

'*Bellona*, this is *Winchester*. Splashed one vampire in the second wave. Heads up one leaker making for the lead ships in the convoy.'

'*Winchester*, this is *Bellona*, roger.'

Bellona's PWO sounded relaxed, as though this was just another drill in the simulators at *HMS Dryad*, or in the exercise areas at Portland.

Winchester's ops room was silent again. Everyone remembered the disaster in the Falklands when the Seawolf failed to engage an inbound Argentine A-4 and *HMS Coventry* was sunk by dumb, iron bombs. Seawolf relied much more upon automation than Seadart, and it had a very much shorter range. It was designed for quick reaction and point defence and had no capability to protect a dispersed force; that was Seadart's job. If the system decided that it didn't have a valid target, it wouldn't engage, and by that time it was all too late for human intervention.

'Captain, Officer-of-the-Watch. There's an explosion at the head of the convoy, not very big, and I can't see what it is.'

Oh God, Mayhew thought, *have I lost a ship*? He had a sudden mental image of *Bellona* desperately trying to stay afloat as the sea came in through a great gash in its side, or *World Antigua* with her cargo of oil burning furiously, lighting up the night sky. Men could be struggling in the water at this moment, or fighting to escape from flooded or fire ravaged compartments. He shook himself out of it, this was no time for self-pity, for that was all that it was.

The ops room was absolutely quiet, not a person spoke or moved.

'*Winchester*, this is *Bellona*,' Bellona's PWO had a languid tone of voice, he almost sounded bored, 'splashed one vampire with mini-birds. It looks like a Javelin was fired too.'

Mayhew was suddenly feeling light-headed. Then *Bellona's* Seawolf had done its business, and maybe the Javelins also.

'AAWO, Javelin. Splashed one vampire from *World Antigua*.'

Well, they could fight it out later, Mayhew thought, but who splashed that last Silkworm would probably never be known for certain. Seawolf or Javelin, at this moment it didn't matter, all that mattered was that there were no more Silkworms in the air, as far as he could tell.

'APS, AAWO. Are there any more fast contacts?'

'Nothing, sir. The P-3 is circling thirty miles to the north now at six thousand feet.'

Allenby checked the track number on his tactical display. The P-3 was probably out of range, but it was worth a try. He felt an unreasoning hatred of the aircraft that spied on them, directed the attack, but wouldn't risk coming close.

'Blind, AAWO. Cover track three-five-two-one with birds.'

'Covering track three-five-two-one with birds. Birds negat track three-five-two-one. It's too low, sir.'

'AAWO, Captain. Keep covering the P-3 but it's a hold fire for now, unless it does something else aggressive.'

'Blind, AAWO. Hold fire track three-five-two-one. Continue covering.'

Allenby didn't want any mistakes now. His team had done well to shoot down two Silkworms with Seadart and one with Phalanx, and a firm order now would prevent a shoot-down outside the rules of engagement.

'AAWO, EWD. All Silkworm rackets ceased. Kuhestak is still transmitting in its targeting mode and I still hold the P-3 racket. No other threat rackets at present.'

Allenby heard the start of a buzz of conversation around the ops room. That would never do, the ship and its convoy was still within range of Silkworms from Kuhestak and

Silkworm

would be for another two hours. *Winchester* still had a job to do. He waved for the ops room supervisor.

'Chief, get everyone focussed on their displays. We're not in the clear yet.'

That was enough. He could hear the chief speaking sharply to the supervisors and directors, and the buzz died down to nothing in seconds.

'APS, AAWO. The threat direction is zero-three-five. Look out for pop-ups inside thirty-two miles.'

Time to talk to *Bellona*.

'*Bellona*, this is *Winchester*. Sitrep. Four vampires fired from Kuhestak, presumed Silkworms, all splashed. The force remains under surveillance from a P-3 to the north, track three-five-two-one, *Winchester* covering, birds negat. Kuhestak might have more than one quadruple launcher and therefore the threat warning air remains red. Threat direction zero-three-five. Report weapons expenditure on tactical UHF.'

'*Winchester*, this is *Bellona*. Roger.'

'*Bellona*, this is *Winchester*. Roger, out.'

***

Chapter Twenty-Three

Saturday, 0500
HMS Winchester, at Sea, Straits of Hormuz
Operation Armilla Daily Sitrep: Exited Silkworm Envelope…

The haze had cleared and for a glorious half-an-hour after the Silkworm attack, the sky was afire with a million stars, and the milky way stretched across the heavens in a vast arc like a diamond-studded bridal veil that had been casually flung aside. It was almost too bright to look at. Saxby looked towards the east where the sky was turning ever so gradually from black to grey as the first light of the new day crept stealthily over the mountains of Iran. It was like the flooding tide on mud flats; if you watched, you couldn't see its progress, but if you turned away then looked again, it had covered a measurable amount of ground. There was another simile that Saxby knew well: it was like a tortoise in an English garden. It appeared to be incapable of moving fast, but if your attention wandered, when you looked again it was at the far end of the lawn or hidden behind a flowerpot. There was a poem in there somewhere, but Saxby was no poet.

The grey turned lighter by degrees until it was tinged with a hint of orange and then the tiniest flat sliver of the rising sun pushed above the peaks. The ship dropped fractionally into the trough of the swell and it was gone, only to reappear twice as large when the ship rose again. He looked up and the stars had vanished as though they had never been, leaving only the brightest planets to shine on for a few minutes. At *Winchester's* mainmast he saw that the highest radio aerial was gleaming gold where the first rays of the sun had caught it. Saxby could hardly remember any lines of verse, but one that he'd learned as a child sprung to his mind:

Silkworm

*Awake! for Morning in the Bowl of Night
Has flung the Stone that puts the Stars to Flight:
And Lo! the Hunter of the East has caught
The Sultan's Turret in a Noose of Light.*

How appropriate that he should be thinking of a twelfth-century Persian poet at this moment. Omar Khyam's descendants had been flinging lethal missiles, not stones, at him only minutes ago, yet somehow his words fitted the mood. Well, poetry might sooth his mind, but he felt tired and unwashed; he badly needed a shower and a shave, and the thought of waiting until the ship stood down from action stations before he could have breakfast was almost more than he could bear. He dropped the command open line microphone to his mouth.

'Captain, Officer-of-the-Watch.'

'Captain.'

Oh why did Mayhew sound so bright and chirpy after a night like that. Saxby suspected that to Mayhew he sounded as tired and jaded as he felt. He tried to perk up his voice.

'Sunrise, sir, five-forty-four. The mountains to the east have blocked the horizon so I couldn't check the gyro compass. The ship is in station five cables on *Eastern Heritage's* beam and we're steering one-six-five at thirteen knots on two Tynes. We'll leave Omani territorial waters in five minutes and exit the Silkworm envelope in forty minutes. The ship's at action station and the ships of the convoy and *Bellona* are all in their proper stations.'

'Very well…'

There was a pause on the open line and Saxby sensed that the captain hadn't finished.

'Is *Sea Surge* still there?'

'Affirmative sir. Their captain called on VHF channel thirteen a few minutes ago, wanting to talk to you. I said you'd be available around six-forty-five. He seemed to understand, sir.'

'Thank you, Officer-of-the-Watch. I'll be up as soon as

we're clear of the envelope.'

Saxby walked to the port bridge wing again. The close range weapon crews were all looking over the port quarter, towards the Kuhestak launching site, and the LAS operator had his high-power binoculars trained in that direction. That was good, because more anti-ship missiles were detected visually than were ever seen on radar. The missile gun director visual gave him a wave then returned to his constant monitoring of his weapons and their crews. The decks were littered with spent shell cases and he had to be careful where he trod for fear of skidding and falling flat. The usually spotless Seagnat launchers were dappled with black sooty stains that twinkled in the early sun where the salt spray had evaporated. A glance over the bridge wing screen showed that the fo'c'sle was no better. The four Seadart missiles had destroyed the launcher's paintwork and the efflux had ripped up some of the deck paint, revealing the old half-inch trip-hazard above the magazine. Two years ago *Winchester* had tried an over-the-shoulder Seadart shot only to find that the efflux got under the corner of the soft patch over the magazine and pulled it up from the deck. Despite its name the soft patch was a massive plate of steel that would blow upwards in the event of a magazine explosion, and it was secured by a strong chain, to prevent it going overboard. The force of the efflux had bent it and the smooth deck of the fo'c'sle was never the same again. Well, *Winchester's* fo'c'sle was Gavin Beresford's responsibility, and although there was no new structural damage he had one heck of a painting job on his hands.

He looked out over the sea, towards the Iranian shore again. It was only twenty miles away, and the narrow coastal plain quickly gave way to higher land that stretched away to the Pakistan border. The sun was a hand's breadth above the highest mountains now, and the planets had all disappeared. The light breeze raised tiny wavelets whose crests caught the sun's low, slanting rays and created a moving pattern of scintillating points of light. It was good to be alive and even better to be at sea, and in that moment he pitied his landlocked friends who never witnessed a spectacle such as this, nor did they ever have the satisfaction of prevailing over a determined enemy.

***

Mayhew too was thinking of breakfast but he couldn't leave the ops room while they were still within range of the Kuhestak launching site. The intelligence assessment suggested that it took thirty minutes to load each replacement Silkworm missile, so it was possible that the Iranian soldiers were even now feverishly craning on the third, and they could achieve a fourth before the convoy was out of range. In fact, he didn't think it was likely. Most probably they had only the four missiles to hand, and on the principle of shoot-and-scoot, they would already have hitched the launcher to its tractor and hidden it away in some cave or warehouse that they'd earmarked for the purpose. He'd bet a substantial sum that an overflight would show that the Kuhestak launch site was empty, and only a row of four parallel scorch-marks would bear witness to the night's drama.

Yet he wasn't thinking about his convoy. He was certain now that it was safe and he was only staying at action stations because he was inside the MOD-directed Silkworm envelope. He was thinking of the Filipino tanker, and of the vital importance of global trade and the right of free passage on the high seas. Few nations could afford the cost of protecting their merchantmen – the expenditure of ammunition last night was proof of that – and it was vital that the free trading nations of the western alliance that could afford a blue water navy stepped up to the plate. He'd miss *Sea Surge*.

***

The hour passed. The P-3 had long ago returned to Bandar Abbas, probably for its mission commander to report that as far as he could tell, none of the radar contacts that represented the convoy and its escort had disappeared from his radar, nor had any of them fallen out of the formation or reduced their speed. All the radars that he'd detected were still operating, and he'd heard no distress calls on any of the frequencies that he was monitoring. If any of the Silkworm missiles had found their target, then it wasn't at all evident. On his radar he'd have caught a glimpse of those Seadarts racing towards the inbound Silkworms at terrifying speed, and the pilot would have reported the brief flashes of their impact. He'd want nothing to do with such defensive systems and he'd be resolved to treat the British and American air defence ships with even greater respect in the future. If he was feeling brave he might add that if the high command thought that he could do a close flypast to get visual confirmation that the convoy was intact, they could think again. But perhaps that would be a dangerous thing to say in a humourless theocracy like Iran.

'Captain, Navigator. We've left the Silkworm envelope.'

'Captain, AAWO. There's no sign of enemy airborne surveillance and no threat radars transmitting except Kuhestak in surveillance mode. Air and surface threat warnings yellow.'

Mayhew breathed a sigh of relief and clapped Allenby on the shoulder.

'Officer-of-the-Watch, Captain. Revert to damage control state two condition yankee. Port defence watch close up. I'll come up to the bridge in a few moments.'

***

The conversation with *Sea Surge* had been brief. The captain – Mayhew was still unsure whether he was a Filipino or from some other Asian nation – offered his gratitude and a hope that they might meet some day, then with a double blast of his siren he hauled out of line and started edging away to the east. Mayhew watched for a few minutes, speculating on where the tanker was bound, but it was hopeless. With the tiger economies of the east all thirsty for oil, the potential ports numbered in the hundreds. He walked into the bridge, ripped off his anti-flash hood and settled into his chair. Then he reached out and very deliberately touched the wood of his binocular box, and he didn't give a damn who saw him do it.

***

The Author

Chris Durbin grew up in the seaside town of Porthcawl in South Wales. His first experience of sailing was as a sea cadet in the treacherous tideway of the Bristol Channel and, at the age of sixteen, he spent a week in a tops'l schooner in the Southwest Approaches. He was a crew member on the Porthcawl lifeboat before joining the navy.

Chris spent twenty-four years as a warfare officer in the Royal Navy, serving in all classes of ships from aircraft carriers through destroyers and frigates to the smallest minesweepers. He took part in operational campaigns in the Falkland Islands, the Middle East and the Adriatic and he spent two years teaching tactics at a US Navy training centre in San Diego.

On his retirement from the Royal Navy, Chris joined a large American company and spent eighteen years in the aerospace, defence and security industry, including two years on the design team for the Queen Elizabeth class aircraft carriers.

Chris is a graduate of the Britannia Royal Naval College at *Dartmouth*, the British Army Command and Staff College, the United States Navy War College, where he gained a postgraduate diploma in national security decision-making, and Cambridge University, where he was awarded an MPhil in International Relations.

With a lifelong interest in naval history and a long-standing ambition to write historical fiction, Chris has completed the first sixteen novels in the Carlisle & Holbrooke series, which follow the fortunes of a colonial Virginian and a Hampshire man who both command ships of King George's navy during the middle years of the eighteenth century.

Chris has used his own first-hand experiences to take an excursion into the late twentieth century with this dramatic description of four days in the life of a guided missile destroyer in the Gulf Tanker War of 1988.

Silkworm

Chris lives on the south coast of England, surrounded by hundreds of years of naval history. His three children are all busy growing their own families and careers while Chris and his wife (US Navy, retired) of forty-three years enjoy sailing their Cornish Crabber on the south coast.

***

The Carlisle & Holbrooke Series

Chris has created the first sixteen in a series of books set in the middle years of the eighteenth century. The series starts with *The Colonial Post-Captain* which tells the story of the fall of Minorca in 1756 and the commencement of Britain's involvement in the Seven Years War. The narrative flows from the Mediterranean to the Caribbean, from the Faeroe Islands to Portugal, and from the forests of the American colonies to the coast of France.

The series will continue, carrying its chief characters into the American War of Independence.

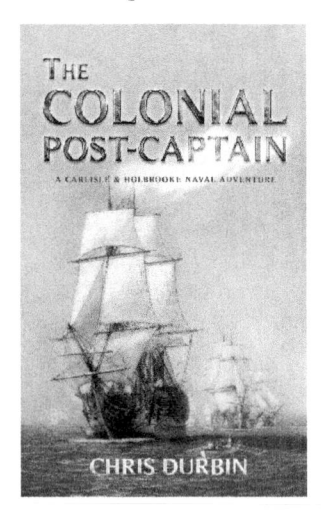

You can find the Carlisle & Holbrooke books on Amazon or by pasting this link into your web search engine:

https://www.chris-durbin.com

***

Feedback

If you've enjoyed *Silkworm!* please consider leaving a review on Amazon.

Look out for the seventeenth in the Carlisle & Holbrooke series of eighteenth century naval adventures, coming soon.

You can follow my blog at:
https://www.chris-durbin.com/blog/

***

Printed in Great Britain
by Amazon